G000065731

Sum Net Gain

– CHARLES FENN –

FASTPRINT PUBLISHING
PETERBOROUGH, ENGLAND

SUM NET GAIN
Copyright © Charles Fenn 2010

ISBN 978-184426-851-1

First published 2010 by
FASTPRINT PUBLISHING
Peterborough, England.

Printed in England by
www.printondemand-worldwide.com

Charles Fenn

Chapter One

'So, basically, we're fucked?'
'Shafted!'
'The Fat Lady's singing?'
'That's not me; that's the radio in the kitchen.'
'The dinosaurs happily roamed the planet for a hundred and fifty million years with no more technology than nest building. They might still be here but for an unlucky meteorite strike. But we, Homo sapiens, are evolutionarily conditioned to wipe ourselves out after a mere ten thousand years of civilization because we have opposable thumbs?'
'Yup. It's a bummer, isn't it? Evolution is exponential.' Richard pushed back his chair and stood up excitedly to demonstrate. He flung his arms as wide apart as they would go. 'Picture the whole history of life on earth on this scale. Each millimetre represents a million years. The two metres between my hands represents the two billion years that it took to advance from simple protoplasm to simple fish.'
Richard looked round the table, swaying slightly and waving his outstretched hands like a goalkeeper preparing for a penalty shoot-out. He locked eyes and nodded to each of us in turn to assure himself that we were all following his analogy until he reached David who had fallen asleep, slumped sideways in his chair. Richard glared at him, started to say something, and then thought better of it. He moved on to Becca who appeared, much more promisingly, to be waiting for Richard's attention with eager anticipation. She fluttered her long eyelashes in a parody

of puppy-like devotion. A lascivious grin crept onto Richard's face, a grin which was dashed almost before it had started as Becca stuck out her long tongue and blew him a soggy raspberry.

Richard abandoned the circumspection of his audience, straightened up, clapped his hands together for attention and then held them out in front of him, now just twenty centimetres apart.

'This distance represents the two hundred million years that it took to progress from fish to dinosaurs.' He turned his body left and right so that we could all appreciate the much smaller distance now being demonstrated. Becca giggled suggestively when the eight-inch gap was proffered to her; Richard studiously ignored her. He tried, and failed, to slip his left hand into his dinner-jacket pocket, steadied himself by leaning forwards against the cherry wood tabletop and ploughed on.

'On my Richard Davies scale of evolution, apes came down out of the trees just four millimetres ago.' He held his right hand up to his eye, the thumb and forefinger so close together that he had to squint as he surveyed his audience through the gap. When he was convinced that we fully appreciated the tiny distance separating us from our arboreal ancestors he dramatically plucked one wavy brown hair from his beard, winced, and held it up triumphantly as Exhibit A.

'Over the last two hundred thousand years Man has developed tool making capabilities. We have developed language. We have mastered fire.' Richard was in full flow. He was almost shouting in his excitement. Becca put her hands up to ward off the flying spittle. 'But... ' Richard suddenly stopped. He dropped the hair onto his pudding plate and continued in a hushed tone. 'But... it is only in the last ten thousand years that we have discovered agriculture, enabling us to move from itinerant hunter-gatherers to domiciled civilization. That's the last one-hundredth of a millimetre in the two metres of the Richard Davies evolutionary scale.'

Richard scanned the remnants of the five-course meal, his eyes flitting desperately from the cheese board to the jug of celery and then on to the salt grinder.

'I'm afraid that I don't have anything small enough to demonstrate ten thousand years on the Richard Davies scale,' he concluded sadly. He slumped back into his chair, deflated by the realisation that his whole presentation had ended in anti-climax for want of a convenient microscope.

William Searle clapped sarcastically from the head of the table. 'Thank you Richard. Very enlightening. Now pass the port.'

'Bugger the port. Who's got the dope?'

'Yes, where is Angus? You said he was going to join us later.'

'And is Anne coming with him?'

★ ★ ★

Why did I come?

I hadn't met any of the people in the wood-panelled dining room for over ten years, but if I closed my eyes I could have been back at Cambridge University in the Robinson College refectory sitting with these same people discussing which lectures we had missed that day. We had been thrown together by the lottery of the college room-allocation system; as first year undergraduates we had been assigned neighbouring identical rabbit hutches to live in on one of the number of identical corridors in the college building. We had different backgrounds, we were reading different subjects, but the seeds of our friendship were sown on the very first evening as we waved good-bye to our chauffeuring parents and got viciously drunk together in the college bar.

We had held each other's hands, both literally and metaphorically, through the chaos of Freshers week. William and Hannah, as the only ex-Public School boarders amongst us, were our early leaders. They introduced us to the peculiar half-communal, half-independent lifestyle which is university life. I had never lived away from home before. I was worried that I would not know anybody, that I would be lonely, that I would not fit in, but my shyness was blown away by their hearty camaraderie. I must have shut the door to my room occasionally to study and sometimes to sleep, but for most of that first year Hannah enforced a strict open door policy down the corridor, which meant that there was always a coffee break or a cocktail party in progress in at least one room at any given time of the day or night. It was more like living in a commune than living alone. By day three, William had organised the first corridor party. Attendance was compulsory; no excuses. It became traditional for non-attendance at such events to be punished by "trial of the flooded carpet". A plastic dustbin was half filled with water and balanced precariously against the non-attendees door while they were inside. A Dispenser of Justice would then knock and warn the guilty party that Court was in session. Rubber-neckers in the corridor took bets on whether the victim would be agile enough to ease open their door and slip an arm though the crack to catch the bin before it crashed forward and emptied twenty gallons of water onto their study floor.

By day five, Hannah had asked William out; by day ten he had accepted.

Our group grew and changed during the three years of undergraduate life. We made other friends at tutor groups, at sports clubs, at extra-curricular societies. In the second year we moved out of the college residential accommodation and into our own digs. A few of the more peripheral members of our corridor clique drifted away, but the A-team managed to rent both halves of a semi-detached town house. In a truly depressing validation of gender stereotyping, the girl's half of the building remained an oasis of neatness for the whole year while the boy's half slowly descended into a dwelling barely fit for human habitation. And it wasn't just because we threw the better parties.

By year three the game of musical beds appeared to have run its course. Most of us had settled into stable relationships with partners either inside or outside the group. We moved in our pairs into a variety of flats around the city according to our various budgets, but we still mainly socialised as 'The Group'. It had been friendship of such depth and quality that I had assumed it would last forever.

I looked round at their faces ten years on. We had all aged physically, but during the canapés and aperitifs I had been surprised by the ease with which I was accepted back into their company. I had steeled myself for their pity but detected only genuine interest in their questions. There was a comfortable familiarity about their mannerisms and their speech patterns but as the meal progressed I picked up the subtle changes in their personalities. Their lives had moved on. As Cambridge undergraduates we had believed that we could achieve anything that we put our minds to; when I had last seen these people we were still bubbling with the optimism and confidence of that ambition. Now they had become established. They had served their apprenticeships in their chosen professions and, even as high-flyers, their lives had been straight-jacketed by the mundane limitations of their jobs. The conversation had turned to commuting, and mortgages, and comparing holiday entitlements. The group dynamic had orientated itself around the most financially successful members. Now as the quality and quantity of William's wine cellar began to take its toll the old naive enthusiasm was returning.

'But Richard, I don't follow the steps of your argument from the exponential rate of evolution to the inevitability of human extinction,' said William.

William Searle, our portly host, was successfully accumulating his fortune in the City. He had married Hannah, of course, as soon as he was properly established at his first Merchant Bank, long before "banker" had become a dirty word. For her part, Hannah hadn't quite settled on any particular career before the arrival of the first of their three girls had provided her with a more suitable occupation. Richard Davies was now a lecturer in Environmental Policy and researching Sudden Man-made Environmental Disasters, or SMEDs as he called them. He had not married Jane, which was interesting. Instead, he had married Sarah, a ravishing Latin beauty who was demonstrably expecting their first baby. So poor old Jane had married someone called Simon Mabbutt. Simon was absent without explanation. Hannah had said stoutly "We don't talk about Simon" when she over-heard me asking about him but I noticed that Jane was still wearing a wedding ring.

★ ★ ★

Why did I come?

These people were still each other's best friends. Jane was Godmother to David's son. William was providing free consultancy for Becca's new venture, a financial advice web-site. Sarah had been round for tea with Hannah last week and gone home with a black bin-bag full of second-hand baby clothes. All of them were sitting comfortably in their black ties and evening gowns. All of them at ease, except me, Jim Turner, dispatch rider, in my denim shirt and black Levis. I had dropped out while they had moved on.

'I can't believe you lot. This is first year undergraduate stuff.' Richard was becoming indignant. William was making the mistake of trying to engage in a serious debate, whereas Richard appeared to be only capable of repeating the same words in a slightly different order. 'One hundred thousand years ago Homo Erectus had a cranial capacity of about a litre. Most of us round this table have brains half as big again.' He paused and looked pointedly at Jane. 'The rapidly changing environmental conditions during the ice ages favoured those species which had the capacity to co-operate, to organise, to communicate. Big brains were favoured over big teeth. The trend only stopped when baby's heads became so big that they started killing their mothers at childbirth, but just as we reached that point our brain size reached the critical mass required to support the complexity of language. It is the key differentiator. The development of language lit the blue touch-paper which caused the explosion of Homo sapiens development, leaving all other species behind us in our dust. We think in language; we conceptualise in language. Suddenly we could theorize about the world around us. We could test those theories and learn from our mistakes. The benefits of instinct which had previously been ingrained over generations of successful mutations could now be achieved by an intelligent man in an afternoon of trial and error.'

'Or by an intelligent woman in half-an-hour.'

★ ★ ★

Why did I come?

Five days ago I'd been sent to make a pick-up at the Gresham's Investments building in Canary Warf. When I got there I had been summoned to the twelfth floor by a certain William Searle. It did occur to me as I stepped out of the lift into the plushly carpeted reception area that it would be an awkward coincidence if my pick-up turned out to be from the William Searle of my long distant Cambridge days. He was, but it wasn't a coincidence and it was only slightly awkward. William had been as friendly as his obviously busy day had allowed and the pick-up turned out to be a gold embossed invitation for me to this ten-year reunion dinner. I had no idea how he found me; Jim Turners are two a penny. I was touched to be invited but initially non-committal. I wasn't sure I wanted to rake up the past. It was only this morning that I had phoned Hannah and said that I would come.

★ ★ ★

'I understand that bit,' said Becca. It dawned on me rather belatedly that she and William were just winding Richard up. The dumber they played, the more exasperated Richard became. 'Homo sapiens just happened to be the first species to develop language in a way which is qualitatively different from other animals. If the apes had got there first then we might all be starring in an ironic tribute to their supremacy called "Planet of the Humans". But why does it follow that because we can now blow ourselves up, we necessarily will?'

I was sitting between Becca and David. They were both in long-term relationships with women who, as outsiders, had understandably declined join the party. I had learnt that David's partner, Carol, was in PR. David, with his 2:1 in Process Engineering, was now a full-time house-husband and in charge of the day-care of their two year-old son which, by his own admission, mainly entailed sitting on the couch with him and watching day-time TV. Becca claimed that she and her partner had made and then lost a paper million with an Internet start-up company during the dot.com glory days. They had developed a computer program which converted a simple web-camera into a motion-sensitive burglar alarm. When you registered with snatchwatch.com you could download the software so that while you were out your web-cam would detect any movement in the room and trigger your PC to automatically open up a connection to the Internet and transmit the pictures to the watching world. Subscribers to snatchwatch.com could log on and watch real-life burglaries in progress, not just in their own homes but in the homes of all the other subscribers. Burglaries and family pets which had got loose, and the sexual antics of the occasional exhibitionist who conveniently "forgot" that the cameras were on them. Becca's partner, Ginny, was the techno-wizard; Becca was the one who wooed the City financers. She had become very self-assured. Her hair was now platinum blonde and she was wearing a figure-hugging evening gown which confirmed her regular gym sessions. I could imagine how the blue-suits had lapped up the idea of snatchwatch.com.

★   ★   ★

Why did I come?

I pushed my chair back against the wall and watched the impassioned, drunken debate going on all round me with a poignant nostalgia. Richard, pontificating as always; Becca, coarse and witty; William, solemn but articulate; Jane looking slightly bewildered but smiling defiantly. We could have been having exactly the same conversation ten years ago.

'We are the end product of the evolutionary process,' Richard continued patiently. 'We have won the race. No other species can compete. We don't even have to adapt to the environment; we adapt the environment to us. But ten thousand years of intellectual capabilities have been superimposed on two thousand million years of competitive instinct. One hundredth of a millimetre compared to two metres of evolutionary struggle. Survival of the fittest rewards selfishness. A locust population will explode until it has destroyed its entire food supply; then all except the strongest will starve. There is only the thinnest veneer of civilization separating us from the savage beast; a few thousand years against the eons of evolution. What hope is there that we can curb our innate selfishness now that we have the power to destroy the environment for our short term goals?'

'A grand point, Richard, and well made', said Angus McManus. We all turned to look at him. Nobody had noticed him arrive. Angus was leaning nonchalantly against the doorframe with his arms folded across his broad chest. The faint Scottish burr was still noticeable in his sardonic drawl. He was wearing a traditional city pin-stripe suit as if he had just come from his office. It was immaculately tailored. Angus had always given the impression of being much larger than his five feet ten inches. We had played rugby together for Robinson College. Angus was our scrum half. I, four inches taller than him, had played open-side flanker, but when we walked into a pub together it had always been Angus who had turned heads and hushed conversations with his roguish self-confident swagger.

'Hannah, darling. I'm so sorry we're late. Business dinner with the Colonel; three line whip, I'm afraid. Anne is just parking the... Fuck me. James Fucking Turner.'

'Hello, Angus'. I said quietly. I had drawn back from the table and Angus had evidently not noticed me at first; now he came pushing behind the other chairs and I just had time to stand up before he enveloped me in a smothering embrace.

'James Fucking Turner! How the fuck are you?'

'I'm good, Angus, good. But I'm not going to bore the others with my life story all over again. You should have been here earlier.' We looked at each other and our eyes were still locked when the door-bell sounded.

'That will be Anne I suppose. Let us retire for coffee,' said William, and then he added in a puzzled tone 'How did you get in, Angus?'

'Ways and means, dear boy. Ways and means,' Angus replied enigmatically.

While William and Hannah went into the hall to welcome Anne, Angus took it upon himself to usher the rest of the party before him down the corridor towards the drawing room. Somehow he contrived to greet all the other guests by name during the short walk while still keeping his left hand on my shoulder. He was wearing gold cuff-links, his aftershave was fresh and light, and with every step I was internally repeating the mantra: "Why did I come? Why did I come? Why did I come?" Then I heard Anne's voice behind me saying, 'James. Is it really you?'

I had been anticipating this moment for five days while pretending to convince myself that it would be no big deal. Now that the moment had arrived I desperately wished that it hadn't. Ten years since I had last seen Anne; since I had last kissed her. Ten years of deliberately suppressed thoughts and slowly ebbing emotions shot straight back to the surface as if she had left me only yesterday. I asked myself one last time: 'Why did I come?', shrugged Angus's hand from my shoulder, and turned. I knew the answer.

Anne had stopped at the far end of the corridor, framed by the doorway and back-lit by the brighter light from the hall. She ran both her hands through her hair, scraping her strawberry-blonde mane back from her forehead. It looked like a deliberately rehearsed gesture but I knew it as a nervous mannerism, executed with the exact level of distractedness as in all my memories. She started towards me and I was struck by her poise. She was wearing a plain white blouse tucked into tightly-belted jeans. I had forgotten how erect she held her self. She had always been supremely comfortable about her own body. I once joked that she held her shoulders back provocatively, challenging the world not to stare at her breasts. She had been surprised and hurt by the implications of my suggestion. The truth was that at the age of twenty Anne had known that she was labelled "beautiful" - how could she not? - but she had found her own way of dealing with this millstone by making no allowance for it what-so-ever. She did not dress down and slouch apologetically, but neither did she wear the glamour-model clothes or vogue fashion haute couture that she could undoubtedly have carried off. She never flirted, but she had learnt that even her old friends could misinterpret her interested-but-innocent conversation as such - because she was beautiful. She never held this against them and she didn't stop having interested-but-innocent conversations either. She had just learned to live with it.

Anne took a step forward and the light in the corridor lit-up her broad, tanned face; the high cheekbones; the full, smiling lips and her startlingly blue, laughing eyes.

'James. You came. I'm so glad. When William suggested a reunion, no one thought that you would come. But I knew that you would.'

I couldn't speak. Her voice was slightly deeper and huskier than it had been but her clipped Northern Irish vowels still broke through the newly acquired Received Pronunciation. She came skipping down the corridor and I actually braced myself for her to throw herself into my arms. She didn't, of course. She just took my hands in hers and squeezed them tightly before reaching up on tip-toe to kiss me lightly on both cheeks. Her breasts brushed against my chest.

I breathed in. She was wearing a sweet, subtle perfume; not the sandalwood which still evoked her so strongly that I sometimes caught myself closing my eyes and inhaling the scent from complete strangers in the street. But her smile was the same. Her eyes had a few more laughter lines in their corners but they held mine with a familiar intensity as ten years of unspoken questions passed between us.

'I take it that you two know each other then?' Angus asked sarcastically to break the lengthening silence. He completed the mock introduction: 'James, this is my wife, Anne McManus, lawyer and human rights expert. Anne, meet James Turner. Jim, I hear, rides motorbikes for a living.'

I dropped Anne's hands. I swallowed and ran my tongue over my lips to try to unglue my mouth. I knew that Anne would notice; she used to be able to mimic mannerisms which I didn't even know I had. Her smile deepened and she tilted her head slightly to one side, a gesture which I knew meant "I'm waiting". She was enjoying this. I became aware that the longer it took me to say something the more significant the utterance would have to be. I was terrified of saying something corny.

'Anne, you are more beautiful than ever.'

'Thank you, James. And you are obviously still looking after yourself,' Anne replied easily. Her tone was lightly mocking and I realised that she was referring to the vestiges of purple bruising under my left eye.

'I am playing rugby again,' I explained. 'Just semi-professional stuff; for Rosslyn Park. But we had the BBC cameras down last week.' I was beginning to function.

'Excellent,' said Angus. 'Now, why don't we all join the others in the drawing room?'

William and Hannah had bought this Hampstead town house a year ago but Hannah had supervised its entire refurbishment before allowing them to move in last month. The dining room had been all dark wood panelling and subdued lighting; the drawing room was bright and spacious with a massive modern mirror over the mantelpiece. I felt like I was stepping out onto a stage as we entered the room. Sarah and David were sitting together, talking babies. Jane and Becca were giggling over William's CD collection, having discovered Abba Gold hidden between Rachmaninov and Tchaikovsky. The others had made a bee-line for William's drinks cabinet. All their faces turned to us expectantly as we entered.

'Angus, Jim and Anne: the Holy Trinity,' said David. 'It's just like old times.'

But it wasn't, and it never would be again.

William came in and supervised the liqueurs. I refused a whisky, just as I had previously refused the gin, the Chablis, the Rioja, the port and the brandy. More than ever I needed the comfort of knowing that at any time I could just grab my crash-helmet and leave.

Later, when we had all settled into a circle of sorts, Angus rolled up a joint and passed it round.

'You are wrong, Richard, about natural selection', he said. It was typical of Angus to pick up on someone else's specialist subject. He had always loved playing devil's advocate. You could never tell what he really thought; he just loved a good debate. 'Darwin didn't say that it was the selfish which survive. He said it is the fittest, the best. We need to stop doing ourselves down as a species and start applauding our own achievements. Our ability to adapt the environment to our own convenience is something to be proud of. Unless you want to go back to living in an ice-cave, wearing rotting animal skins, and having a life expectancy of twenty five?'

'So you don't believe in global warming then?' Sarah asked, shocked by the apparent heresy.

'I accept that average temperatures are going up. There are records going back hundreds of years to prove it. Ninety-eight percent of the world's scientists can't all have misread their thermometers. I also accept that the rising temperatures are probably the result of human actions. I wouldn't normally be so confident that a consensus of ninety-eight percent of the world's scientists means that they have necessarily come up with the right hypothesis, but in this particular case it's pretty obvious. In the space of a few years we have released all the carbon dioxide back into the atmosphere which it had previously taken hundreds of millions of years to capture underground as oil and coal deposits. There has got to be a price to pay for a change of that scale. Scientific theory predicts that the impact of such a change would be an increase in global temperatures and - what do you know? - there is empirical evidence that global temperatures are rising. It would be rather churlish not to accept that the boffins have got the cause and effect right this time.'

'Then how can you be so sanguine about it?' Sarah asked angrily, caressing her bump as if to protect her unborn child from this dangerous talk.

'Do you know how much of the chemical potential energy is actually turned into power for every litre of petrol sold at the pumps?' Angus asked. 'Five percent. The other ninety-five percent is spent on geological surveys, extraction, refinement, distribution and the current inefficiencies of the internal combustion engine. Five percent. Even if we only increase that to ten percent it would still be the same as halving our carbon emissions at a stroke. Have a bit more pride in your species. Survival of the fittest, remember.'

'We may be alright in the West,' Sarah persisted, 'but in the third world hundreds of millions of people will die prematurely because of climate change.'

'And we need to do more to help them through the transition from an oil-based economy. Of course we do. But it is intellectually lazy just to jump on the doom-and-gloom bandwagon. The lives of most of the people in the world are better now than they have ever been in human history. Historically we will look back on the twenty first century not as the century which unleashed global warming but as the century which stopped squandering the one-off bonanza of cheap energy, burning up millions of years worth of oil in a few generations just to give us cheap flights to the Costa Brava. We need to start preparing for when the oil runs out. Carbon emissions will stop then for sure. It is entirely legitimate to use up a finite resource but only if it is a deliberate pump-priming exercise which moves us on to a more sustainable technology. That's our real challenge.'

'It's not just environmental issues we've got to worry about,' said Anne. She was sitting on the floor and leaning back against Angus's legs but her statement was directed at Richard. 'Your contention is that we are the first species to effectively make ourselves immune from evolutionary pressures because we can now change the environment to fit our needs instead of the other way round. But because we are still shackled by pre self-consciousness survival instincts we care more about having a warm house today than a frazzled planet tomorrow, so it's inevitable that we're going to fuck up the world. That's what you're saying, isn't it?'

'Did I say that?' Richard asked, taking a drag on the communal joint. 'Cool. It sounds pretty convincing to me.'

'You may be right. We may trash the planet in the end; but my fear is that those same selfish, short-term tendencies will screw up our civilisation long before we screw up the planet. People say that "History is dead" because liberal democracy and a regulated free market have won the battle between competing political and economic theories. Soon we will all be living like Denmark. Try telling that to the autocracies in Russia and China, to the Islamic fundamentalists, to the starving millions in India. Do any of us really stop to wonder why four fifths of the world's wealth is in the hands of one fifth of its population? It is not inherently ours, we don't deserve it, unless you are some sort of white supremacist. And it is not because our countries have greater natural resources. Far from it. It is the legacy of colonialism, and our systems of government and multinational corporations which perpetuate the inequality.'

'I apologise for my wife,' Angus said formally to the assembled company. 'She does like to bring her work home from the office with her. Of course, my dear, we might be successful precisely because we have implemented those liberal democracies and regulated free markets which you distain so much.'

Anne smiled sheepishly.

'No, Anne's right.' Jane said stoutly. She had been lying on the floor in the middle of the circle, apparently asleep. Now she struggled up into a sitting position and we all waited expectantly for her to continue.

'Well...she just is,' she said lamely, and slumped back onto the floor.

'Thank you for that vote of confidence,' Anne said, but she continued in a more measured tone. 'Every civilisation since the Indus Valley has fallen at its apparent peak, toppled by barbarian hordes who didn't understand that they were expected to conform to the same laws of behaviour as their supposed superiors. Democracy may be the best system of government that we have yet come up with yet, but it isn't perfect by a long chalk. The five year democratic cycle is fundamentally incapable of redistributing wealth on the scale required to buy off global terrorism on a catastrophic scale. It's down to short-term individual selfishness again. People don't vote for jam tomorrow, they vote for jam today. They don't vote for jam for others, they vote for more jam for themselves.'

'Doomed. We are all doomed,' said David in a mock-tragic voice.

'Nation state democracy cannot work in a truly globalised economy.' Sarah said, picking up Anne's theme. 'America lends billions of dollars to people who could never have paid it back and the whole world goes into recession. Soon we will all be fighting each other over fresh water.'

'So we need a world government to arbitrate?' Angus said interestedly. 'I can't see that happening in our life time, but who knows? That's just my point: our political and economic systems are evolving to meet the crisis. Look at the European Union. It is anathema to our parent's generation but our children will take it for granted. It's not the finished article - whatever happened to subsidiarity? And some element of proportional representation is inevitable to keep people engaged in the democratic process - but as you requested, the nation state is evolving before our very eyes to meet the challenges of a global economy. The change might not seem as dramatic as in the twentieth century because twenty million people aren't dying in the trenches to achieve it, but these are exciting times. Your problem is that you compare the current state of the world with how you would like it to be, not with how it has been. Life has always been pretty grim for most people. It still is, but it is getting better, not worse. Yes, there are millions of people starving in India; but there are four billion more people in the world right now who are not starving than there were a hundred years ago. Isn't that something to be proud of?'

'What do you think, James?' Anne asked suddenly, looking at me.

'I don't know, Anne,' I said. 'As you may have gathered, I do not walk in the rarefied circles of political policy making. Most of this discussion has gone straight over my head.'

Anne held my eye, forcing me to commit myself.

'It may not be original,' I continued reluctantly, 'but my own view is that we all have opportunities to make a difference: to challenge the racist joker, to tolerate the drunken tramp, to recycle our newspapers. In our own small ways we can all choose to do it. Or not. Deep down we all know what is right; to add our light to the sum of light.'

Chapter Two

*"If you take the racing line on a right-hand
bend your bike will remain on the correct side
of the road. But your head won't. This is
known as the decapitation zone."*
From: "Ride Well and Prosper".

I left the party shortly after one o'clock. Anne and Angus were
dancing to "Thank you for the music" and it was obvious that
the other guests were all planning to happily outstay their
welcome, even the ones with proper jobs to go to in the
morning. William and Hannah saw me out and as the door
closed behind them it was like a door closing on a glimpse into
my life as it might have been. A life of company cars, wine bars
and office gossip; flats in town and weekends in the country. In
to the office by 8:00 o'clock, and home in time to kiss the kids
good night. A parallel life, one that I had always known could
have existed but that I had never been forced to confront before.

I turned away. It was a beautiful September night. A warm,
almost Mediterranean wind stirred the plants on the upper
balconies. Over Hampstead Heath the London nightglow was
sufficiently subdued to see the stars faintly twinkling. I had left
my play bike padlocked to a sturdy streetlight. I unlocked it and
straddled it while buckling on my crash helmet. For work I ride
a Suzuki GSF600 Bandit. It is old and simple and robust which
means it is easy to maintain and spare parts are cheap. It is light
enough to weave in and out of heavy traffic but it still has

enough acceleration to beat anything on four wheels
standing start. It also has a relatively upright sitting]
which, as a large-framed man, I find more comfortabl
whole day in the saddle; it is better for seeing and being ⌐ıı.
There is a theory that Honda do not make bikes for real bikers.
Hondas, the theory goes, are designed for commuters and
weekend, fair-weather, born again bikers. I have driven most
makes of bike over the last four years and when I wanted
something for just the pure exhilaration of riding I had bought a
second-hand Honda Blackbird. My play bike. Not too flash but
fiercely fast. I rolled her forward off her stand, pressed the
starter button, and felt the thrill as the 1100cc engine purred into
life. The sheer power which was leashed under my right hand
always made me want to whoop out loud. I gunned the motor in
neutral just to hear it roar, twitching my right wrist lightly on
the grip. Then I engaged the clutch, kicked the engine into first
gear, looked instinctively over my right shoulder, and drew away
from the curb.

Riding through London at night is a wonderful experience.
Sometimes, after eight hours riding the Bandit for work, three
hours gruelling rugby training, and a curry of vast proportions, I
take out the Blackbird and ride through the West End as the
pubs and clubs are closing up. The whole human condition is
portrayed all round me; a Rolls Royce picking up the key note
speaker from a Dorchester gala evening, black cabs ferrying
home the drunk and disorderly, ladies of the night waving
hopefully, the homeless bedding down under the arches. On a
motorbike your surroundings are much more immediate than
from inside the cocoon of a car. You are aware of the state of the
tarmac, wary of manhole covers greasy after the rain, the smell
of a late night bakery preparing the morning bread, the sound of
shouting from inside a 24-hour convenience store.

Even in light traffic a bike rider needs to concentrate
unceasingly. Anticipate everything; assume nothing. Just because
the car in front is indicating left do not assume that it is actually
going to turn left, rather than right, or speed up, or stop
completely. And your mindset has to be that if it does, and you

don't allow for it, it is your fault. I know that sounds melodramatic. It feels melodramatic. Every time I start up a bike I say out loud "concentrate or die", and every time I say it I feel melodramatic. But I am still alive. In the four years in which I have been riding for a living I have seen one of my colleagues die and watched another one somersault down the road who will never walk again. Neither of the accidents had been directly the rider's fault but as the most vulnerable party on the road the biker has to take responsibility on behalf of everybody else as well as themselves. It is no good thinking "he didn't follow the highway code" as the cold steel of a car bonnet slams into your thigh. So: "concentrate or die". Not only melodramatic, but arrogant, and suspicious, and superior. Amen. Concentrate for every second of every minute of every hour. And even then it might not be enough.

So as I rode home I pushed thoughts of the party, of my old friends and my old life, of Anne, to the back of my mind. I was grateful for the ingrained discipline of "concentrate or die" which prevented me from dwelling on them now. I detoured via Shaftesbury Avenue and Trafalgar Square just because I could, but so many half-glimpses of couples kissing in doorways threatened my ability to banish all distractions whilst riding. I suddenly just wanted to get home and to bed as quickly as possible.

I crossed over Waterloo Bridge and headed down Kennington Road. All the roads south of the river were deserted but I was forced to stop at the traffic lights at the T-junction with Kennington Park Road. In the park ahead of me, through the narrow railings, I watched a small group of revellers making their way home. The streetlight did not penetrate far into the park but I could make out five youths, all of Asian origin, all dressed in some variation of the oriental youth uniform of jeans and denim jackets. As the lights changed to green I noticed that the smallest figure was actually a woman, her arms linked through the arms of the two men next to her. A car draw up behind me, forced to stop because I had not yet reacted to the green light. The car driver tooted his horn half-heartedly, knowing that it would not hurry my actions but impatient to be on his way. The woman in the park looked up, twisting her head round, and looked straight at me. She tried to shout something but the man on her left pulled her to him. The car behind me pulled out round me and headed south down Clapham Road. I shifted the weight of the bike onto my right leg, freeing up my left foot to kick the bike into gear so that I could follow him. I also wanted to get home. Across the road the kids had disappeared into the trees. I squeezed in the clutch handle to engage first gear and pull away but my visor had steamed up. I let out the clutch again, centred the bike, and flicked open my visor.

'Fuck', I said out loud. She was just fooling about, right?

'Fuck'. I said again. She wasn't shouting for help, was she?

'Fuck'.

To add my light to the sum of light. That's what I'd said, wasn't it?

I left my visor open, kicked the bike into gear and pulled slowly across the junction. The park in front of me was bounded by a low concrete wall above which black vertical railings were topped by ornate spikes which looked sharp enough to dissuade all but the most drunk of merrymakers from climbing over. I turned right and drove slowly down the road with the park on my left looking into the trees for some sign of the Asian party. After a hundred yards I came to a crossroads. To my left Camberwell New Road continued to flank the park and at the corner where the two roads met there was a pair of large metal gates blocking a service road into the park. The gates were locked.

They had not scaled the railings so there must be a way in somewhere. I looked down Camberwell New Road. I could see no other entrance that way. I gunned the engine. I was so nearly home. But I hadn't imagined the plea for help in the girl's face. I backed the bike up awkwardly, turned, and bumped it up onto the curb. I rode back the way I had come, but this time up on the pavement beside the park fence, and faster. I passed Kennington Road again on my left. At the furthest end of the park I found a pedestrian entrance. A footpath emerged with a metal bollard in its middle to prevent unwanted vehicular access. By playing the throttle very carefully I managed to inch the Blackbird through the gap.

My headlights, which had been swamped in the bright city street lights, picked out the path in the darkness of the park. I switched them on to full-beam and everything outside of their arc was thrown into even deeper shadow. I followed the path back to the spot where I had first seen the youths and then I turned off and rode slowly over the soft grass between two flowerbeds in the direction that I had seen them go. I didn't know what I was doing or why I was doing it. They would be long gone by now. Then suddenly they were in front of me: two men holding the woman between them by her outstretched arms. She was naked. Her head lolled forward listlessly. There was a gag in her mouth. Blood was running from her nose and from a cut on her hip. Ripped clothing lay all about her. An older, thickset man with his hair in a short pony-tail was standing in front of her with his back to me. He spun round and squinted into the full glare of my headlights. A knife glinted in this hand.

For a second no one moved. I revved open the throttle and pressed my thumb onto the horn button and held it there. The only modification I had made to the Blackbird against the odd days when I was forced to use it for work was to supplement the factory-fitted horn for an illegally-loud mini-beast air horn. The noise shattered the quiet of the night as I accelerated towards the group in front of me. The men fled. The girl, suddenly released, staggered forward. She nearly fell but finding her balance she tore the gag from her mouth and bent forward to wretch violently onto the ground. I skidded to a halt beside her and took my thumb off the horn.

'Get on the back,' I shouted. I was shaking. I had seen four men in the group but there were only three of them here in the trees. Had they all run? Did they know that I was alone? My headlights only lit up a narrow tunnel ahead of me in the darkness. If they should rush me from the side, push the bike over....

The girl seemed to understand. She straightened up and took a stepped towards me but looked down at her own nakedness.

'Get on!' I shouted at her, even louder. 'And keep your legs away from the exhaust pipes or you'll melt your feet.' She wavered. Then, putting one hand onto my shoulder, she swung a leg over the saddle and hopped onto the seat behind me. I had no idea which gear the bike was in and the last thing I wanted to do was to stall the engine. I forced myself to methodically kick down through the gears into first and then clicked back up into neutral so that I could release my clutch hand. I felt for the girl's hands on my shoulders and lowered them so that she was hugging my chest. I kicked the bike into first gear. The rear wheel spun on the soft ground as I opened up the throttle, and then bit in.

My only thought was to get away. I wove through the trees, expecting at any moment to see someone come charging out of the darkness. The only exit I knew was the way that I had come in. As I edged the bike through the pedestrian entrance I felt pathetically vulnerable, but there was no ambush. Kennington Park Road was still deserted and it seemed incredible that I had been sitting at those same traffic lights just ten minutes before. I shot straight across the road, turned left, right, and left again down some anonymous side street and stopped the bike.

The girl behind me was sobbing quietly but she was still holding me tightly. I unclasped her hands and waited as she dismounted awkwardly. I got off and without looking round rested the bike on its side-stand. I took off my leather jacket and passed it over my shoulder. I felt a slight tug as she took it from me. I took off my helmet.

'Can I turn round now?' I asked.

There was no answer. After a pause, I turned. I was surprised by how tiny she was. My jacket came down to her knees and the cuffs completely covered her hands hanging slackly at her sides. Blood was still oozing from her broad, flat nose. Her jet-black hair was bunched into a ponytail; her fringe fell into almond-shaped eyes which looked back blankly at me. Her brown face was expressionless.

'How badly are you hurt?' I asked. The question sounded trite even as I asked it.

There was no response. No flicker of understanding. Did she even speak English?

'Do you need an ambulance or can you ride to the hospital?'

'No hospital. No police.' She spoke quietly, but steadily. She pronounced the 'l's with an oriental breathiness.

I looked around. I had driven less than half a mile from the park, conscious of the spectacle of driving through London with a naked pillion passenger behind me. Suddenly I felt scared again. Where were all the normal people tonight?

'We have to go to the police.' I said. 'They have to catch those bastards. Jesus. Just look at you.'

'No police.'

I looked at her. Her bare legs. The bruising on her face was already beginning to swell. I tried to imagine the fear that she must have felt, must still be feeling standing humbly before a complete stranger.

'Where do you want to go?' I asked.

No answer.

'What do you want me to do? Is there someone I can call?'

Nothing.

I thought for a long time before saying quietly, 'I have a spare room where you can stay tonight.'

★ ★ ★

All houses are a compromise between location, facilities, and cost. Conventional wisdom insists that of these parameters location should be ranked first, second and third, so when I was looking for a place of my own I looked for the least fashionable location I could find. My price ceiling was fixed so I reasoned that by minimising my location I could maximise my facilities, and you couldn't then have got a much less sought-after location than Brixton Road. I bought a two-bedroom house conveniently sandwiched between a laundrette and a Chinese takeaway for half the price of William Searle's garage in Hampstead. Admittedly it is virtually underneath the railway bridge but the noise of the trains is mainly drowned out by the incessant noise of the traffic on the arterial road outside my front window. On the plus side there is a small backyard where I can hang out my clothes, freshly laundered from one neighbouring establishment to absorb the deep fried aroma from the other, and it is only fifty yards to the lock-up under the railway arches where I keep and maintain my motorbikes.

I rode slowly by the back roads and pulled up round the corner from my house; having made the offer of sanctuary I did not want the complication of explaining to anyone why my half-clad passenger was riding through the streets of London without a crash helmet. Brixton never sleeps. Even on a Tuesday night Jimmy's "Best Chinese Fish and Chip shop" stays open until after two o'clock and a large group of party-goers had spilled out from Jimmy's onto the pavement outside his shop clutching their portions of chips. My barefooted companion provoked some wolf-whistling and suggestive banter as I unlocked my front door but she was so swamped by my jacket that she was modestly attired compared to many others wandering home from the clubs that evening. I ushered my new-found waif into my home and closed the door behind us.

I turned and found her watching me warily. I suddenly felt inappropriately close to her in the confined space of my tiny hallway.

'There is a shower-room downstairs, but it is full of motor-bike clobber at the moment.' I pushed past her and started the up the stairs. 'There should be a first-aid kit of sorts in the bathroom up here. And a spare toothbrush. Do you want me to search it out, or are you happy to just root around and see what you can find?'

I turned on the landing and watched her climbing up the stairs to join me. She was holding my jacket tightly wrapped around her, lifting the hem carefully so as not to trip on the steps. She looked very small and very vulnerable.

'This is the bathroom. Sorry about the state of it. The door on the left is my room. The door on the right is the spare room. I used to have a lodger in there so there is a lock on the inside of the door'.

'You are very kind,' she said. It was the first words she had spoken since Kennington Park. She looked up at me and held my gaze briefly before walking into the bathroom and closing the door.

I dug out some grey jogging bottoms, my smallest tee-shirt and an old dressing gown and took these through to the spare room. I hadn't changed the sheets since my Mum had come to stay the month before, but it was too late to do it now. Fortunately my Mum's visit had forced me to throw out most of the junk which had accumulated there since the departure of my last lodger had provided me with the luxury of a spare room. I laid the clothes and a clean towel on the bed and ostentatiously clomped back downstairs in my heavy riding boots.

I filled the kettle and switched on the radio while I washed up the previous day's dirty dishes so that I didn't hear her again until I noticed her hesitating nervously outside in kitchen door. I beckoned her in and she came uncertainly into the kitchen. The swelling round her nose still looked very sore but she had washed the caked blood out of her hair and it now hung straight and wet down to the small of her back. My jogging bottoms were rolled up almost to their knees, held up by my dressing gown cord tied tightly round her waist. My white tee-shirt made her arms look very dark, almost black, and as thin as sticks.

'You saved my life,' she said simply.

'Maybe.'

'No. Definitely. They would have raped me. And then they would have killed me.' Her English was heavily accented but her sentences were formally structured by the straight-forwardness of her statements rather than any limitation of vocabulary.

'You don't know that.'

'I do. I know those people. And I know that you will have many questions that you want to ask me. I owe you my life. I owe you your answers. I will repay you anything else you ask but I cannot answer your questions.'

'You don't owe me anything,' I said forcefully. 'Anybody would have done what I did. But look, I don't even know how badly you are hurt. Did you find what you needed upstairs? I have got some diazepam somewhere from my current rugby injury habit if you need something stronger than paracetamol? And here, I have made some tea. Do you want anything to eat?'

She smiled. Her cracked lip made her wince, but the smile remained. 'You see, you do have questions. But thank you. I just need to sleep.'

She pressed the palms of her hands together in front of her as if in prayer and bowed to me. I copied her gesture and bowed back self-consciously. She stayed bowed as she walked slowly backwards out of the kitchen. It was an exotic gesture which should have looked completely out of place in my scruffy Brixton kitchen but she moved with such self-assured grace that it seemed the most natural thing in the world.

'Just one question,' I called after her.

She halted on the stairs.

'What's your name?'

I didn't think that she was going to answer me but after a short pause she said, 'You can call me Abbie.'

★ ★ ★

I drank my tea and let the banality of late night radio wash over me before going back outside to move the Blackbird into the security of my lock-up under the railway. When I got back the light was off in the spare room.

I woke once in the night. Soft footsteps paused on the landing outside the bathroom door and then padded quietly down the stairs. I heard the faint chirp as the telephone receiver was lifted from its cradle and one side of a short conversation in a language which was so unfamiliar that I did not even recognise the phonetic sounds let alone any individual words. Abbie crept back up the stairs and I heard the key turn in my spare room lock.

Chapter Three

Counter steering is the only way to take a corner at speed. Turn your handlebars in the wrong direction and 'fall' through the corner. Honestly!"
From: "Ride Well and Prosper".

I saw Abbie only fleetingly the next morning. I was awoken as usual by the news headlines on my radio-alarm clock. I showered, dressed and ate a bowl of muesli without hearing any sound from the spare room. I began to wonder whether Abbie had slipped out in the night. Or died. I poured out a second cup of tea, climbed the stairs, and knocked gently on the spare room door. I was surprised by the strength of my relief when I heard her indistinct response. I waited while the door was unlocked from the inside and went in. The curtains were still drawn. In the semi-darkness I saw Abbie sitting up in bed with my dressing gown wrapped haphazardly about her. I had obviously woken her and she was still disorientated by sleep and the unfamiliarity of her surroundings. I asked with concern how she was feeling and she replied with formality that she had slept well. So far, so good. Then I become suddenly flustered, wondering - completely unbidden - whether she had slept naked. I passed her the cup of tea and beat a hasty retreat. When I got downstairs I found a spare front door key, wrote her a note, and left for work.

★ ★ ★

'You soft eejit!' Charlie laughed wickedly.

Charlie Connor is twenty years older than me. He is my employer; he is also my best friend. Charlie blames his Irish ancestry for his small wiry frame and ginger hair. I blame Charlie's Irish ancestry for his remorseless good humour, his indefatigable enthusiasm, his incessant energy, his infuriating ability to be optimistic about every thing and everybody... in fact I blame Charlie's Irish ancestry for pretty much everything about him.

In his early twenties Charlie had set up Dublin's first dispatch-riding company while Ireland was still, by its own admission, an economic backwater. But it was a backwater with a disproportionately well educated population; a population which had traditionally found release from its homeland limitations by emigrating to the more rewarding economies of the UK and the United States. Then European Union subsidies enabled the country to embrace the high technology service industry in a great, big, fat, lucrative way. UCD and Trinity College graduates suddenly had opportunities worth staying at home for. Ten years later the Celtic Tiger economy was the hot-house of Europe, putting up interest rates to curb inflation while the French and German economies were stagnating and having to slash their interest rates to stimulate growth at home. Charlie's business rose with the Irish bubble. He expanded to London at the start of the nineteen-eighties boom-years. He sold his company with perfect timing, just before the dot.com crash decimated stock-markets worldwide. At the time he had over five hundred riders working for him.

Charlie retired on the proceeds of Speed-Couriers at the age of thirty-five but soon accepted that he did not have the temperament for retirement. Six years ago he started again with Pigeon Post. Where Speed-Couriers had captured the brash entrepreneurial spirit of the eighties, Pigeon Post is branded on loyalty and personal service. Dispatch riders are normally paid piecemeal – so much per drop successfully completed. When courier companies started desperately under-cutting each other in an ever-shrinking market during the nineties, dispatch riding had became like casual bar-work for students and college dropouts. The resultant image of unreliability did not help an industry trying to compete with the new technologies of email signatures and video conferencing. Charlie started Pigeon Post with just two riders, friends from his old days. He wined and dined his old client-base, promising them quality service, staffed by riders who would be polite and courteous, riders who could actually read and write, riders who understood the importance of personally delivering documents into the hands of the addressee. Service, but at a margin. The blarney runs strong in Charlie and he was soon taking on more salaried riders. He recruited those who were prepared to work regular hours for a modest return because they loved riding, rejecting those who were out to make a quick buck and move on. Many were mature riders who had retired early from successful desk-bound existences and so had the security of mortgage-free houses behind them and were just looking for a fun way to supplement their company pensions.

I still don't quite know why Charlie offered me a job, but then I still don't quite know why I accepted. Four years ago I had found myself alone in London. I had no money, I had no friends, and I had no plans to make either. On the spur of the moment, and in an act of almost masochistic nostalgia for old playing days which I thought were long gone, I had gone to watch a rugby union match. I had arbitrarily chosen the match between London Irish and Saracens, probably just because it was relatively cheap and easy to get the Madejski stadium by public transport. I had not played, or watched, or really thought much about rugby in the previous six years, but it had been a huge part of my life during my halcyon Cambridge days. Watching rugby again was going to be an emotional experience and I know how to insulate myself against emotional experiences. Half-an-hour before the kick-off I was fighting my way to the stadium bar when I literally walked into Charlie. He is a foot shorter than I am, and at least four stone lighter, which might be some excuse for not noticing him were it not for his striking ginger hair. In fact he was so much smaller than me that although I apologised for spilling his drink it did not occur to me to offer to refill it until I became aware that everybody else in the bar seemed to be on first name terms with the man.

'Is this oaf troubling you, Charlie?', 'Will I be asking him for another drink for you, Charlie,', 'Want me to throw him out for you, Charlie?'

'No bother. Leave him be,' Charlie said in a surprisingly high-pitched voice for someone who seemed to command so much respect from all those around him. He smiled up at me. 'I was just buying a round for a few friends. You'll be having a Guinness I assume?'

'Um, thanks. No, really, let me,' I offered belatedly.

'You can get the next one.' Charlie said. He turned back to the bar and shouted through the three rows of impatient customers waiting to be served, 'Hey! Sophie, dear! Another pint of Guinness for this gentleman. On my tab if you please.'

The seas parted to let me through to collect my pint and by the time it had settled the little man with the ginger hair and his attendant entourage had gone.

I remember the rugby match as a typical blood-and-thunder Premiership game with no quarter given or looked for. The atmosphere round the ground was partisan but jovial, the more so when London Irish dropped a goal in the last minute to win the match. As the two teams shook hands and their fans clapped them off the pitch I made my way back to the bar. Charlie was already there telling Sophie-the-barmaid and everyone else within earshot that, to be sure, it was great to win but it wasn't the same now that there were only three true Paddies left in the team.

'We have to rely on foreign mercenaries from South Africa, for feck's sake.'

'My round, I believe,' I said, interrupting Sophie as she handed Charlie his Guinness. He did not look in the least surprised that I had returned to repay my debt.

By our second pint Charlie had started talking about his second passion: bikes. I had learnt to ride scramble bikes on my parent's farm at the age of 14 and passed my road test within a month of my seventeenth birthday, but during my second year at university I had reluctantly traded in my old Honda Superdream for the four wheels of an even older TR6; Anne had made it quite clear that she was tired of arriving everywhere cold and wet and it was equally clear that we could not afford to run two vehicles on our combined student budgets. The hood of the TR6 had leaked so badly that Anne still arrived everywhere cold and wet but I hadn't ever missed riding a motorbike enough to save up for another one. When, eight years on, Charlie had asked about my biking experience I had admitted that, like my own rugby career and much else beside, I had consigned my bike riding days to the bin labelled "happy memories".

By our third pint Charlie had offered to loan me one of his bikes and to keep back ten percent of my wages until I had paid off the loan.

By the fifth pint I had agreed.

Charlie calls Pigeon Post his family business. This time round Charlie has kept it deliberately small-scale. The Head Office is one tiny ground-floor room in a grimy four-story building down a small cul-de-sac in Holborn. This is where Gloria presides, answering phones and updating the computers which continually re-calculate the optimum delivery schedules for all the riders. The Holborn office is where Charlie schemes his schemes when he is not down the pub or taking prospective clients out to the races. Charlie calls Pigeon Post his family business not because he has any offspring to inherit it but because he assumes a paternal attitude to all his employees. He calls all his riders "son", even those considerably more senior in years than him, and everyone else calls him "the old man", or just "the gaffer". But even by his own stratospheric standards of generosity Charlie has been ridiculously kind to me. Four years ago he lent me that first bike to get me started and when he heard how much I was paying for my Earls Court broom-cupboard digs he offered me lodgings at the same rate in his luxurious St. John's Wood flat. A year later he matched my father's loan to help me buy a place of my own in Brixton. He said it was the only way he could be sure I would actually move out of his flat but there was no contract for the loan. I shook hands with Charlie on an agreement that I would pay him interest at a rate which was half-way between the highest rate that he could find for a deposit account and the lowest rate which I could find for an interest-only mortgage. This means that Charlie and I share the delta between what the banks charge for the money they loan and what they pay out for the money they borrow. It sounds fair; Charlie could obviously make a much higher return if he invested his capital in a more traditional way but that would mean declaring the earnings to the tax man which would be contrary to one of the few missions left in Charlie's life. Our agreement also states that when I eventually sell my house I will pay Charlie back the original forty grand in cash plus a quarter of any increase in the house's value. Gloria's advice that I should buy south of the river was currently making his investment in my bricks and mortar look like a very shrewd bet indeed. My father's loan is interest free. I square this with my conscience by offsetting the interest I should be paying him against his gross under-payment of me for those years I worked on the family farm.

Even more importantly than his financial generosity, Charlie showed belief in me at a time when I had lost all belief in myself. From the very beginning he sought out my opinions, he showed interested in my thoughts on company strategy and personnel, he bounced ideas off me over a pint of Guinness in the Wheatsheaf. Maybe initially he just liked the idea of a Cambridge graduate doffing his hat to him, a poor Dublin boy made good, but last Christmas Charlie had asked me to look after his company for him while he headed off to the Bahamas for his month of winter sun. I was stunned.

'What about Gloria?' I asked.

Pigeon Post is Charlie's company: Charlie nurtures the business clients, Charlie balances the books, Charlie hires and fires the staff. But Gloria runs the office.

Gloria is another one of life's flotsam and jetsam that, like me, Charlie picked up through some chance meeting. The story goes that Charlie read a newspaper article in the Racing Times which claimed that Ireland was the most racist nation in Western Europe. The next day Charlie reviewed the ethnic mix of his riders and then phoned up the Brixton job centre to ask for two-and-a half black riders to make up his quota. The job centre accused Charlie of being racist for stipulating the colour of the candidates and anyway they didn't have any aspirant dispatch riders on their books. What they did have was any number of aspirant personal assistants. Charlie was not aware at the time that he needed a PA but he agreed to interview one anyway. Charlie and Gloria have been working, and rowing, and sleeping together – off and on – ever since.

Gloria is nearer to my age than to Charlie's but despite her lack of any computing experience, or indeed academic qualifications of any kind, she has slowly revolutionised the day-to-day running of Charlie's company. Gloria discovered a flair for IT which Charlie initially indulged and is now openly in awe of. She started by buying a simple PC with a basic word-processing package to keep track of Pigeon Post's invoices. Then she installed a finance package and taught herself how to use it to run the company payroll and manage the company accounts. Now the office is a wifi zone, much of the business is transacted via the company website, she uses speech recognition software to send her spoken words as text messages to any mobile phone in her address book, and she is currently beta testing the latest route-finder and delivery-scheduling software packages on behalf of a grateful blue-chip international computer company.

Gloria is also nearer to my size than she is to Charlie's. She is a lithe, Amazonian beauty, a black belt kick-boxer and self-confessed house music junkie. She changes her hair on a monthly whim from outrageous afro to beaded dreadlocks and has been known to turn up to the office wearing everything from men's pinstripe suits to running shorts and leg warmers. Gloria's on-off relationship with Charlie has never stopped her flirting openly with me.

'Leave Gloria in charge of the company?' Charlie had asked incredulously. 'She'd be buying some new computer gizmo or other before I'd even got to the airport. Anyway,' he added as an apparent afterthought, 'I can't be leaving the two of you alone together for a month; I've seen her flexing her biceps at you. She'd eat you alive. Gloria's coming with me.'

Gloria gave an exasperated chuckle from behind her desk. Without looking up from her computer screen she moaned, 'It would kinda be nice for a girl to be asked first, before you tell everyone else that she's going with you. Could you do that for me, Charlie, do you think? Just once in a while?'

So I had enjoyed a one-on-one crash course with Gloria on the fundamentals of the office computers and then spent four weeks answering phone calls instead of riding bikes.

'You soft fecking eejit', Charlie repeated when I finished giving him a brief account of my knight-in-shining-armour heroics of the previous night. 'You dumb, thick, ball-bag! You've taken in an illegal immigrant, that's what you've done.'

'What was I supposed to do?' I challenged him. I knew that Charlie would never willingly involve the police in anything short of murder. Possibly not even then.

'You left that lass sleeping in your spare room and you don't even know her name? You even left her a spare key for feck's sake. Get back there before she cleans out the place. Not that you've got anything worth nicking in that bachelor pad of yours.'

'I do know her name. She's called Abbie,' I said, 'and she's only a child.' As I said this I had a flash of memory from the night before: Abbie's naked body stretched out before me in the glare of my headlights. It was a very small body and very thin, but definitely not the body of a child.

'I think it's very sweet,' said Gloria in a honeyed tone.

'Thank you, Gloria,' I said. She blew me a kiss from the other side of the office.

I don't normally go into the office in the morning. Normally I just text Gloria when I clock on and she texts me back with the details of my first pick up and I ride straight there. But I always seek out Charlie when I need someone to talk to. I can talk to Charlie about everything. Everything except politics; when

Charlie gets drunk he still has a tendency to blame the English for every evil under the sun. That morning I had ridden to Holborn rather than text Gloria for my first pick up details but Charlie was preoccupied by a prospective client meeting. He was intrigued by my story, but he was also distracted.

'I'll tell you what, Jim. I'll buy you lunch in the Wheatsheaf. I should be back by then and we can work out what to do with your Abbie. And you can also tell me how you got on with Anne. I hadn't forgotten that you had a hot date last night.'

'I never said it was a date,' I protested, rising to his bait.

Charlie cackled delightedly and I caught Gloria smirking at me from behind her desk.

'Then you can tell me just how much unlike a date it was over lunch,' Charlie said. 'Now haven't you got work to do? I don't pay you to stand around gossiping all day, for fecks sake.'

'Thanks Charlie, you're all heart,' I laughed. 'Ok, I'll see you later. Gloria, where do I start today?'

I pulled on my helmet as I left the dingy Pigeon Post office. Charlie only stays on there because it's within easy walking distance of the Wheatsheaf public house which he claims serves the best pint of Guinness in the City of London. As I backed the Suzuki Bandit out from the rank of other bikes parked outside the building I promised myself that while I was riding I wouldn't think about Abbie. I promised myself that I wouldn't think about Anne either. 'Concentrate or die,' I said aloud. But it wasn't easy. At eleven o'clock my third drop took me south of the river and I phoned Gloria and asked her not to line up any more work for me for a while.

'I wondered how long it would take you to go home and have another look at her,' she said knowingly. 'Good luck, and let me know how you get on.'

I parked the Bandit in the relative security of my lock-up under the railway. As I walked the fifty yards up Brixton Road towards my house I steeled myself to find it trashed and Abbie gone. It had not occurred to me that she might take off with all my worldly goods until Charlie had suggested it, but ever since then the little seed of doubt which he had sown with such glee had been growing so that as I walked up the road I was completely resigned to the worst. I was even preparing a speech for my lunchtime meeting with Charlie, admitting that I had been a mug again. I wondered whether Abbie, or whatever her name really was, had just got up that morning and left or whether she had taken her pick of my more easily pawnable possessions first. Then I wished that Charlie's delighted cynicism had not affecting me so completely. I wanted to believe that even if I found my cupboards bare and my hi-fi gone I would still do the same thing again in the same situation. But I wasn't sure.

We all make judgement calls in life based upon our best understanding of the information available to us at the time. That is what personality is: the aggregation of the sum total of our experiences to inform the risk-versus-benefit judgements which are implicit in every action that we take.

Every action has some risk, and every risk has both a probability and a scale of impact. The probability of being hit by lightning while playing golf is tiny, but the impact if it were to happen would be enormous. The probability of being rained on while playing golf is, in my limited experience, a racing certainty, but the impact of being rained on is relatively trivial.

Similarly, every action has an anticipated benefit or loss, and every benefit can be either immediate or distant. Accepting an invitation to play golf with the lads at the weekend should bring some enjoyment (although, in my limited experience, surprisingly little) but that short-term enjoyment needs to be balanced against the longer term benefit of, for example, not requiring your partner to make her own entertainment at the weekends. That juggling of risk-versus-benefit is what decision making is.

As a species we have developed the ability to balance likelihood and impact against long and short-term benefits to an unprecedented level. What makes us unique as individuals is that, because we all have different personal experiences to draw on, we all weight these factors differently. Each person's past history influences their future behaviour: some people's first instinct on catching your eye is to smile back, other people look away; some people tell the truth for its own sake, other people work out what it is in their personal interest to say; some people act as if a stranger is a friend, other people treat a stranger as threat.

I know all this because my psychoanalyst once patiently explained it to me. Being "normal" means making rational decisions. Making rational decisions means accepting an appropriate level of risk for a perceived level of benefit. An appropriate level of risk means falling within the bell-curve of the normal distribution of risk-takers and the risk-averse. Psychoanalysts love to categorise people: introvert or extrovert, optimistic or pessimistic, self confident or insecure. My analyst explained that the experiences of my life should have led me to believe that people are generally good with the odd bad apple, rather than the other way around. People do not generally kick others when they are down; people do not generally take advantage of unguarded generosity. But more importantly than that, she explained, the experiences of my life should have led me to believe that my life is better if I behave as if I believe that people are generally good, irrespective of whether or not they actually are, and even irrespective of whether or not I believe that they are. To behave in any other way closes too many doors.

So as I walked up Brixton Road I tried to behave as if I did not expect my hospitality to have been abused and my house to have been turned over, but it was still a relief to find that my front door was not hanging off its hinges. There was no sound from inside. I knocked loudly before putting my key into the lock. I did not expect Abbie to still be there but I found myself hoping that she might be. I opened the door and the smell of frying onions greeted me. Abbie came into the hall from the kitchen.

'Hello James,' she said tentatively.

My tee-shirt still looked ridiculously over-sized on her and my jogging trousers had unrolled over her tiny bare feet. She waved her arm vaguely towards the kitchen. 'Your note said to make myself at home, but it did not say when you would return.'

'How do you know my name?' I asked. The question came out rather more bluntly than I had intended and Abbie took a step backwards.

'There were letters on the doormat. Mr. James Turner. Is that not you?'

'Most people call me Jim now. Only Angus and Anne used to call me James. But never mind, you can call me James too. That would be nice. How are you?'

As my eyes adjusted to the gloom in the hallway I saw that she had plaited her hair into a thick braid and tied it off with a rubber band that she must have found somewhere around the house. This exposed the battlefield of her face: her left eye was almost closed by a swelling above her cheek-bone, her bottom lip was split, and there was a graze and bruising all the way down her right cheek. She accepted my appraisal with her arms crossed over her chest and looked back at me defiantly.

'We must look like a right pair, you and I,' I said, feeling the bruise on my own face. 'I just hope that you don't feel as bad as you look.'

Abbie smiled.

'Still no hospital, I take it?'

The smile faltered so I didn't pursue it. 'What are you cooking?' I asked instead.

The smile returned. For someone with a face in her state, she smiled a lot.

'Everything in the house which is edible,' she said. 'Which is not very much.'

Abbie ducked back into the kitchen. I followed her and saw that my big kitchen swing-bin had been placed in the centre of the room. Abbie was standing in front of it in a futile attempt to block it from my view; futile because the bin was nearly as big as her. The lid had been taken off and was lying next to it on the floor and most of the contents of my kitchen cupboards seemed to have been crammed into it.

'I wanted it to be a surprise. I have thrown out everything which is past its sell by date,' Abbie said with pride.

'No wonder you couldn't find anything to eat.'

'Are you angry? Have I been presumptuous?' she asked, hopping anxiously from foot to foot.

'No, you have not been presumptuous. I have been meaning to do a sort out for months.' I moved over to the stove. 'So. What are you cooking?'

'Fish curry. From frozen fish fingers. There is just enough rice for two.'

'Fantastic. Let me get out of my leathers. And Abbie…'

'Yes?'

'Thank you'.

I like to think of myself as a practical person - being brought up on a farm forces you to turn your hand to most things - but having a house of my own has allowed me to indulge my handyman fantasies far further than my building abilities remotely justify. The previous occupant of my house had been an elderly lady who had come to England from Jamaica with the first tranche of post-war immigration. She had been dead in her bed for more than a week before Jimmy from next door had noticed the smell. I got the house cheaply because her distant family had wanted to realise their asset as quickly as possible and I was not in a buying chain. I had been able to pay out-right in cash thanks to the loans from Charlie and my Dad. The old lady's granddaughters had reluctantly arranged for the removal their grandmother's photos, her ornaments, and her 1960's furniture but they had left the floral curtains and the wood-chip wallpaper and the pink bathroom suites. I had spent my first summer in the house stripping it back to its essentials. I had scraped off six layers of wallpaper to reach the original plaster. I had replaced roof tiles and topped up the loft insulation. I had painted inside and out with plain, sensible colours. My greatest extravagance had been to take out the draughty metal window frames and install double-glazing throughout. My Dad had helped with the work but the window units alone had cost me a year's over-time, but it was worth it to be able to shut out most of the noise from the trains and the traffic. By the autumn of that first year I had reassured myself that my house was structurally sound, but I had also learnt that I am much better at tearing things down than I am at getting round to replacing them. When I ripped out all the carpets I discovered that downstairs they had been laid directly onto the foundation concrete and that the upstairs floor boards had never been varnished. I spent the entire winter tip-toeing gingerly over rough concrete and getting splinters in my feet before the financial incentive to make the place habitable for a lodger had forced me to do something about it. Before tiling the kitchen floor and re-carpeting the lounge I had knocked though the dividing wall between them. It had been great fun at the time, but the subsequent chaos was something which only somebody living on their own could have tolerated for as many weeks as I did. I did eventually construct a supporting arch where the dividing wall had been but it took many more weeks before I could bring myself to pay a professional plasterer to make good the mess that I had made.

I watched Abbie put the water on to boil for the rice before leaving the kitchen to change out of my riding gear. As I climbed the stairs I looked at my house through her eyes and accepted that despite all my efforts it was a very poor shadow of the sumptuous elegance that I had seen in William and Hannah's town house the previous evening. Had it been sensible to renew the acquaintance of those ghosts from my past? I could imagine Angus and Anne fitting out their dockland home from boutiques in Knightsbridge whereas my kitchen units came from an MFI sale. My pine dinning table was a present from my parents; it is a beautiful antique farmhouse table but I had had to cut off one end of it in order to fit it into my kitchen area. The carpet in my lounge is another parental cast-off, a deep-pile Axminster which they replaced on their insurance after the excesses of a New Year's Eve party. I have cut it to the right length but it is still rolled up down one side of the room because I haven't yet got round to cutting it to the right width. In the lounge there is one sofa and one armchair and one standard lamp for reading. I have never owned a TV. I only ever watch sport and films. I can watch all the sport I want down at my fitness club without having to pay a digital broadcaster for the privilege but it is not just a question of money; it is more a deliberate choice to insulate myself from the temptation to coach potato. My theory is that not having a TV gets me out of the house once in a while, round to a friend's house to watch the big sporting events or out to the cinema to watch films on the big screen. I can't remember the last time that I actually did either of these things, but I still believe the theory. I did keep Grandma's gilt-framed mirror over the mantelpiece above the gas fire but there are no pictures on my walls, just one framed photograph in my bedroom. The most valuable thing in the house is still my old college hi-fi. What I do have is books. Lots and lots of books. The living room is lined with them all along one wall. Not in bookcases, just books sitting on rough planking lain between columns of house bricks. I don't think that I have ever thrown away a book. Everybody must have bought or been given a book at one time which they were subsequently embarrassed to own because it lowered the tone of their library but I keep even these witnesses to my eclectic tastes. Science fiction, half-read historical romances, pretentious political autobiographies and the distressed purchases of "adult novelettes" hurriedly bought from seedy bookstores before long coach journeys. I may never read them again but I keep them all as testament that I must have wanted them when I bought them.

My downstairs bathroom is the pinnacle of my DIY career: my wet room. I stripped out all the inherited fixtures and turned the whole room into one enormous shower by tiling the walls from floor to ceiling and re-concreting the floor so that it now slopes gently from every corner towards a central plug hole to take away the waste water. The shower-rose in the middle of the ceiling is the size of a dinner plate. I've installed an industrial-strength extractor fan beside the window to battle the humidity and the chrome radiator is plumbed to the hot water system rather then the central heating so that the room stays warm all the time. My three sets of biking leathers usually hang in this room on the kind of laundry-rail-on-wheels that you see in dry cleaning shops. When I come home from riding in the winter, cold and wet to the core, I wheel the previous day's drying clothes out into the hall and stand under the steaming shower for as long as it takes to get some warmth back into my limbs. It takes two days for a sodden set of leathers to dry out completely in my shower-come-drying room so if I rotate my three suits through consecutive wet days I can just about manage to pull on dry trousers each morning.

But that first morning with Abbie was not wet. The day was dry and warm. No shower-room thawing required. I went up to my bedroom, pulled off my boots, peeled off my leather trousers and my rugby shirt and used the more conventional power shower over the upstairs bath instead. By the time I came down again Abbie had lain out knives and forks and glasses of water on the table and was draining the rice over the sink.

'Smells good,' I said as I entered the kitchen.

'Tastes awful,' Abbie replied dispiritedly.

I sat down and felt awkwardly formal as Abbie served me a plate with a mountain of rice and a small topping of curried fish sauce on top. She sat down opposite me and watched expectantly from beneath the dark fringe of her hair as I lifted the first forkful to my mouth.

'This is delicious,' I said. It was, but it sounded horribly contrived to say so. Abbie looked down at her own plate and grunted but as she raised her own fork to her mouth I saw that she was smiling again.

We ate in silence. I did not want to look crass by appearing to interrogate her and every topic of conversation that I could think of seemed to lead straight to some personal question or other about her. Abbie ate quickly. She had served herself with as much rice as me but by the time her plate was half empty mine looked as if I had only just started. I stole glances at her with each mouthful. She kept her eyes down but she did not appear to be finding the silence nearly as uncomfortable as I was.

Eventually I put my fork down.

'Abbie,' I started. She looked up warily. 'I know that you don't want me to ask you any questions about what happened yesterday. Or about your past. Or, presumably, about your future. I know that, and I want you to know that I know that, and I want you to know that it's ok.'

Abbie held my gaze but didn't speak. My statement had not come out quite as eloquently as I had hoped but I carried on.

'Of course I've got questions. Hundreds of them. As you can see from my humble abode it's not everyday that I have a chance to... you know... help someone... like you. But I respect your right to your privacy. The problem is that I am so worried about not asking you any questions that I can't think of anything else to talk about. I will try my hardest not to pry but if I do accidentally ask you something personal I want you to know that it's not deliberate. You can stay here for as long as you need to, but I don't even know if you would be offended if I asked whether you have any idea how long that might be.'

I stopped. Abbie still held my gaze.

'Say something,' I said. I tried to make a joke of it. 'Please.'

Abbie took a deep breath. 'I am sorry that I make you feel awkward. I will not be offended by any questions that you ask; I was just frightened that you would be offended if I do not answer them. You have been so kind to me. So, it is agreed? Neither of us will take offence? I will not be offended if you ask me questions and you will not be offended if I cannot answer them. If I can stay here for a while I promise you that I will repay your hospitality as soon as I can, but I do not want to outstay my welcome. I will leave now if you ask me to.'

So Abbie stayed. We finished our curry and I found that I actually had lots of things I could talk about. I told her about my work as a dispatch-rider. I told her about my re-found passion for rugby. Then I told her in a haphazard, round about way about the university reunion that I had been riding home from the previous night and I told her about my reservations about meeting my old friends again.

'I'm not sure it was such a good idea to go,' I said.

'I am very glad that you did,' Abbie answered.

In the afternoon we walked together to Brixton market where bruised-faced, barefooted Asian girls in over-sized men's clothing do not even register a second glance. I withdrew fifty pounds from a cash dispenser. It was as much money as Abbie would accept. She promised again that she would repay me as soon as she could. While Abbie shopped for clothes of her own I was sent to stock up on some of the basic food stuffs which I was informed were now sadly lacking from my kitchen. Abbie caught up with me as I was being processed at the supermarket checkout. She was now dressed in a plain black sweatshirt, tight calf-length jeans and white sneakers. A flowery hair band was holding back her hair and her bright glossy lipstick attracted attention away from the worst of the bruising on her face. I caught a delicate perfume as I smiled a welcome.

'I have bought you a present', she said excitedly. She delved into one of her shopping bags in which I could see my folded up jogging bottoms and some feminine toiletries and came up with a small, neatly wrapped package.

'Aren't you going to open it?' asked the checkout lady. She stopped scanning my food shopping to watch me unwrap my present. I was aware that the two women in the queue behind me were also watching me indulgently until they caught sight of Abbie's bruised face; then they exchanged meaningful glances and tutted. I prised open the Sellotape and took out a pair of Ray Ban sunglasses. They were obviously not genuine but even so they must have made a significant dent in her fifty pounds. I put them on. The lady behind the till looked from my bruised face to Abbie's.

'I think she needs those more than you do,' she said.

That evening I cooked a Spanish omelette in deference to Abbie's vegetarianism. After the washing up we sat on the carpet in the lounge and she picked tracks at random from my CD collection and challenged me to tell her a memory that I associated with each song she played. There were a few awkward moments when I inadvertently veered too close to her private world. I asked her once where she had learnt to speak English so well. She was fluent but it was obvious that English was not her first language. Another time I asked her what type of music she listened to at home. On each occasion she just smiled and said, 'No offence?'

Later I helped Abbie to choose a book to read. She wanted something to escape into. After half-an-hour of discussion she spotted "Rebecca" by Daphne Du Maurier and immediately insisted that it was the book for her. She took it upstairs to bed while I poured myself an Irish whiskey. We had spent one afternoon together. She had always been courteous but she had revealed nothing at all about herself, yet as I heard the lock click shut on the spare room door I no longer felt like there was a stranger in my house.

Chapter Four

Evel Knievel holds the world record for breaking the most number of bones and surviving. It is a record he is welcome to."
From: "Ride Well and Prosper".

I was woken the next morning by the sound of rain pattering against the bedroom window. I love riding in the rain. I have to. If my enjoyment at work depended on the British weather I would have given up dispatch riding years ago. Rain ups the ante: visibility is reduced, braking distances double, congestion increases, the premium on anticipation is ratcheted up a further notch. But the satisfaction in overcoming the elements goes up too. Concentrate or die! Rain and wind are challenges that I enjoy, it is the all pervading cold of riding on a bitter winter's day which may one day force me to pack away my riding leathers for good.

I stared at the ceiling and let my mind drift through the events of the previous day until the news headlines kicked in. I reached over to turn down the volume on the radio-alarm clock and caught sight of the only picture in my house. It stands on the writing desk on the far side of my bedroom. It is a framed enlargement of an old black and white photograph. The quality is grainy because I've blown up the picture more than the original resolution can comfortably support. I had taken the photograph on a spring day in Prague on a cheap disposable camera which I had bought a minute before from a street seller.

I had caught the subject in an unguarded moment; Anne looked back at me with eyes overflowing with love.

I turned off the radio and listened for any sound from the spare room. There was none. I showered and dressed and ate a bowl of muesli in silence and left for work. I didn't even bother to leave a note.

As I walked down to my lock-up I realised that at some point the previous day I must have turned off my mobile phone. I never turn off my mobile phone. The arrival of cheap mobile communication has removed one of the major cost over-heads in the dispatch-riding business. Bikes no longer need to be kitted out with expensive two-way radios. Pigeon Post requires all its riders to provide their own mobiles. Gloria's PC has the latest texting software. The details of the next assignments should always be in a rider's mobile phone in-box before they complete the previous drop so in theory we should be able to just text back an acknowledgment and move on, but it doesn't always work out like that. Before my stint in charge of the office last winter I used to keep a running score of the number of times each week I completed one drop-off before Gloria had sent me the next pick up. Now I have much more sympathy with the complicated juggling act which she performs every day. The profitability of the company depends largely upon optimising every rider's itinerary. My four weeks in charge last winter coincided precisely with a significant dip in the company's utilisation efficiency graph. I didn't keep score any more.

I cradled my helmet in my left arm and switched on my mobile inside it to protect it from the rain. The phone beeped loudly to indicate that I had new text messages waiting for me but I didn't read them until I was inside the dry of my lock-up under the railway arches.

Received from Charlie at 11:49 yesterday morning: G says u knocked off early. Keep me posted.

Received from Ben at 19:27 last night: Where r u.

Ben is the Rossyln Park scrum half, my team captain, and the closest of my new rugby friends. As a semi-professional club we train together on Monday and Wednesday evenings. On Tuesday and Thursday evenings we are expected to follow our own fitness regimes. Friday is a rest day before match day and Sunday is for recovery after match day. It had crossed my mind several times yesterday to warn Ben that I would be skipping training but somehow I had never got round to phoning him. I'd make up for it down the gym tonight.

Received from Gloria at 8:12 today: Assignment 93474, Vaux to CM1 3TS. PS whats the story... morning glory? Give me the goss!!! xxx :)

Charlie had recently clinched a deal to deliver car parts from a central depot to a huge number of car dealerships all over the South East. This one client had practically doubled the business over-night. Gloria was having to sub-contract some drops each day to other courier companies while Charlie tried desperately to recruit more riders, but it was unusual to get a parts delivery so early in the day. Normally these drops were in response to frantic afternoon calls because a car had been brought in for servicing in the morning and the mechanic had only just realised that he had run out of the right air filter or fan belt. Gloria's scheduling software would normally recommend one rider to pick up several parts to be dropped off at a succession of garages. I recognised the Chelmsford post code for this drop but I checked it anyway in my post code atlas before hitting the appropriate short-cut key on my mobile phone. The short-cut key creates a standard acknowledgment text to which I just need to add the assignment number before sending it back to Gloria, but this time I included a personal message just to wind her up: 'Gossip makes you blind,' I added.

As I set off for the Middlesex depot to pick up whichever spare part was needed in Chelmsford I reflected that the trip to Essex would take me onto the A12, past the spot where I had witnessed my first biking death. Jack had taken a lucrative redundancy package after twenty years working in insurance. He didn't need to work any more, he just loved riding. He had been in the Holborn office flirting with Gloria on my first day in the job.

'Jim,' he'd said, 'you are joining the happiest band of brothers in the world. We should pay Charlie for the privilege of working for him instead of accepting the pittance that he pays us.'

Jack had taken me under his large and avuncular wing; he would call me up during the day and arrange to meet for a pub lunch or for a quick drink after work with a few of the other riders. I was following him back into the City after one of these unscheduled lunch breaks when he was sandwiched between two double-decker buses. The A12 is not quite a dual carriageway at that point but there are two wide lanes in both directions. The lanes are so wide that there was plenty of room between the two buses driving west in parallel for two motorbike dispatch riders to filter between them. It was a sunny day. The bus on my left cast a deep shadow so that looking ahead from between the two double-deckers, past Jack's bike, it had felt like I was looking forwards out of a tunnel. I saw a car parked ahead of us on our side of the road. I started to brake. The car should not have been parked on a red route; but it was. The driver of the inside bus knew that there was another bus outside him; he knew that he couldn't pull out immediately. He knew that he would need to brake first and drop behind the other bus in order to pull out round the parked car ahead. But, because the lanes are so wide, the outside bus was not right on his elbow. Because the lanes are so wide, there was that slight gap between the buses; the gap that we were filtering through. The driver of the inside bus anticipated his subsequent need to change lanes by drifting out slightly, moving nearer to the bus outside him. That was all it took. He didn't brake viciously. He didn't swerve recklessly. He just didn't look in his mirror first. If he had he would have seen two bikes in the space between him and the outside bus that he was about to fill.

By braking hard I dropped out from between the two buses before the space between them disappeared. Whether Jack didn't brake because he knew that I was behind him, or whether he thought that he could accelerate forwards through the gap, I couldn't tell the coroner. He did sound his horn at the last second but even I could barely hear it above the noise of the traffic and the squeal of metal as the ends of his handlebars punctured the skin of the buses closing in on either side of him. It was over very quickly. One second I was wondering whether I should replace my visor because there was a big scratch on one side which was catching the sunlight, then I was aware of the cool and the darkness between the two buses, and then Jack was beneath their wheels.

'Why couldn't it have been you instead of him?' Jack's widow, Christine, asked me at his funeral. I didn't answer. My instinct was to say that it could easily have been me; to say that "there but for the grace of God go I". Any other answer was to imply that Jack's death and Christine's grief was partly his own fault, if not because of anything that Jack had done, then because of some lack of attention or anticipation that he could have done.

Would I have fared any better than Jack if I had been leading and he had been following? It seems egotistical to think so, and such pride comes before a fall. But the alternative is a fatalistic conclusion that Jack had just been unlucky; that accidents happen to us all and that there is nothing that we can do about it. Whereas there is everything which we can do about it. I looked at Christine and I remembered my psychiatrist's lecture: life is risk assessment. Crossing the road can be risky, but so can not crossing it. Accepting a job, kissing a girl, planning a holiday, lying in bed, playing rugby all have a measure of risk which we sub-consciously weigh-up to guide our actions. And then suddenly in life we encounter a situation where all the accumulated wisdom of our experiences dictates that we walk away, every fibre of our being screams "put it back, don't go there, leave it alone, don't get involved", but with quiet deliberation we over-ride the instinct which has served us so well up until that moment and intentionally embrace an unreasonable risk. Maybe the potential prize is too tempting, or the chase is too intoxicating, or the life that we are living is too mundane. We all have moments when we do things which, even as we are doing them, we know we may regret forever. But riding a motorbike is not like that. Riding a bike is more like kissing a girl, part of the fun is the danger but, if you play by the rules, it doesn't have to be life or death. Jack died because he got himself into a position from which he could not get out. But I could not say that to Christine.

I paid a silent homage to Jack as I passed the spot where he had died. I nearly missed it; there was nothing to mark it out from any other stretch of the A12. 'Concentrate or die,' I said out loud.

The heavy rain had eased to a persistent drizzle by the time I got to Chelmsford and by my third drop at mid-morning it had stopped completely. I took off my all-weather over-suit and crammed it into my top box to let my leathers breathe. The text banter from Gloria was intensifying with every assignment text.

Received on arrival in Chelmsford: Assignment 93625, Document, Ryan Air Stansted to Mr. John Stim, Ryan House, SW3 9SX. Was she still there?

Received 10:35: Assignment 93711, Document, Sotheby's Bond st W1A 2AA to Ms Shepherd, Sotheby's Olympia W14 8UX. I know she still there. Call me. Dont be spoil sport.

Received 11:05: Assignment 94120, software, Phil Danny studios W8 9EU to Mr. Will Thomas, Beacon House RG8 12SS. Did u get 2 1st base?

I conscientiously texted back my acknowledge of each assignment but I did not add any further personal details to my replies. I had vaguely planned to drop into the office for lunch to see whether yesterday's offer from Charlie to buy me lunch in the Wheatsheaf was still valid but I was enjoying thwarting Gloria's curiosity too much. I took a break for lunch in a transport café after the Reading drop. As I waited for my spaghetti bolognese to arrive I phoned my home number. My phone rang for a long time and I was just about to hang up when the receiver was picked up. There was no immediate answer at the other end.

'Hi, Abbie. This is James,' I said.

'Oh. Hello James.'

I belatedly realised that I did not have anything specific to say.

'I am just phoning to check that you are ok,' I said rather lamely.

'I slept much better last night. I am feeling much better today.'

I pictured Abbie's battered face and smiled sceptically.

'Good. I wrote my mobile number next to the phone. Call me if you need anything.'

'I don't need anything.' She sounded much more reserved than I had expected but maybe it was just because of the impersonal nature of telephone conversations.

'All right, then. I'll see you later.'

'Good bye, James.'

I spent the rest of the afternoon coyly declining to rise to Gloria's texts but when I got another car parts delivery to Chatham at the start of the evening rush hour I added a short comment to my acknowledgement reply: 'last drop tonight, shagged out'. I knew the double entendre would infuriate her, allusion with no substance. It was a cheap joke but it made me chuckle.

The rain returned from the west as I arrived in Chatham and handed over a new fuel pump to a relieved service manager but it was just light drizzle so I didn't bother struggling back into my waterproof over-suit. I rode back to London into a setting sun and with a glorious rainbow in my mirrors. Despite the heavy traffic my speed on the M2 went a long way towards keeping my leathers dry but the evaporation was also cooling. The rain stopped before the sun went down but the air temperature dropped quickly under the clearing skies. It was dusk by the time I got back to Brixton. The neon lights of "Jimmy's Best Fish and Chips" flickered on as I walked home from my lock-up and as I passed the open door Jimmy caught sight of me and beckoned me inside. I looked on past Jimmy's chip shop to my house. The upstairs windows were open. I was cold. I wanted to get home. I wanted to find out how Abbie was. But Jimmy had been a good friend to me, once we had established that just because I shared his name did not mean that I wanted to share his bed. He is about my own age, my width but a foot shorter, and we spar constantly about the relative merits of soccer verses rugby. His greatest ambition is to get me to join his 5-aside soccer team.

'Hi Jimmy. How's business?' I asked as I stepped inside the shop and walked forward to warm my hands on the hot serving counter that was displaying the first battered fish and savaloys of the evening, pre-cooked in anticipation of the early evening rush.

'Business is frying,' Jimmy replied. I had been asking the same question and Jimmy had been giving the same reply, laughing at his own inability to articulate the difference between "l"s and "r"s, since the first time I had stopped by to ask for the real gen on the neighbourhood before making an offer on the house next door. 'You got new Chinese girlfriend. What you done to her?' he asked bluntly.

'She is not my girlfriend,' I replied, rather too quickly.

'She very cute. Small tits. Just like a boy.'

'Jimmy.'

'Yes, boss?'

'Fuck off!' But I couldn't help laughing as he continued to make suggestive contortions with his face and hands. 'She is not my girlfriend and I did not give her those bruises, but she is a guest in my house so if you value my thrice weekly custom you will treat her with respect and you will keep your hands off her arse.'

'Cute arse, too,' Jimmy said as I turned to go. 'You want set meal for two? On the house?' Jimmy always had to have the last word.

I walked on next door to my house. 'Abbie, it's me, James,' I called out as I let myself in the front door.

'I'm upstairs.'

I put my helmet on its rack in the hallway and went up to find her. The door to the spare bedroom was open. I paused on the landing and looked in. A small animal was crawling around under the rumpled duvet on the double bed. The animal giggled and Abbie's hot but smiling face peered out from inside the duvet cover through the poppered opening.

'There must be an easier way of putting the cover back on,' she said.

'There is. You have to start with the duvet cover inside out. Then you put your arms right inside it and grasp the corners of the duvet... Look, get out of there and I'll show you.'

Abbie slithered out and jumped down from the bed onto the floor. She was wearing her pedal-pusher jeans and a white sleeveless vest. As Jimmy had said, she did have a boyish figure but her vest was tight enough to confirm that her breasts would be large enough, for instance, to fit snugly into the palms of my hands. Breasts are amazing things. I don't know any women who really understand why two lumps of fatty tissue should hold such an attraction for men. Pert bums are nice too, but breasts seem such arbitrary bits of the anatomy, like an afterthought stuck onto a plasticine model. As I caught myself looking at Abbie I remembered an infamous research project in the nineteen eighties which fitted a hundred people with camera-glasses which tracked the eye focus of the wearer. The study revealed a lot of fascinating things, but the most fascinating of all was that every single man looked at every single woman's breasts within five seconds of meeting them. Without exception. All the men claimed to have no recollection of having done so; indeed they all denied it vehemently until presented with the recorded evidence. The program concluded that this sizing up was entirely subliminal. Men are evolutionarily conditioned to evaluate the fecundity of members of the opposite sex. Feminist groups were outraged until a reciprocal study found that every single woman glanced at the groin of every single man. Without exception. That shut them up for a while. It was proclaimed as official: subliminal ogling is an instinctive inevitability and therefore nothing to be ashamed about, like the imperative to turn towards a movement in your peripheral vision in case it is a sabre-toothed tiger preparing to pounce. However, after the first surreptitious appraisal there was a wide difference in the number of times that the volunteers returned their glances to the reproductive areas of the people they met. Some men stared fixedly into the faces of the women they were talking to while others, even knowing that their eye movements were being analysed, let their attention wander freely over the bodies before them. The first glance might be instinctive but anything more was purely self-indulgent. I looked up from Abbie's breasts just in time to catch her watching me watching her.

'Thank you for the offer to teach me,' she said, 'but I think that I have managed a good job by my method.'

Abbie picked up her black sweatshirt from the floor and I made a deliberate show of looking away while she pulled it over her head. I hoped that Abbie had heard the theory explaining the evolutionary difference between involuntary breast-appraisal and letching. She bent to smooth the duvet on the bed.

'Have you washed the sheets?' I asked to her back. 'There was no need to do that.'

'It was fun. You have a great laundry room.'

'I don't have a laundry room.'

'The shower room downstairs. I spread out the sheets, sprinkled some powder and jumped about on them in the water. I could have stayed in there for hours.' Abbie turned and looked up at me earnestly, 'I will do your sheets tomorrow if you like?'

'Abbie, you do not need to clean my house to earn your keep.'

'It is all that I can do for now to pay you back for your kindness. It makes me feel better to do something.' She looked down humbly as her bare feet toyed with the carpet but then suddenly looked back up at me defiantly through the dark curtain of her fringe and added mischievously, 'Anyway, someone needs to clean your house. It is quite tidy, but it is not quite clean.'

I opened my mouth to object. I do make an effort. I clean the kitchen and bathrooms quite often but it was true that the vacuum cleaner had not been out since my mother had stayed over a month ago.

'We can talk about this later.' I turned to leave. 'I am very cold and very hungry and very late.'

'Late for what?'

'Late for gym. I should have been at the squad training session last night. I am normally pretty conscientious so it won't have mattered that I missed one session but I really do need to go to the gym tonight. I can't miss squad training and two gym sessions in the same week. I should have gone to the gym on Tuesday evening as well, instead of going to that bloody dinner party in Hampstead.'

'I am still glad that you went to that bloody dinner party in Hampstead instead of going to your Tuesday gym session,' Abbie said.

I paused in the doorway. Abbie was smiling again now.

'Actually, I'm glad I went, too. I'm just grumpy because I don't want to go out again tonight but I know that I'll enjoy it once I get there.'

I realised that Abbie had not articulated an opinion on my going out; it was me that didn't want to go. It had been a long time since I had had someone at home that I wanted to stay in with. I walked through to my bedroom and sat on the edge of my bed to take off my boots but I left my door open. I called through it to Abbie, 'I am going to have a hot shower – in my newly christened "laundry room" – and then I'll grab something from Jimmy's next door. What do you want?'

She appeared in the doorway. 'I have cooked something already.'

I looked up.

'I found a recipe book. It said that pasta is very good for athletes. I do not know pasta very well, but it seemed easy enough. Tuna bake. It is in the fridge but I can warm it up very quickly.'

She looked so unsure of herself that I wanted to hug her.

'Abbie. I don't know what to say. Thank you again, I guess, would be a good start.'

★ ★ ★

To call my rugby career semi-professional may be misleading. Do the maths. We get between one and three thousand paying spectators at our twenty home matches; paying five pounds a head this generates an income of about two hundred thousand pounds a year. The bar takings contribute another fifty thousand which just about pays for the ground and clubhouse maintenance. Our advertising income just about covers the cost of the match programs; they are not great collector's items. Except for last week when we could promise everybody five minutes exposure on national television because we were to be featured on a BBC program about grass-roots rugby. The takings for advertising on the hoardings round the edge of the pitch from that one match should pay for the whole of next year's floodlighting bill. The ground is used for other sporting activities and the clubhouse can be hired for social occasions, but there are not many takers. Sponsorship pays for our kit, balls, and some training equipment, but we are not yet in the league where dealerships are fighting over each other to give us their cars. Against this there are four salaried staff on various levels of part-time work: Dave-the-groundsman; Samantha, the fitness-coach/physio/nutritionist/masseuse, and long-suffering object of lust and machismo posturing from the younger players; Peter Taylor, the chairman and, more importantly, our accountant; and Suzie-the-secretary. If you take out their wages it does not leave much to go round a squad of twenty-five players. The club is not contracted to pay us anything. It insures us. It pays us appearance money in the guise of very generous expenses, and it "contributes towards loss of earnings" for time spent training, and the club pays my gym membership costs. It all adds up to a significant bonus on top of my day job but no one could accuse us of playing for the money.

Rugby, of either flavour of the code, is the ultimate team sport. At the local level there is still a role for every shape and size of player. Squat props, lumbering locks and nippy wingers can all contribute in their different ways to a winning team. At the elite, fully professional end of the scale every player is both very big and very fast. I am somewhere in the middle. Physical size is a given, but higher skill levels, greater fitness and, above all, better teamwork can still triumph over bigger and faster individuals. If your team mates are all so finely trained that they will unthinkingly thrust their face between a flying boot and the rugby ball if that is what is required to prevent the opposition from scoring then you will be pretty nigh invincible. Skill levels come from practice. Practice, practice and more practice until the basic actions of kicking, catching, passing, side-stepping and tackling are so ingrained into muscle memory that they become second nature. Only then can the rest of the mind be freed up for the bits around the margin which actually win the match: reading the game, playing the referee, keeping a cool head, bringing the best out of your team-mates, exploiting the rules, reacting first. These are the attributes which make the difference between an average player and a good one, and these are the things which go first when the lactic acid builds up and the adrenaline wears off towards the end of a game. The fitter team does not win because they can keep running longer. All teams are sufficiently fit these days that they can go through the motions for eighty minutes. The fitter team wins because it can still be creative, do the unexpected, during those last twenty minutes when the opposition reverts to the predictable.

Brixton Rackets and Fitness Centre is a gleaming new steel and glass private complex whose very existence testifies the rejuvenation and re-found confidence of this part of London. Six indoor tennis courts, four squash courts, two basketball / badminton / five-a-side courts and an out-door all weather surface which can be switched from football to hockey to netball. The fitness facilities are centred around a raised, glass-walled swimming pool known invariably as the goldfish bowl. The banks of running, cycling and rowing machines are lined up on three sides of the pool so that the aerobic workers can chose between watching the soft pornography of MTV on the big wall-screens or the soft pornography of watching the swimmers from underwater as they plough determinedly up and down their swim lanes. There is a mirror-lined dance studio for yoga and pilates and kick-boxing lessons. There is a sauna, a jacuzzi, a bistro, and a coffee lounge with all the satellite sports TV channels you can think of. Then there is the weights room.

Private leisure centres have a code of etiquette all of their own, an inevitable consequence of so many young people congregating in pursuit of the body beautiful. There is an un-stated pecking order amongst the sexes. Women do not have to be attractive, but they do have to be thin. The thinner they are, the fewer clothes they are expected to wear. The new members who sign up in the enthusiasm of their New Year resolutions make their way tentatively to the treadmills in loose fitting track suits, their eyes staring fixedly ahead, zoned into their own worlds and excluding all distractions with the help of their MP3 players. Very few of them make it to February, chalking up the annual subscription as another failed fantasy. The few who do stay gradually shed their clothes throughout the year as they shed their pounds so that by the time next January's intake step gingerly from their communal changing room in their sweatshirts and jogging bottoms the old lags are strutting confidently around the corridors in hot pants and latex crop tops.

With the men it is slightly different. The premium is not so much on thinness as on physique; there is a complete divide between the serious training athletes and the mid-life crisis gentle joggers. The unspoken pecking order bestows a licence for the most muscle-bound men to mingle with the thinnest of women. If you are well toned and glistening with sweat you are allowed to talk to any women on any pretext at any time. I have watched my mate Ben, who is a member of the same gym, stop midway through one of our bench-press sessions and walk all the way across the room to engage a complete stranger in conversation about the relative merits of her cross-country ski machine. There was no introduction or pretext, he found her attractive and so he went to talk to her. Because he could. After five minutes he returned and carried on the bench-press reps from where he'd left off, muttering "she's married" by way of explanation for his early return.

I am not completely immune to the body cult even though I know that it appears both sexist and shallow to those who have not experienced it. If these same people met as strangers at work they would not overtly judge each other by their physical appearance, but there is something about the atmosphere in a gym which cuts through cultural pretences and exposes some very basic compulsions. The pecking order exists; it is accepted and nurtured as much by the women as by the men. The women may claim to join the club just to improve their health but there is also a seed of desire in them at some unconscious level to become a more sexually attractive object. Sorry, but it's true. There may be a few honourable exceptions who are genuinely unaffected by all the pheromones in the air but there are many more who openly revel in their new-found ability to turn heads as they strut by. I do not know the specific pressures of work, or family, or friends which prevent most of the newcomers from seeing through their New Year resolutions, to get fit, to get thin, to expend more calories then they consume, but I do have a respect for the few who make it, who stick the course and accomplish whatever it is that they have set out to achieve however vain they may become in the process.

Rugby flankers have to be a bit of everything: anaerobic endurance combined with occasional explosive upper-body strength. Or as Ben disparagingly puts it, we are jacks of all trades but masters of none. Most of the bulking up is done during pre-season training when our bodies do not need all week just to recover from the previous match. Samantha prescribes steak and tuna diets with protein supplements and weight-lifting-to-failure sessions. Now that the playing season had started again in earnest my diet sheet and workout regime had changed to prioritise speed and stamina over power. More pasta, less meat. More aerobic exercise, less weight lifting. It didn't make the gym sessions any less boring but it did allow my mind to range freely while my feet pound out the miles on the running machine: Abbie. She was about to spend her third night in my house. Did it matter that I didn't even know her second name? Or why she was staying? Did she literally have nowhere else to go? And if so, what would happen next? Next week, next month, next year? No one likes to be taken advantage of. In purely financial terms it would cost me very little to support her indefinitely but once the novelty had warn off would I find myself left with a foreign au pair to meekly clean my house and wash my clothes? And did it matter that my questions were continually interrupted by memories of her naked body?

I had a long work out and then showered at the club. Abbie's light was off when I got home.

Chapter Five

*Don't let car drivers intimidate you. Take up
your fair share of the road. If you feel rushed,
slow down. You've paid your road tax as well.
Haven't you?"*
From "Ride Well and Prosper" .

Friday morning was dry and bright. I listened to the news
headlines, the sports summary and the weather forecast
before getting out of bed and pulling on my dressing gown. I
went through to the bathroom to clean my teeth and pee before
heading downstairs. My usual routine: first into the kitchen to
put on the kettle, then into the drying room to select a set of
leathers for the day ahead. Except that now I thought of it as my
laundry room instead my shower room. I smiled to myself as I
imagined Abbie dancing about under the shower with my sheets
spread out on the floor beneath her. As I took my leathers back
upstairs to dress I paused outside her room and knocked gently.

'Tea?' I enquired through the door.

There was no answer. I tried the handle. The door opened
onto an empty room but before I entered I heard the power
shower spluttering into life in the upstairs bathroom behind me.
I hadn't intended to shower that morning, or even to shave, but
I momentarily remembered the nagging intrusions of previous
paying lodgers who had disrupted my settled routines so much
that I had eventually foregone the extra disposable income in
return for freedom from timetables for morning ablutions and

rotas for kitchen cleaning duties. And my own solitude. I walked on to my room and dressed. By the time I got back to the kitchen the kettle had boiled. I made two mugs of tea and brought them both upstairs but Abbie was still in the bathroom. I left her mug on her bedside table and left my house without breakfasting.

Work was work. It was mostly local City of London drops that morning. Gloria had stopped adding her personal enquiries onto the end of her dispatch texts so I knew that she wasn't finding my radio silence funny any more. When I started feeling hungry towards noon I pulled up by a deli bar to pick up some sandwiches and then called into the office to put Gloria out of her misery. Charlie was out again. Gloria initially greeted my appearance by pretending not to notice me until I went over and dropped the sandwich that I'd bought for her onto her keyboard as she typed. She reluctantly looked up at me.

'Hello stranger,' she said with mock disinterest. Then, 'I hope you've come to spill the beans 'cos if you're still not talking to me I'll stuff your sandwiches where they won't taste so good.'

'Talk to you?' I asked innocently. 'Talk to you about what?'

I received a kick-boxer's trained forearm jab in my stomach in reply.

'Ok! About Abbie? Yes, she is still in my house. And before you give me the third degree, I know nothing more about her than I told you on Wednesday.'

'You must do! God. Men. You are so obtuse. What is she like?'

'I told you what she's like.'

'No. Not what does she look like. What is she like? With you? Does she follow you around the house? Does she mimic your body language? Does she flutter her dark mysterious eyes at you?'

So as we ate our sandwiches I spilled the beans. I told Gloria that Abbie had cooked me a fish finger curry and tuna pasta, that she was in bed when I get home in the evenings and that she didn't get up until after I had left in the morning. I told her that she had vacuumed my lounge and washed my sheets, that she was reading "Rebecca", and that she had bought me some sunglasses.

'Apart from that I have no idea how she spends her days,' I finished. 'But she doesn't flutter her eyelids at me.'

'Oh dear,' Gloria said, ominously.

'What?'

'Nothing.'

'You can't just say "Oh dear", and not explain what you mean by it.'

'You didn't call me for two days.' Gloria smiled triumphantly. 'I want you to send me some new titbit about Abbie with every acknowledgement text today. Keep me updated over the weekend. I want a text every evening. Then, if you're lucky, I'll explain what "Oh dear" means on Monday. Now get your bony ass back in the saddle. There's a pick up waiting for you in Notting Hill. Oh, and Jim…'

'Yes?'

'Nothing.'

'Bitch.'

★ ★ ★

I received a text mid-afternoon which was not from Gloria: 'Fone me. Luv Jane'.

I know at least three Janes. One is a fellow rider whose number is programmed into my mobile phone address book; her name was not displayed as the sender. There is another Jane who, for historical reasons, I am not expecting to hear from again, and certainly not "with Luv". Which left Jane Mabbutt, nee Trafford, who I had not thought about for ten years until I saw her again at our Cambridge reunion party three nights before and who I now knew to be a Methodist minister somewhere in the east end of London. I scrolled down and selected the "phone back" option.

'Jane Mabbutt speaking'.

'Jane. Hi. Jim.'

'Jim. Hi. Thanks for getting back to me. It's Jane here by the way. But then you know that don't you, because you phoned me.'

'Yes, Jane. I phoned you.' Jane had always been the scatty one.

'Sorry. Of course. Anyway, Jim, I wanted to ask you what you're doing tonight?'

'Are you inviting me out?' I asked, amused by her straight-forwardness.

'No. Yes. No. Well… it was fantastic to see you again on Tuesday, but I didn't really get a chance to talk to you properly. It is my job to be interested in people. I meant to call before but I had to phone William first to get your number and… anyway, do you want to go out for a drink or not?' she ended defiantly.

'I'm only teasing. Of course I would love to go out for a drink. Is it going to be just the two of us?'

'Yes. At least I haven't planned to invite anyone else.'

'Can I bring a friend?' I asked.

There was a slight pause before Jane replied. 'Of course. But would you both be able to come out my way. I haven't got my own transport at the moment.'

'I am sure that will be fine. Where and when?'

'Great. Do you know the East End?'

'Jane. I'm a dispatch rider.'

'Sorry.' Jane thought for a while and then gave me the address of what she called her local wine bar. I withheld my surprise that such an establishment existed in East Ham

'We'll see you at seven-ish' I said, and rang off.

I phoned my home number to ask Abbie if she wanted to join me that evening. I let it ring until it stopped but there was no reply.

My next text was from Gloria but instead of the normal succinct delivery instructions the text asked me to phone her after my next drop, which normally meant that the handover instructions were too complicated to text or that the client was a new customer who needed special treatment. I pressed the speed-dial number. Gloria answered immediately. She explained that she had been called by a very distressed lady who had got the Pigeon Post phone number from Talking Pages. The lady was about to set off on a week's sailing holiday from Portsmouth and she had forgotten her bed-time reading – the annotated first draft of her company accounts. She wanted to know if there was anyway that Pigeon Post could pick them up from her office and get them to her yacht before the tide turned at six. I looked at my watch and contemplated the M3 during the Friday early afternoon rush-hour.

'Not a problem,' I said confidently.

'Thanks Jim, but ride safely.' Gloria said. I was about to ring off when Gloria asked, 'And your new information is…?'

'My new information is that Abbie doesn't spend all day inside. Or at least if she is at home she's not answering the phone,' I said.

'And do you normally phone home so often?' Gloria asked innocently. Before I could reply she mischievously added, 'Oh dear!' and cut the line.

I tried calling Abbie again anyway. There was still no reply. There was also no reply from Jane's mobile so I left a message apologising that I might be late for our drink and set off for Heathrow Business Park to pick up some company accounts.

The M25 was nose-to-tail and a shunt on the M3 had closed the inside lane so the traffic was backed up all the way to Basingstoke. I wondered as I filtered through the stationary traffic why people put themselves through this every week; some people did it every day. Once I got past the accident the traffic thinned out. I rarely ride the Bandit at more than 90 miles per hour on the motorway; my licence is too important. Most speed camera vans photograph the front of speeding vehicles and motorbikes, handily, do not have number plates at the front but there are still the unmarked police cars to worry about. To say nothing about the fact that it is just plain wrong to break the law. But it was a perfect September evening and I suddenly had a real young-at-heart feeling. I opened up the throttle and indulged in a mad twenty minutes of overtaking and undertaking at 120. It was exactly the kind of behaviour of which I am normally so contemptuous. It is not only dangerous, it is inconsiderate to other road users. But, man, it's good fun. I arrived at Port Solent marina at 5:45.

There was no obvious reception or security guard. I parked the bike and walked over to look through the gate at the forest of gently swaying masts. The gate was operated by a numeric key pad but there was nothing in my instructions about a code to open it. I was about to phone Gloria when an elderly couple came striding purposefully over from the car park. I asked them if they knew the Foxy Lady and they cheerfully let me through the gate and pointed out two tall masts at the far end of the pontoon. It was one of the few yachts with any sign of activity on board and as I approached the foxy lady herself jumped nimbly down from the deck.

'Please say that you are from Pigeon Post. You are a bloody lifesaver if you are. They won't open the lock gate after six and I'll have a mutiny on my hands if we don't get away tonight.'

I handed over the documents and she signed the delivery note.

'I'm not quite sure of the etiquette, actually. I was told I could send a cheque later but do I need to offer you a tip or anything?'

'Thanks, but it is all part of the service.' I said. 'You'd better get going.'

'Right-o. You couldn't just cast us off forward could you?'

I watched the foxy lady climb back on board and pass her documents down to someone inside the yacht. The engine was already running. She took up her place behind the steering wheel and barked out a few orders which sent the rest of the crew scampering over the deck, coiling ropes and stowing fenders. When she gave me the nod I loosened the last mooring line and pushed the boat gently away. The foxy lady smiled distractedly as I waved her off. She was already thinking about the voyage ahead, shouting down to somebody to call up the lock keeper on the VHF radio. She was no more than in her late twenties, somehow managing to look gorgeous even in her oilskins and safety harness, and from a world so far away from mine that I couldn't even begin to feel jealous of her. There was a wedding ring on her finger.

When the yacht had passed out of sight I fished out my mobile phone to report my successful final delivery and picked up a voice mail reply from Jane: 'Jim, it's Jane. Sorry to hear you're going to be delayed. I hope you can still make it. Why don't you come straight to the manse so that neither of us is left hanging around drinking Chardonnay on our own. 13 McIntyre rd. I'll expect you before nine, unless you get back to me to the contrary. Bye'.

I tried home again. Still no reply.

I got my battered A-Z out from the bike top box and looked up McIntyre road. It would not be much of a diversion to go home first and it would allow me to change out of my day leathers. I rode back to London in a more restrained manner than on my outward journey which allowed me to enjoy watching in my wing mirrors as the sky behind me reddened into a beautiful sunset.

It was dusk when I pulled up on the pavement outside my house but there were no lights on inside. I called out to Abbie as I went in and made my way upstairs to the spare room. The bed was neatly made-up and apart from the faint hint of her perfume there was no sign that she had ever slept there; the room was as bare as when she had arrived. I walked over to the dressing table. The top two drawers were empty but in the third drawer down there were two pairs of white tanga knickers, carefully folded. So my guest with no identity and pathetically few possessions had not left just yet. I wanted to open the other drawers but I left the room and shut the door behind me.

I had a leisurely shower and then pulled on a collared shirt and some heavy denim jeans. I always wear full leathers for work but on social occasions if the weather is set fair and I am not riding far I sometime compromise to avoid sitting around in leather trousers all evening or having to change when I get there. I dressed as slowly as I could but Abbie had still not returned by the time I was ready to go. I wrote a message on the back of an envelope and left feeling disappointed to be heading out alone.

The East Ham manse is not at all like the village vicarages of my childhood. My paternal grandfather was a parish priest up until the day he died. Some of my earliest memories are of croquet-and-tea parties on the lawns of his chocolate-box vicarage near Exmoor, handing round the cucumber sandwiches to elderly parishioners. By contrast Number 13 McIntyre road did not look as if it had a rose-garden in the back sloping down to a babbling brook. Number 13 was in fact identical to numbers 11 and 15. A two-up, two-down white pebble-dashed terrace house, with a pad of concrete in the front for off-road parking.

'Your Church has done you proud,' I said as Jane opened the door.

'Hi, Jim.' We kissed cheeks. 'You will have passed the lovely old manse at the top of the road. It was sold off a few years ago to help to pay for the salaries of the likes of me. The result of a management consultancy review into our finances: "Priority in People". I'm not complaining; I am sure they were right.'

At Cambridge, Jane had always called herself the frumpy one of the group, an image which she had tried to compensate for by wearing floaty Indian-print dresses when everyone else was wearing jeans. On Tuesday evening she had worn an ill-fitting black velvet evening dress. Now she looked far more comfortable in faded jeans and a baggy tee-shirt. Her brown hair was split in a centre parting and gathered into haphazard bunches behind her ears. All my memories of Jane were of her laughing, often at herself, but always laughing, always smiling. Now her eyes looked tired.

'Are you alone?' She asked, looking past me.

'Yes, I'm afraid so. I appear to have a new lodger who I thought might like to come out with us. It is a long story, but I've just got back from Portsmouth and she was already out.'

'You must be knackered. You should have said. We could have done this another night,' Jane started in a concerned voice. She had also been the mother figure of the group. The mother figure, and the most open, honest and gullible person that I have ever met. She believed everything she heard and everything she read because, as she said, why would anyone want to lie to her? To which the answer was, obviously, pretty much any one of us who happened to need an easy butt for a puerile practical joke. Jane had read books for the wrong courses, bought tickets for imaginary gigs, and sought out picnics which weren't there all because one of us had wanted to see if she would really fall for it again. And we all loved her to bits for it. Such a fundamental incapacity for critical analysis was not the surest foundation from which to tackle the rigours of a university degree course but she also possessed a propensity for dogged hard work which had eventually seen her graduate with flying colours.

Jane showed me into a narrow front room with pink wallpaper, a sagging brown Draylon sofa and a chipped gas fire. The room had none of the vibrant personality of the old Jane. The environmentally friendly light bulb cast the corners of the room into gloomy shadow.

'What exactly is the plan for this evening,' I asked, 'apart, of course, from giving you an opportunity to interrogate me again about my last ten years?'

'Jim, how can you be so cynical? Sorry, I should have offered you a beer.' We moved together into a tiny kitchen with a double-glazed door opening out onto a half-lit patio. I wondered if my house looked as bleak as this to fresh eyes, and then wondered what Abbie was doing. Jane got two cans of lager out of the fridge. 'First we drink to renewed friendships. Then you have a choice. We can either go out for a Chinese or I can cook you beans on toast'.

'Jane,' I laughed, 'I'm glad that some things about you haven't changed.'

We sat on Jane's patio and talked about the old times. I explained that when I had finished my Finals exams I had gone back to Devon to help out my Dad on the farm, initially just for the summer, but somehow I had stayed there for two years. Then I had travelled: Europe, Africa, South America. I ended up working in Thailand. Four years ago I found myself back in London and bumped into Charlie.

We drank more beer.

Jane described how she had split up with Richard almost immediately after graduation. Richard had gone off to do his PhD at St. Andrews, Jane had got a job at the British tourist office in London and there just hadn't been enough left in their relationship to justify the long train journeys between them. Then she had met Simon. Simon had already been contemplating taking up holy orders when they had met. They had got married five years ago and gone to ordination school together.

'But it didn't work out for us,' Jane said simply. 'Simon is doing something in marketing now.'

'So you're just separated, not divorced? How does your church view that?'

Jane laughed bitterly. 'My congregation here are wonderfully supportive. Shit happens, and they know it. They all tell me secretly that they never thought Simon was bright enough for me. They're probably right. The higher echelons still talk about rapprochement counselling but we are beyond that stage. As long as I don't openly take up with somebody else I'm not doing anyone any harm.'

'But you can't live your whole life separated.' I said, shocked.

'Oh, I don't see why not. Celibacy used to be a fundamental part of the vocation. It still is for the Romans. Simon might have a different view; I'm sure we will divorce eventually but until someone else comes along I don't see that it makes much difference. And I don't see anyone else coming my way in a hurry. Anyway, I don't see a wedding ring on your finger.'

I looked down at my hands. It was true. I didn't think about it very often, but when I did I knew that I would never marry now, never have my own family, never cuddle a tiny baby and watch it grow from childhood into adolescence and guide them into adulthood, never sit a grandchild on my knee.

'I've just never found the right person.' I said. 'Sex, yes. Love, no. Not of the happy-ever-after-kind anyway.'

'I think you did once,' Jane said. 'I found the right person once, too.'

She was looking at me with great sadness and I had a sudden premonition of what she was about to reveal: 'The first time I saw you, Jim, I fell in love with you. I had never seen anyone as tall as you who could move with such grace. It was the way you walked which first got to me. I can still see you walking towards me down the corridor in Robinson college on that first evening. You had that huge red rucksack on your back. Do you remember it? You carried it so effortlessly. You were trying to find your room and nonchalantly sent people flying all round you every time you turned. I don't think you even noticed me, but I fell in love with you in that moment: hook, line and sinker. You are the real reason that I joined the Ministry. All those philosophical discussions we used to have in your room, just you and me after all the others had gone to bed. You were the first person of my own age who could actually explain why they were a Christian without embarrassment. I can still remember what you said then: "Because it makes sense." Not because you were brought up that way, or because of some divine revelation or deep theological proof. It was an act of faith, so of course it couldn't be proved or disproved. For you it was simply that the sum total of your experiences up to that point made more sense if there was a God than if there wasn't, but in some profoundly separate way than the way in which science explains the material world. We don't need God for that any more; your belief in God was rational because you believed that life was more than just our humdrum physical existence. You believed that God explained the "what is it all for" question.'

'But what about Richard?' I asked aghast.

'Oh, Richard. He is a decent enough man. I don't regret going out with him. We had a lot or fun together at Cambridge – it was convenient for both of us - but Sarah is much more tolerant of his buffoonery than I ever was. Sarah's good for him. But you were always the star amongst us. You and Angus. Our first amongst equals. And it was obvious from the very first day that Anne was the only one for you. How could I compete with her?'

'I didn't start going out with Anne until the second term.'

'No you didn't, you great lummox. All that first term I had to listen sympathetically as Anne told me of the increasingly obvious hints that she was dropping you, but to which you seemed to be completely oblivious. She couldn't understand it. She had never had trouble getting her man before. And all the time I was thinking that if you didn't rise to Anne's bait what chance did I have. In the end Anne got Angus to help her. You remember when you schemed with Angus that you would pretend to go into Anne's room one night by mistake, accidentally, as if you were drunk? You came back together from rugby training, singing and swaying all the way down the corridor, and Angus appeared to guide you accidentally to Anne's door instead of your own? And there was Anne waiting up for you. Well, Angus was a double agent all the time. The whole thing was set up by Anne. She would never normally have been in bed that early or have left her door unlocked. Did that never occur to you as strange? We all knew about it.'

I looked back at Jane but I was seeing again that first night with Anne. It was true: I had been confiding my feelings about Anne to Angus for months but I was so in awe of her beauty that I could not believe that she would want me, and I hadn't wanted to risk our friendship on such a hopeless cause. Angus had assured me that Anne was just as keen as I was, but I wouldn't believe him. Eventually Angus had come up with the plan for me to blunder into Anne's room while seemingly drunk, 'that way, if she does throw you out you can both pretend in the morning that nothing happened.' I was as nervous as a kitten. I would have backed out at the last minute if Angus had not manhandled me down the corridor. 'Go on, man. She's gagging for it. Just go to her room and see what happens.' There was just one lamp lit on the bedside table. Anne was in bed. She was wearing a white cotton nightdress and her golden hair was shinning brightly on her pillow like a halo. The heady scent of sandalwood filled the room. Anne did not say anything; she just smiled and opened her arms wide in welcome.

'The irony is,' said Jane, breaking my reverie, 'you are now the atheist, I'm the Methodist minister, and Anne married

Angus. Come on inside before I start crying. It's getting cold, and I have beans on toast to make.'

'Can I do anything?' I asked.

Jane sighed, theatrically. 'If only…'

'I mean can I do anything to help with dinner.'

'I know what you mean. No thank you. And it's not really beans on toast. There is salad in the fridge and baked potatoes in the microwave. I just need to grill the steaks.'

I perched on a high stool at the breakfast bar as Jane cooked and lamented her current crisis of faith.

'The sad thing is that even though I am personally going through a period of doubt, I am as zealous as ever about preaching the Gospel. All that guff about "If God didn't exist, it would be necessary to invent him". It's absolutely true. It is not just the moral code which religion provides, although you only have to open a newspaper to see how badly society functions without it. It is much more than that. A belief in some purpose for life, some higher good. A goal for life in general, and a point to one's own life in particular. Look at our Cambridge crowd. The brightest of the bright, and not a Christian amongst them. Yet are any of them happy?'

'You tell me,' I said. 'You are the one who is still in touch with them all.'

'I don't think so. They are all excelling in their chosen fields. All working frantically from dawn until dusk, but all, ultimately, filled with the same feeling of un-fulfilment. We all have such enormous expectations from life. The stress of too much choice, of worrying that we do not have the perfect lives which we are led to believe that we deserve. Anne and Angus had a fearful row after you left on Tuesday. Now, open this wine and tell me about your new flatmate. If you haven't found love, you can at least tell me about the sex.'

'If I have any more to drink, I won't be safe to ride home,' I said doubtfully.

'Don't think I'm not counting your drinks. You can sleep here. It's Saturday tomorrow so presumably you won't need to get up for work.' Jane saw my expression and laughed. 'In the spare room, dummy. Don't worry, I'm not going to eat you. I've lasted thirteen years without jumping on you, I think that I can manage another night alone. If you think your new lodger can manage without you, that is.'

We stayed up until midnight drinking and talking and drinking some more. I realised that my initial opinion of Jane had been wrong. She was not as disillusioned as she pretended. She genuinely loved her job and she was a lot more worldly wise and self-confident than she used to be. She recounted stories of genuine deprivation amongst her community which were no less shocking just because the root cause was always the same, a lack of any real education and a commensurate lack of any real opportunities. A teenage girl who deliberately got pregnant by a friend of her fathers because she saw it as the only way to escape from her abusive family, only to find herself completely incapable of coping on her own with her screaming baby in the squalor of a lonely council flat. She abandons her baby to the care of social services and takes to the streets because she finds more comfort from the prostitutes on the street corner than she does from sitting at home on her own watching day-time telly. Young men pumped full of testosterone and drugs roaming the streets with nothing to do and no hope of a future outside the destructive brotherhood of their gang culture. A respectably married man who loses his dustman's job at the age of forty five for a minor misdemeanour and cannot see the possibility of ever working again. After three months of apparently peaceful idleness the prospect of just sitting at home with his nagging wife for another thirty five years drives him over the edge. He beats up the next person who turns up to empty his bins, who just happens to be a young Pakistani boy doing a week's work experience with the council before going off to college to study economics. None of Jane's stories were particularly unusual, they were probably no worse than the stories of hundreds of people who I passed every day in Brixton, but, unlike me, Jane knew these people personally.

If Jane had currently lost her faith in the Almighty she had certainly not lost her faith in her fellow man, despite all her evidence to the contrary. She was full of schemes to help or energise her congregation. Most of her plans seemed to me to be hair-brained to the verge of absurdity but she described them with such enthusiasm that my practical objections seemed prosaic in comparison. Enthusiasm is such an under-rated quality; it is so much easier to be cynical and negative. Jane was engaged in so many local initiatives that the contrast with my own relatively isolated existence stirred a few pangs, first of guilt and then of outright jealousy.

After the second bottle of wine I launched into a long description of how after my thirtieth birthday I had engaged in a flurry of one-night stands. I'm not quite sure why I told her. Obviously the alcohol made it possible, but I wasn't slurring my words yet. Partly, no doubt, it was a desire to repay her confidences. We had once been friends but that was a long time ago; when we had re-met at the start of that evening we had been acquaintances at best and yet Jane had opened up her life to me, with all its successes and failures, just like she used to do in the old days. I wanted to repay those confidences with something suitably intimate. But mainly, I fear, I wanted to shock her. I was not showing off, but Jane seemed to have such a good and wholesome life, she was so thoroughly nice, that I wanted to surprise her out of the complacency that she knew and condoned all the foibles of the human condition.

'It started on my thirtieth birthday,' I told Jane. 'I went home to my parent's farm in Devon for the weekend and spent a lovely day with them. My sister drove over with a birthday cake. But I ended up walking by myself up on Exmoor at 3 o'clock in the morning. I'd drunk quite a lot, enough to be maudlin but not enough to fall asleep, and I asked myself some deep and uncomfortable questions in the cold dark hours before dawn; questions about what I was doing with my life and how it was all slipping away from me without me even noticing.'

'We've all done that,' Jane said. 'My conclusion is that no one should be allowed to be alone on their thirtieth birthday.'

'My conclusion was that from then on I would "Seize the Day". I actually painted those words onto the ceiling above my bed when I got back to London in the hope that just because it was a cliché it didn't mean it wasn't valid. I made a conscious decision during that night on Exmoor to start enjoying my life again. Some people make a hobby out of collecting stamps or flying model aeroplanes; some people are fanatical football supporters. They spend half their salaries on season tickets and travelling to matches all over Europe. I tried my hand at one-night stands. I'm still not sure why it's such an unusual hobby. In laboratory experiments mice starve themselves to death when offered a choice between pressing one pedal to get food and another pedal to cause an electrode to stimulate the pleasure centre in their brains. They wouldn't starve themselves for a pair of cup final tickets. Why should we pretend to be any different? We should de-mystify the sexual urge and accept that it's a human imperative, just behind the need to eat and sleep and keep warm. Now that the eating and sleeping and keeping warm bit is a given we should embrace the opportunity to indulge in the other. Richard said on Tuesday night that ten thousand years of civilisation is a very thin veneer separating us from two billion years of genetic conditioning, and if we are genetically conditioned to do anything then it is to perpetuate the genes which have been thus conditioned. The fact that modern contraception has enabled us to satisfy the imperative without having to live with the consequences should be an even greater incentive to have sex as often and with as many people as possible. If you take God out of the equation, if we really do only have this one allotted lifespan, then everything else is just social convention. We may have different metabolic rates: some people may be satisfied once a month while others want to gorge themselves every night, but it should be an argument about the relative merits of junk food verses a wholesome, balanced diet, rather than a denial that we all get hungry. Make hay while the sun shines, I say.'

'Me thinks you do protest too much,' Jane said. 'I'm not judging you. You're pushing against an open door with me after all, but I'm sensing a "but" somewhere along the line...'

'I did the thing properly,' I continued. 'I approached it like a project, just to see what would happen. I turned out my lodger and tarted up my spare room: satin sheets, a mirror on the ceiling, and handcuffs on the bedstead. Then I cruised the nightclubs and picked up able and consenting adults. Normally we would go back to my house but sometimes I would go to hers, or we would find a cheap hotel room, or a disabled toilet, or a dark alley. There were no formalities. We would have sex for as long as it took and then I would send her home in a taxi. That was always the deal: no exchange of phone numbers, no staying the night, no surnames. It was surprisingly easy to do. These were normal, attractive, articulate young women. There seemed to be a lot of other people who had come to the same conclusion that emotion-free, mutually enjoyable exchanges of lubricant and friction doesn't harm either party as long as there are no expectations on either side. Maybe it helps if you are six feet two and have all your own hair. It certainly helps if you don't care if you fail, but I reckon that anybody could do it if they just had the bottle. Find a group in the disco just before closing time which is still composed only of women. Single out the one who seems the most independent, the most up for it, and ask them if they want to have sex. That's all there is to it. Maybe I'd dance with her a bit first but sometimes I'd just shout the question into her ear as she went to the bar for her last drink. Half of them would slap me round the face, but the other half would giggle, look over at their friends, and then shrug and say, "Alright". Simple as that.'

Jane listened to me with interest but with no apparent shock. 'You talk as if you don't do it anymore,' she said.

I thought about it. 'I haven't had sex in over a year.'

'Why did you stop? Were you worried about the risks?'

'HIV? Chlamydia? No. I took all the usual precautions. I give blood twice a year and they screen it for STDs so I know I'm clean. It may have been a factor, I suppose; it's always there at the back of your mind. But mainly it was just affecting my rugby too much. No, seriously, don't laugh. That was my other thirtieth birthday resolution, to take up rugby again, and I realised that my two new hobbies were mutually incompatible. One of them had to go, and the rugby won. Sex without the meaningful relationship to go with it was just elaborate masturbation. I got a buzz from it for a while. The chase was exciting. The anticipation made me feel alive, but in the end it lost its novelty and I wasn't getting enough sleep to play rugby to the standard I wanted. As a rational human being I am responsible for my own happiness, its duration as well as its intensity. We can take the immediate drugs hit now, or abstain in the hope of a contented old age. I'm abstaining from my one-night stand highs in favour of the more durable enjoyment that I get from rugby. If I break my neck during the match tomorrow I'll feel pretty pissed off, but it's a judgement call we all have to make. I don't even miss it. Maybe it was just a phase I had to go through and now I've got it out of my system. Currently I get my kicks out of playing rugby, pretty much to the exclusion of everything else.'

'You still haven't really got over Anne yet, have you?' Jane asked quietly.

'God, Jane, where did that come from?' I said angrily. 'One minute I'm confiding to you about all my recent conquests and the next minute you drag up someone I went out with a decade ago. I did love Anne, yes. Very much. At the time I thought I loved her more than anybody had loved anyone. Ever. Maybe I loved her too much. But that was over ten years ago. I've moved on since then. I don't even know who Anne is anymore.'

'She hasn't changed very much,' Jane said. 'She is still annoyingly lovely and charming and sweet and fun and beautiful.'

'And that's supposed to help?' I asked.

'I preached a sermon on remembrance Sunday about Nebuchadnezzar's birthday present,' Jane said. 'Do you know the story?'

I looked at her blankly, discombobulated by the sudden change of subject.

'Nebuchadnezzar was the king of Babylon who conquered Jerusalem in the sixth century BC,' Jane continued. 'He was the richest person on the planet. He could have anything he wanted on a royal whim. His court became synonymous with sumptuous excesses of every kind. One day the Grand Vizier asked Nebuchadnezzar what he wanted for his birthday. The king replied that he didn't want anything; he had everything that he could possibly want. The Vizier persisted so Nebuchadnezzar challenged him to find something which could make a happy person sad and a sad person happy. The Vizier scoured the land for a potion or an artefact which would achieve this result but without success. As the Grand Vizier was making his way empty handed to the royal chambers on the king's birthday he saw a small boy playing with a wooden toy in the dusty street. He took the toy and presented it to the king. Nebuchadnezzar thought at first that it was a joke. He looked again. Then he looked around at his glorious gardens and his great palace and all his happiness drained away. Written on the wooden toy was one simple truth: "this too must pass".'

Jane looked at me expectantly.

'You're trying to tell me that change is the only certainty and that I should embrace it rather than resent it. Nothing is ever quite as good or quite as bad as it seems and that I should just get over it,' I said. 'Thanks, Jane, but I really don't need the lecture.'

'When Simon left me', said Jane, 'I bought the biggest, blackest vibrator you've ever seen'.

I choked on my drink.

'Don't scoff,' Jane giggled. 'You men are so egotistical about sex. You were quite happy telling me about all those women you've had but you go all coy when I get personal about myself. I think that the state should provide girls with a vibrator on their sixteenth birthdays, like a telegram from the queen when you reach a hundred. That would do more to stop teenage pregnancies than any amount of contraception education.'

I realised that Jane was trying to lighten the mood after her heavy-handed sermon. It occurred to me that the Nebuchadnezzar speech might have been pre-planned; Jane might have just been waiting for the right moment to give it and now she was regretting it. Or maybe Anne had put her up to it, getting Jane to organise this whole evening with the sole purpose of warning me that what we had once had was over.

'I'm thinking of peroxiding my hair,' Jane continued. 'What do you reckon? Becca told me on Tuesday that there is no longer any excuse for anybody to have brown hair anymore, now that everyone can be naturally blonde for fifty pounds a month.'

'Now I know you're drunk.' I said. 'That's not the kind of thing that you can hide from your parishioners.'

'I know.' She smiled. 'I couldn't justify it anyway. I can think of so many better things to spend fifty pounds a month on - if I had fifty pounds a month to spend.'

We looked at each other. We both knew, in our various degrees of drunkenness, that this was the moment at which it could become inevitable that we end up in the same bed. It could have gone either way, but it was Jane who broke the spell, 'I guess that we will both be embarrassed about this conversation in the morning, but I hope not. We all have secret lives; hopes and fears and scandalous thoughts which convention forces us to suppress but which sometimes slip out when our guard is down. If we were all more honest about our deviancies we might discover that there is no such thing as "normal" to deviate from, only those who conform better in public. I think that is what I most miss about being single, not having somebody that I can share things with without worrying about the consequences or how it might be perceived. Someone that you don't have to act for, that you can truly relax with, knowing that they will love you unconditionally and forever despite whatever stupid things you say or do.'

Jane caught me looking down at her wedding ring and smiled wistfully. 'Maybe that's where we both went wrong. Confusing "unconditional love" with "taking love for granted". Which is where I guess God comes in again.'

Chapter Six

"Don't drop your bike. If you do drop your bike, don't hit anything. If you do hit something, don't use your head."
From: "Ride Well and Prosper".

There was no awkwardness in the morning, but that did not prevent me from making my excuses and heading home after only a perfunctory cup of tea. It was a match day. I never normally drink on the night before a rugby match but I had topped off a week of missed training by waking with a storming hangover.

'Seize the fucking day,' I told myself ruefully as I rode slowly back to Brixton.

I got home before nine o'clock and found that Abbie had written 'I am here, where are you?' underneath my message on the kitchen table. I climbed the stairs and knocked gently on her door.

'It is locked' she said sleepily.

'Fancy a cup of tea?' I asked back.

I heard the key turning. Abbie opened the door looking remarkable wide-awake. She was back in my tee-shirt and jogging pants which she was holding up with one hand.

'Where were you last night?' she asked. The swelling had almost completely dissipated from round her eyes and they were twinkling mischievously.

'I could ask you the same question,' I countered, 'but of course, you are not allowed to answer my questions.'

She looked immediately hurt. I had meant it as a joke, but it had come out with all the subtlety of my sore head.

'I'm sorry Abbie. I didn't mean it like that.' I started instinctively to apologise, but suddenly I was fed up with always being the one tip-toeing around her as if I was walking on egg shells. 'What happened to our agreement? You won't take offence at me asking questions, as long as I don't take offence if you don't answer them? I'll tell you where I was last night: I was visiting an old friend. A Methodist minister actually. I even thought that you might want to come too, to get out of the house, to meet some of my friends. I drank too much so I crashed out in her spare room. Alright? That is where I was. Is that ok? Now, where were you? What the fuck do you do all day that is so secret that you can't tell me? You know, I would really like to know.'

Abbie looked down at the floor.

'I would like to tell you, James,' she said in a small voice. 'I really would, but it is not my confidence to tell.'

'Really! Isn't that just very convenient.'

Abbie was quiet for a long time while I glared at her. Without looking up from the floor she said quietly, 'Do you want me to go?'

'Fuck. I don't know Abbie. No. I don't want you to go. Look, I've got a headache and I shouldn't have drunk so much before a match so this is probably not an ideal time for this conversation. But this is hard for me. I've been stuck in a bachelor rut for too long. I do pretty much what I want to, when I want to, so I am not used to being asked to account for my movements.' I paused. 'Shit. I'm sorry, Abbie. Look at me.'

Abbie glanced up at me and then looked down again at her bare feet. I put my hands on her shoulders and held her until she looked up at me again.

'I do not want you to go,' I said slowly and deliberately.

She looked back at me blankly.

'Come with me,' I said eagerly. 'Come and watch the match this afternoon. I can get you the best seat in the house... actually we'll probably have to find a box for you to stand on or you won't see anything at all.'

Abbie smiled falteringly. 'I don't think so, James.'

'Why not? No, scrub that. It doesn't matter. Ok Abbie, don't come. I want you to know that I would like you to come and that is all that matters. But will you promise me something?'

'No, James. I will not promise you something.'

'Will you promise me,' I persevered, 'will you promise me that you will not leave me without saying good bye?'

Abbie thought about the question seriously, her expressionless brown eyes staring into mine. I did not look away.

'Yes,' she said at last, 'I will promise you that.'

'Thank you.' I said. I hugged her.

'I will make the tea,' Abbie said struggling out of my embrace. 'You need a shower.'

★ ★ ★

Rugby should be a very simple game: you have to get the ball from one end of the pitch to the other without throwing it forwards. That's it. All the seemingly complicated rules have been invented to encourage players to run with the ball in their hands rather than kicking it. And to stop so many people getting killed. Scrums, lineouts, penalties, twenty-two metre drop-outs, these are simply different ways of restarting the game after one of the complicated rules has been broken, but if you pare the game right back to its basics you just pick up the ball and run - which is why it is such a fantastic game for children. You don't need to have great ball control or hand-eye co-ordination to pick up a ball and run. Once their Mums have got over the fact that there is actually physical contact, that you are actually allowed to grab hold of someone to stop them from running, I have seen seven and eight year olds who couldn't dribble a football to save their lives charging up and down a mini-rugby pitch as if Sony had never invented the Playstation.

The fact that rugby is a contact sport is what forces you to play as a team. There is nothing quite like a mild battering in a common cause to build up camaraderie; the knowledge that none of you can thrive without all of you being prepared to put your bodies on the line for each other can engender a great feeling of self-worth. And it is the "putting your body on the line" bit which I like best.

The game that afternoon was typical. It was as near to a home derby match as Rosslyn Park can get in the current league set up. After several false starts, the English Rugby Board has eventually got the structure about right. In the initial gold rush when rugby union first turned professional it was assumed that there would be easy millions for everybody. Then came the harsh reality that because clubs were allowed to pay their players did not necessarily guarantee more money at the turnstiles. After a few high-profile club mergers and some lower-profile bankruptcies the message finally got through. Rugby union just does not have sufficient bread-and-butter, week in, week out, grass roots support to sustain more than a handful of fully professional clubs. The paying public wants to watch a successful national team on the TV and a few big clubs round the country. Anything else is just wishful thinking. Even soccer, the national game, is struggling to support more clubs than it can really afford. In rugby union the lesser clubs have gone back to their proper place, providing fun for their players and a little light entertainment for the local community. At the lower levels they have reverted to regionally based leagues which do not force amateur players to spend every weekend travelling the length and breadth of the country to play in front of half empty stadiums. Somewhat unfortunately for us at Rosslyn Park we won promotion the previous year up to League Division 3 South, which means that we now have the prospect of trekking two hundred and fifty miles to Cornwall at the beginning of February for a match which will inevitably be cancelled when we get there because of a water-logged pitch.

The move up to the southern league was proving to be a far bigger step than we had hoped. It was still early in the season so the pitches were dry and firm. In the lower divisions a hard pitch had always suited our expansive style of running rugby; we backed our superior speed and fitness over the brute strength of the opposition. League Division 3 South was proving to be a different challenge. We had been heavily defeated in our first two matches, mainly because we hardly ever got our hands on the ball. Heavier opponents won the scrums, taller opponents won the lineouts. At squad training sessions we vowed to keep faith with our attacking rugby philosophy, 'better to go down playing the way we enjoy than to stay up using the boot' was how Ben put it, but keeping the ball alive – running into space rather than into oppositions, and passing just before being tackled rather than going to ground with the ball - puts a lot of onus on the scrum back row players, and on the open-side flanker in particular. Me. Whenever one of our players has got the ball I need to be on hand to receive a pass; whenever one of their players has got the ball I need to be on hand to make that first bone-crunching tackle, driving their player backwards or wrapping my arms round their legs to bring them down to earth.

Esher are the only other London-based team in our division, which ensured a bigger than average crowd and a worse than average referee. Esher are not exponents of expansive rugby. Their style suited their bigger physical size; kick the ball into our half, and then pound out the remaining yards by running straight into our players in the hope that we would eventually run out of tacklers. As one giant was tackled he would slip the ball to a colleague who would lumber forward a few feet before he in turn was tackled. For us to defend against this type of play we needed to maintain a high standard of discipline and organisation; we needed to know who was responsible for the next tackle. If it took two of us to stop one of them it would leave a gap for their next player to exploit, so as soon as we had made one tackle we had to get up and run back to make the next one. When we did occasionally manage to grab the ball we passed it as quickly as possible to our slighter, faster back players, whose less bludgeoning approach depended on avoiding their tacklers rather than just running through them.

It was bruising, it was exhausting, and I loved it. Within the larger team game there are also personal challenges as each player tries to out-play their immediate opposite number. The Esher open-side flanker was a big man, my size or bigger, and showed no hesitation in ensuring that his studs left their mark on my shoulder when I was foolish enough be caught lying with the bulk of the scrum between me and the referee. As I stood next to him at the next lineout I caught his eye and smiled.

'You scratch my back, I'll scratch yours,' I said. He knew what I meant, but he did not smile back.

As the match progressed I found that I was getting to the break-downs a vital two or three seconds before my opponent, enabling me to wrestle the ball from the tackled player and secure the all important turn-over ball. He was also beginning to take wrong options with the ball in hand, his decision making slowing down as he got tired. In the first half he had made a number of incisive runs through our defence, in the second half I was able to second-guess him so that whichever way he turned I was there before him.

With five minutes left to play in the match we had both made a number of big hits on the other. The honours in our private battle were pretty even, but Esher were ahead on the scoreboard: 9 - 15. Suddenly the ball squirted out from the side of a maul. Instinctively I dived on it and then sprung back onto my feet. Ben was behind me, screaming for the ball; I flicked it back to him. He darted past me and just as my opposite number crunched into him, Ben kicked the ball high, far up the field. I put my head down and sprinted after it. The ball seemed to hang in the air for an eternity before dropping down out of the sky towards the Esher fullback. I had outstripped the rest of my team and the rest of the Esher defence. I was still too far away to challenge the fullback as he jumped up to catch the ball but as he landed he looked up and saw me bearing down on him. The ball slipped from his grasp, bounced kindly so that I could scoop it up without breaking stride, and there was no-one left to stop me running on to score a try under the posts. Ben kicked the conversion and we won the match 16 – 15.

'Well played, mate. I owe you a pint for that back scratch,' said the Esher flanker as we clapped each other off the pitch. 'Win some, lose some,' he added philosophically.

The courtesy of the post match drink with the opposition is as much a part of the rugby tradition as the "no quarter given or taken" attitude on the pitch. It is also traditional to lampoon your own players in direct proportion to how well they have played so I received a fair amount of stick that afternoon as we changed out of our rugby kit.

'I thought you were meant to have a hang-over today,' said Ben. 'Maybe you should try drinking before every match.'

'Yeah, what exactly were you drinking?' asked our hooker. He was universally known as "Clubby" because Ben had once glanced at him in the shower and remarked casually, 'that's not a cock, that's a club.'

'We should get your urine tested.'

'Whatever it was, bring it along next week so we can all have some.'

'Maybe we should all try missing training next week, too,' Clubby suggested hopefully.

'You can miss training once you have played that well,' said Ben, 'not before.'

I was more embarrassed by the plaudits from the blazer-and-tie brigade in the clubhouse than I had been by the ridiculing of my team-mates in the changing room. I sought out my opposite number from Esher who I discovered was called Dave and who, true to his word, had a pint of bitter waiting for me at the bar. I found out during the first pint that Dave was a chartered accountant who travelled an hour into London from his country house in Surrey for every training session. I was forcing my way through the crowd at the bar to repay Dave's pint when Angus McManus slapped me heartily on the back.

'Fantastic game, James. Let me get these drinks.'

'Angus. Hi. What are you doing here?'

'I was watching the match. And it was a much better standard than I expected actually'.

'Well thank you very much; we aim to please. You've hung up your boots, haven't you? Ben had a shocker today. He needs someone challenging him for his place to keep him sharp. Training is on Tuesdays and Thursdays if you fancy joining us.'

'I haven't played since Cambridge.'

'Is Anne here?' I asked.

'No' said Angus, and passed me a beer.

I sipped my pint as Angus and Dave exchanged constructive criticisms on the match. When I went back to the bar for my third pint Dave drifted back to his own team-mates and Angus made a slow tour of the room shaking hands and telling jokes. This was my second season at the club and I was still very deferential towards the chairman and the older ex-players but Angus seemed to mix with them as easily as he did with the opposition players and the adoring barmaid. Small talk is not something that comes naturally to me, let alone a mixing with a large group of total strangers, but Angus showed no sign of awkwardness as he worked his way round the room. He had always been gregarious. At Cambridge Angus had always been the first to offer to meet a friend's parents at the train station, the first to volunteer to lead a student representation to the chancellor, the first with the killer question prepared in advance for a visiting lecturer. He admitted that he was not a natural networker; it was a skill which he had worked on quite deliberately since he was a teenager. Now he seemed to have it down to a fine art. I had asked Jane about Angus the previous night.

'Angus? I thought you knew. Angus has become a spy.' Jane had said.

'A spy?' I asked incredulously. It was late in the evening, long after our session of personal revelations and the subsequent coffees and the washing up. The drink had definitely taken its toll and I had not been sure if she was being serious.

'Oh yes. He has to tell everyone that he is a researcher at the Foreign Office but we all know that he's really a spy. I'm not sure if it's actually MI5 or some other anti-terrorist organisation, but it is definitely something very spooky. He doesn't admit it but I think he secretly likes the fact that we all know about it. So of course we all pretend very hard not to appear in the least bit interested. They even advertise those jobs in the Times these days, so I suppose that it is not that surprising. Somebody has to be a spy. I just feel sorry for Anne really.'

As I watch Angus in the Rosslyn Park clubhouse glad-handing the crowd I reflected that Jane was probably right. Angus had specialised in Mathematical Statistics at Cambridge. His forte had been for marshalling facts and spotting trends. He never presumed to works of great originality but he had been superb at seeing through all the background noise to the nub of an argument and encapsulating it in one succinct statement. He would be very good at analysing huge amounts of data to spot the one anomaly which might be important in the global war against terror. It was very reassuring to know that people as bright as Angus were on the case. And he would love the glamour of it all. I saw him introduce himself to Ben who looked up suddenly and beckoned me over.

'Angus tells me you have a new girlfriend,' Ben said accusingly as I joined them with my pint in hand. 'Some foreign bird. So that's why you played so well. It wasn't anything to do with your hangover. Nothing beats a good shag before a match.'

I looked at Angus who looked back straight faced.

'How do you know?' I asked.

'Ways and means,' said Angus smugly, tapping the side of his nose.

'Jane.' I said and Angus smiled.

'Jane?' asked Ben. 'Funny name for an Asian girl.'

'No, Jane's not my Asian girl. Jane's the one who must have told Angus about my Asian girl. My Asian girl is called Abbie. Abbie is the asylum seeker who is temporarily seeking refuge in my spare room. Abbie is the one who I am definitely not shagging.'

'Is Abbie here?' Angus asked. 'Did she watch the match?'

'No, and to tell you the truth I have no idea what she does all day.'

'Do you want me to find out for you?' Angus asked mischievously.

I smiled. 'Thank you, but I think that she has more need of Anne's specialist skills than yours. Whatever yours might be.'

Angus was about to reply but Dave came over to talk to Ben. As part of the post-match drinking ritual each captain nominates a "BFG" from the other team, their Biggest Fucking Git, or the player from the opposing team who has caused them the most grief during the match. It is a tradition which has long gone in the professional leagues; in the professional leagues the Man of the Match is nominated by a be-suited television pundit and receives a bottle of Champagne and a cut-glass vase, but in League Division 3 South we still do things in the traditional way. Two chairs were placed in the centre of the room and I was not particularly surprised to find myself being called forward by the Esher captain.

Dave shook my hand as I went past. 'Let this be a lesson to you, young man. Stop running about so fucking much. It shows up the rest of us in a bad light. I want you to remember that when we play you back at our patch after Christmas.' He smiled until Ben nominated him as Esher's BFG. Dave protested half-heartedly but he was shouted down by his team-mates. Dave and I climbed onto our chairs and Angus passed each of us a pint glass with half a pint of Guinness in it, topped up with a shot from each of the optics behind the bar. I clinked glasses with Dave, silently raised a toast to Angus as he cheered me on, and drank the mixture to the traditional chants of "Get 'em down, you Zulu warriors." It was the only race that day which I did not mind losing to Dave.

I always travel to the club by public transport on match days. Angus left after another hour. I completed my gallon of beer and then made my way unsteadily to the underground station. There are never enough trains running on Saturday nights so I was feeling very cold and very drunk by the time I arrived at Brixton station. The anaesthetic effects of the alcohol is usually enough to counter-act the bruising effects of a match until I wake up stiff and sore on Sunday mornings. Now I just wanted to fall into bed and let the recovery process start, but as I walked up the hill from the station I saw that my downstairs lights were still on. Abbie was reluctant to intrude into my laddish routine, but that very reluctance to intrude was beginning to grate. As I unlocked my front door I heard my CD of Gregorian chants playing in the living room. I put down my kit bag and walked quietly in through the kitchen. She was asleep on the sofa, curled up on her side with my copy of Rebecca still open in her hand. She had drawn her knees up to her chest and my track suit bottoms had slipped down over her hip. Her hair was loose and covered her face as she snuggled into the cushions. She had become cold while asleep; I could see the goose pimples at the base of her spine where her black sweatshirt had ridden up. I knelt down beside her and gently stroked her hair. She started and her eyes opened wide with shock.

'Shhh. It's alright. It's James. I am going to carry you to up to your bed.'

Abbie looked back at me. She reached down and hitched up her jogging bottoms but she made no attempt to sit up. I slipped my hands underneath her and lifted her in my arms. She weighed no more than a child.

'You're drunk again,' she said. 'Don't drop me.'

She put one arm round my neck and pressed her face into my chest. I stood up and carried her carefully up the stairs, cradling her in one arm as I opened her bedroom door, and lay her down on her bed. She slithered under the duvet and bunched it up round her neck, shivering.

'Good night,' I said. 'I am sorry that I am drunk again.'

Abbie smiled, but did not reply. I crossed the hall to my own room and fell fully clothed onto my bed.

I slept the sleep of the dead for four hours and then drifted in and out of consciousness until my dreams were disturbed by the conflicting imperatives a full bladder, a raging thirst and a nascent erection. The full bladder finally won through and imposed itself sufficiently to send me staggering to the bathroom. I drank a pint of water first and then sat on the loo so that I could clean my teeth while peeing into the bowl beneath me. Back in my bedroom I stripped off my clothes and examined the damage from the day before. There were fresh grazes on my legs, bruises on my chest and the evidence of Dave's stud marks all the way down my back; so nothing unusual. Certainly nothing to trouble my sleep when I crashed back onto the bed.

I came to again shivering, lying naked on top of my bedclothes. The smell of coffee and frying bacon sent my stomach churning. I opened my eyes and closed them again quickly as the sunlight streaming into the bedroom through the open curtains stung my eyes. I crawled back under the duvet and listened abstractedly to the noises from the kitchen until my mind focused on the sound of footsteps coming up the stairs. Abbie knocked on the door. I grunted and she came in balancing a plate and a mug on my largest chopping-board.

'You need fluids to re-hydrate you, carbohydrate to absorb any residual alcohol, animal fats to give the stomach something to work on, and caffeine to kick-start the system. Sweet coffee and bacon sandwiches.'

'I need drugs,' I said.

'And paracetamol,' Abbie agreed.

'What time is it?'

Abbie walked over to the bed. She was wearing my dressing gown with the cord tied very tightly so that the middle section could be tucked in to keep the hem from dragging on the floor. It would have looked comical if the face above it was not so stern. I sat up against the headboard and the duvet folded back onto my lap. Abbie looked down at the bruises on my chest but she didn't comment as she passed me the chopping-board tray. I noticed three paracetamol tablets sitting on top of the bacon sandwich.

'Thank you.'

'It stinks in here. I'm going to run a bath,' she said. She opened a window as she left.

I managed to wash the painkillers down without scalding myself on the coffee and nibbled at the bacon sandwich while I tried to work out whether she was running a bath for me or for her. I wasn't sure if I was elated or alarmed by Abbie's sudden matronly concern and I decide to postpone forming an opinion until her administrations had run their course. The coffee was certainly very welcome.

Abbie came back into the room and sat down on the side of the bed.

'How are you feeling?' she asked.

'I thought I was the one who was meant to ask you that.'

'Your bath is ready. I will get you some more coffee.' She collected my crockery. Halfway to the door she added, 'If you would like some?'

'Thank you. It seems to be working. No sugar this time.'

When she was gone I got gingerly out of bed. My clothes were scattered all over the floor where I had discarded them in the middle of the night. I considered transferring them from the heap on the floor to a heap on my desk but decided against it. I glanced at the bare hook on the back of the door and smiled at the memory of Abbie engulfed in my dressing gown. I walked naked across the hall to the bathroom. I didn't possess bubble bath, but Abbie had added shampoo to the running water so that there were a few desultory bubbles amongst the steam. The window blind was down. I turned off the light to return the room to twilight, stepped into the bath, and lowered myself slowly into the water until only my nostrils were showing above the surface. The grazes on my knees and elbows stung as the water touched them but my muscles slowly relaxed in the heat.

I lay in the dark and listened to the blood pounding in my head.

Even underwater I was aware of a momentary brightness through my eyelids as the door was opened and closed. I didn't move; I smelt the coffee and I was aware of Abbie's presence as she leant over me. I heard the mug being placed on the corner of the bath beside the wall and then her presence was gone. I slowly straightened my legs and slid my head above the surface. Abbie was sitting on the floor with her back against the side of the bath looking away from me. She had shaken her hair lose and it was trapped between her shoulders and the side of the bath just where my hand would naturally lie. I let the back of my hand rest against her neck and felt her press back against it. I gathered her hair in my hand and let it fall into the water. I placed my hand under the collar of her dressing gown and ran my fingers through the roots of her hair at the nape of her neck. Abbie wriggled her shoulders so that the dressing gown loosened; I leaned forward and place both my hands round the base of her neck.

'Abbie?'

'Yes?'

'Is this right?'

'It is inevitable.'

'That doesn't make it right.'

'No. It makes it inevitable.'

'Look at me.'

Abbie pulled away from me so that she could turn round. Her dressing gown fell open and I saw the outline of her breasts in the semi-darkness before she knelt forward, folding her arms onto the edge of the bath so that she could lean her chin on the back of her hands. She looked me in the eye and then very deliberately looked down into the water in front of her. Her right hand dropped into the water and I felt her fingers walking down my chest, down my stomach, down the inside of my thigh. My cock twitched and she caught it and held it firmly.

Abbie looked back up at me. 'You are not demonstrating too many objections to the proposition.' She smiled at my expression as she slowly worked her hand up and down. The cuff of her sleeve unrolled into the water. Abbie let go of me and shrugged off the dressing gown. I reached out for her and drew her face to mine. We kissed for a long time; her mouth tasted minty to my coffeed tongue. I ran my hands over her shoulders and down to her breasts. She leant forward so that they nestled into my palms. She shivered.

'You're cold,' I said. Without waiting for a response I stood up in a shower of water and lifted Abbie into the air, crushing her cold dry body to my wet warm one. She laced her hands behind my neck and wrapped her legs around me, clinging to me like a limpet. I could feel her heart beating against mine.

'You are as light as a puppet.'

She snuggled into me more tightly. I scratched my nails down her back and cradled her buttocks in my hands. I sensed the warmth of the cleavage between them. Abbie nuzzled into my neck, tensed, and then sighed as my fingers entered her. Her tongue probed into my ear as she rocked backwards and forwards in my hands, my erection jerking against her bottom.

'There is something in the dressing gown pocket,' she whispered.

I set her down in the bath, leant over the side and groped for the dressing gown. I felt in the pocket and took out a condom.

'Pass it to me,' Abbie said. She knelt down in the water as she tore open the packet with her teeth. I sat on the edge of the bath and she rolled it on to me. Without speaking again Abbie stood up, turned away from me and bent forwards to put her hands on the head of the bath. I moved behind her, urgently now. She reached a hand between her legs to guide me to her. Abbie gasped as I pressed into her and then matched her motion to mine as I moved inside her. I knew suddenly that I could not prolong this feeling. I grabbed her hips and I pulled her roughly against me in the spasm of orgasm.

We stayed like that for a very long minute as a tumult of emotions swept through me. Eventually Abbie straightened up and I slipped out of her. She leant back against my chest and I wrapped my arms around her.

'You didn't come, did you?' I asked.

'Hush. It was fun.'

'I haven't had sex for a very long time,' I said by way of excuse.

'I said "hush". It's not a competition.' She wriggled backwards against me.

'You didn't have to do that, Abbie.'

'I said "hush". And think very carefully before you say anything else. Do not imply that I would do this for any other reason than because I wanted to. Anything else would be deeply hurtful.'

I turned Abbie to me. I took her elbows in my hands and lifted her up until her eyes were level with mine. She started to speak. 'Hush,' I said this time, and kissed her.

Abbie shivered again. I stepped out of the bath with her in my arms, wrapped her in a bath towel and carried her through to my bedroom.

'I would like to formally register my approval of your hangover cure,' I said as I let her tumble out of the towel onto my bed. 'You should patent it.'

I dried myself perfunctorily with the towel and joined her under the duvet.

'You're still wet!'

'Do you want to talk?' I asked.

'Just hold me,' said Abbie.

I cuddled her to me, her head on my chest, and let my post-coital lethargy over-whelm me. I don't know how long I slept. I came to briefly and opened my eyes warily. Abbie was sitting up next to me, reading. I snaked an arm behind her back and snuggled my head into the pillow on her lap. Abbie stroked my hair as I drifted back into unconsciousness.

When I woke again she was still reading.

'How's Rebecca?' I asked.

Abbie looked up from her book and smiled. 'Hello, sleepy head.'

'Put that down,' I said.

'Why?' There was a playfulness to her question.

'Because I have woken up with an appetite,' I answered, and ducked my head under the duvet.

★ ★ ★

Later, when it was Abbie's turn to drift into slumber, I retrieved my dressing gown from the bathroom floor and went downstairs. Abbie had tidied the kitchen at some point during the morning and over the last few days a few more exotic ingredients had appeared in my cupboards, but essentially my house was no different from any previous Sunday. But it felt like everything had changed.

I warmed some soup, buttered bread, and hunted out my only tray from under the sink. When I got back upstairs Abbie was sitting up in my bed wearing her white vest.

'Lunch.'

I passed her the tray, took off the dressing gown and got into the bed beside to her. Abbie balanced the tray on her lap and passed me back a bowl of soup which I cupped in my hands and sipped from like a large mug.

'This changes things, you know,' I said.

'This changes nothing, James,' said Abbie.

'You can't mean that. You have to start trusting me now with some more of your life.'

Abbie put down her bowl down. 'Listen to me, James. Listen to me very carefully.' Her voice was suddenly very serious. 'In a few more days I will have to leave you. I do not know exactly when it will be, but I will have to go. It does not make any difference whether you want me to go or not. And, although you may never understand this, it doesn't make any difference whether I want to go or not. I will have to go.' Abbie took hold of my hand and squeezed it. 'For what it is worth, at this moment, as I sit here now, I cannot think of anywhere in the world that I would rather be. I did not want to be here. In your bed. I did not plan it. There are well documented histories of victims becoming infatuated with their saviours. I have tried very hard to resist it. But I have failed and here I am. I am happy to be here. Maybe as happy as I have ever been. But this changes nothing.'

I did not immediately respond. We finished our soup in silence; then I took the tray from her and put it on the floor beside the bed.

'Come here,' I said. I wrapped an arm over her shoulder and pulled her to my side. Abbie lay quiescently with her head on my chest and ran her fingers idly through the thicket of hair there. I took her hand and traced her fingers over the fresh bruises on my shoulder and then down my chest to the hair on my stomach. Abbie made to continue downwards but I stopped her hand just above my belly button.

'What to you feel there?' I asked. Abbie ran her fingers lightly over my stomach. I pushed down the duvet so that Abbie could examine the pockmarked scarring that runs from my solar plexus to my pelvis. She propped herself up on her elbows and combed through the hair with her nails.

'What is it, James?'

'My broken heart.'

Abbie said nothing.

'Have you ever been to Thailand?' I asked.

Again Abbie did not respond.

'I've told you about Anne, haven't I? My girlfriend at Cambridge?'

Abbie nodded.

'When she left me, my life ended. She left during our final year exams. I was more certain that she loved me than I was about anything else in my life. And I was wrong. It made it hard to write convincingly about European Medieval History. I honestly believed that I could make her happy for the rest of her life, and the next day she was gone. I sat my final two papers on autopilot. Then I went back to my Dad's farm because I couldn't think of anywhere else to go. My Mum had to go up to Cambridge to pack up my flat for me, all the things from our flat which Anne didn't want. I was on anti-depressants for a year. They do help. They sort of insulate you from all your feelings, the highs as well as the lows, but they don't actually cure you. They just buy you time in the hope that time itself will eventually work its magic. After a while I realised that I was just "existing", so I ran away. But I took my emptiness with me. In the end I settled in Bangkok. It is the only proper job that I have ever had; I was an assistant editor of the Bangkok Times. I had a proper salary, I rented a flat, and I got another girlfriend. Jasmine. Jasmine Thong.' I gave a half-hearted chuckle but Abbie did not join in.

'I know. It's not a very funny name in Thailand either,' I said. 'Jaz was lovely. She was nearly ten years older than me and she had worked her way up through the journalist ranks. Everyone called me her toy-boy. We lived together for two years in her flat in downtown Bangkok and had some great times; sailing, tennis, parties, sex... We went to Phuket for Christmas. Do you know those spectacular islands? You see pictures of them all the time on travel shows? We had a chalet on one of those beautiful islands. Perfect white beaches, Gin and Tonics in the bar pool at sundown, fresh orchids on the pillows every evening, spectacular cliffs above the crystal blue water.' I trailed off into silence.

Abbie laid her head back on my chest. 'What happened, James?'

'Futility. So much more dangerous than despair. Despair paralyses you so that you cannot take any decisive action; futility wears you down, keeps chipping away. I woke up one morning and watched Jasmine sleeping peacefully beside me and realised that my life could not get any better than it was then. And that is when I gave up on hope. If I could have all that, and still not feel anything, then I couldn't envisage ever being happy again. "Faith, hope and charity" is the usual translation in the bible, but "charity" can actually be translated from the Greek as "love". "Faith, Hope and Love, and the greatest of these is Love". Without love we are nothing. Loving someone who loves you back is not just the most important thing in life. It is the only important thing in life. It is the thing which gives meaning to everything else. You can have all the money in the world, but if you don't love, then what is the point of it all? Everything else is just window dressing. And if you have no faith, as I didn't then, then you have to at least have some hope. Hope that one day you will love again. But I didn't have that hope. It wasn't that I was unhappy, but I just couldn't see any point in going on. I kissed Jasmine and left the chalet. I swam out around the bay and climbed to the top of one of those spectacular cliffs. Then I threw myself off.'

Abbie moved her hand back onto my stomach and caressed the scars gently.

'I'm not sure why I lived. When I came to my lungs were full of water and the sea was red with blood. A minute before I had wanted to end it all but now some sort of self-preservation instinct took over. I put my hands down and felt my stomach split open right down the middle. I don't remember any pain. Not then. That came later. But I remember choosing to kick for the surface, choosing to live, and that first sweet, choking gulp of air. I doggy paddled back to the rocks with one hand while trying to hold my guts inside with the other. I was found half an hour later because of the cries of the seagulls circling over me.'

'Poor Jasmine,' said Abbie.

'Yes. Poor Jasmine. I don't even remember saying goodbye to her. I was air-lifted to Bangkok hospital and then medi-vacced home a week later. One hundred and sixty five thousand pounds it all cost. I had a visit from the insurance loss adjuster about a year afterwards. I was pretty much better by then and back working on the farm. Mr. Gregson, his name was. He asked me a lot of questions and tape-recorded all my answers. He said very early on in his visit that it was a great shame that I could not remember anything about the actual day itself. Post-traumatic stress, evidently. He had even been out to interview Jasmine, Mr. Gregson told me, but she hadn't been able to explain why I had climbed up that cliff. He asked me if I could now remember what I was doing up there. Before I could answer Mr. Gregson stopped his tape recorder and said very deliberately, "I take it that you are aware that any expenses incurred from an attempted suicide would not be covered under your insurance policy?" Then he switched his tape recorder back on and carried on with the interview.'

Abbie hugged me tightly.

'Who else knows that you can really remember?' she asked.

'No one,' I said.

'Not even your parents?'

'I am sure that they suspect, but I have never told them.'

We lay in silence; there didn't seem to be anything else to say. I had been planning to build a case for Abbie to trust me with whatever secrets her life might hold by revealing my darkest secret to her, but it didn't seem important anymore. After a while Abbie asked me whether I wanted to talk about it. I didn't have any objections so I answered her questions as well as I could, but neither did I have any expectation of unearthing any new revelations about myself. I had had six years to dwell on what I had done. I was thinking more about what Abbie had said before, that she would soon have to leave me whether she wanted to or not.

'Abbie,' I said suddenly, interrupting her line of questioning. 'Kiss me. No not there. Here!' Abbie giggled but complied. 'You bought a packet of six condoms,' I said to her bare bottom, 'so we have four more to get through today.'

Chapter Seven

The secret of a happy life is regular servicing.
From: "Ride Well and Prosper".

We spent Sunday in bed.
We didn't talk much; it is kind of hard to keep up an intimate conversation when you can't ask questions and you can't speculate about the future. I went downstairs, loaded up the CD player on random-play, switched the speakers through to the bedroom and dozed while Abbie finished reading Rebecca beside me. I went out and bought some Sunday newspapers. Abbie lay with her head in my lap while I read out crossword clues. Abbie made pots of green tea and hot buttered toast. Abbie blindfolded me and gently messaged all the bruised bits of my body with moisturiser. We played "dirty word" scrabble. Abbie ruled that she should be allowed to spell words phonetically as English was not her native tongue and won the game by placing the letters 'phuqkwit' on a triple-word square. Her unashamed gloating inevitably escalated into a full-on pillow fight, which inevitably ended up with me tying Abbie's wrists and ankles to the bedposts with dressing gown cords and licking her all over. I called Jimmy and ordered the set banquet for three and went next door in my dressing gown to pick it up.

'I told you she has a cute arse,' Jimmy said.

Abbie and I sat cross-legged on my bed and fed each other garlic prawns and then washed the results from each others bodies under the cascading water in my downstairs shower room… all the usual stuff you do on a first date.

The best thing about going to sleep with Abbie was waking up next to her. I had got an overwhelming feeling of contentment from just cuddling her as I fell asleep on Sunday night, and a sudden surge of excitement when I stretched out in the night and encountered the warmth of her body, but the nicest bit was waking up with the soft, regular sound of her breathing beside me. I turned onto my side and watched her sleeping. Abbie looked serene and vulnerable now, and entirely beautiful, but she had slept fitfully. I had woken twice in the darkness to find her whimpering in her sleep. Both times I had gathered her into my arms and stroked her hair gently until the nightmare had passed and her mewing had subsided. It had been a reminder that the memories of her recent ordeal would take longer to fade than the bruises on her face. I was not sure whether staying with me would help or hinder that recovery.

Abbie opened her eyes and looked back at me.

'What time is it?' she asked.

'Time for me to get up. Some of us have got work to do. Do you want tea?'

She reached for me and pulled her body against mine.

'You appear to be up already,' she said.

'Are you insatiable?'

'You need zinc,' said Abbie. She turned over and wriggled her bottom back into my lap until my erection slipped inside her. 'If a man ejaculates more than three times in a twenty-four hour period his body will divert all his available zinc into the production of more semen,' Abbie said to the wall.

'Is that a fact?' I hugged her to me, cupping her breasts in my hands.

'Yes.'

'How do you know that stuff?'

'Cosmopolitan magazine.'

I moved my hands down to her hips and started moving to her rhythm.

'I will buy some zinc tablets today,' Abbie said and I suddenly realised that for the first time we were not using a condom. I stopped moving inside her.

'What?' Abbie asked.

'What about protection?'

Abbie stopped too.

'Protection from what? I'm not going to get pregnant.'

I pulled out of her.

'And I am not going to infect you with anything,' Abbie said. 'Don't you trust me?'

Did I trust her?

'It's not that.'

'What then?'

What was it? Why was having sex without a condom such a much bigger commitment than with one?

'All right then. You asked for this,' I said, trying to make a joke of it. I threw off the bed clothes, rolled her onto her back and held her wrists so that I was pinning her to the bed.

'Are you sure about this?' I asked, looking into her eyes.

'Yes.'

I lowered myself against her and slowly pushed into her again.

'Sure?' I asked.

'Yes.'

I released her wrists and bent to kiss her mouth.

'Sure?' I murmured.

'Yes.'

I nibbled her ear and whispered, 'Sure?'

'Yes.'

I pulled away from her and then thrust again, 'Sure?'

'Yes.'

'Sure?'

'Yes.'

'Sure?'

'Yes.'

★ ★ ★

'You did what?' demanded Gloria.

'I had unprotected sex with someone who I have known for less than a week, who wont even tell me their full name let alone whether they are riddled with a combination of syphilis, gonorrhoea, and HIV, and who is probably an illegal alien hoping to trap me into fathering their child so that they can obtain residency in the UK and fleece me for maintenance for the rest of my life.'

'That is what I thought you said.'

Gloria put down the sandwich which I had brought her as a peace offering. I had dropped into the office again, ostensibly to show Charlie that I hadn't forgotten his offer to take me out to lunch, but I was secretly pleased to find that he had once again had a better offer. Charlie would have wanted to help me fix my problem with Abbie; Gloria was just happy to help me enjoy the problem. As demanded, I had given Gloria a blow-by-blow account of my weekend.

'And I am going to do it all over again tonight,' I finished happily.

'She won't be there tonight,' Gloria said. 'Right now she is battering herself with an iron and giving herself chafe marks on her wrists so that she can present herself at the police station as some escaped sex slave. Your semen is being DNA matched from her vaginal swab even as we speak. She'll blackmail you for Charlie's share of your house or press charges which will send you down for life. Why are you smiling?'

'She was already battered when I found her, but I admit that the chafe marks on her wrists are mine.'

'Whoa, Jim! Way too much detail.'

'That's a first. When has too much detail ever been enough for you before?'

'Don't you think this is all just a little bit too perfect? A mystery woman turns up who cleans your house, washes your clothes, cooks your meals, and then shags you senseless, but still requires no commitment from you. Is there anything she doesn't do?'

'I haven't found anything yet,' I said. 'She's a pocket contortionist. I never imagined that the human body could be so flexible.'

'Stop right there. I don't want to know the details. But there has to be a catch.'

'You're just jealous.'

'Jealous of Abbie?'

'No. Jealous of me. You want someone to clean your house, wash your clothes, cook your meals, and shag you senseless.'

'Hey. I've got Charlie, haven't I? One out of four ain't bad. No. I'm not jealous of you; I'm worried about you.'

'I thought you would be pleased for me. You were the one who thought Abbie was sweet before.'

'That was then. This is different. You are going to get hurt this time. Promise me that you are just using her, Jim. Don't go and fall for her.'

'Don't you see? That is just the point. Abbie is going to leave me soon, no matter what I do. No matter what I think, no matter what I feel. So I might as well enjoy it while I can, shouldn't I? And give me some credit. There is always the possibility that she might be enjoying it too.'

Gloria's reply was interrupted by my mobile phone whistling the dam-busters theme tune. I was tempted to ignore it, but I knew from the tune that it was a call from a landline number which was not already in my phone's address-book. Maybe it was from Abbie. Gloria watched me as I flipped open the phone.

'Hi, Jim Turner,' I said.

'Hello James.'

I felt my stomach lurch.

'Hello? James? Can you hear me?'

I still didn't answer. I noticed that Gloria was watching at me inquisitively.

'Bloody mobiles.' Anne's natural Irish lilt had always been most pronounced when she swore.

'Hi, yes, I can hear you, I just wasn't expecting a call from you,' I said in a rush before Anne could cut the connection. Across the desk I saw Gloria's curiosity deepen.

'Oh, good. Hello James,' Anne said again. 'Can you talk? You're not on your bike or anything at the moment?'

'No, I can talk.' But I had nothing to say to her.

'I got your number from Jane. She said you were in good form on Friday. It was good to see you again last week.'

'It was odd for me too,' I replied, deliberately mishearing her.

'Odd? Yes, I suppose it was odd, but I hope you didn't find it too awkward. I didn't find it awkward. There has been a lot of water under the bridge for all of us since Cambridge but after you had gone we all said how in some ways you hadn't changed at all. In others ways you seemed a completely different person.' There was a slight pause before Anne carried on, 'It would be nice to get to know you again.'

'I don't know, Anne.' Gloria started at the name, and then caught my eye and smirked. At the other end of the phone I sensed Anne falter. 'I'm not saying "no",' I continued, 'I'm just not saying "yes".'

'Oh. Ok. I understand, I suppose. Well, we are all going to the theatre tomorrow night. Becca and Jane and a few others. That modern "Hamlet" at the National. It's been absolutely panned by the critics so there should be returns available on the door if we get there earlier enough, and the worse the reviews the better the show in my experience. We wondered whether you wanted to come with us? And Jane told me about your new lodger; you can bring Abbie if you want.'

'I'll ask her.'

'Ok. Well… give me a call at work. You've got this number now; it rings straight through to my desk. Tomorrow will be fine. We'll probably try to meet up for a drink beforehand so I'll let you know when and where. Assuming you're coming of course.'

'You know that I'll come, don't you. I should be in the gym tomorrow, but my whole routine seems to have gone out the window since… anyway, I'm sure I'll make it. I can't speak for Abbie, though. She doesn't venture out of the house very much but I'll ask her.'

'Speak to you tomorrow.'

'Ok. Bye Anne.'

Gloria burst out laughing as I snapped shut my phone.

'What?' I asked, but I knew very well what.

★ ★ ★

It started raining in the afternoon, heavy, persistent rain, so that by the time I knocked off after the evening rush-hour it had begun to permeate even through my supposedly impervious over-suit. My last drop-off was at the Foreign and Commonwealth office so my route home took me over Westminster Bridge and down Kennington Road. I was forced to stop at the same traffic lights opposite Kennington Park as I had stopped at the previous week. I opened my visor to prevent it steaming up and looked across the junction and into the dark sodden trees of the park, but there were more cars behind me than there had been last time. When the lights turned green I pulled away without a second look and made for the relative shelter of my lock-up.

I spent a few minutes wiping down the Bandit before locking her away for the night. As I walked up to my house I wondered whether I could default on yet another rugby training session that evening. If I was going to the theatre the next day it would be missing another gym session as well, but that evening's choice seemed to be between two hours running around in the rain or snuggling up on the sofa with Abbie? Tough call. It made me realise just how little social life I had had for the last two years.

Abbie met me at the door and reached up on tip-toe to give me a kiss. It was a generous kiss, a friendly kiss, her small tongue nuzzling mine, but it was not a passionate kiss. It was a welcome-home-from-the-office-dear kiss, not an I-have-been-thinking-about-you-all-day-and-can-no-longer-keep-my-hands-off-you kiss.

'Ugh. You are all wet,' Abbie said recoiling from me. She was wearing her white vest and a short blue pleated skirt. Her feet were bare and her hair was bunched into two long pigtails tied with red ribbons. She looked every inch like a mischievous schoolgirl trying to act older than her age. 'Get out of those wet things and dress smartly for dinner. I have cooked something special for you.'

She skipped lightly away from me and sat down halfway up the stairs. I looked up at her. Abbie smiled at the forlorn expression on my face, her first smile since I had arrived home, and took pity on me. She slowly let her knees fall open so that I caught a flash of white gusset before she clamped her legs tightly shut again. 'Maybe for dessert. . . if you eat up all your vegetables,' she said teasingly.

I fetched the drying rail out from the shower room and sat down on the stairs a few steps below her. As I pulled off my boots I felt Abbie's toes curl into the hair at the base of my neck. I caught her ankle and turned my head to kiss her foot. She did not pull her foot away but I resisted the urge to continue my kisses up the inside of her calf. The uninhibited intimacy of the previous day seemed to have gone.

'What's for dinner?' I asked instead. It would have been normal to also ask whether she had had a good day, but I knew she wouldn't answer. Our situation wasn't normal.

'Wait and see. And you are not allowed into the kitchen until I say so. Ok?' Without waiting for an answer Abbie jumped up and ran up the stairs to her room.

I padded across the hall to my newspaper re-cycling pile, my matted, wet walking socks leaving pools of footprints behind me, and stuffed three scrunched-up pages of yesterday's Observer into each sodden boot before struggling out of my saturated outer layer of clothing. The next layer was damp rather than wet but the leather clung clammily to my legs as I peeled off my trousers. I hung my leathers up on the drying-rail and went to stand under the shower in my sweat layer of rugby shirt, boxer shorts and socks. As the hot water wash over me I hoped that Abbie would join me in the shower as she had yesterday but

I knew that she wouldn't. The atmosphere had changed. Eventually I turned off the water and let my usual end-of-wet-day routine kick in. I towelled myself half dry, switched on the dehumidifier and retrieved the drying rail from the hall. I bundled up my wet clothes and headed naked for the washing machine before the closed kitchen door reminded me of Abbie's embargo. I threw the clothes back into the shower room and as an after thought I self-consciously wrapped a towel around my waist before climbing the stairs to my room.

I opened my wardrobe and looked at the pile of jeans and sweatshirts inside. Last Tuesday it had been a fashion statement to be the only one in jeans when everyone else was in dinner jackets; now I wanted to be able to please Abbie by appearing in a shirt and tie at least but I resigned myself to denim again and my one smart Polo shirt. My deck shoes were muddy and scuffed and I had no shoe cleaner. It suddenly felt like a terrible indictment of my life that I couldn't even demonstrate that I had made an effort to look smart.

There was a tentative little knock on the door.

'Come in,' I said, giving myself a last rueful look in the mirror.

Abbie opened the door. She was wearing a pale blue, high-necked, silk evening dress that reached just below her knees; on her feet were stiletto-heeled shoes in matching blue. There was a delicate silver chain around her left ankle, a heavier silver bracelet on her right wrist and the set was completed by an elegant silver chocker around her neck. Her thick hair was piled up on her head in an elegant French plait. She had used make-up for the first time to hide the last remnants of her facial bruising and her lips shone a deep, glossy crimson. Even her fingernails were painted to the same duck-egg blue as her dress. She had used dark eyeliner to make her almond-shaped eyes look almost Egyptian.

'Dinner is served,' Abbie said in little more than a whisper and made to close the door.

'Abbie.'

She paused. I went to her, took her in my arms, and as she started to protest I kissed her lightly on her lipsticked mouth.

'Shhh. I am not going to ask you any questions. I am not going to say anything... except... you are very, very beautiful.'

Abbie allowed me one proper kiss before she took my hand and led me downstairs. She had moved the kitchen table into the living room and draped a clean white sheet over it as a tablecloth. The table was neatly laid with a small bowl of flowers as a centrepiece and two candles burning in eggcups at either end. A bottle was standing in a casserole dish with ice packed round its base.

'Open the champagne while I bring in the oysters,' Abbie said. I caught her round the waist and tried to kiss her again, but she shrugged me off and headed for the kitchen. I realised that her earlier reserve had been nothing more than concern that her special meal would be successful. She must have spent all day preparing it.

When we were both sitting in front our plates of oysters I raised my champagne and offered a toast. Abbie lifted her glass.

'To zinc,' I said seriously, 'and to that all comes from it.'

Abbie giggled, relieved that I had remembered her assertion from that morning. Now that the meal was starting she was suddenly her girlish self again.

'You know what?' she said secretively. 'I don't really like them. And I couldn't believe how much they cost here.'

There was an infinitesimal pause into which I could have asked how much oysters cost in other places she had been. I could have asked her where the money for this food and her clothes and her jewellery had suddenly come from. I could have asked her whether that personal comment, her first slip, was a genuine accident or whether I was meant to read anything specific into it. But Abbie was holding my gaze firmly with no suggestion of wanting to retract her words. I let it pass.

'Well I love oysters,' I said.

'It wouldn't matter if you didn't,' said Abbie. 'I have prescribed them for you as medicine so if you don't eat them all you won't have any dessert.'

The main course was a variation on a Thai green curry, made with fish and coconut milk and lots of lemon grass but served with noodles rather than rice. It was absolutely delicious and just about as hot as I can enjoy. We finished the champagne and I moved on to cold lager. Abbie wouldn't let me clear the dishes so while she cleared the table I put on some background music. She reappeared from the kitchen carrying two bowls of fresh strawberries. She had kicked off her shoes and brushed out her hair so that it hung straight and glossy down her back.

'Your first dessert,' she said.

'I'll let you know later which tastes better,' I said. I caught her eye and I waited for her say it, to tell me that she was leaving, for surely this was all by way of a farewell meal. But the opportunity came and went. Maybe she thought that actions spoke louder than words but I knew that I was not going to be the one to precipitate that discussion.

'Tell me what you dream of,' she asked suddenly.

'You have fulfilled all my dreams,' I replied, keeping my tone jocular.

'No. Tell me a fantasy. A real one. A weird one. A dark secret that no one could ever guess without being told.'

'There are two types of fantasy,' I said warily. 'There are the silly things which are alluring just because they are impossible or taboo, the "forbidden fruit" fantasies. Fruit which would probably turn out to be rotten if you ever actually got hold of it but which is fun in make-believe. Becoming Prime Minister, ruling the world, playing rugby for England, winning the lottery, having sex with Marilyn Monroe.'

'She would definitely be rotten fruit by now.'

'Yeah ok, but any current pop star or film actress. I wouldn't have a clue what to say to them if I actually met one of them in real life, let alone be able to muster a respectable erection. They are probably all precious and arrogant and atrocious lovers anyway.'

Abbie smiled sceptically.

'Or a harem of sex slaves,' I said, warming to my theme. 'Surely a perfectly respectable male fantasy, all oiled orifices and shaved fannies, but what would it actually be like in real life? The play-acting of master and slave is fine if it adds spice to a flagging repertoire but to get pleasure out of someone you own? Not my cup of tea.'

'What about the other type of fantasy?' Abbie asked quietly.

'A real fantasy is one that could possibly happen. Just possibly. It is still so unlikely that it would be irrational to build your hopes around it, but it is reasonable to be enthusiastic about. It is a dream, but it is a dream of how your life could be.'

I stopped.

Abbie looked at me expectantly. 'So, not playing for England but winning the league with Roslyn Park? That could really happen. Or riding your motorbike to Cape Town?' She suggested.

'Yeah. Those would be good things.'

'But they aren't what you really long for are they? Tell me a real fantasy.'

'Real fantasies spoil if you speak them out loud,' I said.

'Coward,' Abbie teased.

'I'm not very good with words,' I said, 'but if you will help me push the table out of the way I have a real fantasy about dancing with a beautiful woman in a silk kimono.'

★ ★ ★

Later, as Abbie lay with her head on my chest and we both stared with unfocused eyes at my bedroom ceiling she asked me why I had not asked her about her fantasies.

'It never occurred to me that you would tell me,' I answered.

'I have a "forbidden fruit" fantasy,' she said. 'One that could never happen. One that would turn out to be rotten if I ever really tried to fulfil it.'

I didn't say anything but stroked her hair gently in the darkness.

'I would like to fall in love with someone and have children and watch them grow up into healthy, happy adults.' There was suddenly such bitterness in her voice that I was shocked into stillness. 'Is that such an unreasonable thing to want?' she asked.

'No,' I said quietly. 'Why can it never happen?'

Abbie did not reply. I held her tightly and she leant into me, but then she suddenly shook herself free and sat up in the bed.

'I have a "real" fantasy as well,' she said brightly. 'One that could actually happen.'

'Don't say it out loud,' I said, 'or it will spoil.'

I didn't want to hear it, whatever it was. There was such a desperation about her that it filled me with dread.

She looked at me and said very deliberately, 'I want you to fuck me in the arse while I'm asleep.'

I felt numb. She wasn't joking. Abbie had flipped from the tenderness of sharing with me her maternal longing to the most transparent demonstration that she despised me as just another sexual predator in her tortured life. I put my arms out to comfort her but she deliberately misconstrued my meaning. She threw herself down on the bed with her back to me.

'Didn't you hear me?' she shouted. 'I have to be asleep first. Keep your hands off me until then. Then you can do to me whatever you want.'

I watched her silently trembling back, her whole body shuddering with suppressed anguish. I felt physically sick. Had the whole romantic dinner just been an elaborate charade designed to act out her perceived view of me as her sexual abuser? But I wasn't like that. Was I?

There was nothing I could do. I got out of the bed and walked across the room but I stopped with my hand on the door handle and looked back. Abbie had not moved. I realised that if I left her then it would be an irrevocable step; there would be no way back for either of us.

'Abbie,' I said, 'I know that you can hear me. I do not expect you to answer me, but I want you to listen to me. I don't know whether you hate me personally or just as the personification of something else that you hate. Whichever it is I am very sorry. I am sorry if you feel that I have taken your feelings for granted or if you have interpreted my respect for your anonymity as a lack of interest in you. I do care about you. And I know, right now, better than you do yourself, what is in your best interests. I am going to come back to you for five minutes. I will not kiss you. I will not caress you. I am just going to hold you. And then I will leave you and go next door and sleep in your room.'

Abbie did not move as I lay down beside her. She did not protest as I drew her to me but neither did she respond. She lay stiffly in my arms. I held her gently and then, as I had promised, I left.

Chapter Eight

Your spinning rear wheel provides a gyroscopic stabiliser. Lock your wheel and you lose your stabiliser."
From: "Ride Well and Prosper".

It took me a long time to get to sleep in Abbie's fragrant sheets. I must have dozed off in the end because I was not conscious of the door opening or of Abbie slipping into the bed beside me but her head was on my shoulder when I woke in the cold grey light of dawn. I drew her to me. Her eyes fluttered open but she closed them again and smiled as I stroked her hair. I did not go back to sleep. I held her to me until the pins-and-needles in the arm under her head forced me to move. She didn't wake as I wriggled out of the bed. I walked through to my room. It was nearly seven. I switched the radio-alarm off before it had a chance to disturb the peace. I showered in silence and ate a few spoonfuls of cold rice and curry in the kitchen and left the house without waking her.

It was a glorious autumnal day, crisp and bright. Most of my deliveries that morning involved decent runs to the outer suburbs or to Home Counties market towns which reminded me why I enjoyed my job so much; being paid for the thrill of riding.

I phoned home mid-morning. I didn't expect Abbie to answer but she surprised me by picking up the phone immediately and launching into a chatty discussion about that morning's guests on Woman's Hour as if nothing had happened the previous night.

'And you're sure you don't want to come to the theatre with me this evening?' I asked as soon as I could get a word in edgeways.

'No, I don't think so.'

'What if I said, "please"? I don't know these people myself anymore; I haven't seen them for ten years. I would welcome your support.'

'Thank you. But I don't want to intrude on your evening with Anne.'

'It's not like that. Anne is happily married to someone who used to be my best friend.' I paused. 'So, actually, if it was like that it would be all the more reason why I would need your support.'

'I'm sorry, James. That is your life, not mine. But I presume you will want something to eat before you go out? Shall I have something ready for you?'

As I selected Anne's work number I was still undecided about whether I would go that evening.

'Hi Anne,' I started, 'it's....

'Hi James,' Anne interrupted me. I was pleased that she recognised me from the sound of my voice. 'Thanks for calling back. Is Abbie coming tonight?' she asked.

'No.'

'I am sorry, but you're still up for it aren't you.' It was a statement rather than a question.

I opened my mouth to say, 'I'm sorry, I have changed my mind,' and instead heard myself saying, 'I'm looking forward to it.'

'Good. No one can think of a single decent pub near the National Theatre so we're going to meet at the theatre bar. Ginny is going to get there at six to queue for tickets, so anytime after that. Curtain up at seven thirty.'

'Great. See you later,' I said vaguely. Anne was laughing as I hung up.

The sun was still shining. I managed to push any considerations about a second meeting with Anne to the back of my mind for the rest of the day. 'Concentrate or die' has its uses. In the middle of the afternoon I phoned Gloria to say that unless she was really snowed under I wouldn't mind knocking off a bit early. I got the retort that I deserved – 'you seem to be knocking off quite a bit recently' - but she let me off on the promise that I keep up my newly acquired habit of bringing her lunch every day to keep her fed with gossip. By five o'clock I had locked the Bandit away in my lock up and was walking back up Brixton Road to my house.

'Honey, I'm home, and I've had a bad day,' I sung out as I opened the front door. I realised that Abbie was unlikely to recognise the Shania Twain song, especially the way that I sang it, but it felt appropriate for the exuberance that I felt. I shivered. The house felt cold. I knew instantly that she was gone, but the certainty did not stop me from shouting out as I climbed the stairs.

'Abbie. Hi. It's Jim. Where are you?'

Her bedroom door was open. The bed was made-up and my tee-shirt and track suit bottoms were neatly folded on top of the duvet. I checked the bathroom and my bedroom before returning to the spare room. I opened the wardrobe and the chest of draws. All sign of her was gone. My dressing gown was hanging on a hook behind the door. Even the pockets were empty.

I went downstairs, half hoping and half fearing to find a note left on the kitchen table. The room was clean and tidy. All the detritus from the previous evening's meal had been put away. The surfaces had been wiped down and the makeshift tablecloth had been washed and ironed and put back over the table. There was no note.

I got a beer out of the fridge, walked through to the hall, took off my jacket and sat down on the stairs to pull off my riding boots.

'Oh well,' I said out loud.

I took the beer upstairs and paused outside her bedroom. I had always known that she was going to leave. I went back into her room. As I sat down on the bed I caught the scent of her perfume again but it was very faint. This time she had really gone. Twenty minutes later I had long since finished the beer, but I was still lying on Abbie's bed.

'Bugger,' I said to the ceiling, trying to laugh at my own self-pity, 'she said she would have dinner waiting for me.'

I didn't feel like eating. I thought of phoning Anne to say that I would not be coming but I guessed that she would have left her office for the day and I didn't have any other contact number for her. I could phone Jane. I could just go down to the gym, return to my usual Tuesday evening routine and to hell with the lot of them. But I knew that I wouldn't. I knew that I would go to the theatre. It was the right thing to do.

I got up and went downstairs to shower. I wheeled the drying rail into the hall and hung up my riding gear. It was the same ritual that I had performed a hundred times on my own and just once with Abbie sitting halfway up the stairs watching me. I hoped that the familiarity of the routine would be comforting and shake me out of my maudlin mood but if anything the feeling of abandonment grew as I showered. My perfunctory attempt to dry myself brought back memories of Abbie chiding me for similar half-heartedness two days, and another lifetime before.

I smiled as I bundled my sweat-layer of clothing into the washing machine. 'At least I am allowed into my own kitchen this evening,' I consoled myself.

I climbed the stairs and opened my wardrobe again.

'I guess it has to be the old denim outfit again,' I told the mirror in my room. I'd been planning to ask Abbie to come out with me and help me do some clothes shopping.

'I'm old enough and ugly enough to do my own clothes shopping,' I said to my reflection. But I knew that I wouldn't.

I locked up my empty house and walked the half mile to Stockwell underground station. The evening rush hour was in full swing. The great preponderance of humanity was flowing out from the centre of town and back towards the suburbs, bustling to be home in time for their TV dinner-dates with East Enders, but even battling against the tide I was inevitably jostled by strangers who strayed into that square metre of personal space which in all other circumstances except on the rugby pitch is considered sacrosanct. I had to stand for the three stops up the Northern Line to Waterloo.

It is only two hundred yards from Waterloo station to the heinous concrete complex of the National Theatre but I dragged out my approach by walking first to Westminster Bridge and then coming back along the Thames Path beneath the London Eye. There was one large group of Japanese tourists and a smattering of families queuing up for their evening ride in the world's slowest ferris wheel but compared with the hordes on the underground the river bank was relatively tranquil. This felt like my last chance to break free from the current which was sweeping me back into the circle of my old friends. It wasn't that there wouldn't be subsequent opportunities to walk away from them, it was that after tonight I knew that I might not want to. I hoped that by the time I had made my way to the theatre I could have worked through the conflicting emotions which were warning me off and urging me on. I wanted to think through what I was doing so that my choice, whatever it turned out to be, would be the result of some conscious decision on my part.

I failed. I didn't even get close.

I found myself back at Waterloo Bridge no happier than before. I stood leaning on the concrete balustrade that surrounds The Terrace outside the National Theatre looking out over the quiet waters of the Thames and I had still not even worked out whether I was making a mountain out of an emotional mole hill. What was the worst that could happen? Either it would be a fun evening, in which case it would have been the right decision, or else it would be a bit awkward and I would know that there was no mileage in pursuing it. But at least I would have been out to the theatre which hadn't happened for quite a while. I wished Abbie was with me now. I wondered where she was, what she was doing at that precise moment…

'Don't jump.' Anne whispered suddenly into my ear.

I started in surprise as she laughed guiltily.

'Sorry James, but I couldn't resist it. I thought I was going to be late so I was rushing up the steps when I saw this hunk of a man staring moodily out to sea which, as you know, would be enough to catch my attention at the best of times, but lo and behold it turns out to be you doing your old impression of Rodin's "The Thinker". Now don't you go looking at me like that; it was a joke. Ok?'

I smiled down at her.

'Hurrah. A smile. Come on. Ginny's phoned me twice already on my way down here. She's worried that she's going to end up with too many tickets.'

Anne held out her arm to me and I could do nothing except link my arm through hers.

'We've got ten minutes until curtain up but you should have a pint of Guinness waiting for you. I told Ginny to get one in for you because I was sure you would come.'

I felt very self-conscious as we walked up the stairs arm-in-arm and pushed our way through the crowded foyer towards the bar. Anne was wearing a shimmering black dress with the thinnest of thin straps barely visible beneath the cascade of her golden-red hair which tumbled over her shoulders and down her back in a halo of ringlets. She was still the slight waif of a girl that I had known but there was also something more substantial about her now. Maybe it was just in comparison with my companion of the last two nights. Anne walked with an assurance which turned heads as we moved through the throng. Becca waved at us from across the room. She was sitting at a small table with Jane and another woman who I took to be Becca's girlfriend, Ginny. Both Ginny and Jane were in jeans and jumpers. Becca, predictably, was virtually spilling out of a leopard-print suit which was dazzlingly accessorised with crimson lipstick and chunky silver ear-rings to complement her platinum bob.

Anne waved back and called out, 'I've found him.'

'What? So I'm to be the token bloke tonight am I?' I asked as we joined the others.

'Token? I do hope not,' said Becca. 'The whole point of this evening is to give us girls a chance to find out whether, unlike all our effeminated city friends, you have managed to remain a real man after all this time.'

Jane looked embarrassed by Becca's forwardness, whether on Ginny's behalf or mine I wasn't entirely sure, but Ginny smiled at Becca indulgently and stood up to offer me her hand.

'Hi Jim, I'm Ginny, in case you haven't already guessed. I am very pleased to meet you. I've heard so much about you already.' It was clear that she was well used to Becca's outrageous flirting with every man in the room.

'Hi Ginny,' I said, taking her hand. 'I've heard a lot about you too.'

'I doubt that,' Ginny said, looking over at Becca and casting her eyes to the ceiling. Becca might be the extrovert of the two but it was immediately clear that it was very much a partnership of equals.

'A pint of Guinness for you, as requested by Anne on your behalf.' Ginny indicating one of the two un-started drinks on the table. 'Hi Anne. The other one's for you, although how you can drink a pint in five minutes and still make it through to the interval without a pee is quite beyond me.'

Anne and Ginny kissed cheeks. I wasn't sure if I was expected to kiss Becca and Jane or whether I could brush over those formalities but Becca came to my rescue by kissing me full on the mouth and then making a great play of wiping her lipstick off my lips with her fingers. I gave Jane a hug which seemed to me to be the most genuine thing to do.

'Good, I'm glad that's all over with,' said Ginny, sitting down again. 'I couldn't get five seats together but I've got a three and a two right in front of each other. Jim, have you heard about this production? The guy playing Hamlet is meant to be great, a real up and coming star borrowed from the Royal Shakespeare Company, but the whole play has been set in the modern day.

The Prince of Denmark has become the right hand man of some modern media mogul. It all sounds terribly contrived.'

The five minute warning bell sounded. Anne and I made significant inroads into our drinks while the others discussed the seating arrangements. After much debate, during which my views were entirely ignored, it was decided that I should sit between Becca and Ginny for the first act with Anne and Jane in the two seats directly behind us. I asked Becca if she wouldn't rather to sit next to Ginny but she just looked at me as if I was mad.

The performance was nearly as dire as had been predicted but at least there were two intervals. After the first break I found that Jane had taken my seat, leaving me to sit with Anne in the next row back. Becca kept looking round as if to check that we weren't holding hands. I guessed that the game of the musical chairs was just a small part of some much wider elaborate joke in which they were all conniving to make me feel as uneasy as possible. If so it was certainly working. I had forgotten how uncomfortable theatre seats could be. There was not enough room between the rows for me to sit with my legs straight ahead of me. I had to choose between facing half-right, and imposing on the elderly gentleman next to me, or facing half-left and risk accidentally resting my knee against Anne's. I chose half-right but I am sure that Anne was conscious of my discomfort because she kept smiling to herself and there was nothing remotely funny happening on stage.

I had also forgotten how long Hamlet is. When the lights came up for the second interval I jokingly asked Anne whether, as I knew the ending, I might be excused from the final act. Becca overheard me and took my suggestion seriously.

'I have never been so bored in my entire life,' she said, yawning theatrically.

'Let's jack this in and go for curry,' Ginny suggested.

'Ginny, I love you already,' I said, suddenly realising how hungry I was. 'Anybody got any idea where we can eat round here?'

'Race on!' shouted Becca gleefully. While they dived for their Blackberries – Becca from her Gucci handbag and Ginny from her jeans pocket – Jane explained that Becca and Ginny were trying desperately to convince everyone that there was actually some advantage in having a 3G phone other than for playing games.

'Rajput. 14 Cornwall Road,' said Ginny triumphantly.

'Bugger!' said Becca. 'I was nearly there.'

'Which would be quite impressive, if any of us knew where Cornwall Road was,' said Anne.

Fortunately I knew the way to Cornwall Road. Becca swore that she could download a local map to her mobile if we just gave her a couple more minutes but she was shouted down. As we set off I dropped behind to walk with Jane.

'What's really going on?' I asked, somewhat more aggressively than I had intended.

'What do you mean?'

'The whole contrivance of getting me to sit next to Anne.'

'Oh, sorry. I didn't think about it,' Jane said. After a pause she added, 'Despite whatever Becca may have said, this evening has not all been organised in your honour, you know. At least, not as far as I'm aware. We do all try to meet up occasionally and it's not usually an all girl affair. Angus comes sometimes, and William. Richard occasionally. I assumed that this was just somebody's off-the-cuff suggestion. I'm sorry if you feel set up.'

'Don't worry about it. You know I nearly didn't come tonight? Abbie left today and I am meant to be down the gym training for rugby, but I am genuinely glad I did. You're not such a scary bunch after all.'

The Rajput looked seedy even by my standards but Ginny led the way in undeterred and the proprietor reluctantly managed to find a free table for the five of us in his otherwise empty restaurant. While we waited for the papadums and lager to arrive I asked Ginny about her latest venture with Becca.

'The power of the internet,' she said, 'is that it is available to everyone. It is also its vulnerability, but that is another story.'

'Don't get her started on how hackers are killing off the very thing that they claim to love by making everyone so security conscious that they are frightened to host their own web-sites,' warned Becca.

'If you want to make money out of the internet, and we do,' continued Ginny, 'you need to leverage a mass market. It is much easier to make one pound from a thousand people over the internet than it is to make a thousand pounds from one person. There are a few high-value commodities which can be successfully traded, like cars, where the build quality is a given. You can test drive the car you want at your local dealership and then go home and order the duty-free imported version of the same model from the comfort of your own armchair and you can be confident in what you are going to get. But no one is going to spend ten thousand pounds on a unique Persian rug without feeling the quality of it first. Most of the successful early start-ups dealt with books or CDs where the mark-up may be minimal but delivery is cheap and you have the benefit over your bricks-and-mortar competitors that you don't have to pay for any shops.'

'Or porn,' said Becca.

'But you also need to build and maintain a reputation if you are going to be more than a one day wonder,' Ginny carried on, ignoring Becca's interjection. 'There is so much competition out there, and it is so quick and cheap to copy everybody else's good ideas, that you need to provide a quality service at a price that people don't object to paying. You don't make money in the long run by ripping people off. I am still making a decent amount out of the first web-site that I ever built. It is still running quite happily from a server under our spare bed.'

'What does it do?' I asked.

'It sells number plates,' Ginny said.

'Personalised number plates?'

'Of a sort. Within months of the number plate licensing laws being liberalised in the eighties there were literally hundreds of web-site offering to buy or sell your number plate. What they really did was just hold your details on their database and then make them available for everyone else to look at. The clever number plates went for fortunes, but a lot of other people got caught up on the bandwagon. You may not have thought that there was any value in a number plate of J812TPD, but it might be worth fifty quid to Jonathan Twisten Puddle-Davies, or whoever, so people registered their details just in case. And the point of those web-sites is that the sellers don't have to commit anything until a buyer is found. There are no over-heads, so once the site is up and running it's just money for old rope.'

'What is your site called?'

'Mirrorplates-dot-com,' said Ginny.

'Ginny wanted to call it setalprorrim.com,' said Becca. She looked round at our blank faces. 'You see, Ginny, I told you. You might have a technical brain the size of a planet, but you have no flair for marketing. Thank god. Leave that bit to me.' She reached across the table and squeezed Ginny's hand. 'S-E-T-A-L-P-R-O-R-R-I-M,' Becca spelt out again. 'Come on, Jim, Ginny has already given it away. It spells 'MIRRORPLATES' backwards. That's the point of her web-site. But setalprorrim is way too subtle for the mass market. Personalised number plates, but which only spell words in the mirror. It's become a real cult in the gay community. We got five thousand pounds last year for YO8 PI8.'

'For what?' Jane asked.

Becca wrote it out on a serviette and then held it up backwards over the light.

'Imagine seeing that coming up behind you in your driving mirror,' I said.

'The eights doesn't really work,' said Jane.

'Which is not actually my point,' said Ginny. 'My point is not about the five grand we got for that plate; that was the exception. My point is about the ten pounds which we make on the thousands of other plates which we sell without having to do a thing. A small amount of money from a large number of people. Most guys just want to display the initials of their latest partner backwards. Nobody knows about it outside the gay circuit but it's a kind of signature thing. And if it only cost them a hundred quid it makes a nice Christmas present. With a high churn rate of partners we have a few regulars who buy themselves a new plate two or three times a year. We take a ten percent commission for putting the buyer in touch with someone with the appropriate lettering. It's normally only five or ten pounds per transaction, but week in, week out, over eight years it has paid for all our holidays.'

The papadums arrived.

I looked up and saw Anne watching me from across the table.

'You are being unusually quiet,' I said, and realised that I was judging her by my memories of ten years ago. Anne had lived half her life again since then. Maybe she had mellowed.

'I was just thinking that considering this evening was meant to be about us all dissecting your life you are doing a very good job of avoiding the inquisition,' Anne countered with a laugh. I was glad that she still laughed a lot.

'Fire away,' I said, 'I've got nothing to hide.' But I had a temporary reprieve as the waiter returned with five pints of Kingfisher. I sank half of mine in one quaff and put in a repeat order before he had finished distributing the first round. There was then a pause while we all consulted menus. I thought I had got away with it.

'Are you happy, James?' Anne asked.

The menu consulting stopped abruptly.

'What sort of a question is that?' Jane asked into the protracted pause. 'At least let the poor boy order his main course first.'

'Chicken jalfrasie, pilau rice, garlic nann, and a sag aloo,' I said, playing up to the part. 'Or maybe I should have the Madras? Let me just have half-an-hour to think about it and I'll get back to you. Is that alright, Anne?'

Anne laughed. We all laughed.

'Ok. You can take your time,' she said, 'but I want an answer from you before we leave.'

'Tell me about you, Anne. You don't have to tell me that you are happy. I can see that for myself. But what does a human rights lawyer actually do?'

'You're doing it again,' Anne said. 'Deflecting the question. The rest of us all know what we all do. It's called keeping in touch for the last ten years. You're the mystery man amongst us.'

'No, go on, Anne,' Jane chipped in. 'I see you all the time, but I don't really have a clue what you do all day.'

'Well, it's pretty much what it says on the tin.' Anne said. 'I am a very small cog in a very large machine. We specialise in cases where there is an alleged infringement of the European Convention on Human Rights. Everyone thinks that we spend all our time defending illiterate refugees, but we take on all comers. I am in court tomorrow arguing that my client's rights have been denied by West Ham district council – he may be a parishioner of yours Jane - because they have cautioned him for flying an old IRA flag in his back garden. He argues that as the garden is enclosed it is no one else's business what he does in it. I happen to agree with him, however objectionable he may be as a human being, but the law is not about whether something is morally right or morally wrong, it is about whether an action is prohibited by an act of the legislature – in our case by Act of Parliament. If the UK law prohibits something which the European Convention deems to be a basic human right then we can challenge it. If we win, the UK law has to be re-drafted so as to comply with the convention. Interestingly in Britain we start from the premise that our citizens can do anything they like and then list some specific exceptions. Over the centuries we have gradually built up a long list of acts which the legislature deem to be sufficiently against the common good to outweigh an individual's personal freedom. By contrast the Napoleonic legal code comes at it from the other end. Most European constitutions start by stating all the duties expected from its citizens and then list the specific exceptions where a person's individual freedom over-rides their obligation to the state. That's why it's easier for them to incorporate Human Rights into their constitutions; they can just add them to the list of things which an individual is entitled to...' Anne had been looking at me as she talked but she trailed off as she noticed Becca pretending to yawn. 'Sorry to lecture you, but you did ask.'

'Don't take any notice of Becca,' I said. 'I'm riveted.'

'Yeah, right.' said Becca. 'Anyone flying an IRA flag should be banged up. End of story.'

'That's not really what you think, is it?' Jane asked. I wondered whether Jane knew that Anne's Catholic father had been a staunch apologist for the IRA during the Northern Ireland troubles.

'That's exactly the point,' said Anne, 'it doesn't really matter what you think. The judiciary doesn't make up the law. In an ideal word the legislature would pass laws which were completely unambiguous. The police would determine the facts of the case beyond dispute and it would be completely obvious whether a law had been broken or not. That is why the vast majority of cases never go to court. And the vast majority of cases which do go to court are because the facts of the case are in dispute, not because the law is ambiguous. The jury has to decide whether or not something happened; not whether, if it did happen, the Law was or was not broken. Over the centuries we have built up a history of test cases which pretty much set the precedent for every occasion so once the jury has agreed what, beyond reasonable doubt, happened, there is nearly always a previous example which defines whether or not that action constitutes breaking the law. There is no place for bleeding hearts. We can't argue whether something is morally right or wrong, just whether or not the action is prohibited by some previous case law.'

'And is there a law against flying an IRA flag in private?' Becca asked.

'So you are still awake?' Anne asked. 'You should be. Precedent covers most cases but as new laws are passed, especially shoddy, rushed legislation, there needs to be new test cases to define how the fine words on the statute book are meant to apply in the real world. What was the intent of the legislature when it passed the law? So, importantly, there is still no place for lawyers to question what is morally right or wrong, or what the legislators should have meant if they had thought about it properly. Test cases just have to work out what behaviour the new law was passed to prevent. It is the making of any lawyer's career to win a high profile test case. And where these laws are being tested most frequently at the moment is in cyberspace. It crosses national boundaries, it can be totally anonymous, it can ride roughshod over intellectual property rights. I bet with Snatchwatch you had your own company lawyer.'

'Complete shark,' said Ginny.

'Complete fuckwit, more like,' said Becca.

'Are you ready to order?' asked the waiter.

As the waiter cajoled some consensus from us I looked round at the faces of my friends from a decade ago. There was little in what Anne had just said that I didn't already know, but for me that knowledge was just theory and pub-quiz answers. For Anne it was her life. It is what she did. Jane ministered to the needs of a parish of thousands; Becca and Ginny owned their own internet company. I thought back to last week's dinner party. Richard Davies: a university lecturer; William Searle: something in the City; Angus: something in spooksville. It all seemed so grown up, but it could have been me. Was I really happy with where I had ended up?

'But what do you actually do?' Jane asked Anne again.

'Hands up who cares?' Becca asked, shoving both her arms under the table.

'It's not at all glamorous,' Anne continued. 'I rarely even get into a courtroom. It's probably like most office work: fun because of the people I work with - my colleagues not the clients - and a bad day is when the coffee machine is broken. I mainly research background information on clients or the opposition before the trial actually starts but if I'm really good I get to sit with the advocate team in court and look decorative.'

'It doesn't sound like you to accept such tokenism,' I said.

'Oh, the means justifies the end, James. My idealism has long since gone out the window. You wouldn't believe the affront of those bastards in big business. If I can tip the scales of justice by smiling sweetly at the judge, what's that to me?'

'You're joking, right?'

'Well I do find it funny but, no, it's not a joke. Some of the judges are more susceptible than others. Judge Tobias is my real pet. If Tobias is assigned to our case the other team rolls over without a fight. I've only got to absent-mindedly cross my legs or touch my breasts in court and Judge Tobias nearly has a heart-attack.'

'You old trollop,' said Becca.

'So how does the absent-minded breast touching route go exactly?' Ginny asked mischievously.

Anne pushed back her chair, crossed her legs and stared thoughtfully towards the restaurant door. She brought up her right hand, ran her fingers through her hair and then stroked her chin thoughtfully before letting her hand drop casually onto her chest. Still gazing out into the darkened street Anne gently cupped her left breast and let her thumb idly stroke the thin black silk of her dress.

'Thank you, Anne. I think that we've all got the idea,' Becca said tartly.

'No, I'm afraid you lost me there, Anne.' I said. 'Could you just go over that last bit again.'

Anne laughed but looked down at her Madras, suddenly embarrassed.

'We were talking about our new web site: IFA.com,' Ginny said into the silence. 'I'm not quite sure how we got sidetracked onto Anne's erotica. IFA. Independent Financial Advice dot com. We will save you money year on year, or your money back.'

'That's too cumbersome,' said Becca. 'If this is going to work we need people signing up in their tens of thousands. The hook has to be right. It is the only important thing. William was suggesting something about shitting on city slickers, get your own back for all those times you've been ripped off in the past.'

'What? So the technology to run the site isn't important. The absolute guaranteed security. All our deals with the finance product providers. In fact all the bits that I manage aren't important? Just your publicity work?'

'Of course your bits are important, darling. But they're a given. You can do all that stuff standing on your head.'

'Anyway, I wasn't trying to muscle in on your branding strategy,' Ginny said, not at all mollified by Becca's extravagant praise. 'I was trying to explain to Jim what we are actually trying to do.'

'You can't tell them. It's still supposed to be secret,' Becca stated solemnly.

'For God's sake, Becs!' Ginny seemed genuinely exasperated. 'The whole world knows what we're doing. You've been tapping up your old friends for seed funding for months.'

'I don't know what you're doing,' I said to break up the domestic spat which was brewing before our eyes.

'Sorry,' said Ginny, tearing her glare away from Becca. 'IFA. Independent Financial Advisers. They'll come to your house with a lap top, ask you a succession of life style questions, and bingo, out pops a recommended financial product that you simply must buy. The trouble is that these guys are not actually independent. They get a kick back for every ISA, pension or life insurance policy that they sell you.'

'Ginny, you're not allowed to say that,' said Becca, but it was a half-hearted warning and Ginny ignored her.

'So, we've set up a web-site where you can answer the same lifestyle questions – marriage status, age, salary, mortgage, current pension arrangements etcetera – at your leisure, and then our secret algorithm determines which financial products you should switch to. We charge you a hundred quid for the privilege and if we don't save you at least that much over the next year you can claim your money back. But when you come back to our site to check out our sums at the end of the year we are guaranteed another shot at selling you something equally vital. What could possibly go wrong?'

'You could go bust before I get a chance to redeem my guarantee?' I asked.

'We haven't actually decided the pricing model yet,' Becca put in quickly.

'Why aren't all the High Street Banks doing this already, if it's such a good idea?' Jane asked. 'Where's the catch?'

'Its illegal,' Ginny said.

'That's not strictly true,' Becca said. 'It's not illegal but there are very stringent regulations to prevent mis-selling. You need to give the client a cooling off period to re-consider. You need to ensure that they understand not only their commitment but also your commission and any penalties or strings attached, which is currently interpreted as saying that you need to speak to them face-to-face and get them to sign a disclaimer.'

'But Becca is talking to the right people at the Financial Services Authority so that we can be the first web-site to do all that remotely.'

'I am sure that she is,' I said laughing.

'Do you really not have an email address?' Ginny asked.

'I don't have a telly, let alone a computer. What would I want with an email address?'

'I could send you all my jokes,' Becca said.

'I begin to see the attraction of being without,' Jane said.

'Are you not tempted to join the rest of the human race?' Ginny persisted. 'Don't you feel excluded?'

I thought suddenly of Abbie. 'No, I don't feel excluded.'

'What do you do for porn?' Becca asked.

'Don't ruin the evening,' Ginny said. 'Have you drunk too much already?'

'I've not drunk too much, I'm just interested. Porn is the new masturbation. Our parent's generation all denied pleasuring themselves even after Masters and Johnson revealed that 99 percent of all men do it. Now everyone accepts it as an integral part of a healthy sex life. And a healthy sex life is an integral part of a healthy everything-else life. Now pornography is the new taboo. The porn industry is worth twelve billion dollars a year in America alone. That's declared income, not counting the amateur 'Horny Housewives' videos which get flogged round the pubs in brown paper bags. So everyone must be watching it, we're just not ready to come out of the closet and admit it yet.'

'Just because it's popular does not make it right,' Jane said. 'Pornography is exploitative and a sad reflection on us all.'

'I didn't say it was right. I am not making a moral statement, just saying that porn is the real way to make money on the Internet. I bet that everyone from Saint Augustin to Mother Theresa had, at some point in their lives, the same epiphany; that sex is the real driving force in society. Happily married men throw it all away for their twenty-year-old secretary. Politicians risk their fame and fortune for a quick tumble in the bushes on Wimbledon common. Prostitution isn't called the oldest profession for nothing.'

'And your point is…?' Anne asked.

'It's all hypocrisy. Pure and simple. It may currently be exploitative, Jane, but it would be a lot less exploitative if we stopped pretending that it wasn't happening.'

'Drugs, porn, prostitution. It's always the same argument: that because there is a market for these things we might as well make them legal so that society can at least regulate them,' Jane said. 'But some things are just plain wrong. There will always be drug addicts, there will always be prostitutes, but that doesn't mean we should condone it, even if in the short term it would be the best way to control it. That would send out the wrong signal and demeans society. You may never win the war but sometime just keeping the lid on something constitutes success because it is literally the best that can be done. The price of freedom is eternal vigilance.'

'Is it true that men really think about sex every six seconds?' Becca asked.

Suddenly all four women were looking at me. I looked down at my watch and started counting out loud: 'One, two, three, four… Yes. It appears to be true,' I said.

They all laughed. I looked up from my watch and made the mistake of catching Anne's eye first. It was entirely co-incidental; she just happened to be the one sitting opposite me. It could have been any one of the others that I happened to look at first. Except, as we were all suddenly thinking, I hadn't had sex with any of the others. Up until that point it had just been a joke. I hadn't actually been thinking about sex at all, let alone remembering a specific occasion. But I was now. And we all knew it.

Anne looked away.

'It's amazing that men get anything done at all, then,' Ginny said into the embarrassed silence.

'They don't,' Anne said without looking back at me.

'What does it actually mean?' Becca continued to me, quite seriously. 'Is it for one second out of every six, or do you think about sex for one sixth of the time? Four hours every day?'

'Give Jim a break,' Ginny said. 'If you really want your own porn site you'll have to find a new partner.' And I don't think any of us thought that she just meant a new business partner.

'You're not making a very good job at convincing me to rush home and sign up to the great internet revolution,' I said, trying to lighten the atmosphere.

'I'll tell you why,' Ginny put in. 'What are you really passionate about, Jim?'

'Rugby,' Jane said.

'Let him speak for himself,' Anne said. 'I have a feeling I am about to get my question answered. Come on, James. Be honest.'

Four pairs of eyes looked at me expectantly again.

'Drivers who don't indicate.'

'What?' Anne asked, disappointed by the triteness of my reply.

'You told me to be honest. I very rarely suffer road rage; I can't afford to. But when I am sitting at a roundabout and the approaching car turns off in front of me without indicating, thus denying me one of a very limited number of opportunities to pull out, it drives me crazy. How hard can it be to flick an indicator stalk? It's selfish. And lazy; it shows that the driver isn't concentrating properly. And arrogant. The whole point of indicating is to warn other people of your intentions - Doh! That's why it is called "indicating"! - so that if you haven't seen someone before you pull out they have a fighting chance of avoiding you anyway. If you don't indicate when changing lanes on the motorway it is like saying "I'm infallible. I know where every other car on the road is, so I don't need to bother expending even one calorie of energy on the off chance that there is someone in my blind-spot who I haven't noticed".'

'He is passionate about it.' Ginny said excitedly. 'So, what are you doing about it?'

'I'm not that passionate about it. I'm not writing to my MP, if that's what you mean.'

'I'm very glad to hear it,' Anne said.

'Writing to your MP wouldn't do any good. You need to educate people. Make them think. Send them an email.'

'A viral,' said Becca.

'Like an email chain-letter; one that people will want to send on to all their friends,' said Ginny. 'It's got to be funny.'

'And cool,' said Becca. 'A driving game. With some edge to it. If you forget to indicate the old lady gets squished. Horribly. And sexy. If you get a high score you get to see the totty behind the round window. We could use a clip from that video you took of me last month.'

'I have no idea what you are talking about,' I said.

Becca ignored me. 'But we don't want to be preachy.'

'Got it!' said Ginny. 'The crusade starts here. This is the twist. We don't chastise people for not indicating. We kindly inform them that their equipment must be faulty, because, surely, that could be the only reason why such an otherwise courteous driver would have failed to indicate. I can hack up that pirate driving game from last year. It's too heavy to email, but I can build a web site at the weekend and include a link to the site in the email. The subliminal message is: if someone fails to indicate, don't get angry. Take pity. Politely inform them that there must be something wrong with their indicator by beeping your horn lightly three times. Beep-thrice-dot-com. It will enter youth driving culture within a month.'

'People are starving all over the world,' said Jane, 'and you are starting a campaign to encourage people to indicate more often?'

'Would you like to see the dessert menu?' the waiter asked. Instead we asked for the bill and there was a sudden awkwardness when it arrived. Becca offered to pay for all of us which Jane interpreted as being patronising – whether towards my income or hers I wasn't sure. Anne thought Becca was showing off, and Ginny said Becca was just being plain stupid.

'We are probably the poorest of the lot of you. We're living off the money which we've borrowed to invest in IFA.com. Someday soon there is going to be a reckoning.'

The illusion of equality which had built up during the evening was shattered.

'At least let me drive Jim home,' Becca pleaded.

'I'm going to take him,' Anne said.

'Since when has Brixton been on the way to the Docklands?' Becca asked.

'Since when has Brixton been on the way to anywhere?' Anne replied.

'Jim won't fit into your car. It's tiny.'

'James, would you like a lift,' Anne asked me, turning to me.

'Thank you, Anne. For the offer. But why don't you take Jane. East Ham is more in your direction. I am quite happy making my own way home.'

'That would great,' said Jane. 'I don't really like taking the underground this late at night. It gets a bit seedy after Bow Church.'

In the end we split the bill equally between the five of us, although Becca ostentatiously left twice her agreed share of the tip. We left the restaurant together. When we got to the point where the routes to Becca's and Anne's cars diverged it seemed completely natural for me to kiss Ginny and Becca on both cheeks as we said our good-byes. They set off chatting animatedly and after a dozen steps Becca's hand found Ginny's and she rested her head against Ginny's shoulder. I turned away and offered my arm to Jane. Anne took my other one and we made our way with our arms linked back towards the National Theatre.

'You still haven't answered my question,' Anne said quietly.

'Do you know that the expectation that we should be happy is a very recent phenomenon? The claim that we have an inalienable right to the pursuit of happiness was the most revolutionary thing about the American Declaration of Independence. Prior to that people expected to be unhappy, or didn't think about it at all. Now there is two hundred times more money spent on research into depression than there is into happiness, yet happiness has become the Holy Grail. It is all that parents want for their children. Never mind wealth and power and physical beauty, as long as they are happy. Then somewhere along the line we get corrupted into thinking that wealth and power and physical beauty are pre-requisites to happiness, which is a small step from ditching happiness all together and making wealth and power and physical beauty the objectives in themselves.'

'I knew I shouldn't have given you time to consider the question,' Anne said.

'Go on Jim,' said Jane. 'That's not an answer.'

'Don't you start, Jane. I thought you were on my side.' Jane squeezed my arm, but didn't say anything.

I took a deep breath. 'The interesting thing is that no one can define what happiness is. It means different things to different people. It's subjective. Something which makes one person happy can make another person sad. No one knows why two people in very similar situations can report very different levels of happiness. Which is why there's no secondary school course on the three steps to perfect happiness. It's not that easy. What we do know is that people who generally report themselves as being happy generally share the same personality traits: they don't have unrealistic expectations from life, they try to see the best in every situation, and they are genuinely interested in helping other people. It's not rocket science really.'

We walked along in silence for a few steps before Jane asked, 'Is that it?'

'Shut up, Jane,' Anne said. 'James won't be able to resist elaborating if you just let him dangle for a while.'

I laughed. Anne knew me too well.

'Have I told you about Jasmine?' I asked. 'My girlfriend in Bangkok?'

Jane nodded. Anne said nothing.

'Jasmine sent me to see her Mum every week to improve my Thai. It didn't do my Thai much good, but I did learn a lot of other stuff from her. For instance, do you know that Buddhists believe that we are responsible for our own personalities. They do not accept that we are genetically pre-destined to be optimists or introverts or selfish or shy. We have the capacity, even the responsibility, to mould ourselves into the person we want to be. If we count our blessings every night, look on the bright side enough, try to think of ways in which we can make the people around us happier, then we will become happier ourselves. Even if it doesn't initially come naturally. You have to fake it to make it. That is our real objective in life. You don't get there by trying to be the way you want to behave, you get there by trying to behave the way you want to be. You don't have to become a more generous person before you can give more charitably, it is by giving more charitably – even if it goes against every fibre of your being – that you will eventually become a more generous person. If you feel sad, smile.'

'Is that why you smile so much?' Anne asked, half jokingly.

'I know this sounds like one of Jane's sermons, and I don't claim to always practice what I preach, but I do believe it quite strongly. In the West we are encouraged to believe that we can achieve anything if only we try hard enough. But our incentives are just more worldly goods; a faster car, a bigger house, a more beautiful wife. The American Dream: Irish immigrant becomes President of the United States. The fairy tale Happy Ever After: Cinderella marries her Prince Charming. The Protestant work ethic: the industrious shall inherit the earth. It's all bollocks. The vast majority of people do not win life's lottery – they are just made to feel miserable and slighted by having the false hope of winning repeatedly dashed. If we put as much effort into trying to be content with what we cannot change as we do into trying to improve what we can, we would be a much happier society. We're worn down by fears of global warming and international terrorism, but most of us have more immediate problems to address. From the age of fifteen Ma Thong gave birth to a child every year for ten years. She lived in a squalid shanty town, the whole family sharing a corrugated-iron hut on the banks of an open sewer. Six of her children died in childhood, yet Ma Thong is the most serene person that I have ever met.'

'Seriously, do you want to do my Sermon for me on Sunday?' Jane asked. 'That was bloody brilliant.'

'No,' I said, more forcefully than I meant to. I was feeling irritated and slightly foolish at having been manoeuvred into delivering such a monologue.

Anne pressed her key fob and the hazard lights of a maroon Audi TT squawked its greeting. 'It was brilliant, James' she said. 'A brilliant lecture on altruism and the nature of happiness in general. But you still haven't answered my specific question: are you happy?'

'Nice car,' I replied. 'But I thought only bottle blondes and balding men drive soft tops.'

★ ★ ★

There are not many trains on the Northern Line after midnight so I had plenty of time to think back over the evening as I made my way home. It had been fun. I tried to leave it at that and not analyse it too much.

It started to rain as I walked up the hill from Brixton station and I sunk deeper into my thoughts.

'So she left you, boss?'

I looked up. Jimmy was shutting up, wheeling in the big public bin from outside the shop door which he had to take responsibility for as part of his business rates. 'Never mind. But she did have a nice arse.'

'Shut up, Jimmy,' I said, and let myself into my house.

I had allowed myself to hope, just fleetingly, that Abbie might have come back while I'd been away. She hadn't, of course. I walked through into the kitchen and put the kettle on out of force of habit but wandered upstairs without making coffee. I looked into Abbie's room while cleaning my teeth; the bed cover was still rumpled where I had lain on it earlier. I banished a sentimental thought of sleeping there that night and shut the spare room door.

Chapter Nine

"Considerate riding is safe riding. Pussies have nine lives."

From: "Ride Well and Prosper".

I woke to the breaking news story of a failed Islamic fundamentalist terrorist attack on the London underground. The excited radio newscasters explained that a bomb had exploded on a train somewhere between Waterloo and Westminster stations. The early speculation seemed to be that the primer had detonated, successfully accomplishing the suicide element of the mission but, for reasons unknown, the thirty kilograms of high explosive in the rucksack had declined to follow suit. The two or three passengers closest to the bomber, including a six year old boy, were in a critical condition in intensive care. There were several carriages-worth of flying-glass injuries but there was general consensus that it was a miracle that there had not been greater loss of life. Various experts gave their wise-after-the-fact opinions, disagreeing on whether the intended objective had been to structurally weaken the underground right beneath the river Thames or whether the bomber had been on his way to the Houses of Parliament when the detonator had triggered prematurely. I showered listening to a phone-in program with the usual mix of indignant xenophobes calling for the deportation of all immigrants and some resigned Londoners bemoaning the inevitable disruption to their public transport systems.

As I ate breakfast the first eye-witness reports started coming in. The bomber appeared to have been a blonde girl wearing a tee-shirt and hot pants with a badge of the American flag sown onto the back of her rucksack. The Islamic fundamentalist theory was being hastily re-appraised.

The previous evening's drizzle had intensified into heavy rain during the night so at least the choice of riding gear was easy: full waterproofs, and then some. I sent a text to Gloria before leaving the house, logging in for the day. I then stowed my phone in its waterproof pouch for the walk in the rain down to the lock-up. By the time I got there I had received Gloria's response with the details of my first pick-up and the additional message: 'How's Aby, luvaboy?', followed by a screen full of full stops and semi-colons which cleverly built up a pointillism picture of a stick man with an erection of Bacchalian proportions. I smiled ruefully as I set off towards Sevenoaks.

The Sevenoaks pick-up resulted in a drop near Maidstone and my next pick up was from Gatwick airport so I had the joy of motorway riding in heavy rain and spray for the first part of the morning. It wasn't until I tried to make my way across London to Euston Station to deliver the Gatwick pick-up that I began to appreciate the full impact of that morning's bombing. I phoned Gloria who explained that all the undergrounds were working to a reduced schedule, and that the police had closed all the bridges across the Thames from Waterloo to Lambeth and cordoned off great swathes of Westminster to non-emergency traffic. The result was total gridlock from the Old Kent Road onwards. I tried all my favourite rat-runs but even they were virtually impassable; I wasn't the only person with an A-Z. I eventually wiggled my way over Blackfriars Bridge but a police roadblock stopped me from going up Farringdon Street. I turned west down Fleet Street. The rain had petered out without me noticing and I suddenly realised that I was about to expire in my boil-in-a-bag waterproof over-suit. I turned into a cul-de-sac at random to de-layer and found that I was just round the corner from the Royal Courts. Right at that moment Anne might be summing up the defence of her IRA sympathiser. I wondered whether the morning's news would make it harder for her to defend the unconventional; I wondered whether the court had even managed to convene at all with all the traffic congestion; I wondered whether Anne ever stopped for lunch.

I parked the Bandit between two cars in a residents-only bay and took off my helmet. I sat on the kerb and struggled out of my redundant water-proof over-suit. Then I phoned Anne's office number. Her voice, sounding uncharacteristically stressed, apologised that she would not be at her desk until late afternoon and helpfully gave me her mobile number which she suggested I try for any matters which could not wait until then. I sent her a text.

'I'm in WC2. Do u lunch?'

I expected that it would take a while for her to respond but my phone buzzed almost immediately.

'Might do. Who r u?'

I smiled. I had assumed that Anne would have logged my mobile number into her phone. Evidently not.

'Tall dark handsome', I texted back.

'Jethros 12.15,' was all she replied.

I looked at my watch. Fifteen minutes to find Jethro's. I texted Gloria to warn her that, contrary to company guidelines, I was stopping mid-assignment for lunch. It was an emergency. I stuffed my damp over-suit into the top box, locked my helmet behind the saddle, and headed off on foot towards the plethora of bistros and wine bars which I knew clustered around the court buildings.

I found Anne with five minutes to spare. Jethro's was packed but Anne was the only person braving the al fresco seating on the pavement outside. Some of the chairs next to her were still wet from the earlier rain but she had pulled out a dry seat out from under the awning and was sitting with her head tilted back and her eyes closed, basking in the autumnal sun.

'Hello James,' she said without opening her eyes as my shadow fell over her. 'Get out of my sun.'

'Hello, Anne.'

I pulled up another dry seat and sat beside her.

'Have you been following the news this morning,' she said to the sky.

'The bombing? Not since seven o'clock. It seemed at the time that we had got off pretty lightly.'

'Only two people died if that's what you mean. The bomber. And her six-year old son.' Anne let the significance of the last sentence sink in before adding, 'What desperation drives someone to such an extreme of evil?'

I took advantage of Anne's closed eyes to look at her. She was wearing a white, embroidered, short-sleeve cotton tunic. Her thin arms were folded across her chest and her strawberry blonde hair was swept back from her forehead and hung loosely down behind her. Her olive green linen trousers were perfectly pressed but the right trouser-leg had become un-tucked from her ankle-boot as she stretched her legs out before her in the sunshine. A sliver of pale and freckled calf was left exposed. She was not wearing any make-up apart from a strikingly dark red lipstick, or if she was it was too subtle for me to notice. She still looked every inch the delicate Irish rose that I had known so well as my irreverent, giggly, mischievous girlfriend that it was hard for me to think of her as a high-powered human rights lawyer. I wondered whether she was dwelling on the knowledge that she had defended people accused of such terrorist outrages in the past. Or was she thinking about the society which spawned them.

'Angus says that she was a second generation Pakistani from East Peckham called, incongruously, Rose Smith,' Anne continued. 'Her white husband used to beat up her Muslim Mum but he left her a couple of years ago. None of Rose's friends knew that she had been radicalised and she was not on the radar of any of the security services. She was quite fair skinned; she just looked tanned. She bleached her hair blonde and was apparently travelling with her son to counteract the attention she would have generated by carrying such a large rucksack. Angus is still not sure what the real target was. What a waste.'

'Is your trial suspended?' I asked.

'Yup. Until next week at the earliest.' Anne suddenly sat up and looked at me. 'That doesn't mean that I haven't got a stupid amount of work to do back at the office, but to hell with it. I'm hungry. Is this your treat?' She asked flirtatiously.

'No,' I said.

'Shame. Angus may be joining us later.' With that cryptic remark she stood up. 'I have reserved a drier table inside.'

I followed her into the relative gloom of the wine bar. It was filled with mainly be-suited, earnest-looking young men clutching pints of beer or balloon-sized glasses of wine. The throng parted to let us through but our progress was hampered by the fact that every man in the place seemed to know Anne and they all wanted to greet her personally. She laughed, apparently genuinely, at the comments shouted in her general direction, comments which became increasingly more suggestive as we moved towards the back of the room until at last we reached a table for two in the furthest corner with a reserved sign on it. Anne flopped down in the chair with its back to the room and the cheery mask slipped from her face.

'It's all gone to hell,' she said as I lowered myself into the seat opposite her.

'With friends like that...' I sympathised, assuming that she was referring to the misogynistic welcome she had just endured.

'What?' Anne looked puzzled. 'Oh, them. No, they don't mean any harm.'

'Then what's gone to hell, Anne?'

She held my gaze momentarily and then just shook her head. 'Let's eat. I had already booked this table from one o'clock before I got your text. That's when Angus was due to arrive, but I don't think we should wait for him. I recommend the scallops, and just to be clear this is on me, ok?'

'Then I'll have two of whatever you're having,' I said. 'You're not eating enough; you're too thin. But I don't drink when I'm riding.'

'Yes, I know,' Anne said. 'And my waist-line is the result of five hundred sit-ups a week I'll have you know, not Mr Atkins or Mr G-plan or whatever the current celebratory fad is. I've never been able to diet. You should remember that.'

'You haven't changed at all,' I said.

Anne looked as if she thought I was teasing her; then she threw her head back and laughed freely for the first time.

'James, you are priceless.' Anne smiled at me and stretched her arms up above her head, oblivious to the admiring glances she was provoking from the tables around us. 'Take a good look and then tell me that I haven't changed,' she challenged.

I looked.

'Why?' I asked.

'Why? Why have I had my breasts enlarged?' Anne asked. 'They were a birthday present from Angus.'

'A birthday present for Angus,' I muttered.

'No James. Absolutely not. Angus has many faults, but he is incredibly empathic. Most men have no understanding of the pressure women feel under to stay young, to stay pretty. Other women are just as guilty as those cat-calling men behind me. When I look at myself in the mirror in the morning I tell myself that I am still attractive, but what I see first are the blemishes and the imperfections: the new lines on my forehead; a new plumpness to my cheeks; the dryness of my hair from too much blow drying, the rawness above my upper lip from the previous night's waxing, the sinews in my neck and the looseness of the skin over my stomach. Despite all the sit-ups.' Anne was speaking lightly, but there was obviously more that she wanted to say. 'I had a bit of a crisis last year. It suddenly seemed like life was all down-hill for me. Hey Presto! Two cup-sizes bigger and a bit more pert and suddenly it doesn't seem that bad after all. These breasts represent four thousand pounds well spent if they make me walk tall again.'

'Ok,' I said, putting up my hands. 'I was wrong. You are a totally different person from the one I knew.'

I had meant it as a joke, but even as I said it I sensed that I had made a hurtful remark.

'Fuck you,' Anne said defiantly. 'You think you're some kind of noble savage, uncorrupted by the stresses and strains of modern life just because you flunked out of a professional career. Dispatch riding! Half of me rejoices that you have escaped the great rat race. I never knew what you were going to do with your life, but I knew it would be something different. But the other half of me despairs. The great James Turner. All that intellect wasted. You were the one we voted "the most likely to achieve whatever they wanted". Have you achieved what you wanted, James?'

The waiter arrived at the table. 'Three main-course scallops and three large tomato juices, Peter,' Anne said to him without taking her eyes off me.

'I hate tomato juice. But of course you know that.'

'Then you shouldn't have asked to have two of whatever I'm having. That's what you get for being lazy.'

'Your breasts look lovely from over here,' I said. Anne smiled. 'I did suspect. I nearly asked Jane last night after our Indian meal, but it just seemed so unlikely that you of all people would ...' I trailed off as I realised that I was re-digging the same hole, but Anne had overcome her sensitivity.

'I know,' she laughed. 'You never used to think that I cared about how I looked, did you? Can you imagine how hard that was for me? Not only did I have to look stunning for you, but I had to make it all appear so effortless. Even scraggy jeans had to be scraggy in just the right way.'

'I never expected you to make an effort for me,' I said defensively.

'No?' she left the question hanging in the air.

'So, what's gone to hell?' I asked Anne again. She started to shake her head but I forestalled her denial. 'Don't you think you owe me anything at all for dumping me without any explanation?'

'That was ten years ago, James.'

'What has gone to hell, Anne?'

Anne closed her eyes. She was silent for a long time before saying simply, 'Can you imagine what it is like not to love the person you have committed your life to?'

The silence hung between us. Anne opened her eyes and looked at me.

'My marriage is a sham, James. Angus and I have been sleeping in separate beds for a year.'

'Don't do this to me, Anne. This isn't fair.'

'No one else knows, but I don't think there is any going back for us.'

'I cannot imagine what it is like to fall out of love with the person to whom you have committed your life,' I said, 'but I do know what it is like to be left by the person that you wanted to commit your life to. Angus was my best friend. After you.'

'I know.'

'You had a Catholic wedding didn't you?'

'Yes.'

'You promised to have and to hold him, for richer for poorer, for better for worse, in sickness and in health, forsaking all others, until death do you part?'

'Yes.'

'There was no promise to love him forever?'

'No.'

'Just to have and to hold?'

'Yes.'

'They know a thing or two about human relationships, those Christian patriarchs. You cannot love someone forever. Not that young, lustful, romantic, idealised, honeymooning type of love. The marriage vows should be re-written to explicitly commit you to staying together even after that first love dies. That is what happens. Then you work at it and, if you're lucky, a different kind of love comes back.'

'I know that.'

'I think my Mum had an affair once. I'm not sure, but my parents lived fairly parallel lives during my early teens. The isolation of the farmers-wife role got to her. It wasn't all the cheery country life that she had signed up for, especially when the money got tight. She said to me once, quite flippantly, that she now lived her life as if loving my Dad was her only option, which I took to imply that she had considered and declined other options. People who leave their partners often justify it by saying that in the long run it is in neither party's interests for them to stay; if they are both unhappy then the best thing is for each of them to look to their own happiness. What my Mum was saying was exactly the opposite; she had come to the conclusion that her own best chance of happiness was to work for her husband's happiness. That is what marriage is, the reciprocation of living for each other. There is no greener grass over the fence, just another round of that young, lustful, romantic, idealised, honeymooning type of love. But that won't last either. You have to work at making your old grass as green as possible; to find the contented, supportive, mutually-respecting, empowering love. My parents are very much in love again now.'

'I could work through the loss of love, James. But what happens when the trust goes?' Anne asked. 'Don't judge me too harshly.'

'Anne, I am very, very, sorry. Sorry for you, and sorry for Angus. But I'm not the right person to confide this in.'

'Who better, James?'

'Then tell me, Anne, why are there no little McManuses?' I wanted the conversation to stop or, better still, never to have started, but I couldn't help myself. 'Have you and Angus tried to have children?'

'Angus thinks that I can't conceive.'

'But you can, can't you, Anne?'

'I don't know.'

'You do know. Does Angus know that you aborted our child? Just after you turned down my proposal of marriage and just before you said that you couldn't see any place for me in your life anymore?'

'Jesus, James.' Anne looked furtively over her shoulder as if Angus might have snuck up behind her while I was talking.

'I'll take that as a "No" shall I?'

I pushed back my chair and stood up. 'I have to go, Anne. I don't want to be sitting here eating scallops with you when Angus turns up.'

'He's not coming, James. I phoned him just after your text and put him off. Sit down,' Anne said pleadingly. 'Please.'

'I still have to go,' I said again.

I pushed my way past her and left the restaurant without looking back.

★ ★ ★

As I walked back to my bike I automatically fished out my mobile phone to let Gloria know that I was back on my way to Euston but having forfeited lunch with Anne I added: 'What sandwich u want?' I got an immediate: 'Stood-up? Making do wiv me? Brie n strwbry. Plowmn 4 c. After Euston!'

I was not surprised to learn that Charlie had deigned to show up in the office for a change. The traffic mayhem would mean that all hands were needed. When I arrived twenty minutes later he greeted me with his usual gruff, 'What the fuck are you doing here?', but he let his phone ring to a stand-still on the desk in front of him which was an enormous concession for him. Gloria got up from her bank of computers and came across the room to wrap me in a big hug. It started in a motherly fashion but I must have squeezed her a bit too hard or a bit too low down because she broke away laughing, saying 'I can see you're not too broken hearted.'

'Is your concern for me about Abbie, or about Anne?' I asked surprised.

'You tell us,' Gloria countered.

'Abbie's gone. I miss her; it was great sex. But I always knew she was just passing through my life. There's plenty more great sex out there.'

'Don't count on that,' Charlie said. I threw his baguette at him.

'So what's the story about Anne?' Gloria asked.

'I don't know. I think that she has just invited me to have an affair with her, but I really don't know. She is obviously not happy, but that's not the kind of involvement I wanted.'

'Jim, what gives with you? Is this the same Anne? The great lost love of your life? The Anne that you have bored us stupid with for so many years?'

I smiled sheepishly back at Gloria.

'And now she offers you her butt on a plate, but you've suddenly developed a new moral timidity? Or has she grown an extra head since last week?'

'Give the lad a break,' Charlie said, coming to my rescue.

'What, so that's it?' Gloria asked. 'You guys are no fun any more. If this isn't what do you want, Jim, what is? What did you expect to happen when you met Anne again? She would ask you to be Godfather to her next baby?'

'Do you want your sandwich or not?' I asked aggressively but I couldn't suppress a chuckle. 'And if either of you had the courtesy to show any interest at all in my troubles I would talk you through my day, but as you only want to talk about yourselves I don't seem to be able to get a word in edgeways.'

Gloria opened her mouth to protest but then closed it again and meekly held out her hand for her sandwich. I spun out the suspense by insisting on brewing a pot of tea first to have with our sandwiches. Then Charlie and I drew our chairs up to Gloria's desk so that she could keep track of the other riders while I talked. Charlie insisted that I start my story again from the night of the Cambridge reunion dinner because he had lost track of what he called my Abbie saga. I couldn't believe that it was only eight days ago, but the retelling of my week did put things back into perspective. It was not all that dramatic compared to the human tragedy which had unfurled that morning on the underground.

'Speaking of which,' Charlie said, after he drained his tea mug, 'we are in the middle of our busiest day for years and you're here inflicting your sordid love woes on us. What's the back-log on pick-ups?'

Gloria typed something into her computer. 'Thirty seven jobs, which extrapolates into three and a half hours with the current active rider list.'

'Is that including Jim, or without him?'

'Jim's scheduled to be at the parts depot in seventeen minutes. He just doesn't know it yet.'

'Alright, I get the message,' I said, picking up my helmet. 'So, no helpful advice from either of you then?'

'What's to advise on?' Gloria asked. 'Abbie's gone. It was fun. It's over. Forget her. Now you need to work out for yourself what you want from Anne. I don't think anyone else can help you with that one.'

'You are, of course, right,' I sighed. 'Ok. I'm off, but Charlie has to make himself useful by washing out the mugs.'

'I don't do washing-up,' Charlie was saying as I left the office. 'I've missed thirteen calls from prospective clients while you've been yapping …'

★ ★ ★

It was a frantic day on the streets of London. The almost total gridlock had the double whammy of increasing our delivery times and vastly increasing our work load as increasingly desperate customers started thinking of new and imaginative ways to use our services. Gloria started receiving enquiries from customers asking if we could provide a motorcycle taxi service to get them home as public transport had all but ground to a halt. She initially dismissed the idea because of the insurance complications, but when customers started offering to wrap themselves up and pretend to be parcels, and with the prospect that many main roads would be closed for days or even weeks, Charlie broadcast a general text requesting that any riders who would be willing to carry pillion passengers should report to the office at 07:00am the next morning for an emergency health and safety briefing. And to bring spare helmets.

I worked well past the normal rush hour time. I told myself that it was to help with the back-log of deliveries but I was aware that I was also putting off thinking about Anne, or Angus, or Abbie, or anything at all. When I texted Gloria at eight for another assignment she responded, 'No gym Jim?' without attaching any pick-up details. I could tell that she was pleased with her homophone because she had bothered to capitalise my name. I called her back.

'Hi Gloria. How are things in the office?'

'Shit. But Charlie's in his element. All the central London prospects that he's been courting for months are begging to sign up to whatever contract he puts before them. He's also sorted out the company insurance to temporarily cover pillion passengers and redrafted the employee terms and conditions accordingly. He's talking about a whole new niche market.'

'Is there anything I can do to help?'

'Sweet. But I think we are both knocking off soon anyway. Early start tomorrow. Get down that gym and workout some of my frustrations for me.'

'I'll do my best. See you in the morning. If you need me to help out on the phones just shout.'

Gloria blew me an exaggerated kiss down the line and rang off.

★ ★ ★

Opening the door in to my empty house was every bit as dispiriting as I had anticipated, but I sat on the stairs, pulled off my boots and hoped that the usual end-of-work routine would kick-in. I stripped off my leathers. My rugby shirt was damp with sweat, but rather than use the shower room I decided to soak in the bath upstairs so that I could catch-up with the latest news of the bombing on the radio. I knew that it would do me good to generate some endorphins down the gym, even if I only went for an hour, but I also knew that it just wasn't going to happen. I bundled my base-layer clothing into the washing machine in the kitchen, took a beer from the fridge, and walked naked up the stairs.

I switched on the bathroom radio. The presenter was cheerfully forecasting a day of changeable weather tomorrow. I turned on the bath taps and then went to shave while the bath filled. One of the advantages of my life is that I am not expected to look any better than just "presentable" for work. A morning shave is not essential, but I tend to scrape my face most evenings because longer stubble chaffs on my helmet chinstrap. My razor was not sitting in its little plastic tray inside the mirrored cabinet above the sink. I looked round and found it where Abbie must have left it, on the edge of the bath behind the economy bottle of supermarket foam-bath which had appeared during the last week. I smiled fondly at the image of Abbie covered from head to toe in pink bubbles and emptied the last inch in the bottle into my bath for old times sake.

The chimes of Big Ben presaged the news headlines as I lathered my face. I turned up the volume but there were no new facts and few new theories. Representatives of moderate Islamic groups were falling over themselves to denounce the atrocity and particularly declaring the use of a small boy as un-Islamic, lending weight to the theory that the primer had detonated prematurely. The bomber must have planned to leave her son on the train when she got off at Westminster station, presumably having arranged for him to be met by someone further up the line. This implied that the Houses of Parliament had been the intended target. Against this argument, structural engineers were postulating that if the entire thirty kilogram bomb-load had exploded when the primer detonated the force of the blast could have been sufficient to crack the tunnel casing right underneath the Thames. Flooding the underground would have been a massive propaganda coup.

I finished shaving, stepped into the bath and lowered myself into the steaming bubbles. My mind wandered as my muscles relaxed, remembering Abbie seducing me three days before in this very bath; Abbie massaging my bruised body, me massaging hers, both of us soaping each other in the cascading water of my downstairs shower; Abbie winning her bet that she could walk across my bedroom on her hands wearing only a pair of bright white pop socks; Abbie swamped in one of my old rugby shirts, curled up in my lap, searching for any grey hairs on my chest; Abbie in her pedal-pusher jeans and white vest jumping up and down on my bed, trying to prove that she was big enough to touch the ceiling. Good memories. But there were so many things that we hadn't done yet. I remembered Abbie standing before me in my tee-shirt and jogging bottoms as I shouted at her on Saturday morning, Abbie looking down at the floor and asking me whether I wanted her to go, Abbie promising that she wouldn't leave me without saying goodbye.

She hadn't said goodbye!

I stood up, cursorily swept some bubbles from my shoulders, stepped out of the bath and without any attempt at drying myself pulled on some jeans and a tee-shirt. I ran down the stairs and out in to the street. The tantalising smell of sweet and sour sauce and frying chips came wafting out of Jimmy's open door. The three customers leaning against the warm frying-counter looked curiously at my wet hair and bare feet but Jimmy just smiled at me.

'What you having tonight, boss?'

'How did you know that Abbie had left?' I asked him bluntly.

Jimmy's smile faded. 'I saw her moving out. Her friends helped her with her bags and drove her away.'

'Which friends? When was this? Tell me exactly what you saw.'

Jimmy looked nervously at his other customers. 'We got to do this now, boss?'

'Jimmy this is really important to me.'

'Ok.' He paused to think. 'Yesterday afternoon. I was shutting up after lunch, so about two thirty, a car pulled up on the double yellows outside. I waited by the door in case they were looking for late lunch but no one got out so I carried in the street bin and tidied up in here. About fifteen, twenty minutes later when I went to lock the door I saw them throwing plastic bags with Abbie's stuff into the boot of the car. Abbie was sitting in the back seat. I waved but she didn't wave back.'

'And then the car drove off?'

'I guess. I didn't stay to watch.'

'What sort of car was it?'

'Mercedes I think. Posh. Big. Silver.'

'Did you see the number plate?'

'Jim, please? I was just locking up.'

'I know, Jimmy. But please think. What about her friends? What did they look like?'

'They look like her. Good looking boys.' Jimmy smiled again in spite of himself. 'But you know us wops. We all look alike to you.'

'And don't tell me,' I said grimly. 'There were four of them and one of them had a pockmarked face?'

'Yeah, that's right,' Jimmy said brightening up. 'So you know them?'

Chapter Ten

"Be seen; not hit. Wear the right gear. Motorcycle helmets have been known to deflect bullets."

From: "Ride Well and Prosper".

I had been in Brixton police station before; I had been picked up the previous year during a police raid on a nightclub in search of the drugged and disorderly. As I had been neither drugged nor disorderly at the time and had been able to remain polite and cooperative throughout I was discharged without even a caution and chalked the whole evening up as an educational experience.

This time round I was not a disinterested spectator. The outside of the building, despite the recent gentrification of the area, was still fortified like the American embassy in Baghdad. Inside I was expecting that 9 o'clock on a Wednesday evening would be as quiet as any frontline station could get but there was still a great intensity in the reception hall; shouting, laughing, swearing, and people of all colours and professions coming and going. Maybe that is as quiet as it gets.

I waited patiently to be seen by a duty officer and tried to compose a suitably alarming story but when I was questioned I had to agree that I was there because of my conviction that someone whose real name I didn't know had been abducted from my house, a conviction based primarily on the fact that she hadn't said good bye before she left. PC Watkins was very formal in his demeanour. He took down my statement without expressing an opinion and then issued me with a leaflet entitled "What you can expect from YOUR police service".

'Is that it?' I asked as he filed my statement with a wedge of others in a folder on his desk.

PC Watkins looked up impassively and nodded at the leaflet in my hand. 'You have got the incident number? There's a telephone number in the leaflet which you can call every day for an update on progress if you want to. We will of course contact you directly if there are any significant developments.'

It was obviously a well-used patter and I felt an almost overwhelming urge to pick him up and physically shake the complacency out of him. Every minute wasted might cost Abbie her life. If it was not too late already. But assaulting a policeman was not the way to help her. PC Watkins closed the folder and then looked back at me; he look suddenly tired. I sensed some vestige of the humanity which had originally induced him to join the police force and I had a glimmer of hope that he might bring himself to deviate for once from his well-worn script.

'I do feel sorry for you,' he said. 'You might even be right about her. But what do you expect me to do? We can't resource a manhunt for every missing girl reported in here, however heartfelt the appeal. She must have had her reasons for not reporting what you call her attempted rape last week.'

'So Abbie is just another statistic? '

PC Watkins shrugged his shoulders.

As I walked home I phoned Charlie's home number. I should have phoned him first. Charlie had some shady contacts; he would know what to do. But Charlie didn't answer. I sent a text to his mobile – 'Phone me asap'. With some reservation I phoned Anne's mobile number. It rang until her cheery voice invited me to leave a message. I declined but before I had even put my phone back in my pocket she rang me back.

'Hi James. Thank you for ringing.'

'Hi Anne. How are you?'

'Feeling a little foolish.'

'Good. Foolish is good. But Anne, I actually need to get hold of Angus. It's about Abbie. I don't think she left me yesterday; I think she was kidnapped.'

There was momentary pause at the other end of the phone and then Anne said very briskly, 'All right. I'll get Angus to ring you. Are you at home?'

'I will be.'

'Goodnight, James.'

I wanted to say something else, something about our meeting at lunchtime, but she had rung off.

I stopped off at Jimmy's on the way home. There were no customers in the shop and he came round from behind the counter to give me a big hug.

'I never forgive myself,' he sobbed into my shoulder. 'I loved that girl.'

He was desperate to help, too desperate. It was immediately clear that he couldn't reliably add anything to the story that he had already told me but he was quite prepared to make up facts in a misguided attempt to be helpful. When he stated that, now that he had had a chance to think about it, maybe Abbie had been bound and gagged in the back of the car I knew that it was time to go. I thanked him politely. Jimmy said he would ask all his regular customers whether they had seen anything. He promised that he would have the car number plate within twenty four hours. I didn't say what I was thinking: that twenty four hours would be too late.

Back in my own house I started a thorough search for anything of Abbie's which her abductors might have left behind. I tried to recall what the house had looked like when I had arrived home the previous evening but as far as I could remember it was just as neat and tidy as I would have expected Abbie to have left it if she had left voluntarily. Her recent food purchases were in the cupboards, her recent music choice was in the CD player; other than that there was no sign that she had ever existed. Even the smell of her scent had gone from the room that she had so briefly occupied. I was sitting on her bed an hour later staring into space when the doorbell rang.

I got up, hoping that the police were calling to collect evidence but fearing that Jimmy had just remembered another implausible fact from yesterday, and found Angus on my doorstep. He was dressed in his office suit, appraising the peeling red paint on my front door and looking very tired.

'Very nice neighbourhood you've ended up in,' he said by way of hello.

'Angus. Come in. I didn't expect you to come in person. You must have had a hell of a day today.'

'I have had quieter days but it will do me good to get out of the office for a few hours. I can't claim that I was passing this way, but I am intrigued by your mysterious girlfriend.'

Angus stopped in the hall and peered into the shower room where my three sets of damp leathers were drying on their rail.

'It smells like the Bat Cave,' he said.

'I'll get you a beer and then give you the guided tour if you like,' I said.

Angus followed me into the kitchen and looked around intently as I got a couple of cans of lager from the fridge. He took a deep draft from his can and then, shifting his Scots burr to a very passable imitation of Basil Rathbone, he said: 'Right Watson, lead on, and tell me the whole story as you show me round. The game is afoot.'

So for the third time that day I found myself recounting everything that had happened since the Cambridge reunion dinner. Angus proved to be more interested than PC Watkins had been, and more challenging than Gloria and Charlie had been at lunchtime. He continually interjected with perceptive questions and replayed parts of my narrative back to me in his own words, emphasising the differences between my assertions of facts and his conjectures of motives. Angus asked a number of questions about the theatre trip which I didn't think were directly pertinent to Abbie's disappearance but I answered them as openly and honestly as I could. I had never been able to hide anything from Angus, or from anybody else for that matter.

'So you worked today as usual. You get home this afternoon, lie in the bath, feel sorry for yourself, and conclude that Abbie couldn't possibly have left you voluntarily without saying goodbye?'

'Something like that,' I smiled modestly. 'There was actually a very specific visual image which started me questioning her departure, but it was only the final straw around which all my previous doubts congealed. She wouldn't have left without leaving a note. The clincher is that Jimmy saw her being driven away by the same men who were going to kill her last week.'

'Some men who may be the same ones which Abbie claimed were going to kill her,' Angus corrected me. I started to protest but Angus waved me down. 'Their exact intent doesn't matter. What matters is, a) whether Abbie needs our help, b) whether she deserves our help, and c) whether we can give her our help. Anything else is just noise.'

'The answers are: Yes, Yes, and Yes,' I said.

We had reached Abbie's room. Angus emptied the wastepaper basket onto the bed and started sifting through the poignantly meagre pile of lipsticked tissues and discarded packaging.

'And key to all three of my questions is: who is Abbie,' Angus continued.

'I'm not sure that it really matters who she is,' I said indignantly, but Angus carried on: 'And key to who Abbie is, is what was she doing in Kennington Park last Tuesday evening?'

'What do you mean?' I asked.

'That is the best lead that we've got. It's the most salubrious borough south of the river. There are no street walkers. No night clubs. It could be an escort agency that delivers to the door.'

'Or maybe, just maybe, she may not be a whore at all. Have you considered that?' I asked angrily.

'James, calm down. I am not assuming anything. But unlike you I am not ruling out possibilities either until we have more evidence to the contrary than your somewhat biased character reference. If you really want to help her you need to detach yourself emotionally. I have never met her. Convince me that she is not an illegal immigrant working, willingly or unwillingly, in the sex trade?'

'I can't believe this,' I said.

'James, I am not saying that her employment determines whether or not we should help her, but we can't do anything without more facts.'

'I can't do anything without more beer,' I said.

'Stay focused, James.'

'Angus, no bullshit,' I said seriously, 'what do you really do for a living?'

'James, no bullshit,' Angus replied equally seriously, 'if I really told you I would really have to kill you.' But he was smiling self-depreciatingly.

It was after midnight when Angus left. We had talked through the situation as dispassionately as I was able to over another few cans of lager. I didn't completely convince him that Abbie was an innocent tourist who may have been caught up naively in some criminal activity but I felt he was softening to that possibility. I said that Jimmy was confident of getting the car number plates but Angus dismissed this. He explained that if Abbie had been taken by an organised gang they would be driving a stolen car with legitimate plates. Steal a silver Mercedes in London and get plates made up that match an unstolen car of the same type that's registered in Manchester. If anyone runs a check on the number plate it wont show up as stolen and the innocent owner will swear that his car was safely in his garage at the time of the crime. Angus promised to do what he could to expedite the investigation into Abbie's disappearance without ever saying exactly in what capacity he could help. I didn't ask again. We avoided any awkward small talk about the good-old-days which might have lead to Anne. I caught myself once on the verge of asking when she would be expecting him home and stopped mid-sentence, resenting the knowledge that she had burdened me with. If Angus guessed the cause of my discomfort he didn't say anything until he eventually said that he had to go.

'There will be very few trains running at this time of night,' I said.

'I'll walk north until I find a cab.'

'Do you want me to walk with you?' I asked.

'I think I'll be safe out on my own,' Angus said. I didn't doubt it, but he softened his remark by adding, 'and I need to think over a few things.'

'I understand, Angus. And thanks for coming.'

'By the way,' he said as I opened the front door for him, 'did you enjoy the scallops this morning?'

I froze momentarily and then turned to face him.

'I didn't stay to eat,' I said. 'I lost my appetite.'

'Be careful, James,' Angus said, and stepped out into the street.

★ ★ ★

I set my alarm for 6.00am in order to get to Holburn in time for Charlie's pillion-passenger taxi service briefing. Privately I thought that it was a crazy idea, but I was keen to give him an outward show of support for his new venture. That gave me just five hours in bed. I feared that I would get a lot fewer hours of sleep but surprised myself by nodding off almost immediately and sleeping undisturbed until I was woken by the six-o'clock headlines. Details about the tube explosion were already being over-taken by spin-off stories about the increased security measures, the traffic chaos, the cost to business, and the anti-Muslim backlash.

I stumbled through breakfast and remembered to dig out a spare helmet before leaving for the lock-up. On the way down the hill I got a call from Charlie on my mobile.

'Sorry I didn't get back to you last night. Everything alright?' he asked.

'No,' I said bluntly. 'I think Abbie was kidnapped. By the same thugs that I saved her from last time.'

There was a noticeable silence at the other end of the line and then Charlie started asking all the obvious questions.

'It doesn't matter,' I said, 'I thought maybe you would have some suggestions on what to do, but I've told the police and I think I've even got MI5 involved now.'

'Your Angus friend?' Charlie asked sceptically. 'Don't mess with the spooks, Jim. From what I hear those monkeys make even the boys in blue look incorruptible and half-competent.' I knew Charlie would hate me turning to any kind of authority for help; in his view that was what friends are for. 'Look, are you coming in for the briefing?' he asked.

'Of course.'

'Ok. We'll talk after that. I'll make some calls. Just don't do anything precipitous in the mean time.'

'Ok, Charlie,' I said laughing. 'And thanks.'

Charlie just grunted and rang off.

The pillion-service briefing was an anti-climax. There were only a handful of other riders standing on the pavement outside the office when I arrived, quite possibly because of the unsociable hour, and their mood was not improved when Charlie explained that there had been a last-minute hitch with the insurance which meant we couldn't start offering the new services yet anyway. Gloria gave us all an update on the latest traffic position so far as she could make it out from the radio and web reports with a promise to include as much relevant advice as she could with each assignment text over the next few days.

'Which summarises as: Westminster is closed and London is fucked,' some wag shouted out from the back of the group. As the other riders drifted away to start their shift Charlie led me into the office.

'Bloody insurance,' Charlie started. 'I'm trying to offer a public service in a time of national emergency, pulling together in the spirit of the blitz and all that sort of thing, and they want to profiteer from it. They're trying to charge me an arm and a leg, but I'll shame them into something more reasonable. It's not as if we're going to go out of our way to kill off our clients.'

'What about Abbie?' I asked.

Charlie looked at me sympathetically.

'I've made some calls and now we just have to wait,' he said. Charlie's faith in the network of people who owed him favours was legendary. 'I'm sure you want to go out and kick butt, but there is nothing you can do at the moment. It's an unwelcome message, but it's the truth.'

I started to protest, but he cut through me. 'Listen. The police – ' he hawked and spat mockingly – 'they haven't got the resources to investigate this properly. And MI5? They'll be kind of busy right now! Or they should be if they didn't have their heads stuck so far up their own arses. But I know people who used to work in these circles. They'll find out what's going on, and then we can decide what to do.'

My mobile phone rang from the inside pocket of my jacket. I nearly left it, but Charlie and I had come to a natural pause; we were both absorbing the finality of Charlie's pronouncement. I took the call.

'Is that James Turner?' asked a clipped military voice.

'Yes.'

'Hello, James. You don't know me. My name is Peter Grange. Angus McMannus works for me.'

I didn't say anything but I looked over at Charlie, who looked back inquisitively.

'I understand that you are concerned about the well-being of a young girl known to you as Abbie?'

'Have you found her?' I asked excitedly.

'Not yet, but we do have some information which you might find interesting. Would you be able to join me at my club for coffee at, say, eleven o'clock? The United Services Club, 112 Pall Mall. You will need a jacket and tie, but the doorman can lend you those.'

'Sure. I'll be there, Mr. Grange. Is she OK?'

'I'll see you at eleven, then?' he said and rang off.

I repeated the conversation to Charlie, who sighed deeply and shook his head. 'I understand that you have to go, Jim, but it will all end in tears.'

★ ★ ★

'Concentrate or die,' I told myself as I wove through the congested London streets, trying to fill the time until eleven o'clock with work and to prevent my mind from wandering. It started drizzling at ten so I felt completely incongruous presenting myself at the hallowed United Services Club dressed in damp riding leathers.

'I'm here for coffee with Mr. Grange,' I told the elderly doorman.

He peered at me through thin round spectacles.

'Colonel Grange,' he corrected me. He did not appear at all perturbed by my unsuitable attire. 'Have you got a collared shirt under that jacket young man? No? Then follow me to the cloakroom and I will fit you up.'

Five minutes later I was sitting in the lobby on the plush leather waiting couch wearing motorcycle leather trousers and boots below the waist and a white shirt, blue club tie and brown checked sports jacket above it.

'James Turner, I presume', called the sharp clipped voice from the top of the thickly carpeted entrance stairs. 'Thank you, George,' he added to the doorman, 'I will take him from here.'

I joined Colonel Grange at the top of the stairs. He was probably in his late fifties with a shock of greying hair swept back from a broad forehead. He was less tall and less broad than me but there was no middle-aged paunch beneath his trim grey suit. We shook hands rather formally and he ushered me along a dark, portrait-hung corridor into a light and airy dining room. The room contained thirty or so linen covered tables. Half of the tables were already laid out for lunch but the smaller tables were set with cups and saucers and side plates. There was one other person in the room, an elderly gentleman sitting at a table by the windows with a newspaper spread out in front of him. He looked up and nodded at us. Colonel Grange returned the nod and steered me into a seat at the corner table.

'Good of you to come, Mr. Turner'.

'Call me Jim, Colonel Grange,' I said. 'Everyone does.'

'Except for Angus. He calls you James, I believe?' he appraised me across the table and then took a folded piece of A4 paper out of his breast pocket. And Anne; Anne used to call me James, I thought. And Abbie.

'Firstly, James, I would be grateful if you would take a look at this.'

He passed over the sheet of paper. I unfolded it. Most of the paper was blank but roughly in the centre of the page and slightly at an angle was a blurred black and white image. Abbie stared back at me. Her picture had obviously been cropped from a larger group photograph and enlarged so that the resolution was grimy, but it was unmistakably a recent picture of her. Colonel Grange read the recognition in my face.

'So,' he said. 'Tell me about this girl.'

I paused. Charlie's warnings about MI5 echoed in my head and I considered whether I should first challenge him about his interest in Abbie. Colonel Grange waited patiently. A waitress approached and took our orders for coffee and biscuits. When she left I recounted the entire story, from driving home from the party at William and Hannah's up to my unprofitable visit to Brixton police station.

'So then you called Angus?' Colonel Grange asked. 'Why?'

I had anticipated that question. Colonel Grange was Angus's boss. Would Angus be disciplined for getting involved in my personal matter, blowing his cover for the sake of our friendship? I had tried to get in touch with Angus since receiving the Colonel's phone call but the home number which he shared with Anne somewhere in the Docklands had rung unanswered and I hadn't wanted to phone Anne again.

'Why is Angus not here?' I asked.

Colonel Grange smiled, a genuine smile which lit up his whole face. His eyes twinkled. 'I wondered how far I would get before you started asking me a few questions of your own. I only ask why you chose to call Angus in your time of need because I am interested to know which version of the truth he presented to you. I gather that many of his friends believe that he, and therefore presumably that I, work for MI5. Is that what he told you?'

'He didn't say, and I didn't ask,' I replied truthfully.

'Excellent. Well then, I can tell you that actually we do. Both of us.' I was surprised by the frankness of this admission and the

Colonel paused to enjoy the effect of his revelation before he continued. 'But we are not in the cloak and dagger business. The line is blurring between counter-espionage and counter-terrorism these days. Our Intelligence comes from many sources, but my own department is not responsible for gathering the raw material. I don't personally run informants or spy-rings or carry out tortuous interrogations. That stuff may or may not go on; I keep well clear of it. My department specialises in processing the data once it has arrived. We trawl though everything, much of it is already in the public domain, looking for trends and anomalies, personality profiling, modus operandi. Lots of computer work. You can probably guess the sort of thing; trying to anticipate the next atrocity against our democracy which doesn't really want to acknowledge that the problem even exists until someone slips through the net and blows themselves up in public. Then suddenly it is all our fault. Angus is exceptionally good at what we do. This latest unpleasantness did not happen on his patch, I can assure you. His trouble is, I fear, that he finds it all a bit dull. I hope that I am wrong. Tell me, did he have a bit of the James Bond about him at Cambridge?'

I shook my head, more in bemusement than in answer to the question.

'Well, no matter. The thing is Abbie has turned out to be a bit more interesting than I expect you expected. I will come on to that, but while we are talking about Angus, you should understand that it is against company regulations to mix friendship with work. That is why he is not here, and I am. Do you see? When we are done here if you should remember anything further that might be of interest, or, God willing, Abbie should actually contact you, I would be eternally grateful if you would come directly to me. Please do not talk to Angus about this again. It would put him in a bit of an awkward situation. Is that OK? You should find that Abbie is a non-subject now with Angus, as far as that is practical within the norms of social intercourse.'

Colonel Grange broke off while our pot of coffee and plate of shortbread biscuits were delivered. When the waitress had left he poured for both of us before continuing.

'So, to Abbie. I will tell you what we think we know. As soon as you leave this room you will start to question whether I have told you the whole truth, or even a version of it. That is one of the ironies of our Service; we exist to protect the nation, yet no one trusts us. It is natural for you to be suspicious. All I can say is that it is not in my interest to lie and to hope that my sincerity shines through.' He smiled briefly, a smile I did not return.

'Last night Angus came straight into the office from your house and ran a check on, amongst other things, your telephone records. He is a very diligent boy. The shit is flying all round us and everyone is screaming "Rose Smith" but he took the time to look a little further into your missing Abbie. There was very little of interest in your calls except for the night that Abbie arrived at your house, or more precisely at three twenty seven on the Wednesday morning. An international call was made from your phone to a number in Thailand. It was not called again. I imagine that Abbie was confused and frightened that first night, which was why she let down her guard. By the following morning her more natural caution had returned. If she made any more calls they must have been from public phone boxes. We have checked all the ones in your vicinity but so far without success. Angus is a good boy. He is very thorough. He had no reason at that stage to suspect that Abbie might be of any interest to us professionally, but he passed the Thailand phone number onto a colleague in Bangkok before going home to his lovely wife. It was normal office hours then in Bangkok. You can imagine Angus's surprise when his colleague called him back on his personal number three hours later. Angus called me immediately and, against my better judgement, I gave him the morning off from Ms. Smith to put the pieces of Abbie's life together. With me so far?'

I nodded.

'Your Abbie is actually Ma Taw Abying, the youngest daughter of General Taw Lay Htoo of the Karen Independence Army, the military wing of the Karen Nationalist Party. You have been to Burma, or Myanmar as its State Peace and Development Council prefers to call itself.'

It was a statement, not a question, but I nodded anyway. 'Yes. I visited Rangoon and Mandalay briefly, four or five years ago. I was working for a Bangkok newspaper at the time and took the standard tourist trip over.'

'So you know that Burma is run by a brutal military junta and has been in a state of perpetual civil war ever since it gained independence from Britain in nineteen forty eight. On the map it makes perfect geographical sense for Burma to be a single nation. It is naturally isolated, separated from India and Bangladesh in the West by the Chin Hills, from China in the North by the Eastern Himalayas, and from Thailand in the East by the Dawna mountain range. This natural horseshoe of mountains surrounds the incredibly fertile flood plains of the Irrawaddy River which empties into the Bay of Bengal just to the east of Rangoon. Geographically it might make sense, but prior to British occupation at the end of the nineteenth century Burma had rarely been a single country. It was a melting pot of various warring states. The majority tribe, the Burmans, make up about two thirds of the population and dominate the central Irrawaddy basin. The Burmans are devout Buddhists. The rest of the population is made up of a myriad of other ethnic groups including Shan, Chin, Kachin, Mon, and Karen, who occupy the peripheral mountain regions. The tribal states were animistic but proved to be more susceptible to the Christian Missionaries of the British Empire. Independence for the unitary state of Burma was bestowed to a democratically elected Burman-dominated government with some Shan, Chin and Kachin representation. These tribes only accepted the new constitution because it gave them a guaranteed opt-out from the union after ten years if they did not feel that it was working for them. Surprise, surprise: when they came to cash in the opt-out, the Burmans said that they had had their fingers crossed when they'd signed that bit of the deal. It was a powder-keg arrangement from the start and there has been civil war ever since.'

I sipped my coffee, and waited for the punch line to the Colonel's history lesson. He may have noticed my studied patience because he asked suddenly, 'Why is this of any interest to us?'

I wasn't sure whether 'us' meant the two of us at the table, his secret service, or the UK population in general.

'Drugs,' said Colonel Grange, answering his own question. 'Burma is the arm-pit of Asia. It is a potentially hugely wealthy country. It possess great natural assets: oil, gas, teak, rubies, yet it has been classified by the United Nations as the fifth poorest state in the world; brought low by its own internal bickering. Children are starving in a country which used to export rice across the world, but why should we care? They are the ones who have closed their own borders, drawn down the shutters on international aid and development. Good luck to them. We may have bequeathed them an unsustainable constitution but that was more than seventy years ago. We certainly left them a thriving economy and a substantial rail and road infrastructure, both of which have long since gone to rack and ruin. So, in short, not much different from thirty other half forgotten ex-colonial states which I could name. So what makes Burma different?'

'The Golden Triangle,' I answered.

'Very good, James,' said Colonel Grange, nodding encouragingly. 'Yes. Basically cocaine comes from South America and heroin used to come from the poppy fields in the mountains of Burma, Laos, and northern Thailand. Of course, other rogue states have long since cashed in, most notably Afghanistan, but a significant percentage of the smack on our streets still originates in South East Asia. And for a very good reason: the lack of recognised state control. The drug barons of Columbia and the warlords of the independence struggle in Burma all need money to buy their arms. They have no other commodities to sell so, despite their public lip-service to the contrary, they control the cultivation and processing of the poppy harvests.'

'I know all this. What has it got to do with Abbie?' I asked.

'If you know all this then you will also know what a loose rag-tag of coalitions and self-interested factions these independence movements always are. They are all supposedly fighting for the freedom of their people but in practice they just replace the Burman repressive non-elected government for a tyranny of their own in any territory which they hold. The poor tribesmen are levied for the independence war effort by the insurgents with every bit as much brutality as the central government extracts its taxes to maintain the status quo. Seventy years is a long time to fight a war, James. Can you begin to imagine it? Whole generations which know no other existence. General Taw Lay Htoo is just the latest in the long line of self-proclaimed leaders of the Karen Nationalist Party, which probably means he assassinated his predecessor, General Klan. We don't have much background on him at the moment, but we do know that the last few months have witnessed a particularly bloody counter-offensive by the Karens against the Burma state army, which seems to have coincided with General Taw's appearance on the scene. We also know that the KIA controls the most significant smuggling routes between Burma and Thailand. General Taw, as the current ruling warlord can be guaranteed to be taking the largest slice of the drugs pie.'

'And Abbie?'

The Colonel sighed. 'Not really sure actually. One would have thought that General Taw would have had his personal family safely nestled away somewhere in Thailand. We are very interested to know what his daughter, Ma Taw Abying, is doing on the streets of London. Our best guess at the moment is that she was sent as an envoy to the quite significant Karen refugee community here, possibly seeking further funds for the war effort. We might also assume that her assailants, if she has been kidnapped as you say, are members of Burmese Military Intelligence, but that is just supposition. The BMI are a particularly unsavoury lot, as brutal against their own Burman people as they are against the insurgent tribesmen, but there is more intrigue and in-fighting within these various groups than there is within our own Conservative party. Abbie's kidnappers may be supporters of the ex-General Klan seeking revenge for his assassination. Either way, I hope that I have said enough for you to lose no further sleep on Ma Abying's behalf. I have colleagues who will carry on the investigation, but I would not hold your breath for a further update. As you may have noticed we have more pressing interests at the moment with our fundamentalist Islamist friends.'

Colonel Grange smiled again. He drained his coffee cup and pushed into the middle of the table. The meeting appeared to be over. The message was clear: if I should stumble on any related information I was to pass it directly to the Colonel but other than that I was to forget the whole incident.

'I am in any personal danger?' I asked.

'Oh, I shouldn't think so. These chaps are much too busy fighting each other to hold a grudge against you. There is a propaganda war going on as well; both sides are keen to be seen as the slighted peace mongers. They wouldn't want to involve a foreign national. Which reminds me; please don't go running to the press. Angus assures me that you are a sensible lad, but I probably ought to spell it out. This meeting would be denied – I am actually in Paris attending an anti-terrorist conference as we speak. This club is the soul of discretion. More importantly it would jeopardise any chance my colleagues might have of tracking Abbie down in one piece. Which is, after all, what we both want, isn't it?'

I looked down at the photograph of Abbie lying face up on the table. 'Assuming that she was taken by Burmese Military Intelligence, where would they have taken her?'

The Colonel looked at me suspiciously. 'Could be anywhere. Possibly the Burmese Embassy if they plan to smuggle her back to Burma. She would be worth more to them as a live hostage than a dead one. No. 19 Charles Street, if you are interested. We are having it watched of course, but don't get any ideas of storming the building single handed. Stop thinking of her as a damsel in distress and start thinking of her as a drug trafficking terrorist.'

He took a slim silver propelling pen from his jacket pocket and wrote a phone number on one corner of the piece of paper which had Abbie's photo on it. He tore off the corner and handed it to me, putting the rest of the photo back in his pocket.

'Here's my private number. I cannot say that I expect to hear from you, but you never know. Now, we must give that hideous jacket back to George on your way out.'

★ ★ ★

Back outside on the pavement I was astonished to find that it was only eleven thirty. I wanted time to assimilate what I had just learnt but I had a living to earn. I fished out my mobile to see what Gloria had lined up for me and found instead a text from Charlie telling me to phone him immediately.

'What did the spooks have to say?' he asked without even saying hello.

'I'm not entirely sure. Abbie's Dad is some kind of Burmese terrorist apparently.'

'Shit. I don't suppose you'd consider just walking away from this whole scene now, would you?'

'No. I don't suppose I would,' I replied.

'Shit. I didn't think so, but I don't like it, Jim.'

'Why did you ask me to phone you?' I asked.

'Come back to the Wheat Sheaf and we can discuss it with the benefit of Guinness,' he said with an effort at jocularity.

I didn't respond. I heard Charlie sigh at the other end of the line. 'I've had a call from a friend that I used to ride with back in my Dublin days. He says he may know someone who may know something about your missing girlfriend.'

'What's his name?' I asked.

'My friend's name is Brian Davey. He wouldn't name his source, so don't be getting your hopes up,' Charlie said. 'It's probably nothing and I wouldn't be troubling you except that Brian was just about sleazy enough to dabble in human trafficking. Or to know someone who knows someone who is.

Brian wants to meet you, so it will be about money. Do you want me to negotiate for you?'

'Where does he want to meet?'

Charlie sighed again and then read out an address.

'I'll let him know you're coming' he was saying as I cut the connection. I realised belatedly that I hadn't thanked him.

The address was in Cricklewood, northwest London, and turned out to be on a large industrial estate just off the North Circular Road. I rode slowly round the industrial estate until I found the right building, a large portacabin next to a distribution warehouse which appeared not to have opened up for the day. There were no lights on inside and the blinds were still drawn on the large frosted-glass windows. I parked the Bandit and walked over to the front door. It was locked. I rang the doorbell.

'Who is it?' came the mechanical voice from the speaker above the bell.

'Jim Turner. I'm looking for Brian Davey.'

'Give me a minute. When you hear the buzzer, push the door.'

As I waited I took off my helmet and held it under the crook of my arm. When the intercom buzzed I turned the handle and opened the door. It was still dark inside. I took a step in, saw a movement in front of me and doubled up as a heavy weight smashed into my stomach. The attack was so unexpected that I staggered forward bewildered, my helmet slipped out of my hands. Something exploded onto the back of my head and I crashed to the floor.

'That's enough,' said a soft Irish voice.

I rolled into a ball and cradled my head between my arms to protect it from the next blow, but none came.

'Will someone put on the fucking lights,' said the voice.

An overhead florescent light flickered on. I peered up through my arms and saw a big, thick-set man in a dark donkey jacket caressing a baseball bat.

He grinned down at me. 'Nothing personal, English,' he said. He had a deeper voice, but the same strong Irish accent.

'Get up, Mr. Turner, and take a seat', said the first voice.

I looked past the donkey jacket and saw a thin, balding man in a short-sleeved pastel shirt leaning back in what would normally have been the receptionist's chair. He had his hands clasped behind his head and his feet up on the desk in front of him. There was a third man behind me, leaning against the closed front door with this arms folded across his broad chest.

I got slowly back to my feet. The thin man took his feet off the receptionist desk and pointed towards a chair on the other side of it.

'Take a seat,' he said again.

I looked at him and then deliberately turned away and stooped to pick up my helmet. My head swam and I almost wretched. The baseball bat prodded me sharply in the back. Fuck the helmet. I left it where it was and walked passed the door-guard to the desk and sat down apprehensively opposite the thin man.

'Now then, if you're quite comfortable, shall we begin?' he asked. 'I believe you know why you're here.'

I said nothing.

'We want to know what has happened to Miss Taw.'

'I don't know anything.' I said with slow deliberation.

The thin man smiled.

'How did I know that you were going to say that?' He nodded to the brute in the donkey jacket. 'Pat. Say good morning to Mr. Turner again.'

The big man hefted the baseball bat as he walked towards me. He wasn't smiling anymore.

'There is no need for this,' I protested shrilly as I scrambled up to face him, 'I genuinely don't know anything.' And then the bat swung. I jumped backwards against my chair and raised my arms in an attempt to ward off the blow. The strike connected with my left forearm and battered me against the desk. The pain was shocking. Then my whole arm went numb. Before I could react the bat had swung again into my unprotected ribs and then again onto my shoulders as I slumped across the desk. They were not frenzied blows. If anything they were slow and measured, but full strength, like you would chop at a fallen tree-trunk with an axe. And professional. Donkey-jacket had done this a hundred times before to other people just as bewildered as me that this was actually happening. I heard myself shouting as I tensed for the next blow and remembered a confession from a Serbian prison guard during his trial at the European Court of Human Rights in The Hague. He had said that the ones who screamed during torture were not near to their breaking point; it was when they went quiet that he knew he had them. And then I remembered his interviewer asking him why he had made no attempt to conceal his identity. The Serb had replied quite calmly that he had not expected any of his prisoners to survive to bear witness against him. I stopped screaming and looked up into the cold eyes of the thin Irishman across the desk. For the first time I felt truly afraid.

'Thank you, Pat,' he said calmly. 'Please feel free to shout, Mr. Turner. There is no-one here to hear you.'

'What do you want to know?'

'That's better. Sit back down, Mr. Turner. I want to know everything, of course.'

'I don't know anything about her,' I whimpered as I slumped into my chair cradling my left arm. 'I saved her from what I took to be a gang rape and let her stay in my house for a few days. Then yesterday she left. I don't know anything about her.'

The baseball bat was raised again.

'For fucks sake, that's all I know!' I shouted desperately. 'I'm just someone caught up in all this. I don't even know what "all this" is. And I don't want to know. Just let me go.'

The thin man held his hand up and the baseball bat drooped. As the donkey-jacketed man took half a step backwards I sprang out of my chair and drove my right fist into his surprised face with every ounce of strength left in my body. Blood burst from his nose. He staggered backwards but he didn't fall so I kicked out with a heavy leather boot and caught his right knee cap. I heard a snap and he crumpled. The man by the door was putting his hand into his jacket pocket but I didn't wait to confirm which type of weapon he would pull out. I ran straight at the side window and launched myself headlong at it. The aluminium frame crumpled under my weight, the windowpane shattered and the roller blind was torn from its bracket. I crashed through. The jagged glass at the edge of the frame ripped into my leather trousers. I put my hands out in front of me to break my fall but my left arm refused to absorb any weight so I nose dived into the concrete but I dragged myself straight back onto my feet and ran.

The Bandit was parked right outside the portacabin door. I couldn't possibly get back to it and get it started before the door opened. The corner of the next building was twenty metres from where I had landed. I ran towards it, the space between my shoulder-blades prickling in anticipation of a bullet but none came. As I rounded the first corner I heard shouts from inside the building and the sound of the door being thrown open. I ran for the next corner.

I have a pretty tidy turn of pace on a rugby pitch but running in full leathers and riding boots is another matter. The industrial estate was a maze of small warehouses but they were all shut up or derelict. I dodged left and right down the narrow alleyways between them. There was a stabbing pain from my ribs every time I gasped for breath and all the time I was listening for any sound of pursuit. I came to the service road which encircled the estate. Running along the far side of the road was an eight-foot high wire-meshed fence. I stopped for the first time and looked behind me. There was no one else in sight. I looked up and down the road. I could not remember which way I had come in. Then I heard a car engine starting up. I sprinted across the road and leapt at the fence. The toes of my boots were too broad to fit between the meshing and my left hand refused to grip. My right hand closed over the top of the fence and I hung there for second. The sound of the car was coming closer. I hauled myself up with my right arm, kicking and scrabbling with my feet, and flopped over the fence into the grassy ditch outside. A white van came round the corner of the service road and accelerated towards me. I scrambled out of the ditch, pushed through the bushes beyond, and found myself in a quiet residential side street. I heard the van screech to a halt and doors slamming but I did not look round. I ran up the street as it curved gently round until it joined the main North Circular road. The traffic was moving quickly considering it was the height of the morning rush hour and my prayers were answered when I saw a vacant taxi approaching. I waved frantically. It pulled up beside me and started off again before I had even settled into the backseat, not wanting to pause too long on the busy road.

'Where to Governor?' asked the driver good naturedly, and then, 'Bugger me! You fall off your bike?'

I looked out the back window but there was no sign of the white van.

'Central London,' I answered, just to keep him driving.

'Anywhere particular in Central London? It's a log-jam in there today.'

I looked down at my left arm, hanging by my side; 'Charing Cross Hospital, please.'

★ ★ ★

I am used to being battered. It happens every Saturday afternoon and usually I revel in it. As the taxi made its laborious progress through the newly security-congested streets I realised that this was an order of magnitude different.

I have fallen off my bike once. It happened in my first year of dispatch-riding in the middle of the M25 during the morning rush-hour. It had just started drizzling after a few dry days so the tarmac was particularly greasy; the accumulated oily particulates from a million exhaust pipes had been flushed to the surface by the gentle rain but not yet been washed away by it. I was filtering slowly through the nose-to-tail traffic in that "second-and-a-half" lane; the lane that motor bikers believe exists just for them on crowded motorways between the middle lane and the fast lane. Then a blue BMW changed lanes in front of me and my second-and-a-half lane disappeared.

I don't blame the car driver. It would have been nice if he or she had indicated before pulling out or checked their blind spot, but I expect that to this day they are completely oblivious to the part they played in my brush with death. I should have noticed that there was a relatively large gap ahead in the line of cars in the outside lane. I should have anticipated that a car from the middle lane might pull out without warning to fill that gap. My fault. Concentrate or die.

The fall itself happened so fast that I don't remember it. Or I have selectively blanked out the precise details. There must have been an instant when I jammed on my brakes and realised that I was still closing too fast with the back of the BMW. I might have braked harder until I lost control, or I simply threw myself off. I don't know which. My bike shot across the two inside lanes and ended up on its side on the hard shoulder. I travelled the relatively shorter distance in the opposite direction across the fast lane and ended up on my side in the central reservation. I don't remember the fall, but I do remember the eerie silence as I stood up afterwards and looked about me. To my right, along the direction of travel, the motorway was now completely empty. The BMW and its near neighbours had driven on, blissfully ignorant of the drama behind them. To my left for as far as the eye could see there were three solid lanes of stationary traffic. I stood and looked down into those anonymous headlights for an age until a car half a mile back in the queue started sounding its horn. As I walked slowly across the motorway to the hard shoulder the traffic started moving behind me, flowing past as if nothing had happened.

A Suzuki Bandit weighs 160 kilograms; twenty five stone. There is a particular technique to lifting up a bike from a horizontal position but my adrenaline was flowing and I hauled it up with one hand and set off without giving any thought to the condition of the bike. Or me. It wasn't until I reached 80 miles an hour, still on the hard shoulder, undertaking the traffic which had just passed me that I realised that I must be suffering from some sort of reaction to the accident. I remember an almost overwhelming need to get away from the scene. It took a tremendous act of will to slow down to a sensible speed, to re-join the slow lane, to leave the motorway at the next junction. I had parked the bike in the first lay-by and walked up and down the road for five minutes before the pain from my broken ribs had started to really kick in.

Sitting in the taxi waiting for the pain to come I wondered whether I was experiencing something similar. The taxi driver suggested closer hospitals, but I declined. It wasn't that I was worried that they, the Irishmen, would try to find me. Maybe I should have worried but at the time I just wanted to get away. I fished my mobile phone out of my jacket pocket. It had survived our beating better than me. I had two text and one missed call from Gloria, the first asking where I was and the latter asking if I was ok, but nothing from Charlie. I went over our last conversation – "some people I used to run with back in my Dublin days". I couldn't believe that Charlie had knowingly set me up, but then I couldn't understand why my attackers had asked me where Abbie was, when they knew that I was trying to find her. I also couldn't understand why I was sitting lamely in a taxi going to hospital instead of making my way to Brixton police station to ram PC Watson's "It's Your Police Force" leaflet down his smug throat or phoning 999 to report my assault.

Then the pain did kick in and I stopped thinking about anything else.

★ ★ ★

'When you fell off your bike, did you hit your head?' the triage nurse asked again.

'No, it's just this arm that I need you to look at.'

'Then whose is the matted blood in your hair?' she asked, more wearily than in anger.

I put my right hand up to the back of my head. It was sore to touch and my fingers came away with flakes of dried blood on them.

'Don't mess me about,' the nurse said. 'I don't care what caused your injuries, but I can't assess you properly if you don't give me a truthful history. My time would be better spent treating those who will.' She was a large matronly black lady in her early forties who was obviously far too busy to allow herself any really sympathy for her patients.

'I ran into a baseball bat,' I mumbled quietly.

'That's better,' she said matter-of-factly. 'Any blurred vision, nausea, palpitations, cold sweats?'

I shook my head; it ached dully.

'My arm is sore.'

'Bay nine. Please strip right off and put on the gown that you find on the bed. A doctor will examine you shortly.'

As I stood up to move towards the indicated cubicle the nurse added more kindly, 'By the way, we have representatives from the Met stationed here if you want to talk to someone but anything that you say to me or the doctor will be treated in confidence.'

Getting undressed took twenty minutes. My left arm was failing to obey instructions which made it very difficult to get my rugby shirt over my head and when I bent down to take off my boots my head throbbed. I thought I might have to call the nurse to help pull off my leather trousers. I found myself giggling alarmingly at the image but I managed it on my own in the end. The hospital gown was thinner and shorter than is strictly fashionable and I was sitting on the bed wondering whether I really had to take off my boxer shorts when the doctor drew open the bay curtains.

'Good afternoon, Mr. Turner. I hear that you have been in the wars?' She was young and blonde and blue eyed and had a caricature of a German accent. She smiled to show that she was aware of how incongruous that particular figure of speech sounded coming from her. But it was a tired smile; she had used that ice-breaker many times before.

'I have been hit by a baseball bat in my stomach, my ribs, my head, my back, and on my left forearm. But my leather jacket took most of the flak. It is only my arm that I am really worried about.'

The doctor tutted; she would be the judge of that.

'If you think I look bad,' I said brightly, 'you should see the state of the bat.'

The doctor tutted again.

She was initially only concerned about my head. She fired off a barrage of questions, shone a torch into my eyes, and then called in a heavily gloved nurse to wash the wound area. The disinfectant hurt enough for me to start worrying about my head too, but when the doctor re-examined it she just tutted. There was evidently nothing interestingly serious about it.

She took my left hand in hers and ran her right hand firmly along my forearm, squeezing in pulses. It really hurt. About halfway along it really, really hurt. I tried to jerk my arm away but her grip was surprisingly strong. She tutted.

Then she asked me to take off my gown. I felt vaguely grateful that I hadn't managed to get my boxer shorts off, but primarily I felt enormously relieved to be abdicating responsibility for my body to such a disinterested professional. I lay back on the bed as instructed. She palpated my stomach, watching my face for any involuntary wincing, and listened to my breathing through her stethoscope.

'Nothing appears to be punctured. You may have broken some ribs, but we would treat them the same whether they are broken or bruised so there is no advantage in having them x-rayed. The nurse will strap you up. Your radius, however, is almost certainly broken. Take this form and follow the red line to the x-ray department. I am tempted to keep you in over-night for observation but we have run out of beds. I assume that you have someone at home who can monitor you for signs of concussion?' - I found myself nodding – 'Then I do not think that we will need to detain you. Now then, where is that bat that you want me to look at?'

I stared at her momentarily nonplussed. She gave me her tired smile and turned away to find her next patient.

Two hours later I was standing in the taxi queue with a smart white plaster-of-paris casing from wrist to elbow and the euphoric feeling of distant pain being kept at bay by the dulling effects of strong drugs. Now that I was outside the strict No Mobile Phone rules of the hospital I felt that I should let Gloria know that I was OK and warn her that I was not going to be able to ride for a few days. Maybe I would end up back on the phones after all. Up until that moment I had formulated no plans for the future. If I had thought ahead at all I probably expected to slink home and nurse my wounds until I was fit enough to resume my previous existence. That is what I did when I got injured. But as I sent Gloria her text I suddenly felt overwhelmingly lonely. It would be nice to have someone at home to monitor me for signs of concussion. I thought of calling Ben, my rugby mate, but that would mean telling him that I was going to miss most of the season while my arm healed. And anyway that wasn't the kind of monitoring I wanted. I thought of Jane in her Methodist manse. As I scrolled through my phone address book for her number I found that I was dialling Anne's number instead.

'Hello James,' she answered before I could change my mind and hang up. Her tone was wary.

'Hello Anne.'

There was a short pause before Anne said, 'I may be wrong but I think that it was you that called me? And the caller is often the one who has something to say.' Her voice was more amused now.

'Would you believe me if I said that I'd dialled the wrong number?'

'No. Did you?'

'Yes.' Pause. 'No.' Pause. 'I'm standing outside Charing Cross Hospital Accident and Emergency department.'

Pause.

'Do you want me to come and pick you up?'

Pause.

'Yes. Please.'

Chapter Eleven

"Never, ever, ever brake on a bend. Go in slowly, come out fast."

From: "Ride Well and Prosper"

As Anne drove me in her little red convertible, with the top down and the wind blowing through her un-tethered golden hair, I told her everything. Everything that had happened since we last met. I initially assumed that Angus would have told her about his visit to my house the previous evening but Anne asked me to go over it all again anyway. She asked a few questions but mainly she just let me talk. I told her about my meeting with Colonel Grange which she seemed to think was completely unextraordinary. She had met him several times and described him as a charming but driven man. I told her how Charlie had asked his less savoury contacts if they could find out anything about Abbie's abduction. I told her how Charlie had sent me off to Cricklewood to meet some old Dublin friends of his. I told her what had happened there.

'Do you think they do know where Abbie is?' Anne asked.

'I don't know. This whole thing is not really my area of expertise.' I said. 'That's why I'm hoping Angus will be able to help. What's the point in having a friend in MI5 if he can't help you track down a terrorist suspect.'

'Angus has moved out,' Anne said.

'What?'

'Angus has moved out. He might tell you I threw him out but it comes to the same thing in the end. I thought maybe you knew.'

She glanced at me.

'Don't look so worried, James, it's not your fault. The Cambridge ten year reunion party made me realise just how long I have been unhappy. Can you imagine how hard it has been keeping up the pretence, day in, day out, that everything in our garden is rosy? Seeing you was the final straw. You made me face up to the fact that I do want to have children someday, and as I do not want them to be fathered by an adulterer it was up to me to change my circumstances. Our separation has been inevitable for ages, my only regret is that I didn't do it last year when I first found out that Angus was having an affair. No-one ever thinks that it is going to happen to them but if I'd considered it at all I would have expected myself to be a "one strike and you're out" kind of girl. I mean it's not exactly the kind of thing that happens by accident is it, fucking someone else? There are no excuses and no justifications. It is a deliberate choice, a betrayal of your partner's love. You can only get back from that breach of trust if you both want to. I just demeaned myself by giving Angus a second chance. Maybe I wasn't ready to accept that the dream of happy-ever-after was over, which was crazy because Angus was long past the stage of ever saying sorry for anything.'

Anne was speaking loudly to be heard over the noise of the wind and the traffic. She stopped suddenly and I knew that she was waiting for some kind of endorsement from me.

'I'm sorry, Anne. Sorry for you both.'

'Fuck you, James. Leaving Angus isn't the sorry bit. The sorry bit would be staying together when there is no chance of happiness for either of us ever again. Look at me. I'm laughing. I feel free and excited about the future for the first time in a very long time.'

'No you don't,' I said. 'Happy-ever-after was all that you ever wanted. Right now you are putting a very brave face on a very sad heart. It will get better. Believe me, I've been there. But it takes years, not days.'

'You bastard. What the fuck do you know about it? If I wasn't driving I'd slap your smug face right now - head wound or no head wound.'

'If you weren't driving I would give you a big, platonic, bear hug – broken arm or no broken arm.'

The tears started. Anne made no attempt to wipe them away as she drove. Eventually she pulled over into a bus stop and cried in my arms, oblivious of the on-looking bus queue, until no more tears would come.

I insisted on driving the rest of the way. I made Anne make the gear changes whenever I depressed the clutch and called out the number of the gear that I needed. I could have managed by myself even with my arm in its cast but it reminded me of the driving lessons I used to give her in our old TR6 back in our Cambridge days. By the time we got to the Docklands she was laughing again as we crashed our way through the gear changes.

Anne's flat was everything that I would have expected from two high-earning professionals with no children to support. And then a lot more. The whole top floor of a converted warehouse. The main room was bigger than my entire house, one huge living space divided up into functional areas. The kitchen ran along the east wall, slate work-surfaces and granite floor tiles, a butcher's block and copper-bottomed saucepans hanging on meat hooks from a Sheila maid. A breakfast bar separated the kitchen from the more formal dining space, a circular glass table on a beech-wood floor which morphed into a richly carpeted sitting room area with enormous leather sofas and a plasma-screen TV. His 'n Hers desks faced the west wall, each with their own computer, separated by a communal printer. There was only one window in the room but it constituted the entire south wall and opened out onto a balcony with genuine Thames river views.

'Bugger me,' I said appreciatively as Anne showed me round her flat.

'Been there, done that, thank you,' Anne replied with mock primness. 'Angus came into a bit of unexpected money. I guess it's going to make the divorce a bit messy.'

'Anne, can I be serious for a minute?'

'Now that's a rhetorical question if ever I heard one. You're going to say your piece, whether I want to hear it or not.'

'I feel uncomfortable being here. Or rather, it feels like the most comfortable thing in the world, but I'm not sure it's sensible. You're fucked up emotionally; I'm fucked up physically. It can't just happen like this.'

'What can't just happen, James? I can't just run you a bath? Just cook you dinner? Just tuck you up in one of the beds in the spare room?'

'I want to kiss you,' I said.

'I know. I want you to kiss me too. But not yet. I said some inappropriate things the last time we met. In my defence I was, as you say, emotionally fucked up but I'm not now; at least not in the same way. Things have moved on. We can't pretend nothing happened ten years ago. We'll need to talk it through. We are different people now, we've lived different lives. Nothing is guaranteed. We need to understand each other, become friends again. But we both want you to kiss me, which is a good starting place. There's no hurry to consummate it.'

If I wasn't drugged up to my eyeballs with painkillers I might have argued that last point but the moment passed. Anne sent me off to the kitchen in search of drinks while she started the bath running in the spare-room en suite and then insisted on helping me undress.

'Don't be so coy, James. I've seen it all before.'

I put up only the most token resistance as she fussed over me, examining the gash on my head and the bruising which was coming up on my back and chest. I protested that I was too drowsy and sore to eat anything but while I soaked, trying to keep my plaster cast dry, Anne warmed some soup which I ate sitting at the breakfast bar with a big towel wrapped around my waist.

'Right, its time for your medicine and bed,' Anne said when I'd finished. 'You can borrow my toothbrush. I'll check that you're still breathing when I turn in but what you really need now is sleep. I don't need to rush into work tomorrow so you should try to sleep in for as long as you can.'

Five minutes later I slipped naked beneath the crisp clean sheets. As I drifted into an uneasy sleep I caught the old familiar scent of sandalwood from the pillow.

★ ★ ★

I woke aching and confused and lay staring up at the unfamiliar ceiling trying to make sense of it all until Anne opened the door, flooding the room with light.

'Good morning patient. It's ten o'clock. How are you feeling on this sunny day?'

'I'm stiff and throbbing, nurse.'

'Some things never change,' Anne said, smiling.

She was wearing a simple white dress and carrying two steaming mugs of tea which she set down on the bedside table before stooping to kiss my forehead. It was such a tender gesture that I half expected the kiss to migrate down to my lips but she moved away to open the curtains before returning to perch on the edge of the bed.

'There are a few things I need to get from the office; then I can come back here and work from home for the rest of the day. Will you be alright if I nip out for a couple of hours? I could drop by your house and pick up some pyjamas for you?'

'I have to go to the police,' I said.

'Ok.' Anne said slowly. 'You don't have to. You're seriously injured. You could just lie in bed and recuperate; but I don't suppose you will. If you really want to go I'll take you when I get back. I may even be able to help, you know. I do have some expertise in the legal system.'

'And I also need to talk to Angus.'

Anne sipped her tea.

'I guess you do,' she said at last. 'What will you tell him?'

'I'll tell him about the Irish guys and see if he's made any progress with tracking down Abbie.'

'What will you tell him about us?' Anne asked. The word "us" sounded even more significant because of the casual way in which she used it.

'What is there to tell?' I replied. 'That I want to kiss you and that you want me to kiss you, too? I don't think I need to tell him that, but he'll probably work it out anyway. It's not rocket science. And I've never been very good at lying.'

'I remember,' Anne said. She stood up. 'He's staying at his club for now but he'll know that you've been here. If you've left your mobile phone on he will have traced you to within a few metres.'

'Then he'll know that I slept in the spare room. Can I have his number?'

'Of course. I'll write it down and leave it on the table. If you're sure you're ok I've got to go. Help yourself to breakfast.' She paused at the door. 'I'll be back as soon as I can, James, and I'll bring lunch with me. Don't forget to take your pain killers.'

I lay in bed and sipped my tea until Anne shouted a last goodbye from the entrance hall and I heard the front door close behind her. Half-an-hour later I sent her a text before letting myself out of her flat: 'Hi Anne. Feeling better now I'm up. Making own way home so take yr time in the office. Didn't want to presume on your hospitality.'

Five minutes later I felt the first of her replies arrive in my pocket, 'Don't be martyr/prat!'

Three more messages arrived before I had reached the Thames Light Railway station:

'I bet you've already left, haven't you?'

'I'll pick you up from your house at 14:00.'

'Let me care for you. Please.'

I texted back, 'C u at 2'.

The underground system was still barely functioning. The entire Jubilee line was closed until further notice and the Northern line might as well have been. I eventually managed to find my way home via the Victoria line. There was no reception on the underground but as I walked out of Brixton station I received a concerned text from Gloria, a missed call from Anne, and another text from Anne which just read 'X'.

I composed a suitably ambiguous reply to Gloria as I walked up Brixton Road and stopped outside my house to hunt in my pockets for my keys. My front door was a-jar. I pushed it further open and saw that the jamb was splintered by the lock. I stepped inside and listened while my eyes adjusted to the relative darkness within. Someone was moving in the kitchen. I tried and failed to walk quietly to the kitchen doorway in my heavy riding boots and threw open the door. Jimmy was on his hands and knees with a dustpan and brush.

'Damn, Jim! You frighten me,' he squeaked, scrambling to his feet.

The room had been trashed. Every cupboard had been opened and the contents thrown to the floor. The glass cabinets were smashed. The fridge was on its side.

'Looks like someone has been through here with a baseball bat,' I said.

'Jim, I'm so sorry,' Jimmy said. 'I don't know when this happen. I saw your door open just now and thought I try to clean up a bit before you get home.'

'It's ok, Jimmy. Thanks, that's really kind of you. I presume the rest of the house has had the same treatment?'

'Yes,' said Jimmy, hanging his head as if this was all somehow his fault. 'What happen to your arm?'

'I think it was the same baseball bat,' I said matter-of-factly.

Jimmy glanced nervously at the door.

'You think they come back?' he asked.

'I don't know. Maybe. Look, thanks for helping but there's nothing here that really matters. If you can just give me a hand getting the fridge upright I'll grab a few things and go.'

'You go to the police?'

'Yes. Sorry. I know it will be bad for business to have them sniffing around but I don't expect they'll actually do anything.'

'Course, boss,' Jimmy said miserably.

He insisted on staying to help me straighten the kitchen, which just meant putting everything that was broken or perishable into black plastic refuse sacks, but I persuaded him to leave when I started working on the front door. I couldn't turn my house into a fortress but I did want to at least make the door close again before leaving.

The rest of the house was not as damaged as the kitchen. The lounge looked bad; the stereo was smashed and a there were books all over the floor but the destruction was a bit half-heart. I saw my copy of Rebecca lying on top of the piles of books. I picked it up and put it carefully back by itself on one of the few shelves that was still standing. I left everything else lying where it lay. Upstairs the damage was even more token. My mattress had been over-turned but Abbie's room was virtually untouched. I don't possess much that is worth breaking. But the message was clear enough: "we know where you live". And maybe: "we hope that next time we call we will find you in". I just wished I knew why.

I grabbed a kit bag, emptied out the muddy rugby boots inside and replaced them with a few over-night essentials. I changed out of the bike leathers that I had been wearing, on and off, for the last thirty hours and put on some jeans. From force of habit I took my leather trousers downstairs to hang on the drying rail next to their companions. The rail had been over-turned. As I re-hung my three riding suits I saw the corner of an envelope sticking out of the inside breast pocket of one of my jackets. I took it out. On the outside of the envelop Abbie had written:

To James.

If you have found this envelope and I am still with you, please do not open it. (There are not many people who could resist but I know that you will respect this request.)

I smiled as I opened it. I moved out into the hall and sat down on the stairs to read her letter:

James.

This is the hardest thing that I have ever done. And I have done many hard things. I have just finished writing you a different letter. A fun letter. A letter that I hope to swap with this one if I am allowed the chance to say good bye to you in person. My other letter thanks you for your kindness and your kisses and invites you to visit me one day in my homeland, in the cool season when the mountain valleys are filled with wild-flower meadows that stretch for as far as the eye can see.

But as I sit here at your kitchen table with the sun streaming in at the window I know that we will never meet again. Maybe you are sitting in this very chair as you read? I can picture you in your leather trousers and socks, caught out by finding this letter in the process of getting ready for work one morning, returning to your old life, the one that you led before you saved me. The life that in my fun fantasy I found a way to share with you.

If you are reading this letter rather than the happy one it means that I did not leave voluntarily. But I made you a promise. I do not want you to remember me as having left you without saying goodbye.

My name is Taw Abying. In our culture the family name comes first. I am thirty five years old. Do you remember how I laughed when you guessed that I was twenty three? Were you just being polite? I am older than you! I was born in a tiny village in Kawthoolei, which you would think of as being in Karen state within the country of Burma. My village does not exist any more. It was burnt to the ground by the Burmese army when I was ten years old. Some of my family escaped and we started a new life in northern Thailand. I am glad that you have been to Thailand, even if you did not find happiness with your Jasmine.

I was educated by my father at first but later he sent me to Bangkok where I trained to be a doctor. I spent a post-graduate year here at University College London. I might have stayed and started a new life here but my father could not turn his back on the plight of our people. He returned to Kawthoolei to help organise the resistance. I went with him.

My father has persuaded the Karen people to give up their demand for an independent Karen nation. He has united all Burma's ethnic states into a new coalition which seeks to negotiate a system of democratically elected federal government which devolves just enough power to the regions so that we can maintain our own cultural identities. Unfortunately the very reasonableness of this demand terrifies the Rangoon junta. They know that western governments are trying to impose regional stability in South East Asia and now the junta can no longer depict us as separatist terrorists. So they have started a systematic program of genocide against the Karen in an attempt to re-populate the entire area with 'ethnically pure' Burman people. We are being massacred every day, while the world turns its head away.

We are desperate. I came to England to look for help. If you are reading this letter then I have failed. But I am still glad that I came. Pray that I died quickly.

Abbie

A nice old lady in Brixton library showed me how to log on to the World Wide Web. The hoodies on the terminals next to me were using the publicly provided internet facilities to play a game which seemed to involve racing pimped-up cars over cats and policemen to a backdrop of muffled rap music. It looked fun. They sniggered when I asked if they could help me log onto Google. They laughed even harder when they realised that I was serious but one of the kids, aged about nine, parked his Ford Mustang and gave me a brief tutorial in how to search for strings of key words. There were thousands of hits for the word "Burma". Most were links to web-sites about Aung San Suu Kyi, the imprisoned pro-democracy leader and Nobel Peace prize winner, or cyclone Nargis, or nostalgic stories about fighting in Burma during the second world war and the last days of the Raj. There were fewer hits for a search for "Karen State" but enough for the scale of the atrocities taking place there to start sinking in: pictures of smouldering villages and charred bodies reminiscent of the Vietnam War, smiling children in the refugee camps, statistics of the dead and the displaced.

I searched for "Karen State support groups" and found a number of links for organisations based in Thailand, the United States and in London. Many of the sites seemed to be no longer active: their pages did not display properly or they gave as the "latest news headlines" stories which were two years out of date, but they all contained information on how to sign up to support their cause and email addresses to contact for more information. I didn't have access to email. I found one site which gave a UK phone number. I called it from my mobile but the number was no longer in use.

I kept searching, trying different combinations of key words and following the trails of links-within-links from within each site. A site called WomenOfKawthoolei.com advocated the importance of educating women as the only long term strategy for peace and reconciliation. Their "Contact Us" page gave a Bangkok telephone number. I didn't know if my phone could make international calls but I tried it anyway. The number rang and a woman's voice answered. The Thai words were distantly familiar but I did not recognise enough of them to work out that they were recorded until the beep tone sounded, prompting me to leave a message.

'Hi. Hello. Sawaddee.' I started tentatively. 'My name is James Turner. I am a friend of Taw Abying. I'm calling from England. She has been staying with me and I think that she may be have been kidnapped. I am trying to find anyone who may be able to help me find her. Please pass this message to anyone who may be interested.' I gave my number, preceded by the UK dial code, and hung up.

'What the fuck am I doing?' I asked out loud. The hoodie on the next terminal looked across at me with renewed respect.

My left wrist was aching in its cast, unaccustomed to the strains of typing at the best of times. The nice old lady came by to see how I was getting on.

'I'm not making any progress here,' I told her.

'Oh dear,' she said in a motherly fashion. 'Still it can't be all that bad; at least nobody has died. Why don't you take a break? We've got a new machine in the cafe which makes a lovely cappuccino.'

I declined the coffee and kept on surfing, leaving my desperate message on more and more anonymous answer phones around the world but never once managing to speak to a human being. The racing, murdering, cat-torturing game-players drifted off. I looked at the clock on the wall and realised that Anne would be arriving at my house in less than an hour. I was wondering whether I needed to shut down my internet session somehow before leaving when my mobile rang. I scrambled to quieten it.

'Mr. Turner?' For an instant I thought that it was Abbie's voice. But she would have called me James.

'Yes.'

'Your message has been passed to me. We know who you are and I would like to thank you for the help that you gave to Abying.'

I asked something like: 'Who are you?', 'Where is she?', and 'Is she all right,' all rolled into one sentence.

There was a pause.

'Abying is lost to us. It is probably not safe for me to tell you more. For either of us. But you need to accept that she is beyond your help.'

I looked at my phone. The incoming caller's number had been withheld. Was I imagining a momentary delay in transmission or was this an international call?

'Is she dead?' I asked.

There was a longer pause.

'It would be better for her if she was. We believe that she is being flown to Rangoon this evening. They will try to use her as a bargaining chip but we do not give in to blackmail. Her father will get Abying back one limb at a time.'

'How are they transporting her?' I asked.

'She will be sedated to the point of coma and flown out under a diplomatic passport as a medical emergency. Probably. They have done it before.'

'Then we can go to the police and fucking stop them,' I shouted.

'Your police will not interfere with the diplomatic process,' her voice continued, unperturbed by my expletive. 'We can protest, write to the newspapers, demand inquiries. We are doing all this. It will be too late for Abying but if some part of her story trickles into your western consciousness then her death will not be completely in vain. If you want to help us, Mr.

Turner, talk to your MP. Join our marches. Articulate our cause. We have lost many battles but we are winning the media war. If we descend to their tactic or break your UK law we will just be considered as another bunch of terrorists.'

'Who the hell are you to tell me what to do?'

'My name is Rebecca, Mr. Turner. Abying is my sister. That is why I thank you again for the kindness that you showed her. And why I ask you again to let Abying go.'

The line went dead.

★ ★ ★

What do you do when you receive a phone call like that?

Evolutionary biologists believe that they are close to understanding the selective advantages of a propensity for religious belief. There are a number of competing theories: that the emergence of a structured theology enabled early humans to understand the world around them better and encouraged them to think that they could control it, that metaphysical beliefs provided a solace for the individual from the pains and discomforts of their everyday lives, that the physical activities of religious rituals released sufficient endorphins, nature's opioids, to bond the group together, or that the carrot and stick of a belief in an after-life imposed a moral code which improved the chances of survival of the whole group and thus, by extension, the genes of the religious-believing individuals within that group.

Homo Sapiens is the only species with the cranial capacity, particularly the frontal lobe matter, to be able to indulge in group religion. The vast majority of the animal kingdom has no concept of self-awareness; ants do not know that they exist. The higher mammals exhibit behaviour compatible with what philosophers call first-order intentionality – the ability to 'intend' - which itself entails some sense of self-awareness and an ability to believe something. Pavlov's dogs drooling at the sound of their dinner bell may not be proof of a capacity for belief - behaviour learned through repeated punishment or reward does not require insight into the cause and effect of that behaviour, for example clams open their shells when the tide turns to catch passing plankton but no one would claim that clams know that they are hungry – but a dog which finds her own lead and nuzzles awake her sleeping master is surely displaying more than just learned behaviour. She is displaying an intention, a hope, a belief that her action can influence a particular outcome. That is first-order intentionality.

The Great Apes appear to be capable of at least second-order intentionality: not only do they have their own intentions but they also exhibit behaviour which implies an understanding that other beings have intentions too. Deliberately conveying information implies second-order intentionality because it requires the belief that the recipient of the information is able to understand (and act upon) the information conveyed. Apes deliberately convey to their handlers the information that they are hungry. In doing so they demonstrate that they believe their handlers will respond to that information by feeding them.

True communication though, as opposed to just conveying information, is thought to require at least third-order intentionality. The frontal lobe capacity of early humanoids was definitely sufficient to support third-order intentionality and therefore communication. It might even have supported fourth-order intentionality: the ability to double bluff at poker:

No bluff: I raise the stakes because I believe that I've got a better hand than you. I am not considering how you might interpret my actions. I just want to win a bigger pot.

Bluff: I raise the stakes because I want you to believe that I believe that I've got the better hand (even though I actually believe that I've got the less good hand).

Double bluff: this time I actually do believe that I have the better hand but I want you to think that don't. I raise the stakes in such a way that you think I am just pretending to have a good hand. If you fall for my double bluff you will match my raise and I can smugly reveal my superior cards. I want you to believe that I believe that you believe that you have the better hand. Fourth-order intentionality.

Homo Erectus may have found the bluff a useful device. It would have enabled him to face down a sabre tooth tiger by pretending not to be afraid when in fact he was grateful that he had put on his brown animal skin that day, but the capacity to double bluff would only be useful for pretending to pretend to not be afraid – a subtlety which would be lost on most of the predators of the day. But fourth-order intentionality would support primitive superstition: individual members of the tribe could postulate the existence of a God with independent intentions, and they could communicate their desire that other members of the tribe share their belief in that God.

So why did our frontal lobe expansion not stop there, with the huge evolutionary advantage of being able to win at poker? Because wanting to share *your belief in a God with independent intentions* is not the same as wanting to share *the fact that you want to share your belief in a God with independent intentions*. Communal or Group religion requires this fifth-order intentionality, not just bowing in fear at the eclipsing moon but openly proclaiming the mutual embrace of a shared belief in a supreme being who can influence and be influenced by the tribe. This is what ushers in the religious rituals which bind the tribe together and places obligation on the whole tribe to behave in accordance with a common moral code. A belief in a supernatural being who will punish free-loaders who might otherwise profit from the evolutionary benefits of cooperation (hunting) whilst secretly pursuing their own selfish agenda (keeping the best bits of meat). A belief in a Greater Good which causes individuals to sacrifice their chance of propagating their own individual genes (by wrestling single-handedly with the sabre tooth tiger) in order to enable the genes of the tribe to prosper (by allowing the rest of the tribe to escape). Tribal genes which, incidentally, include that propensity to believe in God.

Game modelling shows that communities cannot grow bigger than about one hundred members unless you factor in some form of a shared moral code. Below that number everyone can see that everyone else is working together for the common good. Above that number it is too easy for the shirkers to hide amongst the honest toilers. The free-loaders are quite happy to take the benefits of the group activity without contributing their share of the hard graft. Then every one starts suspecting everyone else and the whole thing breaks down. But if you programme into the free-loaders a fear of discovery which is greater than the probability of discovery actually warrants (such as the belief in a supreme being external to the group who can discern their private intentions), or if you programme into all individuals a belief that self-sacrifice for the greater good of the group will be rewarded in some other way (such as with a glorious after-life), then the size of the community can literally grow without limit.

The size of a troupe of monkeys does not grow without limit. Once the troupe size gets bigger than about one hundred members, despite the obvious benefit of being able to defend a better territory, factions start forming which bicker and fight and eventually split into separate smaller troupes. Monkeys do not have the cranial capacity for fifth-order intentionality.

But we do. So, according to evolutionary biologists, religion really is nothing more than the opium of the people. We are evolutionarily conditioned to believe in something because those of our ancestors which did believe thrived in their larger tribes whilst those of our ancestors who did not believe fought amongst themselves to their own detriment. The gene which predisposes us to believe was passed on whilst the sceptical gene was not. Which might explain why many people who think that science has done away with the need for God are left feeling empty and unfulfilled. Our nurture, our holistic edifice of interdependent knowledge built up through experience, tells us that we no longer need a supreme being to explain the world around us; but this is at odds with our nature, our genetic pre-disposition to believe. On a personal level something is missing.

And the tribe is in deep trouble.

If troupe sizes of greater than one hundred are not sustainable without a proclaimed shared belief in the carrot and stick of an afterlife to keep the free-loaders in check, it explains why human civilisations crumble at their decadent peak. It is no good trying to re-invent God; it's too late. The genie is out of the bottle. With no fear of super-natural consequences the free-loaders can eat and drink and make merry like there is no tomorrow. And if there really is no tomorrow, who's to blame them? Civilisations without charity will fail, but if there is no Divine Purpose why should that matter?

Charity involves those who have sharing with those who do not; those who can helping those who cannot. But that is not all. The motivation for the act is as important as the act itself. Charity that begins and stays at home is not charity at all. The trickle down effect is not charity. The assertion that by making yourself, your family, your nation, wealthier you will create more crumbs to fall from your rich table to the benefit of those beneath you, that is not charity. It may be true. It may be better than nothing. But it is not charity. Even enlightened self interest is not charity. A wealthy land owner giving a family of travellers a financial incentive to move on; if the action is inspired purely by the benefit to the landowner rather than by a concern for the welfare of the travellers, than that is not charity. It might be the same outcome for the travellers, but it is not charity.

Charity is Sum Net Gain.

Charity is the pursuit of the greatest total benefit irrespective of to whom the good accrues. For its own sake. For the sake of maximising the total benefit of the tribe. Personally, I don't get the fifth-order intentionality explanation of our propensity to believe in God. What about ants? Ants sustain colonies of thousands without feeling the need to incorporate churches into their ant-hills. But I do get the charity thing. Without charity we're fucked. The Humanist agenda is to find some other social-glue for our secularised society to replace the common beliefs which once held the tribe together. It is an agenda which has so far spectacularly failed.

Those of us who have declined to die look at life from a different perspective from the rest of you. We don't all have the same perspectives as each other, but we do all stand apart from those of you who have not yet tasted your own mortality. I have met people who have survived near-death experiences who thank God for giving them a second chance; they commit themselves to good works with a missionary zeal to make up for their past sins. I have met people who think that they survived because they are somehow specially chosen for some particular purpose known only to themselves. I didn't have either of those responses. To me the fact that I did not die with my intestines spilling out of me in that bay in Phuket just reinforced my conclusion that it would have made very little difference if I had. It made a difference to me, obviously, and to my immediate family and close friends, but beyond that small sample of humanity the ripple effect dies out pretty quickly. It would have made little difference to the other thirty six inhabitants of Cuddleton, the tiny hamlet in Devon near my parent's farm which is the place that I most closely call home. It would have made no difference at all to the twenty five thousand inhabitants of Barnstaple ten miles down the road, no difference to the seven hundred thousand people living in Devon, the sixty million people living in Britain, the six billion current population of the world.

But my acceptance of the fact that my life is in some very profound way literally purposeless does not mean that I no longer feel that it has any value. I have been through the futility phase, the what's-the-point-we're-all-going-to-die-anyway phase. I have tried the hedonism phase, the Seize-the-Day-and-to-hell-with-tomorrow phase, and found it shallow. I have reached the Sum-Net-Gain phase, trying to do what is right, not out of piety or for personal profit but just because it is right.

And letting Abbie go was not the right thing to do.

I didn't accept that there was nothing that could be done to help her. If I was bold enough. If I really didn't care about the consequences. I knew all about risk-versus-benefit analysis, but I also knew that this was that moment in my life when I was going to over-ride my accumulated wisdom and intentionally embrace that unreasonable risk, revelling in the knowledge that I might regret it forever. If Abbie was still alive I would do whatever I could to save her. I just didn't know what yet.

Abbie's sister had recommended writing to my MP; trying to get the press interested in Abbie's story and put pressure on the Rangoon junta. I didn't share her faith in the British Establishment's sympathy to the plight of a foreign national, especially one who could be portrayed as having terrorist tendencies, but I would try that. Later. I had no idea where to start - Anne would know - but whatever could be achieved through that route would be too late for Abbie. A posthumous victory at best. I needed to do something now, today, to stop Abbie leaving the country.

Rebecca had warned that any actions outside the rule of the law would be counter-productive to their cause. But her cause, even Abbie's cause, was not my cause. My cause at the moment was very limited: to set Abbie free. Everything after that could take care of itself. I thought of calling Angus, or even Colonel Grange. Whatever his motives, he would be interested in Abbie's situation. He might already know the details of her planned departure. Would he intervene?

I could think completely dispassionately of several Plan Bs. Plan Bs were easy: storm the Burmese Embassy with my bare hands, phone in a plausible terrorist threat to get Heathrow airport closed, run naked round the departure hall until I was arrested, anything to delay her being put on the plane to Bangkok. But my Plan Bs were all acts of desperation; empty gestures with little chance of even generating any meaningful headlines. More like plan Zs. I knew with absolute certainty that I would resort to them if I had to, but I needed a Plan A. However harebrained.

I sent Anne a text saying that there was no need for her to pick me up; I would make my own way back to her flat as soon as I could. I thought of Abbie being drugged and wheeled onto a plane taking her to her death. I thought back to my own medical evacuation six years before. I Googled the British Airports Authority website and clicked on the link for information on travelling with a disabled or injured passenger.

Chapter Twelve

"At some point every rider will go into a corner too fast. When you start drifting out on a bend, look where you want to go, not where you are going. Your body will take you where you're looking."

From: "Ride Well and Prosper".

'Hello, Vanessa. I'm Doctor Thompson, Heathrow on-call duty doctor for today.' I gave the Thai Airways check-in supervisor my most dazzling smile as I read the name badge pinned to her purple sari.

I held out my right hand to her across the counter. Vanessa looked at my crumpled Oxfam suit and my new-second-hand brogues. I had considered finishing off the outfit with a white doctor's coat and a stethoscope draped nonchalantly around my neck but realised that would be over playing my part. I did have my own name badge - Dr. Richard Thompson - in a little plastic wallet hanging from my breast pocket.

'Be confident,' I told myself. The web-site implied that this was normal practice. It was possible that the check-in supervisor had never had to call a duty doctor before herself, but I had to act as if I did this kind of thing every day. 'Be authoritative!'

Vanessa's appraisal took in the battered leather briefcase that I had set down on the concourse floor beside me. I kept my hand stretched out to her but what I was really thinking was, '. . .and if the worst comes to the worst, there is always plan Z'.

Vanessa had the slim figure, high cheek bones, the jet black hair and the beautiful complexion that I remembered of all young Thai women. She also had the air of someone who was not only very busy but who cultivated their air of being very busy; not someone to welcome another disruption to her already disrupted day. She looked at the plaster cast on my left arm.

'Rugger injury,' I said. I withdrew my proffered hand, rapped the plaster cast briskly with my knuckles and shrugged sheepishly before offering my right hand back to her.

I feared that I had overdone the foppishness but Vanessa smiled sympathetically and shook hands.

'What can I do for you, Doctor?'

She hadn't asked for any proof of identity.

'I got a message that you need me to perform a pre-flight check on one of your Bangkok passengers?' Was I talking too quickly?

'Not from me,' Vanessa said, starting to look worried.

'No matter. The thing is I gather that the protocol is rather delicate. You are expecting a Burmese diplomat travelling with her own medical assistants?'

Vanessa nodded. She seemed reassured rather than suspicious that I should know the details of her confidential passenger list. To the lay person, doctors are expected to know everything; I was relying on it. Or maybe she was just relieved that this was a problem that she already knew about and not a new one to add to her long list.

'I understand that there is some, err, scepticism about the thoroughness with which her own doctor may have passed her fit to travel. I know that it's a bit delicate - the diplomatic thing - but, as you know, Thai Airways are responsible for all their passenger's safety whilst in the air, irrespective of whether they have signed the "flying with known risk" waiver beforehand.'

Vanessa shook her head and tutted for good measure, as if this was a familiar worry of hers. Maybe it was. I had quoted verbatim from the BAA web-site so it ought to sound convincing.

'I've been asked to give her the once-over, just to confirm that all is as it should be. It's probably a formality, but better to be safe than sorry, eh?'

Vanessa nodded her vigorous agreement.

'The thing is, she may not take too kindly to my interference. I'm sure that you are much better at smoothing ruffled diplomatic feathers than I, so can I leave it to you to make the explanations when she arrives?'

Vanessa squared her shoulders in preparation for the coming confrontation. I could see her mentally cracking her knuckles in anticipation of the fight. I smiled gratefully at her.

'Right-oh. I've brought some work with me,' I continued, lifting up the briefcase, 'so I'll set up camp in the first-aid room. Give me a buzz when she arrives and I'll scoot across and take a quick squint at her.'

I fished about in my pocket and brought out one of the business cards which I had printed off an hour earlier. It simply read: Dr. Richard Thompson. My mobile phone number was printed underneath the name. Vanessa looked at it and put it safely to one side.

'Thank you, Doctor.'

'You can reassure her that I should only take five minutes of her time, unless of course she is not as fit to travel as she claims...' I left that possibility dangling in the air as I left.

I retraced my earlier steps across the cavernous check-in hall, around the roving security guards cradling their sub-machine guns, down a narrow corridor, past the multi-faith prayer room, and on to the door with the green cross on it. It had not taken much leaning on to burst the lock and the door now stood propped open by the wastepaper basket. I went in, sat down at the desk, and buried my head in my hands. My heart was beating so fast that I thought I was going to be sick.

'Fuck,' I said out loud. 'This is fucking crazy.' And then I giggled. Angus would be so proud of me.

My mind was whirling. My Google research had confirmed that pre-flight medical checks can be demanded by any airline before admitting a passenger. I had thought of phoning up Thai

Airways with an anonymous tip-off, warning them that Abbie might not be fit to travel. Then I had discovered that diplomats are exempt from all the normal departure procedures and I had not had time to resolve which protocol would take priority if these two codes of practice came into conflict. I also had no idea whether Abbie would fail an independent medical check; maybe she would be forced to play along under the threat of some worse reprisal? The thought that I should actually try to play out this charade myself had come to me slowly and had been rejected often during the preceding six hours. I was here now because in the end it was the only Plan A that I had managed to come up with. What had started as a hypothetically thought-experiment had taken on a momentum of its own because it had felt so much better to act than to sit there thinking about acting. There had been so much to prepare and so little time that before I could reconsider I had found myself standing in front of Vanessa, opening my mouth, and hoping that something plausible would come out.

And so far, so good. But that was the easy bit over and done with. So far, at any stage I could have pretended to receive an urgent text and hurried away. The Blackbird was parked two hundred yards away in the short-term car park with my leathers in the side panniers and two helmets locked beside the seat. My plaster cast had made changing gear awkward, and painful, on the ride to the airport but having the bike close by meant that I could still back out. I had given Vanessa my phone number and my face was captured on hundreds of CCTV cameras. If I left now I might eventually be traced but I am not sure that I had yet committed any crime for which it would be worth prosecuting me.

That was all about to change.

I looked at my watch: six-thirty. The Bangkok flight was not due to take-off for another hour and a half and I guessed that Abbie's arrival would be timed for the very last minute. All I could do was wait, pretend to be immersed in my notes, and try not to flinch every time someone looked in as they walked past. A cleaner knocked on the open door. I looked up but before I could start my pre-rehearsed explanation she waved cheerily, said something in Polish, and pushed her cleaning trolley on to the chapel next door.

I wondered what I would do if there was a real first aid emergency while I was sitting there. I wondered whether Vanessa was even now mulling over our conversation and beginning to question who had requested my attendance. Hopefully she was too preoccupied by the normal check-in problems to worry about one which appeared to have a pre-ordained solution. What if someone else had actually invoked a real pre-flight medical check for Abbie? Was it still too late for me to do that, plan B? Should I revert to plan C and just dial 999 when she got here? But as time passed I began to accept that soon Abbie was going to arrive, Vanessa was going call, and I was going to play out my part to the best of my ability, wherever it might lead.

I took my phone out of my jacket pocket to check that it had decent reception and it rang in my hand.

'Shit!'

I forced myself to take three deep breaths before answering.

'Doctor Thompson,' I said quickly.

'Doctor, this is Vanessa. The passenger has arrived.'

'I'll be down in a minute,' I said as casually as I could.

'As soon as you can, please, Doctor' said Vanessa. I could hear voices being raised in the background.

I switched off my phone as I walked back slowly to the Thai Airways check-in desks. As I approached I saw Abbie sitting in a wheel chair flanked by three squat Asian men. I wondered if she would give me away but she appeared to be asleep. A thickset man was waving a piece of paper at Vanessa and loudly repeating the words 'diplomatic immunity'. He turned angrily towards me. Even though I had prepared myself for this moment I still felt a shock of recognition. The last time I had seen his face he had been squinting into the full glare of my headlight in the park in Kennington. He had been standing in front of Abbie's naked body and he had been wielding a knife.

But I had been wearing a motorcycle helmet, I reminded myself. He couldn't possibly recognise me.

My arrival coincided with that of the Thai Airways duty manager, a wiry, fussy looking man, who nevertheless accepted my presence immediately.

'Doctor Thompson. Hi, I'm Tim Whittaker,' the duty manager introduced himself. 'I am so glad you're here.'

'Good evening, Tim' I said. I offered him my hand to shake. 'So, this is the proposed passenger?' I tried to look down at Abbie with detachment; I'm sure that I failed. She was tucked into her wheel chair with travelling rugs. Her head had lolled forward but I could see that her eyes were closed beneath her thick fringe. She was asleep, but there was something about the way that her body was so totally slumped that did not look in the least bit natural.

'They are not at all happy about this,' the duty manager said in an understatement, 'and, to be fair, she doesn't look too bad to me.'

'I'll be the judge of that, I should say,' I replied, trying to regain an air of confident superiority.

'Yes, of course, Doctor. It is just that it could be very awkward if...'

'... if she were to die in your care?' I finished for him, deliberately misunderstanding his concern.

I noticed Vanessa nodding behind him. I turned to her and asked, 'Does Sleeping Beauty have a name?'

'Mary Thacker,' said Vanessa without looking at Abbie, 'and here is her doctor's letter.'

She handed me a type-written document. It was written in English. It looked official; it had a flowery signature and an ink stamp of some sort at the bottom. I had no idea what it said but I pretended to scan through it, glancing up occasionally to look at Abbie. They all watched me closely as I read. When I had finished I sighed and looked down at Mr. Whittaker with a sombre expression.

'I am very sorry to say...' I paused dramatically, 'that everything appears to be in order.'

The duty manager let out a loud sigh of relief.

'However,' I continued, turning to the ex-knife-wielder and holding his belligerent stare, 'I do still need to take her to the first aid room. I was mainly worried about any kind of head injury. From her notes this does not seem to be a risk factor, but I would still like to check her consciousness levels. Having been called I would now be considered negligent if I did not examine her at all before passing her fit to fly.' I had not wasted my internet research time.

The ex-knife-wielder stared back at me defiantly.

'This is Mr. Shaun. He is Ms. Thacker's travelling nurse,' Vanessa told me, and then added in a stage whisper, 'I'm not sure he speaks much English.'

Vanessa turned to talk to one of the other members of Abbie's retinue. I recognised a few of the words but my Thai was far too rusty for me to follow the conversation. The second attendant shook his head and looked at me suspiciously. A small crowd of bystanders was beginning to gather around us at a respectful distance. Vanessa remained calm but insistent. Reluctantly the attendant started translating my request to the knife-wielder. Mr. Shaun grunted dismissively but then noticed our interested spectators. Behind them I saw a pair of patrolling policemen veering towards us. Shaun scowled at me, but nodded curtly.

'Thank you,' said Vanessa brightly. 'Right then Doctor, do you want to lead the way?'

I moved to take up position behind Abbie's wheelchair but Mr. Shaun beat me to it so I turned my back on the lot of them and set off somewhat peremptorily back towards the first aid room. I did not look round until I was half-way across the airport concourse. When I did I was relieved to see that Mr. Shaun was meekly following along with Abbie and that the rest of his team had remained behind at the check-in desk. I took this as a good sign; they were not sufficiently suspicious to expect trouble. I was less pleased to see that Vanessa was trotting along behind him. I paused to let them catch up; Vanessa in her smart Thai Airways sari and Mr. Shaun pushing the passenger known as Mary Thacker in her wheel chair. The dénouement was approaching. Abbie's life would be decided in the next few minutes. I needed some distraction to get me alone with her for long enough to get away but in the meantime I had to reprise my performance as the disinterested duty doctor. I fell into step beside Vanessa and tried to chat inconsequentially with her about a time when I had lived in Bangkok for a few years after graduating from medical school. She seemed genuinely interested. As we were passing the prayer room I stopped again.

'Vanessa, I'm so sorry. I should have brought Mary's doctor's letter with me. I think I left it at the desk. I will need to reference it when I sign her off. You couldn't just nip back and get it for me could you?'

Vanessa looked suspiciously at Mr. Shaun as if afraid that he might intimidate me into sanctioning an unfit passenger to fly if she left me alone in his company for too long.

'If you have any problems with him, wait until I get back,' she said, and set off back to the way we had come.

When she had gone I ushered Mr. Shaun before me through the open first aid room door. He pushed Abbie inside. I entered, kicking the waste paper basket out of the way so that the door swung shut, came up behind him and punched him as hard as I could in the area of his unprotected kidneys. He let out a muffled grunt and staggered around to face me, surprise and pain in his eyes. As he turned, I swung my left arm with all my force so that the heavy plaster cast caught him full on the chin. Pain shot through my arm and my eyes watered so much that I didn't see him staggering forward until he was almost on top of me. I pushed him away and punched him again with my good fist. His eyes rolled upwards and he fell forward onto his knees. I hit him again and he slumped face-forward onto the floor.

That was that. He wasn't dead. But he wasn't getting up again in a hurry. I grabbed the long roll of surgical tape that I had found in the desk draw and wrapped it several times round his head and over his mouth. I pocketed the tape.

I ripped the travelling blanket off Abbie. She was wearing a thin black shell suit and cotton socks. I picked her up and hugged her, as small and light as a child. Her eyes fluttered half-open but there was no sign of any recognition. She struggled to lift her head and look around her but then her eyes closed again and she went limp in my arms.

Mr. Shaun stirred on the floor. I had no time to worry further about Abbie's welfare: she was alive now and if I did not get her away soon she would be dead. Any risk was worth taking but I had my first real choice to make. Vanessa would be back any minute. The rational decision would be to wait for her to arrive and truss her up like Mr. Shaun. This would buy us more time to get away. But I knew that I couldn't do it. Hitting the man who had turned Abbie into the zombie in my arms had been easy but Vanessa was an innocent party. Which meant that every second was crucial.

I pulled open the first aid room door. The passage outside was empty. I turned away from the main concourse and walked briskly the other way carrying Abbie with her head over my shoulder like a father carrying his sleeping daughter. I kept my head down as I skirted round the back of the row of check-in desks. I was vaguely aware of a commotion by the Thai Airways desks but I resisted the temptation to look up. I walked out through the automatic doors, across the road where taxis were dropping off their fares in the last rays of the dying sun, and into the relative darkness of the multi-storey short term car park. The Blackbird was waiting for us by the car park exit. I sat Abbie across the saddle and took her head into my hands. I gently lifted the lids of her eyes with my thumb. She muttered something in Burmese or Karen and shrank away from me. When I let go of her she slumped forward and lay with her head on the instrument panel between the handlebars. I considered carrying her back to the taxi rank but as I looked up one of her other Burmese Military Intelligence minders came running out of the terminal building. He looked up and down the road and then started running along the line of taxis, peering into each of them.

I unlocked the two helmets from the strong-point behind the saddle. I slipped one over Abbie's head and pulled the other one onto mine without bothering to do up the straps. I took the surgical tape out of my pocket and straddled the seat behind her. Sitting her upright and holding her inert body tightly against mine I passed the tape in front of her and then passed it round my back, pinning her to me. I wound it awkwardly round us both five times and shoved the rest of the roll, uncut, into an outside jacket pocket. I leant forward and reached around Abbie to put my key into the ignition; she dangled in front of me like a puppet whose strings have been cut, her head lolling on the instrument panel and her arms swinging down dangerously close to the front wheel. I leaned back. She rose with me. I clumsily taped her arms to her sides and then reached forward again to grip the handlebars. The BMI man was crossing the road as I moved off towards the exit but I was confident that he couldn't see us within the gloom of the car park. I wiggled the bike passed the exit barrier and slipped out into the last of the rush hour traffic.

The road between Heathrow and the M25 was virtually grid locked. As always on a Friday evening. I caught a few startled glances as I slipped between the stationary cars in my Oxfam suit with Abbie lying like a rag doll across the fuel tank in front of me but when we reached the M4 I opened up the throttle and flew past the other drivers too fast to worry about their expressions. It is 27 miles from the M25/M4 interchange to Reading services. I covered the distance in fifteen minutes through heavy traffic. By that time the wind chill factor was beginning to get to me, even with my adrenaline running and with Abbie's body in front of me as a wind break. The sun had gone completely. Hypothermia would definitely push Abbie into a coma. I pulled the bike into the darkest corner of the service station car park, well away from the overhead sodium lights, unwound the tape binding us together, lifted her off the bike, and laid her down gently on the grass verge. I eased off her helmet. Her face was so pale that I feared that she was already dead but her eyelids flickered open and this time she did recognise me. As I took off my own helmet she struggled to sit up but she did not have the strength. I sat down beside her and tried to cuddle her to me but she pushed me away and suddenly retched onto the grass between us. I helped her to turn onto her side and held her head. Spasm after spasm wracked her body but only a thin trickle of bile dribbled from her lips.

'It's going to be all right,' I kept repeating as I stroked her hair. 'Everything is going to be all right.'

Eventually the vomiting stopped. I rolled her on top of me, wrapped my suit jacket around her, and hugged her frozen frame to me. Her breaths were coming fast and shallow but as some of the relative warmth of my body seeped into hers I felt her hands moving against my chest. I sat up. Abbie clung to me, curled up on my lap.

'It's going to be ok,' I said again, hugging her reassuringly. 'But I don't know what those bastards have drugged you with. You're the real doctor amongst us. Should I be calling you an ambulance now?'

She didn't answer, just snuggled into me even more desperately, like a frightened animal burrowing away from danger.

'Hush,' I said. 'It's ok. You're safe now.'

And so I sat, rocking her gently in my arms and kissing her hair until at last she relaxed enough to lift her head and look up at me.

'James?' she said, looking wonderingly into my eyes

'Abbie,' I smiled back at her.

'What happened?'

'Not now. I know you're cold, but we've got to keep moving. I've got some warmer clothes for us if you'll let go of me for long enough for me to get them.'

She squeezed me fiercely but then sat up and looked around her. I lifted Abbie off me and went to retrieve the clothes that I had stowed in the Blackbird panniers three hours before; in a different lifetime. I helped Abbie struggle into a thick jumper and a spare leather jacket which swamped her tiny frame. My leather trousers were far too large for her so I helped her pull on a pair of tracksuit bottoms over her shell suit trousers, the same jogging trousers that she had borrowed on her first day in my house. Then I dressed myself. I felt immeasurably more comfortable back in my normal riding gear. Abbie lay silently watching me as I changed.

'I know it's a stupid question, but how are you really?' I asked.

'I'm going to live. Thanks to you. Again.' She tried to smile. Her first attempt failed but she persevered.

'I need to find some footwear for you. It didn't occur to me that you might be barefoot. They sometimes sell odd things in service stations. I'll see if I can find anything which might do. Don't go away'.

I felt elated as I wended my way between the parked cars towards the noise and bustle of the service station buildings. I had crossed my Rubicon. I had attacked a foreign diplomat; I had impersonated a doctor with intent to deceive; I was now probably wanted by the UK police as well the Burmese and my Irish friends. But Abbie was alive.

Plan A had succeeded.

My euphoria was crushed by the sight of a police car pulling off the motorway. I stopped and watched as it turned off the slip road and cruise unhurriedly round the car park, moving inexorably towards the darkest corner where Abbie was lying on the grass next to my parked bike. The patrol car paused beside her and then moved on towards the bright lights of the petrol station. I started breathing again but as I entered the service station precinct I realised that plan A only took me so far. I looked around at the suited commuters, the beer-bellied truckers and the family groups queuing up at the fast food outlets and milling around in the shop, chatting and laughing about their normal lives. The enormity of what I had done was beginning to sink in. I didn't have a normal life anymore.

The service station shop didn't sell shoes. I bought three pairs of ladies sport socks, two strong sweet coffees, cheese sandwiches, chocolate, and freezer bags. I paid for everything by debit card; it would leave an electronic trail but I figured it would take a few hours at least to track it down. I smiled up at the CCTV camera behind the counter as I left. In the foyer outside I withdrew two hundred pounds from the cash point machine.

Back in the car park I took out my mobile phone. I had turned it off at the airport. I could imagine Angus sitting in front of a computer screen somewhere urging me to switch it back on so that he could find out where I was. It was decision time. Abbie did not want to go to hospital and throw herself onto the mercy of the British establishment but was she really in position to know what was best for her. Should I call Angus and try to cut some kind of a deal with him?

I switched on my phone. While I waited for it to boot up I looked over into the darkness where Abbie must be watching me. My phone buzzed with new messages: from Charlie, Gloria, Ben, and three from Anne - all along the same lines of 'where the fuck are you?' Nothing from Angus. There were voice messages for me too, but I didn't bother to pick them up. As I walked back towards Abbie I passed an empty minibus with Irish number plates and a roof rack. On a sudden impulse I climbed up on its rear foot plate and pushed my mobile phone into one of the bags on the roof.

Abbie tried the coffee and some chocolate but couldn't face the sandwiches. I pulled all three pairs of socks onto her feet and then taped the freezer bags over the top. It looked a bit odd but it would keep the wind off. I helped her stand and then half carried, half dragged her up and down the grass verge until some life returned to her legs.

'We ought to go,' I said.

'Where are we going?'

'Somewhere safe.'

This time I sat in front and Abbie sat behind me in the traditional pillion position. I still did not trust her strength to hold up so I gave her the tape and told her to bind us together again.

'If you need anything just give me a squeeze,' I shouted over my shoulder. She squeezed to show that she understood, sending pain shooting through my injured ribs. I kicked the bike into gear and pulled away.

I pulled off the motorway at the next junction and wiggled my way south on back-roads until we picked up the A303. I wanted to put some miles between us and Reading service station so I rode as fast as the speed limit would allow until I was forced to stop for more fuel. I turned off the main road and cruised through a sleepy West Country market town until I found an open petrol station. I stopped down a side street beyond it. Abbie un-taped us, climbed off the bike and sat on the kerb out of sight while I filled up. When I came back Abbie managed half a sandwich and said that she was alert enough not to be bound to me anymore.

The A303 became the A30 and we skirted around the north edge of Dartmoor to Okehampton. I turned south and after a few miles picked up the signs to the tiny village of Lynchcombe. It was after midnight when I pulled onto the block-paved driveway of a converted barn and drew up under the branches of an old oak tree. Abbie staggered and nearly fell as she dismounted. I was cold to the bone, aching everywhere, and my left arm throbbed ominously inside its cast but I knew that my discomfort was nothing compared to whatever Abbie must be bearing so uncomplainingly.

'All this fresh air has gone to my head,' was all she said when I asked if she was alright. I smiled down at the freezer bags still taped to her feet.

'This is my sister's house. She's a teacher. She doesn't know anything about you yet, but she is a good person.'

Abbie came to me, put her arm around my waist and hugged me to her as I knocked on the door.

There were still some lights on inside and I could hear the sound of a television in the otherwise silent night. An outside light came on and Julia opened the door in a fluffy pink dressing gown and matching slippers. If I owe my dark hair, natural reserve and my big-boned farmer's build to my father's genes, my sister has inherited our mother's petite figure and blonde good looks. So much so that when Angus and Anne had come home with me to work on the family farm during our second summer holiday at Cambridge I had had to remind Angus that

Julia was then only seventeen years old; much too young to have her heart broken by him.

Julia is also the only person I know who can out-mother our mother in the bustling concern and bonhomie department.

'Jesus, Jim. You could have rung me to let me know you were coming. What have you done to your arm? Still, good to see you, I suppose,' she said. 'I see you've brought company with you this time. In plastic bags!' she added seeing Abbie's feet. 'Hi. Come on in. I'm Julia. Come in, come in. You must be freezing.'

'Julia, this is Abbie, Abbie, Julie,' I said, making the introductions. Julia did not appear in the least bit phased by our surprise appearance.

'Do you guys need anything to eat or drink?' she asked as she ushered us into her farmhouse kitchen. I led Abbie over to the warmth of the Aga.

'Julia, this is really good of you. I owe you an explanation. Several explanations, probably. But for now Abbie just needs a hot bath and bed,' I said bluntly.

Julia looked at me closely but didn't press the matter. She turned to Abbie. 'My darling brother is completely bloody hopeless. I hope you realise that? I know what it's like being on the back of one of his bikes even with something warm on my feet. I see he's got some nice sturdy boots for himself, though, hasn't he. What was he thinking of? But you will warm up, I promise you. Jim, when will you learn how to treat your women properly?'

She scowled at me and shook her head. I grinned at her.

'Right,' she carried on briskly, 'Jim, you know where everything is. Why don't you show Abbie up to the spare room and run her a bath while I get out the whisky? There should be plenty of hot water. Then you and I can talk.'

I carried on grinning. Julia carried on scowling. Then she threw her eyes up to the ceiling and smiled fondly back at me.

I led Abbie up the narrow staircase. Julia's house is not much larger than mine but I was struck as always by how much more of a home it is. Whereas my house reflects the functional minimalism of my bachelor existence, Julia's style is much more House and Country – not overly ornate but warm and comfortable, and coordinated. The spare bedroom had an autumnal theme: the burnt ochre curtains, already drawn closed over the large bay window, were flecked with antique gold to echo the gilt-framed mirror over the wash stand, the small candelabra hanging from the ceiling, and the brass bed-knobs of the large bedstead. Two Russell Flint prints of Egyptian washer-women hung against the burgundy wall paper and a beautiful cream, lace throw and chocolate-brown cushions were arranged tastefully on the brick-red counterpane. Julia had constructed a beautiful family home; it was just a pity that no family had arrived yet to fill it. Maybe I'd been too hasty in reining Angus in all those years ago.

I wanted to tend to Abbie, to help her undress, bathe her, dress her wounds and sooth her to sleep, but I sensed a sudden reserve in her. She was swaying with tiredness but adamant that there was nothing medically wrong with her. I hugged her gently and went back downstairs. Julia was filling a hot water bottle as I came back into the kitchen.

'Pour me a drink,' she said without looking up.

There was a bottle of Jack Daniels and three large cut-glass tumblers on the table. I half-filled two of the glasses.

'Did you catch the news this evening?' I asked, handing her a whisky. 'Any more news on the underground bombing?'

'How's Abbie?' Julia asked.

'She's in the bath. She says she's going to be fine and she ought to know. She's a doctor.'

Julia took a sip. 'So. What's her story?'

'Humour me; did you watch the news?' I persisted.

'Yes. No new leads on the underground bomber. The main story was some Euro MP getting caught with his pants down as far as I remember. What should I really have been looking out for?' she asked perceptively.

'A commotion at Heathrow airport.' I said.

Julia looked at me over her glass as she thought back, then shook her head. 'I think you've got away with it so far. Whatever "it" is. Are you going to tell me?'

I did; the full bottle of whisky's worth eventually. But after our first glass, before I had even started assembling the events of the day into a coherent narrative, Julia stopped me while she took the hot water bottle up to Abbie and rustled up tooth brushes, a spare nightdress and some painkillers. I resisted the temptation to follow her up the stairs. Julia was gone for half-an-hour. I could imagine her sitting happily on the side of the bed and chatting away about the weather and the price of fish, nonchalantly putting Abbie at ease. With a twinge of jealousy I accepted that my presence would be an intrusion. When she came back she reassured me that Abbie was comfortable and nearly asleep already.

Julia picked up her glass and lifted it towards me, 'To the knight in shining armour. Abbie says that you saved her life today.'

Julia's absence had given me a chance to gather my thoughts. I realised that I was in danger of neglecting my own injuries and tiredness but above all I needed to talk. I tried to do justice to my last few hours by putting it in some sort of context. I'm not sure if I gave a very lucid account of myself but it was revealing enough for Julia to conclude for me: 'So, basically you've got no idea what sort of a mess you've got yourself into, you don't know what to do next, and you're shit scared?'

She was right on all counts.

'There seems to be only one salient point at the moment, and that is whether Abbie is safe here tonight,' Julia continued. She looked at the kitchen clock and went to switch on the radio for the two am headlines. We listened in silence. There were still no stories from Heathrow. We discussed what this could mean. I couldn't believe that Vanessa would not have reported my assault on Mr. Shaun or Abbie's mysterious disappearance. If the police had been informed, were they suppressing the story? Surely the apparent kidnapping of a foreign diplomat was sensational enough for any news editor? Julia suggested that scar-face may have come round before Vanessa got back to the first aid room and given her some less dramatic explanation of Abbie's absence. I dismissed this idea at first but the more we talked through this scenario the more I liked it. The Burmese authorities would not want the real story to be known. If Mr Shaun had had a chance to gather his wits before Vanessa arrived he may well have just told her that Abbie had rethought her travel arrangements. If so there was not very much that Vanessa could have done about it. She might even have suspected that my examination had found Abbie not fit for flight and that Mr. Shaun had simply whisked Abbie away from the airport in order to save face. Vanessa may have tried to phone me – I wished that I waited long enough in Reading services to pick up my missed messages before sending my phone on its slow trip to Ireland – but as long as no complaints were made the non-outcome of Abbie's disappearance would probably be a relief to Vanessa. It was certainly a relief to me. It meant that the only people actively looking for me were probably the Burmese Military Intelligence and they would have no way of tracing us to Julia's house.

I yawned and tried to stretch but the bruising in my ribs over-rode any anaesthetic effect of the alcohol.

'Bed for you too,' Julia announced. 'I think we've deduced that you're as safe here as anywhere for now. There aren't even any neighbours to snitch on you. Spare room or couch?'

I had evidently not revealed quite as much as I thought.

'Spare room,' I said with a school boy smirk.

Julia nodded knowingly.

Chapter Thirteen

"If it comes to a choice between leaning over further or hitting a wall, lean over further. Trust your tyres."

From: "Ride Well and Prosper".

I woke up with the intense thirst and the dull headache of a mild handover to add to my other ailments. Sunlight was streaming round the edges of the curtains. Abbie was snuggled-up beside me in Julia's borrowed nightdress with one hand lying lightly on my chest. We had slept next to each other with all the platonic comfort of a well-worn marriage. I lifted her hand and kissed it gently then slipped out of bed and walked naked to the bathroom in search of paracetamol and re-hydration. The bathroom clock showed ten minutes to eleven. I wrapped a towel round my waist and went downstairs to the kitchen to switch on the radio. There was a hand-written note propped against the kettle:

Good morning, Lovers.

Sorry to miss you. I forgot I had a PTA jumble sale I promised to help out with!

Make yourselves at home. I've put some clothes out for Abbie on my bed. I'll get home as soon as I can.

J x

I let the tea brew while I waited for the news headlines. When they came there was still no mention of a Heathrow kidnapping. Rose Smith and her six-year old son Billy had recently come back from a holiday in Pakistan. Her extended family there denied any involvement in her radicalisation but friends in London were now saying that she had been very withdrawn since she had got home. I took my first mug of tea upstairs and tried unsuccessfully to keep my plaster cast dry while washing the rest of my body in the shower. Then I went back downstairs and brought a tea tray up to the spare room. Abbie was still asleep. I climbed into bed beside her and drank my next mug of tea while watching her reluctantly surface into consciousness. Eventually she turned over next to me and her eyes blinked open.

'Morning, sleepy head.' I said.

'James?'

There was still sleepy confusion in her eyes. She struggled up to sit beside me in the bed.

'How are you feeling?' I asked. I passed her a mug.

'Happy,' Abbie answered simply. She laid her head against my shoulder as she took her first sip of tea. 'And sore. And confused. And hungry,' she added.

'I think we're safe here for a while. Questions and Answers over breakfast?' I suggested.

Abbie nodded. We finished our tea in silence. Then I dressed and went down to start the scrambled eggs while Abbie showered. She entered the kitchen twenty minutes later looking self-consciously demure in a bright yellow summer dress of Julia's. I had always thought of Julia as my very little sister but her dress still reached down to Abbie's ankles.

'You look gorgeous,' I said truthfully.

Abbie smiled shyly.

'Eggs, baked beans, mushrooms, toast, and grilled tomatoes,' I said. 'The rules are that we take it in turns to ask questions but we stop as soon as either one of us has had enough. There's no rush.'

'Ok,' Abbie said. 'I ask first. Tell me everything that happened since Tuesday morning.'

'That's not a question; that's a command!' I tried to make a joke of it but I was happy to talk first. I hoped that Abbie would be more willing to talk now than she had been during her brief stay in my house but I didn't want to put pressure on her to relive her most recent ordeal. While we ate I told Abbie how I had gone home on Tuesday evening and found her gone. I had not believed that she would have left voluntarily without saying good bye but that this had not particularly impressed PC Watkins. I told her how Charlie had made some enquires amongst his less salubrious friends and sent me to Kilburn where I had been beaten up by some Irishmen. I half expected Abbie to comment at that point but she just reached out and took my injured hand in hers and stroked it gently as I continued. I explained how I had left messages with every Karen web-site I could find and how eventually her sister had called me back and told me that Abbie was being flown out of Heathrow yesterday evening.

'Rebecca called you?' Abbie asked, showing real surprise for the first time. 'Now you know why I chose to read that particular book at your house. It is a lovely story. We all do our bit. Rebecca runs a Karen web-site which publicises our grievances to the world. She still believes that if we can generate enough public support we can stop the Burmans from killing us.'

I did not tell her that Rebecca had advised me along similar lines. Instead I explained how I had used the web to research the procedures for embarking sick or injured passengers and hatched my desperate plan.

'Everyone trusts Doctors, so I impersonated one, knocked out Mr. Shaun, and rode off with you into the sunset,' I finished simplistically.

Abbie sat looking at me in silence and holding my hand for a long time. I had so many questions to ask her but I was hoping that she would volunteer to answer them without being asked.

'It is a lovely day,' she said at last. 'Let's go out for a walk,'

Julia had bought Highfield Barn when she finish her probationary year and started teaching the reception-year infants at Tavistock Primary School. The converted barn is on the outskirts of Lynchcombe village, right on the western fringes of Dartmoor. The previous summer Julia and I had spent a fortnight walking the moor and camping, something we hadn't done together since as a fifteen year-old boy I had taken my little sister exploring Exmoor from our parent's house at Home Farm. It was clear to me why Julia had settled at Highfield. It is not quite as isolated as Home Farm, there are neighbours and a shop within walking distance, but it has the same feeling of being right up in the wilds of the moor - and it is close enough to Mum and Dad's to get home for the odd Sunday lunch.

Our camping trip the previous summer contended with typical English summer weather - hot sunny days alternating with driving, horizontal drizzle - but it had been very nostalgic to spend time alone with Julia again. Prior to university we had been very close, genuine friends despite, or maybe because of, the gender difference and three year age gap. Home Farm is not in a village; not even close. As children Julia and I had had to walk a mile each morning just to reach the main road in order to be picked up by the school bus. And a mile back up the same hill every afternoon, come rain, come snow. We did not often have friends of our own age round to play with. So we worked, always together, either both of us helping Dad with the cows or both of us helping Mum about the house. Our parent's roles were very traditionally defined: Dad worked the farm, Mum kept the house, but I had never felt self-conscious rolling pastry or making jam with Julia, just as it had never occurred to either of us that she should not take her turn to drive the tractor when she was old enough. She would come and watch me play rugby for the school and I would help her muck out the stables after her riding lessons. Then I had gone off to Cambridge and later still I had left to work my way around the world. I had sent her post cards every month, more conscientiously than to Mum and Dad, but when I'd turned up in London four years ago I had found that my very little sister had become an adult without me even noticing.

Last year, after the initial awkwardness had worn off, we talked again as we had not talked for years. Julia opened up first.

It was obvious that she loved her job. Tavistock Primary is a surprisingly large school for such a rural location. It has a huge catchment area with a commensurately huge range in pupil ability and amount of parental support. Children who read their parent's newspapers before school in the morning sit next to children who are still struggling to recite the alphabet. Julia has always been more garrulous than I. As we walked she kept up a constant flow of funny stories of incidents that had happened at the school but without ever disparaging her less able students. She talked of being chatted up by would-be suitors at the school gates and of ex-boyfriends from her teacher-training days – all married now, and parents themselves. I asked her why none of her own relationships had lasted. Julia just shrugged her shoulders.

We discussed Home Farm. Our parents had never put any pressure on either Julia or me to commit ourselves to the farm but they had both suddenly started to look old. The seemingly endless succession of farming crises had taken their toll. Dad was beginning to talk about selling up but farming was all he had ever known. He was understandably frightened. Julia told me that Mum had asked recently whether she knew what my long-term plans were. She told me that she had told Mum that it was none of her business, which sounded entirely plausible. Mum and Julia could spit at each other one minute and cry on each other's shoulders the next.

On the third day of our walk Julia asked me whether I was still in touch with Anne. She talked about that summer after my second year at University when Angus and Anne had come to stay at the farm for the first time. Mum had apparently been in a right lather before we'd arrived, not knowing whether to put Anne and me in the same bedroom. Julia, wise beyond her years, had told Mum that if she wanted me to come to visit more often she should remove every disincentive for me to do so. So Anne had been shown to the spare room with the double bed in it and I had joined her there every night after the rest of the household had retired. That third day of our walk was one of sunshine rather than showers. Julia and I had been sitting with our backs to a craggy tor munching chocolate when she had looked at me very seriously.

'You told me after that visit that you were going to ask Anne to marry you when the time was right. Did you ever propose to her?' Julia had asked.

I had proposed to Anne. The eight months that followed Anne's visit to Home Farm had been the happiest of my life. We seemed perfect for each other. As our Final exams loomed Anne had told me that she was pregnant and it had seemed the most natural thing in the world to me to want to cement that happiness through whatever uncertainties might follow. I had done it properly; romantic evening punting on the Cam, champagne picnic, down on one knee for the speech, engagement ring already in my pocket... Maybe I had left my proposal too late. Maybe I had asked too soon. She hadn't given me an answer straight away. As I climbed hand-in-hand with Abbie up the path which led from the back of Julia's house up onto the moor I wondered whether it was the prospect of motherhood which had caused Anne to come to me the next day and say "no". She had been too young and too excited by the myriad of life's possibilities laid out before her to be straight-jacketed by the domesticity of parenthood. And having said no to parenthood, she had said no to the parent. She wanted a fresh start, a start without my presence perpetually pricking her Catholic conscience over what she did next.

How different my life would now be if Anne had said "yes". I would have some office-based job with a serious salary. We would go skiing in the winter and sailing in the summer. Or maybe I would be the proud houseparent to our six children. I might even have brought Anne back to Home Farm and started trying to modernise the farm, although that would have been hard to square with Anne's professional ambitions. Not just the outward arrangements of my life, but how different would I be as a person? Would I be happy? If I was, if I had invested the best ten years of my life building a relationship with her, how much worse would it be if the relationship were subsequently to fail? Maybe she had been right to leave when she did.

'I didn't know that England could be this beautiful,' Abbie said, breaking into my thoughts.

'I love the moors,' I said. 'People say that they are bleak and featureless, but every area has its own distinct character. This bit is relatively tame. The trees over there are maintained by the Forestry Commission but in the middle of the moor there isn't a tree for miles. When we get a bit higher the bracken will disappear and it will just be peat bog and heather for as far as the eye can see, but changing subtly depending on the altitude or the aspect. And the tors, those odd lumps of rock on the top of the hills. There is a lovely waterfall in those woods which we can walk to tomorrow if you're feeling stronger.'

'My village was by a waterfall,' Abbie said with enthusiasm. 'My father was the clan leader so we had the biggest house, right in the middle of the village. It was a large, airy bungalow, solid, made out of teak. By western standards we were poor. We wouldn't even register on your scale of poverty, but we had everything we needed. Everybody farmed, or crafted things from wood, or hunted in the jungle. There were only a few hundred of us in the village. Everything we owned we made ourselves. We didn't trade much. There were no roads. The next village was a day's walk away. We had no contact at all with the wider world. It was truly a subsistence lifestyle. Everything was communal. Children called all the adults "Aunt" or "Uncle" as a term of respect, but also to reflect the shared responsibility that the community had for looking after us. Everyone looked after everyone else; everyone's house was open to everyone else. Everything was shared. I don't remember ever being on my own. Until the army came.'

Abbie fell silent. After a while she started again, but all the previous gaiety in her voice had gone. 'I was gathering plants in the jungle with Rebecca when we heard the first shots. I wasn't sure what it meant at first, but Rebecca knew. She is two years older than me. I wanted to run home; then I wanted to run away. Rebecca made us hide. We were close enough to identify the screams of the men as they begged for mercy. Not for themselves. Our village was no threat to the Burman army; they had come for sport. The men were made to watch their wives and children being raped in front of them. The women didn't scream. Not then. They screamed when the men were being shot, one after another, a single gunshot ringing out with metronomic regularity. We found them later, lying in a neat row in the village square, each with one bullet hole in the back of their heads. My elder brother, Joa, was there, and his best friend, Peter. That was when the women shouted. They were begging to be shot too. But the Burmese were not that merciful. The women and children were taken away to be fucked to death in some army outpost, or made to walk in front of the advancing troops to clear the land mines out the way. I know my mother was taken because we heard her praying for us as she was led away.'

Abbie paused again, but she needed to finish her story. She carried on a flat monotone, as if she was recounting events which had happened to someone else. 'We stayed in the jungle all that night and all the next day. It was only when the carrion birds started to circle above the village that Rebecca allowed us to venture back. That is where our father found us, sitting amongst the dead bodies with Joa's head on my lap. We were too shocked to even think of routing through the burning houses for food. Father has never forgiven himself. For surviving. Five other men came back from wherever they had been hiding. No one else from the village survived. The men wanted to bury their families but Father wouldn't allow it. He thought the army could come back at any moment and now he had a mission: Rebecca and me. Our lives were the only things which justified his survival. He organised the others to scavenge for whatever they could find from the ruins of the village and then he led us out into the bush. For many months we were on the move, never staying anywhere for more than a few days at a time. Sometimes others joined our group but Father never let it become too big. He wasn't trying to raise an army. He did not want revenge. His one purpose was for Rebecca and me to survive for long enough to cross the border and reach the relative safety of the refugee camps in Thailand.'

'Thank you for telling me that,' I said when Abbie fell silent. I squeezed her hand as I said it. It was a warm day but a wispy cloud had temporarily hidden the pale autumnal sun. I shivered.

Abbie stopped walking and looked up at me. 'And that is now my purpose, too. To help my people to survive. I trained as a doctor so that I could return to the refugee camps and do what little I could. But we are not surviving.' Her voice was suddenly animated again. 'Most Karen are Christians; Baptists mainly. I used to pray that someday the world would stop standing idly by while our people are wiped out; that our Christian brothers would put pressure on the Burmese authorities to stop. That is what Rebecca believes. But now I realise that Jesus doesn't work like that. He empowers us to help ourselves.'

We walked the last mile to Lynch Tor in silence. From a distance the tor looked like a huge crumpled top hat at the summit of a barren hill, up close it turned into a staggered pile of enormous stone dinner-plates. It was a steep climb and I took off my shirt to feel the sun on my back before clambering to the top of the pile and pulling Abbie up after me. She shaded her eyes with one hand and looked out over the moor. There was nothing moving in any direction.

'It is hard to believe that there is such solitude in England. I think of Britain as a tiny over-crowded island. In my culture it is a terrible thing to be alone; that is why we revere hermits as such holy men. To live voluntarily in complete isolation is considered a tremendous sacrifice. Do you know that the Burmese word for "lonely" is the same as their word for "sad"?'

'Are you lonely?' I asked.

Abbie sat and dangled her legs over the edge of the tor. I sat beside her and held her hand in my lap.

'I am *apart*,' she said. 'In Bangkok and then during my year in London I learned to see the world through Western eyes. I appreciate how modern science and industrialised society has raised the standard of living of billions of people. But my heart remains in Karen state. So now I am split in two. People talk of the first-world, the second-word and the third-world, and they are right; we live in completely different worlds. I understand how you view us, "the starving millions of India". We are not real to you; you visit our countries, you contribute to our charities, you sympathise with us, but we do not really impinge on your day-to-day lives. In the same way that even intelligent adults brought up in a Karen village can never truly believe in the existence of a six-lane motorway until they see it with their own eyes. Your problems are different from our problems. You worry about your economy, the global environment, the level of your unemployment. We worry about surviving the next monsoon and whether the path to the next village has been land-mined. Your problems are just as real to you as ours are to us, but there can never be real empathy between us until we share the same problems.'

'So if we won't help alleviate your problems, you will bring your problems to us?' I asked.

Abbie looked at me sharply.

'We live in the Garden of Eden but we are a very poor people. It never gets as hot and sticky in the mountains as it does on the Irrawaddy plains. After the monsoons the hillsides are covered so thickly with wild flowers that the scent makes you swoon. Most people still live off the land as they have done for thousands of years. They have very little access to modern technology. They do not seek it; but they also have very little access to modern medicines. We have a twenty percent child mortality rate. It is a very difficult balance to strike. My father is trying to improve our education and medical facilities without importing the western materialistic values which would destroy our culture.'

'Are there many poppy fields?' I asked.

Abbie took her hand from mine. 'You know who the Irishmen are who beat you up, don't you?' she asked.

'I think I can guess,' I said.

'In South-East Asia many people smoke opium pipes. The authorities discourage it but drug abuse is not the socially destructive problem for us that you have made it in the West. It is not the availability of drugs that is the problem, it is how society deals with it.'

'Our problems are not your problems,' I quoted back to her.

'I am not a drug trafficker,' Abbie said. 'I accept that my two worlds are irreconcilable. I do not wish the western world any harm. I am a doctor. I want to live a peaceful life doing good in the world. I want a husband and children of my own. My few days at your house were like a test, a choice that I could make. Do you remember my last night with you?'

I nodded. How could I forget?'

'If you had asked me to stay with you that night I would have done so,' she said simply.

I remembered back to that Monday evening. As I had walked in the door after work I had sensed that something had changed in her. She had money for new clothes, for oysters and champagne. I had danced with a beautiful woman in a silk kimono. I had thought that she had been steeling herself up to tell me she was leaving me when in fact she had been hoping that I would ask her not to.

'You saved me from the BMI; I wanted you to save me from myself. From my father. From what I have to do.' Suddenly Abbie was crying in my arms, her head against my bare chest and her arms hugging me to her. I hugged her back and stroked her hair as my memory of that evening exploded into fragments which I slowly put back together again in a completely different light. Abbie was a small and frightened woman sent alone into a strange land on a desperate mission to save her people. Maybe all perceived terrorists had such human faces to those who looked hard enough.

'It's still not too late to walk away,' I said when the sobbing subsided.

Abbie sat up and wiped the tears from her face.

'Thank you. But it is. My people are being slaughtered. The Burmese Army have the latest Chinese weapons while we try to protect ourselves with Second World War rifles. For a few days at your house I let myself believe that I could escape from my responsibilities but Mr. Shaun has proved that there is no escape. I cannot walk by on the other side while I know that such evil exists in the world.'

'You came here to exchange drugs for guns,' I said. Abbie seemed about to say something different but after the briefest hesitation she just said, 'Yes.'

I waited for her to say something more but she waited even more patiently. Eventually I put my arm round her and drew her to me again.

'What happens now?' I asked.

'I don't know,' she said, so softly that I barely heard it. I thought she was going to cry again but instead she pushed herself out of my arms and looked up at me defiantly. 'I came here to do something. I failed, but I have to keep trying.' She looked away from me and added, 'Ask me any questions you want. I will not hide anything from you any more.'

So sitting on Lynch Tor in the pale English sunshine Abbie told me everything. How the Karen Nationalist Party had always taxed the sale of opium in the golden triangle but the really big money was made by the international traffickers, the refiners and the distributors in the West. The opium tax was used to fund schools and hospitals and refugee camps. And second hand small arms. It had enabled the Karen people to survive for the last seventy years, but the Burman junta were no longer happy with even this pitiful semblance of existence. They wanted a final solution to their ethnic problem. Opium taxation was not sufficient to buy what the Karen people now needed. Abbie's father needed modern weapons and you cannot buy Rocket Propelled Grenades on eBay. The KNP is not recognised as a legitimate government by the United Nations so they have no legitimate access to arms manufacturers. So they have to resort to illegitimate providers. When you are fighting against genocide it is very easy to make the end justify the means.

Members of the Karen Diaspora around the world had been asked to talk to friends-of-friends. In London these friends-of-friends had made enquiries and left messages and eventually been contacted by an anonymous third party. Abbie knew him as Michael; I knew him as my Irish interrogator from a Kilburn industrial estate. My guess was that Michael was not a senior member of the old IRA high command; more likely he ran some quasi-autonomous splinter group of thugs operating prostitution and protection rackets in London. But he did claim to have access to some of the huge arsenal of IRA weapons which under the terms of the Good Friday agreement were meant to have been put permanently beyond use. Now that the armed struggle for a united Irish republic had lost its respectability, Michael and his type needed new outlets for their entrepreneurial talents. Swapping old guns that they could no longer use for new drugs which they could must have seemed like a pretty good use for all those old stock piles.

Michael had supervised the exchange of a small amount of raw opium for a few hand guns. I didn't ask how the opium had been smuggled into the UK or how the firearms had been smuggled out, but Abbie said that the exchange had sufficed to build up confidence on both sides; confidence in the logistics of the operation, and confidence in the security of the other parties and their ability to produce the goods. Abbie's mission was to negotiate the ramping up of this exchange to provide her father with the weapons he needed to protect his people.

'I was ambushed by the BMI on my first night in London as I arrived at what I thought was a friend's house.' Abbie said. 'I thought that the whole operation must have been compromised but if they'd known who I was they would not have been about to kill me when you appeared on your motorbike so miraculously out of the darkness. They would have taken me back to Rangoon for interrogation, like they were planning to do the second time round. Maybe they just got a tip-off that members of the Karen community were using that address and that was reason enough for them to take out the first person they caught. You saved me. I re-established contact with my Karen friend. He lent me money. I had just arranged a meeting with Michael and I thought everything was going to be ok when Mr. Shaun found me again. They were waiting next door in the laundrette when I opened your front door. They forced me back inside and very methodically collected all my things before taking me away in their car. But they didn't find my note inside your jacket.'

Abbie smiled at her tiny victory before continuing. 'I don't know how they found me that time. Maybe I was betrayed again. Maybe they remembered your number plate and had been watching Kennington Park in the hope that you would ride by again and then followed you home. The second time round they definitely knew who I was.'

Abbie shuddered at some unspoken memory.

I thought about this for a moment. 'When you failed to show up for your meeting with Michael he heard, via my friend Charlie, that I was asking after someone of your description. Michael decided to call me in and beat me up just to see what I knew?' I conjectured.

'I am sorry that you got involved,' Abbie said. 'I shouldn't have stayed so long in your house, but you didn't make it easy for me to leave...'

I thought it was meant as a joke. I smiled anyway.

'And now that your cover's been blown you can go home,' I stated. 'You're father can find someone else to negotiate with Michael. And I can come with you. You can show me the flower-filled valleys of Karen after the rains.'

It was Abbie's turn to smile, but hers was a wistful smile. 'It is a nice dream, James. Maybe someday it will come true. I agree that I cannot stay much longer in England but it is clear to me that I cannot leave now until I have met Michael. He will find out soon enough that I was captured by the BMI; he may already know. He will worry that our organisation is not secure. Only I can reassure him. I need to see him before he calls off the whole deal. That much is clear to me, but how? I don't know. I have twice relied on my Karen contacts in London and twice I have been betrayed. I don't know who I can trust anymore.'

'Who do you trust?' I asked.

Abbie looked at me. 'I trust you,' she said simply. 'I trust you not to betray me. But I cannot ask you to help me.'

We sat side-by-side and looked out over the moor. The warmth had gone out of the sun. I shivered and looked round for my rugby shirt. It was lying on the small cairn of stones at the very top of the tor. I got up and fetched it and put it back on. I sat down again next to Abbie.

'I cannot help you to smuggle drugs into this country,' I said. 'You know this.'

Abbie did not say anything.

'But I cannot turn you over to the British authorities, either. In the end they would just hand you back to those Burman thugs. So I will help you to meet Michael and then I will help you to leave the country. Then I will turn myself over to my old friend Angus.'

Still Abbie did not say anything.

'Angus is a sort of policeman. I will tell Angus everything. Everything that I have done and everything that you have told me. And anything that you tell me from now on. I could say that I would try to hide some things from him but it is more sensible to assume that I would fail. I do not know what will happen to me then but it is the only way that I can think of to get my own life back again. Then I will come and find you in your flower-filled valley.'

I waited for Abbie to respond to my offer, one way or the other. I didn't need to wait long. She took my hand in hers.

'Thank you,' she said. 'I look forward to welcoming you.'

Chapter Fourteen

"More throttle is nearly always a better way to get out of trouble than more brake."

From: "Ride Well and Prosper".

On the walk back down from the moor we tried to work out what to do next. My objectives were easy enough to state: arrange a face-to-face talk with Michael and get Abbie out of the country. The first of these sounded simple enough. Abbie had been given a phone number which she had used before to contact Michael. We just needed to phone him up and set a time and a place for the meeting. The slight complication was that Abbie could not remember the number, but she had written it down in a safe place. It was written on the inside cover of my copy of Rebecca by Daphne du Maurier. I knew exactly where the book was. It was the one book that I had picked up from the scattered pile on my living room floor and put safely back on the bookshelf. I wasn't sure how to get hold of it yet, but at least that was a problem that I could get my head round.

I had no idea how to even start with my second objective: getting Abbie out of the country and back to the relative safety of her own community in the refugee camps on the Burma-Thai boarder. She had no money, no passport, no travel tickets; in fact literally nothing other than the clothes that she stood up in and a toothbrush, and those had been lent to her by Julia. Fortunately Abbie was much less concerned about the second problem than the first. Maybe being a displaced person all your life makes you less particular about the legality of your own documentation.

'My father will sort all that out,' she said confidently. She must have seen my sceptical expression because she added: 'We have money,' as if that explained it all.

'How do we contact him?' I asked.

'We have phones as well, you know. If he's at KNP headquarters, and it hasn't moved, and the phone lines are up, I will call him. I do remember his number. He will know by now that I did not arrive in Bangkok on today's flight but he will not yet know why. He will be able to get more money and documents couriered to the UK within forty eight hours.'

I was struck by the matter-of-fact way in which Abbie pointed out that her father still did not know that she had escaped from the BMI. Even that she was alive. For all her previous show of vulnerability Abbie was very businesslike now that we were discussing the practicalities of our next steps. What sort of a relationship could she have with a father who sent her half-way round the world on a mission which carried a significant risk that she would never return?

I hadn't asked Abbie to relive all the horrors of her second incarceration at the hands of Mr. Shaun but it was evident from the way she spoke that they had not felt in any hurry to interrogate her. If they had been in more of a rush her torture would have been more physical and less psychological. Abbie did not think that she had divulged any details of her mission in England and I had no reason to doubt her. How much Mr. Shaun already knew from his other sources we could only speculate.

Julia was already home from her jumble sale when Abbie and I reached her house. I saw her though the window sitting at the kitchen table preparing lesson plans as we walked up the drive.

'There is a fresh pot of tea on the Aga,' she called as Abbie and I kicked off our borrowed boots in the porch. 'Abbie, that dress really suits you,' she added as we joined her in the kitchen.

'Good turn out for the PTA?' I asked conversationally.

'Average,' she replied in a dismissive tone which implied that she had something more important to talk about. 'Mum phoned as soon as I got home.'

'We agreed we wouldn't talk to Mum and Dad yet. The fewer people who know that we're here, the better.'

'I know that, dear brother. But she phoned me; do you expect me not to answer my own phone? Anyway, I didn't let on that you are here. But it wasn't easy, especially when she said that she had just had a phone call from your old friend Angus.'

I froze halfway through picking up the teapot. I had told Abbie about Angus, but I hadn't told her everything. I hadn't told her that Angus already knew who she was and that he might be trying to find us right now.

'That's nice,' I said after a heart-beat's pause. 'How is the old fart?'

I poured the tea and willed Julia to pick up my air of nonchalance.

'He's fine. He asked Mum if she knew where you were. He said he wanted to get in touch to congratulate you. He says you played a blinder.'

I poured the milk.

'He saw you play rugby last weekend.'

I breathed again.

'He says you won the game single handed. He says you should remember that rugby is meant to be a team sport; that you should make use of all the assets at your disposal.'

I passed a mug of tea to Abbie. She was looking at me quizzically.

'I used to play rugby with Angus at Cambridge,' I explained. 'He was always big on the team ethic.'

'Angus also told Mum that he was keen to get in contact with a mutual friend of yours: A Dr. Richard Thompson. He works at Heathrow airport apparently; ring any bells? Mum passed the message on to me in case you called me first. Although if you did call me, Mum also said that I was to harangue you mightily for not calling her more often.'

I smiled sheepishly but my mind was racing. Julia turned to Abbie and asked her where we had gone on our walk. Angus knew! He knew that I had freed Abbie and he guessed that I would take her to Home Farm. Or had he just tried there on spec? Why had he not phoned Julia? Angus wouldn't have Julia's number, but then he wouldn't have still had the Home Farm number either; it was over ten years since he had last been there. Finding phone numbers would not be a problem for someone with his resources. What were his resources? Was he on his way here now? Could he call out the local constabulary to pay a house call? Was there a satellite camera watching this house right now? My bike would be hidden under the oak tree but had Angus watched Abbie and me strolling on the moor as if we didn't have a care in the world?

The phone started ringing. Julia and I exchanged startled looks.

'It's Mum again,' Julia said looking at the caller displayed on the phone.

'Let it ring,' I said. 'She won't be suspicious. She's just spoken to you.'

I turned to Abbie. 'We can't stay here,' I said bluntly. 'I thought we would be safe for a few days at least, but I don't want to bring Julia into this.' Julia started to object but I carried on. 'We would be fine if it was just your Burmese friends looking for us but if the British authorities are involved it won't take them very long to think of looking here. Its not like there are so many other places I could run to.'

I realised belatedly the incongruity of this abrupt change of heart so I petered out with something close to the truth. 'That call from Angus must have spooked me a bit. He's just an old university friend but the coincidence has made me realise that I shouldn't have come here.'

Abbie looked at me with her serious eyes. 'If you think that I am putting you or your family at risk then I must leave immediately.'

'Don't be ridiculous.' Julia said crossly. 'Abbie, of course you don't need to go. You can stay here as long as you like. I don't know exactly what is going on with you and my brother but I cannot imagine a safer place in England than here in Lynchcombe.'

I stared at Julia. She stared back at me so fiercely that the ridiculousness of the situation got the better of me. 'You're probably right, Julia,' I laughed. 'I am over-reacting. I'm sure there's no need for us to run out the door this minute but being a generally law abiding citizen I had no idea that hiding away would be this difficult. The awful thing is not knowing who is looking for us. Maybe no one. I'm probably giving our seekers much too much credit: scar-face has probably just turned over my house a couple more times and the British police are too busy worrying about underground bombers. I really wanted to have a few days of peace and quiet for Abbie to recover but the clock is ticking. We won't be safe until she is out of the country and until then we need to keep moving. I don't know where yet, but I'll think of something.'

I stopped speaking and Abbie and Julia waited expectantly for me to announce our next move, as if being on the run was something I had been doing all my life.

'There are some people Abbie needs to talk to,' I said to Julia, 'but I don't want her to use your phone. Maybe I'm being paranoid but it's better to be safe than sorry. Can I borrow your car so that I can get into Tavistock before Woolworths closes? I want to buy a new Pay-as-You-Go mobile. When I get back I think Abbie and I should go.'

Julia sighed but did not demur further. 'How much money do you have?' she asked sensibly. Without waiting for a reply she rummaged in her purse for her cash card and handed it over to me. 'The pin number is Twelve, Ten,' she said. 'The twelfth of October, your birthday; not very secure, but it stops me from forgetting to send you a card. It should let you take out two hundred pounds without setting off any alarm bells.'

'Thank you, Julia. I'll pay you back, I promise,' I said vaguely. Sorting out all the loose ends was something that would take care of itself at some unspecified time in the future when my life returned to some form of normality. For now I seemed to be failing to even think ahead one day at a time.

'No. I will pay Julia back,' Abbie said. 'I will pay you both back once I contact my father again.'

'There's no rush,' Julia said encouragingly to Abbie. I could tell that Julia did not entirely believe that Abbie would ever be able to make good that promise. But I believed her.

'I don't think it's sensible to use your phone, but the internet should be safe enough, shouldn't it?' I asked Abbie. 'Julia, can Abbie borrow your internet connection to send an email to her Dad while I'm shopping? At least she can let him know that she is safe and sound.'

'My father does not trust the internet,' Abbie said, 'but I can email my sister, Rebecca. She lives in Bangkok but she should be able to get a message to my father.'

'The computer is in my bedroom,' Julia said. 'I'll log you on. Unless you would rather I did the shopping for you, Jim?'

I declined Julia's offer and also Abbie's offer to accompany me on the grounds that in Julia's daffodil print dress all the male shop keepers would remember her, if only because she would haunt their dreams for weeks. She smiled at the implied compliment and instead wrote me a short list of the things that she needed. She was particularly in need of footwear. She had just about managed on the moor in Julia's wellies with three pairs of socks but she couldn't sensibly wear any of Julia's shoes. Julia added a few things of her own to Abbie's list and recommended I travel north to Okehampton rather than south to Tavistock; it was a bit further but she gave me directions to a hypermarket on the outskirts of the town which should be able to provide for all our needs in the relative anonymity of Saturday afternoon shoppers.

I was gone for nearly two hours. Abbie's shoes were much harder to choose than the mobile phone but I settled on the sturdiest training shoes that I could find in her size. I was conscious of my limited budget but the clothes in the shop were so cheap that I supplemented Abbie's list of minimal requirements with start-of-season ski-thermals in preparation for our next bike ride and I bought a cheap and cheerful bunch of flowers as a token of thanks for Julia. I paid for everything with cash. I was asked if I wanted to register my new phone which panicked me a bit. I gave Ben's name and his London address. Thinking of Ben gave me a twinge of nostalgia for the simplicity of my old life when my biggest worries had been missing rugby training or squandering a try-scoring opportunity at the weekend.

As soon as I was outside the shop I called directory enquires and asked for the number of the East Ham Methodist manse.

★　★　★

When I got back to Highfield Barn the kitchen table was set for dinner and there was a vegetable stew simmering on the Aga. Julia thanked me for her flowers and put them in a vase in the middle of the table. Abbie had sent off two emails to Rebecca. The first just said: "Hi, I'm alive. Mail me back as soon as you get this message". The second was a longer email giving a brief account of what had happened since she had been captured and her suspicion that her contacts in England may have led the BMI to my house in Brixton. Until that was proven one way or the other Abbie told Rebecca not to trust anyone in London. Abbie had asked Rebecca to contact their father and let him know that she was planning to meet Michael as soon as possible and outlined the help that she would need to get home.

So far there had been no reply from Rebecca but it was still the middle of the night in Thailand. It would be a few more hours before Rebecca could be expected to be up and about and checking her emails.

I took my new mobile phone out of my pocket and wrote its number on Julia's kitchen memo board in case she should ever need to contact us after we left. Abbie took the phone upstairs. She was gone for twenty minutes. When she came down she said that she had not yet been able to get through to her father. Apparently this was not unusual; he moved around a lot. Abbie didn't have a phone number for Rebecca but she had sent her sister a third email giving her my new mobile phone number and asking her to call it as soon as possible.

Abbie put my mobile phone down on the kitchen table next to the flowers and we all looked at it expectantly, but it didn't ring. While we ate the vegetable stew I explained to Abbie that Jane, my Methodist minister friend in London, was more than happy to take us in for a few days. I said that I had led Jane to believe that this was a political asylum issue. I told Abbie that Jane was itching to start a campaign on Abbie's behalf but that I had made Jane promise not to tell anyone yet that we were coming. No one; not her favourite supplicant, not her best friend, not even her Mum. No one.

I did not tell Abbie that Jane had been particularly relieved to hear from me because when I called she had only just put the phone down after a long and difficult conversation with Anne. Anne had been distraught and tearful, but eventually Jane had calmed her down and learned that Anne had picked me up from Charring Cross hospital on Tuesday afternoon after I had been beaten up by some Irishmen, and that the next day I had walked out of Anne's docklands flat and just vanished. Anne had had no response to any of her calls to my mobile over the last 24 hours. So Anne had driven over to Brixton and found my house locked up. She had gone next door to Jimmy's Best Fish and Chip shop to ask if anyone knew where I was and been further alarmed by Jimmy's colourful description of my house being broken into. At that stage Anne had been on the point of calling the police but she had reluctantly decided to call Angus first. Angus had reassured Anne that I was ok but said something enigmatic about me having eloped with Abbie. Angus had apparently signed off by warning Anne that if I contacted her she should call him immediately.

Now Anne didn't know what to think.

I did not come out particularly well from Anne's version of events. I should have warned her that I was leaving and I didn't like her thinking that I had eloped with Abbie. I had wanted to call Anne there and then, standing in the sunshine in that Okehampton hypermarket car park with my brand new mobile phone in my hand. I had wanted it to be like the old days when she had been my best friend and we had discussed all our problems together. I had asked Jane to remind me of Anne's number and I had promised Jane that I would call Anne immediately. But I hadn't done so. It was not that I didn't trust Anne but my over-riding priority was to get Abbie out of the country; only then could I come clean to Angus. Talking to Anne would have put her in an awkward position. She said that her marriage to Angus was over but a ten year relationship is a huge thing to walk away from. I was fairly sure that Anne would have kept Abbie's whereabouts a secret, but fairly sure was not sure enough.

'We will be safe with Jane,' I assured Abbie.

'Thank you,' said Abbie simply.

We ate quickly. Now that we were committed to leaving I wanted to be off as soon as possible. The meal took on the air of a last supper; there was nothing of any consequence to say and no one could be bothered with the pretence of small talk. As soon as we had finished Abbie and I went up to the room that we had slept in together, me to change into my riding leather, Abbie to change out of Jane's borrowed dress and into her new ski-thermals, borrowed sweatshirt and a tightly belted pair of borrowed jeans. She turned her back to me as she changed.

The ride to London was entirely uneventful. We waited until it was dark before leaving Highfield Barn even though my earlier concerns about being tracked by spy satellite now seemed one conspiracy theory too far. My paranoia of that afternoon disappeared as soon as we were riding again and now that Abbie was snugly kitted out, with Julia's Gortex jacket as an over layer and two pairs of socks inside her new trainers, she seemed to be enjoying it too. It was a beautifully clear evening. We were not in a hurry. I avoided the motorways, rode within the speed limits, and we stopped frequently for coffees and doughnuts. It did occur to me once as we passed a highway agencies camera that I had heard that some of them were linked up to number plate recognition systems which could identify stolen vehicles but the possibility that MI5, either officially or through the personal interests of Angus, could really be looking for us seemed incredibly far fetched now. I stuck to the A roads along the south coast and it was lovely to be riding through the night with the moon rising over the sea to my right and Abbie sitting behind me, hugging my waist.

I had put my mobile phone in my leather trouser pocket and as we approached Brighton I felt it vibrating. I pulled over and explained excitedly to Abbie that Rebecca might be trying to contact her but the missed call turned out to be from Jane. I phoned her back and warned her that we might be another couple of hours. Despite her many layers of clothing Abbie was beginning to feel the cold and immediately after setting off again we passed a Travel lodge. Last week I would have checked in and we would have made love until dawn; I gave her encircling arms a squeeze with my left hand as we rode past.

We picked up the A22 into London which turns into the A23 and then into the Brixton road. I had not planned it that way but I suddenly realised that this route would take us right past my house. My paranoia came flooding back. I was sure that my house would be being watched by somebody: BMI, IRA, MI5. Maybe all three of them from their different parked cars. But we needed Michael's phone number which meant we needed my copy of Rebecca, and one o'clock in the morning seemed as good a time as any to try to retrieve it. I stopped at an all night café half a mile south of my house and explained to Abbie what I planned to do. Abbie said that it wasn't worth the risk. She said that her father would be able to get us Michael's phone number. I said that we didn't know when that would be; we hadn't even been able to contact her father yet. And I didn't like being frightened to go in to my own house.

I made Abbie stay in the café and rode on alone. I had two options. Jimmy's Best Fish and Chip Shop stays open until two o'clock on Saturday nights. I could park the bike round the corner, walk into Jimmy's as if I was a customer, walk through the shop and out the back, jump over the fence between our two back yards and break down my own back door. Or I could do it the direct way.

I chose the direct way. I rode straight up Brixton road, bumped the Blackbird up onto the curb and stopped right outside my front door. There was the usual traffic on the street but there were no pedestrians and no one was loitering suspiciously outside Jimmy's. I rested the bike on its side stand, jumped off and unlocked my door. It was dark in my hallway but I did not put on the lights. I knew exactly where I had to go. I rushed through my kitchen and into the lounge. In the darkness the room looked exactly as I had left it: smashed hi-fi and scattered cushions. I picked my way carefully over the strewn books. Rebecca was standing alone on its bookshelf. I shoved the book into my jacket pocket and retreated.

My old mobile phone was sitting in the middle of my kitchen table.

I stared at it for a full ten seconds before noticing the note underneath it: 'You misplaced this I believe. Call me.' Angus had tracked down my mobile and brought it back here. I grabbed up my phone and ran from the house.

There was no one waiting for me outside. I was tempted to call into Jimmy's but decided that I might be pushing my luck. I started up the Blackbird and was halfway back to Abbie before I realised that I hadn't turned off my old phone. I pulled over and powered it down, but I knew that it was too late. Angus would know that I was in London. I wasn't sure why it mattered, but it took some of the shine off my jubilant return with Rebecca.

Abbie showed no outward sign of relief when I walked into the café but she thanked me solemnly as I handed over the book. She opened the front page and nodded to confirm that she had found Michael's number.

'I will call him in the morning,' she said.

I paid for Abbie's coffee and we re-mounted the Blackbird. I headed south and picked up the South Circular road, crossed the Thames through the Blackwall tunnel and drew up at No. 13 McIntyre Road shortly before two am.

Jane had obviously been waiting up for us because she opened her door and welcomed us in before I had even got off the bike. She hurried Abbie inside to warm up while I pushed the bike along the concrete path beside Jane's house and parked it on the back patio out of sight from the road. I looked up at the sky and then manoeuvred Jane's garden sunshade over the bike, but I was laughing at myself as I did it. I took the small grip bag containing our few travelling essentials out of the top box and went inside to find Jane talking to Abbie as she put a large jug of hot chocolate into the microwave to warm.

'Thank goodness you got here when you did,' Jane was saying. 'I'd forgotten how dreadful night-time radio can be. You arrived just in time to stop me phoning an awful phone-in programme to counter all the bigots calling for Muslims to be expelled as the only way to keep our country safe. They are saying that Muslims are being radicalised in their ghetto communities and that the continued existence of these pockets of minority culture proves that three generations of multi-culturalism hasn't worked, whereas all it really proves is that we need to work harder at it. There is no alternative. Just look at the riots in France. They've tried to suppress cultural differences rather than celebrating them, and look where that has got them.'

'Hello, Jane,' I interrupted her. 'I see you two have introduced yourselves.' I gave Jane a big hug. 'Thank you for taking us in.'

'Don't be silly. I've left the immersion heater on but Abbie says she is too tired for a bath tonight. She also says she doesn't want anything more to eat, but there's cheese and biscuits if you want? I've put her in the front bedroom and you are in the one you slept in last time. I hope that's alright?'

I looked at Abbie. She smiled at me, but nodded. The disengagement process was complete.

The hot chocolate was welcome. While we drank I explained again to Jane, as previously agreed with Abbie, that Abbie had come to the UK on the promise of a well-paid cleaning job but had found that the nature of the work that she was expected to perform had turned out to be very different from what she had been promised. I had helped her to escape from her employers, for which interference I had received my beating, and now she just needed somewhere to stay hidden for a few days until her travel documents were sorted out and she could go back home to Thailand. I thought that the story was near enough to the truth to be convincing, although I wasn't sure that it fully explained why I did not want Anne or Angus to know where we were. Jane's natural inclination to believe everyone probably helped; she had lots of questions but they were all about our well-being and could easily be postponed until the next day. It also helped that there would have been no apparent motive for the story not to be true.

'Bed time,' I said, picking up the holdall. 'Jane, are you happy for me to show Abbie up to her room?'

Abbie followed me up the stairs and I pointed out the bathroom, Jane's room, and the spare bedroom that I had slept in.

'So I guess this must be your room,' I said, leading her into a smaller room with a single bed and a small window which overlooked the back garden. There was a copy of the Bible on the bedside table. I put the bag down on the bed and divided the contents into two piles as I took them out: Abbie's wash things, spare underwear and Julia's nightdress in one pile, my old Oxfam suit, toothbrush, and clean boxer shorts in another. I pulled my new mobile phone from my pocket. Still no call from Rebecca. I put the phone on top of Abbie's pile.

'I'm sure she will call during the night,' I said.

'Are you ok about this,' Abbie asked quietly.

'About us not sleeping together?' I asked. 'Yes. I think it's right. In a few days time our lives will part. You will go your way and I will go mine. I am glad that we shared the same dream, if only for a while, but it is time to wake up again.'

Abbie took my good hand and squeezed it. I bent to kiss her lightly on the top of her head and then picked up my pile of things and walked to the door.

'But you know where I am if you need me in the night,' I said as I left the room. It was only half in jest.

Chapter Fifteen

"Overtaking at a junction is like playing Russian roulette. With a full clip."

From: "Ride Well and Prosper".

Abbie woke me in the morning with a mug of tea. She was already dressed.

'Did your sister phone?' I asked as I sat up.

'Yes.' Abbie smiled. 'We had several long chats. She asked me to thank you for ignoring her advice.' Abbie sat down on the bed beside me. 'She hopes to thank you in person one day, but more pressingly I need to put some more credit on your phone. I didn't realise it cost money just to receive an international call. I also need to meet someone.'

'Have you phoned Michael already?' I asked alarmed.

'No, not yet. But Rebecca has been busy while you have been asleep. She has come up with another friend in London, someone who has never been involved with our cause before. An English woman. There is no way the BMI could know about her. Rebecca has wired her money. If I can ask you for one more loan to get me to her I should be off your hands very soon.'

'Don't say it like that,' I said. 'Don't ever say that.'

'I was joking,' Abbie said. 'But I shouldn't have. My debt to you is not a joking matter. But I am not leaving for good. Rebecca is working out a new plan to get me back to Thailand, but it may take a few days to organise. I'll try to be back for lunch.'

'Do you want me to come with you?' I asked.

Abbie hesitated and then shook her head. 'I think better not. We can call this new friend Margaret, but I will not pretend that is her real name. It is not that I do not trust you but it is better for you if you do not get any further involved with this. Do you understand?'

'I understand,' I said. I looked at my watch; six thirty on Sunday morning. No wonder it was quiet outside. 'Will you draw the curtains for me?' I asked.

Abbie stood up and crossed the room to let in the morning sunshine. My wallet was on the bedside table. There was eighty pounds left from my sister's loan. I offered half of it to Abbie.

'Will that be enough?' I asked. 'Take more if you need. I'm sure I can borrow some from Jane to tide us over. It won't be long until I can start using my own cards again.' Everything seemed to be winding to a close.

'That's plenty. Thank you again. I will repay you …'

'I know,' I said, cutting her off. 'I suppose you've had breakfast already? Did you sleep at all last night? You're meant to be recuperating too. Is Jane awake yet?'

'I haven't seen Jane. I did get a few hours sleep before Rebecca called but after that I was too excited. I haven't eaten but I'm not hungry. I will buy something later.'

'Have bowl of cereal with me before you go,' I suggested.

'No. I need to go. Do you know the way to the nearest tube station?'

'Let me walk you that far at least.'

Abbie smiled again. 'That would be nice,' she said.

I dressed quickly. We left without waking Jane and walked through the sleepy residential streets to Upton Park station, hand-in-hand like the lovers we used to be. At the station Abbie bought a one day travel ticket and a top up card for the phone as soon as the newsagents opened. That used up almost all of the money that I'd just given her. I made her take another twenty pounds. A few more taciturn early morning travellers drifted onto the platform as we waited for the first west bound train. I bought a newspaper and three Danish pastries and insisted that

Abbie eat one. Her train arrived before she had finished it. She got on and blew me a flaky kiss through the door window as the train pulled away. I wondered if I would ever see her again.

When I got back to the manse Jane was awake and wondering where we'd got to.

'I thought you'd done another bunk.' she said as she opened the door to let me in. 'Where's Abbie?'

'Her sister called in the night. She's gone off to meet someone who may be able to help her get home. I walked her to the station. I've bought a Sunday paper and a Danish for your breakfast.'

Over breakfast Jane asked me all the questions that she had wanted to ask the night before. I answered them as best I could. I asked her again not to tell Anne or Angus that I was here. I could only explain this by saying that Abbie was so traumatised by her recent ordeal that she had made me promise not to tell anyone where she was. It sounded a bit lame to me but sometimes the truth is lame. Jane seemed to accept that a promise is a promise. The conversation was slightly rushed because Jane needed to leave at eight o'clock to take an early morning service.

'Why don't you come along too?' Jane asked. 'It's not really a service; the Family Communion is not until eleven. This is just half-an-hour of quiet contemplation and reflection. I open the chapel every morning at eight-thirty for anyone who wants to start their day with prayer. No fire and brimstone. There are normally only about five old biddies there on a Sunday. No one will recognise you, although they will all be dying to know who you are.'

'That would be lovely, but I'm not sure when Abbie will be back,' I said.

'We can leave a key out for her.'

'I can't call her; she's got my mobile phone.' I said. Switching on my old phone was not an option until Abbie was safely out of the country. 'We can't exactly leave a note on the door saying "the key is under the mat". Anybody might find it.'

'Borrow my mobile and send her a text. Anyway, the service only takes half-an-hour and if Abbie went into town she won't be back for hours. Jim, it's not like you to find reasons not to do something. I do believe you are procrastinating.'

I smiled. 'I do believe that I am,' I conceded. 'Ok. I'll come. I could do with some quiet contemplation and reflection.'

Jane found her mobile and while she went upstairs to put on her ecclesiastical vestments I sent Abbie a text telling her that we would leave a front door key under the back wheel of my motorbike. I added that she could contact me on Jane's phone, the phone I was texting with, if she needed me urgently. There was no immediate reply.

The Methodist chapel turned out to be a new two story redbrick building just around the corner from MacIntyre Road. Jane showed me round before the service. Upstairs there was a crèche-and-Sunday-school area, Jane's office, a library-and-meeting room, and a properly kitted out kitchen. It was clearly a well-used community resource. The chapel proper took up the ground floor of the building and was a world away from all the High Church grandeur of my grandfather's parish church in Dorset. Instead of stained glass, the windows were double glazed against the noise of the traffic; instead of cold flagstones there was a deep blue carpet on the floor; instead of an ancient organ hidden behind its forest of pipes there was an old upright piano against one wall in front of an interactive whiteboard. A plain wooden altar stood at the eastern end of the room with a garish modern tapestry hanging behind it. There was no raised plinth for the choir and no obvious pulpit. There were no high-backed wooden pews. We arrived to find the padded congregation chairs pushed back against the walls, a legacy from the youth club's dance lesson the previous evening.

Following Jane's instructions I was arranging twenty chairs into a semi-circle in front of the altar when the first of her congregation arrived who, contrary to Jane's forecast, was an earnest young man in his early twenties. He greeted me like a long lost friend. He immediately pitched in to help with the furniture re-arranging with a confidence which I took to imply that he was used to having to prepare his own place of worship. By eight-thirty I was sitting in the semi-circle with half-a-dozen under thirties and half-a-dozen over sixties; the mid-range was not represented at all, but everybody seemed to know everybody else and everybody was very welcoming to me. Jane's position, in the middle of the semi-circle but not plumb centre, seemed deliberately chosen to deny any hierarchy, but a hush fell immediately when she stopped chatting to her neighbour and suggested to the wider group that it was time to start with a prayer. Heads bowed as she thanked Jesus for guiding us all there - by whatever circuitous route it had taken for each of us. She asked Him to help us to feel His presence, not just here in His house, but in our work, in our rest, and in our play throughout the rest of the day. I was struck by the intimacy of the prayer. It was as if Jane was talking to someone sitting on a chair next to me.

After the prayer Jane stood up, walked to the apex of the semi-circle and turned to look at me.

'I would like to welcome Jim to our meeting today. Jim is an old friend of mine and my current house guest.'

Murmurs of 'Welcome, Jim' passed round the circle. I smiled back at everyone.

'Jim does not believe that Jesus lives,' Jane said.

I was taken aback by this unexpected public outing of my unbelief. The rest of the congregation seemed equally taken aback. My smile faded.

'What should we do with Jim?' Jane asked. The jocular tone of Jane's enquiry restored the light-hearted atmosphere immediately.

'Make him stand in the corner,' suggested the retired gentleman on my right. A pretty, blonde haired, twenty-something girl shouted out, 'wax his legs!' to general amusement. It was obvious that they were all comfortable with the informality of this gathering; it felt more like a sixth form general studies tutorial than a religious service. Once the ice was broken the suggestions came flooding in thick and fast, a mixture of the funny and the serious: 'ask him why not,' 'break his other arm,', 'welcome him in, and evangelise to him,' 'convert him through example', 'pray for him'. No one seemed too shy to throw in their two-pence worth.

'Maybe we should just pity him,' said the blonde haired girl, smiling across at me.

'Pity him?' Jane asked, and the others suddenly became respectfully silent. 'My first reaction was actually to envy him. I know that every one of you has to make sacrifices every day to live out your convictions in this secular age. How much easier it would be if we could conform to the lowest common denominators of today's society. For starters, we could all now still be in bed.'

'But before we progress with the public lynching, I should point out that although Jim doesn't currently believe, he is one of the main reasons why I found the Lord ten years ago.' Every eye in the room turned to look at me as Jane continued. 'I was brought up in an agnostic household. My parents took me to church on Christmas day and Easter. For them, as for so many middle class people, Christianity was purely a social convention, like washing the car on Saturday afternoon, the Sunday roast, and making contributions during Christian Aid week. There are many such good people who, even if they no longer call themselves Christians, pretty much keep the Ten Commandments and treat their neighbours as they would want to be treated themselves. They "add their light to the sum of light", as Jim calls it. Most of them have just adopted the beliefs and behaviours of their parents. Without Jim here I might have done the same, or probably drifted even further from a committed belief than my parents because it has now become so much more socially acceptable to be atheist. We are all shaped by our experiences; if I had been born in Pakistan rather than Portsmouth would I be a Muslim rather than a Methodist? Without Jim you might have been blessed with a different minister in this circuit.'

There were a few chuckles but everyone was now watching Jane expectantly as she paced back and forth, waiting to see where this address was going.

'Last night I was forced to stay up until the small hours while I waited for Jim to arrive from Devon. To keep me awake while I worked on my address for later I half-listened to a phone-in programme on the radio which was asking what our response should be to last week's underground bombing. Almost without exception the callers were demanding tighter controls on immigration. The more hysterical contributors were calling for all Muslims to be deported. Whatever stigma we incur as Christians for professing our faith in public, it is nothing compared with what other faiths endure in our supposedly tolerant society. It is nothing compared with what Christians are still subjected to in other parts of the world. It made me realise that as Christians we actually have much more in common with members of the other major religions than we do with agnostics, like Jim here. Even Buddhism, which claims to be a philosophy rather than a religion because Buddha famously refused to pronounce on the existence of God, shares the belief in a transcendental purpose to life which is beyond our understanding. All the religions believe that the life we live now is just a journey of personal preparation for whatever it is that comes next. The Christian interpretation is that if we are not prepared, if we do not forge our personality into one that is able to accept God's presence, it is not that Heaven will be denied to us when we die, but rather that we will not be capable of accepting it. We will not recognise Him when he calls us. Then death really will be the end.'

'The different religions guide people up different paths depending on their cultural starting point but they are all trying to climb the same mountain. As a Christian I believe that Jesus is the only guide who can take me right to the top, but if I had been born in Pakistan I could now be following the Muslim path up the same mountain. The journey can be hard, we will often fall down and need to start back up again, but at least we all have a goal to pursue. A purpose for life. How much better that is than wandering around in the foothills not believing that there is anywhere worth aiming for.

I think that we all accept that the theory of evolution explains how we have descended from the apes. But it does not explain why. It does not explain why life started in the first place, why inert atoms formed into the first single molecular life, why life has subsequently evolved from simple plant forms into complex sentient beings, apparently against a fundamental law of nature, entropy, which requires energy to dissipate from areas of concentration. Science can tell us all sorts of things about life, but at the fundamental level it cannot tell us what life is.

I do not believe that all non-Christians go to Hell, but I do believe that the further up the mountain you get, the more likely it is that you will be able to accept Gods infinite grace when it is offered to you. So, yes Sarah, I think that you're right. I think that we should pity Jim. But maybe we should wax his legs as well.'

There was general laughter which Jane let die down before suggesting a moment of peace for each person to reflect upon what it meant to them to be a Christian. I pursued my own reflections. Jane walked quietly over to a PC beside the piano and started it playing a song from Taize. She faded up the volume so slowly that by the time I became aware of the music I realised that the gentle chanting had already been washing unnoticed over my thoughts for several minutes. As the song became more audible several members of the tiny congregation joined in.

When the music finished Jane let the silence deepen for a minute before saying quietly, 'Let us conclude with a prayer based on the plea of Saint Teresa of Avila. It is a prayer for Jim, but it is also a prayer for every one of us here: Lord Jesus, you know that sometimes we do not believe. Lord Jesus, you know that sometimes we do not even want to believe. But Lord Jesus, you know that we always want to want to believe. Help us with our belief, and help us also with our unbelief.'

'Amen,' we all intoned.

As the service broke up various members of the congregation came over to me and shook my hand. It was obvious that they wanted to engage me in conversional conversation. I hope I remained polite but non-committal. The pretty blonde girl introduced herself as Sarah. She was the last to leave, eventually shaking my hand in parting while explaining that she would be upstairs preparing for the eleven o'clock Sunday school if I wanted to talk more. As soon as she was gone I collared Jane.

'Jesus, Jane! You could have warned me that you were planning to make an example out of me this morning,' I said.

'Sorry Jim. I genuinely didn't intend it until I was halfway through introducing you. It just sort of came to me as I was speaking. My meditation for this morning was going to be based on the old Good Samaritan parable; I worked really hard last night trying to come up with a novel angle to the old theme. I guess I can still use it later, unless you want to come to Communion as well? Anyway, you love being the centre of attention; you certainly didn't appear to mind being the centre of Sarah's attention just now.'

'I thought you were going through a period of doubt yourself?' I asked.

'Sssh.' Jane exhorted, looking round theatrically. 'Nobody knows. And actually I think that this morning's service may turn out to be my first step back onto the wagon. You see? You have this effect on me: you drive me to religion. How about you? Any Damascan epiphanies?'

'You're mixing up your allegories shamelessly,' I said, but I was feeling less picked on. 'Are we going home now?'

'Sorry. This is start of my working day. I've got an emergency finance committee meeting before the main service and I need to do a bit of prep in my office first. You can head off though; you know where the key is.'

'Would it be alright if I sat in here a bit longer? It seems like as good a place as any to put one's thoughts in order. Surprisingly enough I didn't manage to get as much quiet contemplation done during the service as you had promised. It must have been the effect of everybody baying for my blood. All their focused prayers must have interfered with my thought patterns.'

'Of course you can stay here,' Jane said looking at me mischievously. 'And when you've done contemplating I'm sure that Sarah will make you a lovely cup of coffee if you go upstairs. If you do head off, I should be home by one o'clock. I normally just have soup and cheese for lunch on Sundays, I hope that's ok? There should be some stuff in the fridge but feel free to have a look and supplement it if needed.'

I sat in the chapel for nearly two hours before heading back to the Jane's house, taking the opportunity to try to think further ahead than just the next few hours. Jane might have called it praying. The early birds were beginning to arrive for the day's main service as I was preparing to leave. Jane came down from her finance committee meeting to greet them. She failed to persuade me to stay on for the service and so gave me her mobile in case Abbie should phone. I asked her for directions to the nearest deli and bought some fresh soup, salad, cheese, and newly baked bread rolls with the last of Julia's loaned money. When I got back to the manse the key was still under my bike wheel where I had left it. I let myself in and made a long call on the house phone which I had only just finished when I heard Jane knocking at the front door.

'Good service?' I asked as I let her into her own home.

'Yes, a very friendly service. Thanks for asking. Is Abbie back yet?'

'Not yet, but she's only been gone a few hours. There is nothing much we can do except wait. And have lunch.'

Jane warmed the soup and re-heated the rolls as I laid out the other provisions. We tried to talk about other things: people from our Cambridge days that neither of us had heard of for years, the underground bombing, even the weather. The last time I had stayed here, before Abbie had left, before Anne had split up from Angus, before I had become a wanted man, the talk had flowed freely and easily but now every topic of conversation seemed fraught with danger. The trouble with lying is that one subterfuge leads to another and if you are not very experienced at it you soon lose track of what you have said before. The conversation drifted to my time in Thailand and then on to Burma and the notorious Death Railway which the Japanese had forced POWs and captured natives to build through Karen State during the Second World War. An awful lot of nearly talking about Abbie, without actually doing so. The temptation to confide everything to Jane grew but just at the point where I might have done so her mobile registered a text message from Abbie: 'All well. On the train. See you soon.' My opportunity for confession had passed.

Abbie arrived half-an-hour later wearing new clothes and carrying a handbag and a new rucksack. She was bubbling over with excitement and new found confidence. 'Margaret has passed on the funds from Rebecca and she should be receiving a new passport for me tomorrow. So I have been able to do a little bit of shopping at last.'

As soon as Abbie got inside the door she shrugged off her new rucksack and did a twirl for us in her crisp white blouse and dark trousers which actually fitted her properly for a change.

'The clothes Julia lent me are in the backpack,' she said, smiling a newly lipsticked smile. I moved to pick it up but Abbie stopped me. 'There is some more stuff of mine in there as well. And there is also a present for you. I will sort it all out in a minute and then I will finally pay you back a little of the huge debt that I owe you.'

'There is no hurry for that,' I said.

'I'm so glad that things are sorting themselves out,' Jane said, 'but I'm afraid I need to head off straight away. I feel very rude leaving just as you arrive but Sunday is my busiest day of the week. You can show me all the rest of your shopping this evening. Have you had any thing to eat?'

'Not since James bought me a pastry this morning,' Abbie admitted. 'I was having much too much fun trying on clothes to think about food.'

It was lovely to see Abbie looking really happy for the first time since her abduction from my house. Jane said her good byes and left to conduct an afternoon service at an old people's home. I resurrected the lunch while Abbie took her rucksack upstairs to unpack all her newly bought goodies. When she came down again she asked whether Jane had gone.

'Yes,' I said.

'I've made contact with Michael,' Abbie said, suddenly serious again.

'And?'

'He wants to meet us at six o'clock this evening. He sends his apologies to you for the earlier misunderstanding and asks if you could take me to Kilburn. He says you will know where to go.'

I didn't say anything as I let this sink in.

'This is just an introductory meeting.' Abbie explained. 'We cannot draw up legally enforceable contracts for this kind of exchange but I need to ensure that there is absolutely no misunderstanding about what is being committed to. The deal needs to work for both parties; it is not ultimately in either party's interests to take advantage of the other; that just leads to mistrust and betrayal. I need to be sure that Michael understands this before I commit to any long term agreement.'

I thought of Michael's donkey-jacketed heavy laying into me with his baseball bat in the very same portacabin on the Kilburn industrial estate that Abbie now wanted me to take her to. I wondered how much longer my beating would have gone on if I had not taken matters into my own hands. I wondered whether I should warn Abbie to walk away now. But she knew my story; maybe such casual brutality came with the territory.

'He specifically asked for me to take you?' I asked.

'Yes.'

'Why does he want me there?' I asked.

'He says he wants to shake your hand. He knows that you freed me from the BMI and he says that anyone who can pull off a stunt like that deserves his respect. But I think that, like me, he wants to understand who he is doing business with. If he is as astute as his reputation he will probably ask you a few searching questions to satisfy himself that you don't pose a security risk to the operation. I've told him that you are an accidental player and that after today you will play no further part, but I imagine that he will take the opportunity to remind you that he knows where you live. If he doesn't hear from you again, you won't hear from him.'

'What happens if I don't take you?' I asked.

Abbie looked back at me steadily. 'I would not ask you to do this if I thought that you would be in any danger, but this is very important to me. If you do not turn up the deal is off.'

My heart leapt. I was being offered a way out for both of us.

'So you could go back safely to Thailand. You could return to work in the refugee camps. I could come and visit you and meet Rebecca. I could take Rebecca's advice and start mobilising public opinion here to put pressure on the Rangoon junta to resolve this issue once and for all...'

'No. There will be no happy ending for me. In six months, maybe a year, there will be no Karen state left to save. This is our last resort. For a long time Rebecca persuaded my father not to resort to this while we waited for public opinion to help us. But Rebecca was wrong. We are beyond the help of public opinion. If you do not come with me I will go to meet Michael alone. I will try to convince him that you are not part of this. If I fail then my father will look for other sources but we do not have the luxury of choices anymore.'

So I could walk away, but Abbie would not. And how far away could I really walk? I did not like the prospect of sitting at home and wondering when Michael might pay me another visit.

'I will take you,' I said at last. Abbie did not say anything but her eyes spoke her thanks. 'If we need to be there at six, we don't actually have that much time to get organised and I've got a personal phone call that I need to make first.'

I suggested that if, as Abbie said, this was just a business meeting we could take a taxi to Kilburn, but on reflection I agreed that it wasn't such a smart idea. I couldn't see Michael approving of the fact that there was a cab waiting outside with the metre running while Abbie and he talked about Kalachnikovs and opium purity indicators. So that meant kitting up again and riding over on the Blackbird. I put my leathers back on and Abbie got back into Julia's old jeans, sweatshirt and hiking jacket. I was so used to seeing her in an odd jumble of ill-fitting borrowed clothes that I actually thought she looked better that way but she insisted on taking her handbag as a sop to her briefly re-acquired sophistication.

'Now that I'm back in charge of my own destiny again I'm not going anywhere without my lipstick,' she said.

I took my new phone back from Abbie and while she was changing I sent Jane a text warning her that we would be out when she got back and that I was not sure when we would be back. I initially typed that I was not sure "whether" we would be back, which did not seem like a particularly auspicious start to the evening.

The journey around the North Circular to Kilburn on a Sunday evening took just as long as I had forecast and kept me fully concentrating on just getting us there safely but then suddenly I was turning into the deserted industrial estate. My old Suzuki Bandit was still standing forlornly outside the portacabin reception building. I had half expected to find it torched or gone but apart from a new piece of plywood over the side window the scene had not changed much since I had left in such a hurry three days before. There were lights on behind the drawn blinds this time, but at Abbie's suggestion I rode the round the industrial estate for five minutes before pulling up beside my work bike. None of the other warehouses looked occupied and there were no other vehicles in sight; not even the white transit van.

'This is your last chance to back out,' Abbie said as she took off her helmet and shook her hair loose. She stuffed her gloves inside the helmet and put the helmet on the ground beside the bike. I laid my helmet beside hers as she opened the top box and took out her new handbag.

'Let's get on with it,' I said with more nonchalance than I felt.

I walked up the steps and pressed the bell beside the door. An Irish voice responded immediately, 'Come in Miss Taw and

Mr. Turner.' Even through the distortions of the intercom I recognised the voice of my interrogator from my previous visit.

The intercom buzzed loudly to indicate that the door was unlocked. Abbie made to open it but I stepped in front of her.

'I'm meant to be your bodyguard, remember?'

I pushed open the door but I did not immediately step inside. Once bitten, twice shy. I looked through the doorway and saw the same three Irishmen. The small man who I now knew as Michael was sitting behind the reception desk as before. The two other men were standing behind him. I was pleased to see that the face of the man in the donkey jacket had a purple bruise spreading from his nose up behind both eyes. He took a step forward and I saw that his left leg was also in plaster.

'No hard feelings, eh, English?' he said, nodding at me.

I lifted my plaster cast arm in reply, 'No hard feelings.'

Michael stood up and held out his hand as he came towards me. 'Mr Turner, come in. And Miss Taw. It is good to make your acquaintance at last. I was worried for a while that we were never going to meet.'

'There was no need for you to worry. Everything is in hand.' Abbie spoke calmly. She made no move to take Michael's hand and he dropped it back to his side.

'That's not what I heard. I heard that you had a one-way ticket to Rangoon already paid for before Tarzan here stepped in.' Michael couched the reference as friendly banter but I wondered if he was trying to unsettle her. Abbie didn't blink.

'As I say, everything is in hand.'

'Excellent. So before we talk about the future let's share a toast to your miraculous escape. If we are going to be business partners we should start out as we mean to continue.'

'I don't drink,' said Abbie.

'Then Mr. Turner can have your share.' Michael chose not to comment on Abbie's deadpan responses. If anything her neutral tone was provoking him to greater excesses of Irish bonhomie. 'James, you'll share a whiskey with me for old time's sake? Pat, go next door and ask our mutual friend to join us for a drink.'

The donkey-jacketed Pat turned to the door behind the desk. He started clomping his way to it on his plastered leg, but before he reached it the door opened towards him. A man came in carrying a tray of glasses and a half empty bottle of Jameson. He placed the tray carefully on the reception desk and straightened up.

'Hello, James,' said Angus.

I blinked stupidly at him. 'I didn't expect you to be here,' was all that I managed to say.

'I would be mortified if you did. But I was expecting you; you are so very predictable. I have been friends with Michael for a very long time. We first met while I was compiling a report on how Britain could divest itself of the nuisance of Northern Ireland before the Good Friday agreement made such drastic measures redundant. My report was commissioned by the Prime Minister himself, so Mick here gave me the first big break in my career. The report was meant to be purely hypothetical, blue skies thinking, but the more I got into it the more sense it made. Opinion polls showed that the vast majority of the English, the Scots and the Welsh didn't give a damn about whether Ulster was part of the UK or not. Their so called Loyalists couldn't even let Catholic school children walk to school unmolested; most people thought that the whole lot of them should be towed out into the middle of the Atlantic and sunk. So I thought if I really wanted to make a convincing case for washing our hands of the whole mess then who better to help me frame the argument than those who have been advocating a united Ireland for eighty years. Michael and I have been helping each other off and on ever since.'

'You see, James, Angus is a good Catholic boy at heart. All those freezing afternoons on the terraces at Celtic Park have left their mark,' said Michael.

'That's bollocks, Michael, and you know it,' said Angus, hotly. 'I am no more motivated by religion than you are, but a united Ireland seemed inevitable at the time. You Catholics breed like rabbits. In the end you'll command a democratic majority in Northern Ireland anyway and you'll be able to vote your sovereignty to Dublin, but in the meantime how many more bombings were going to go off on the mainland? Michael helped me to compile a very convincing report which was then conveniently leaked to certain factions within the Loyalist community. It was only because they believed that the British government was seriously thinking of abandoning Ulster completely that the Loyalists came to the table and started negotiating with Sienn Fein. So you see, Michael and I are personally responsible for the Northern Ireland peace agreement.'

'But what are you doing here?' I asked.

'We are here because you kindly reassured your friend Angus that you had no intention of reporting our last meeting to the police,' said Michael, misunderstanding my question. 'I was all for closing this place down for a while. Angus was very pissed off that we picked you up in the first place, weren't you Angus? But when he told me that he thought you knew more about Miss Taw's disappearance than you were letting on, I sort of took the law into my own hands. Luckily for you Pat went a bit soft on you. It is not a mistake that you will make again, is it Pat?'

Pat grunted.

'I am here to tidy up a loose end,' Angus said, picking up the right emphasis of my question. He brought his hand out of his pocket. The gun looked ridiculously small, like a toy replica of a James Bond pistol. I pushed myself in front of Abbie.

'For fuck's sake Angus! What the fuck are you doing?' I shouted.

'How very touching,' Angus sneered, 'but you don't need to lose any sleep over Abbie. You are not the first gullible young man that she has seduced for the sake of her cause. She is quite the little Marti Hara. But as far as I can see, Ms. Taw does not actually pose a significant security threat to this country. No, this is pleasure, not business.'

The gun was aiming unwaveringly at my chest. I looked into Angus's eyes. He look back with manic intensity.

'Steady, Angus,' Michael said. 'No one said anything about permanent. The plan was just to let Pat get a little bit of revenge in for his previous oversight.'

'You never had any intention to negotiate with me today, did you?' Abbie said to Michael from behind my back.

'Not once you were picked up by the BMI,' Michael replied. 'Sorry, darling. You'd become much too risky. I only set up this meeting to repay a favour to Angus. He said he had some unfinished business with your new boyfriend that Pat might be able to help with.'

'Shut up, all of you,' Angus shouted. He backed himself into the corner so that he could cover the Irishmen as well as Abbie and me. It was suddenly Angus against the world.

'You think you are so fucking clever!' He was talking to me now, but quietly as if we were back having a conversation at the rugby club. 'With your cushy middle-class upbringing and snotty liberal views. You swan in to Cambridge as if it's your god-given right and then you throw it all away. Dispatch riding? And playing rugby for some two-bit amateur side. If I'd had half your talent I'd be playing for Scotland by now. You're a loser, Jim. I worked my arse off to get to Cambridge. I'm the only boy from my school to ever go to University, let alone to Oxbridge. But everybody idolised you. Even Anne, the babe of the year, followed you round with her tongue hanging out. But oh-no, you didn't have the balls to do anything about that without my help. I got Anne for you and I took her away from you too. You pushed her too far and she came running to me. Now, after ten years, you come sniffing around again and expect her to come running back. She's mine. You will never take Anne from me.'

I saw Angus subtly shift his balance: his stance straightened and his grip tightened on his gun. I knew with absolute certainty that he was about to kill me.

The shot, when it came, was deafeningly loud. My mind went completely blank and then I saw the gun spill from Angus's hand and clatter onto the floor. He looked surprised. His gaze moved from my face to Abbie standing at my shoulder, and then he crumpled forward onto the ground. Abbie dropped her handbag and stepped past me holding her gun forward in front of her. It was now aimed at Michael.

If the first shot was deafening, the second bang was unimaginably loud. I felt the shockwave from it tear at my eardrums. There was a blinding flash and the room was filled with smoke. The next thing I knew I was lying flat on my back staring up past an unfaltering machine pistol into the dead-eyes of a black gasmask. The room was full of running, shouting, dark-clothed figures. Slowly the gas cleared and my ears began to function again. I saw polished shoes and a grey pin-stripe suit. Someone tapped on the shoulder of the man crouched over me who reluctantly straightened up and dropped the muzzle of his weapon to the floor.

'Are you alright, James?' asked Colonel Grange.

'Get an ambulance.' I said. 'Angus has been –.'

'– Angus has already left. We had paramedics standing by. Not that he deserves one jot of our frugal NHS resources. We unearthed a lot more than we bargained for here tonight. Shame, I thought Angus was brighter than that. It is always the same mistake: needing more money than you can properly account for.'

Colonel Grange offered me his hand and helped me to clamber weak-kneed back to my feet. 'We recorded everything which was said here this evening but whether it will ever be heard in court remains to be seen. It is possible that your astonishing bravery will never be able to be publicly acknowledged. This country has many more heroes in the fight against terrorism than its people know about.'

'I didn't do it for the publicity,' I said simply.

I looked around the portacabin reception room. Michael had already been taken away. The other two Irishmen were being marched from the room. Pat looked across at me with a look of pure hatred.

'You will never be able to hide from us, English. Have pleasant dreams about my baseball bat. I will smash every bone in your body before you beg me to kill you.' One of the men holding him punched him viciously in the stomach. He doubled up silently but as they dragged him past me he spat at my feet.

Abbie was sitting on a chair, her hand-cuffed hands lying limply in her lap, her sad gaze focused upon me.

'You promised me that Abbie would be allowed to leave the country,' I said.

'I promised no such thing,' Colonel Grange replied. 'I did say that would be the most likely outcome but we have to interview her first. She may have saved your life tonight but she may also have committed man-slaughter. That depends, of course, on whether Angus pulls through or not. However, as I said, it may be in everyone's best interest that some parts of this incident never come to trial.'

'Can I talk to her?'

I made to move towards her but Colonel Grange caught me with a restraining arm.

'Best we do this by the book, James. It would be better if you don't talk to her until after we have questioned her. We all have a long night ahead of us. You too, I'm afraid. We will need to take a full statement before letting you have your old life back.'

He put his arm over my shoulder and guided me towards the door. When we got there I shrugged him off and turned back towards Abbie. She was still staring at me. I raised my outstretched hand towards her in a futile gesture of reconciliation. Her expression did not flicker as I turned away.

Chapter Sixteen

"Don't rely on your mirrors. You may think you are the fastest thing on the street but there's always another biker just sitting in your blind spot."

From: "Ride Well and Prosper".

I spent the next twenty-two hours at Paddington Green police station catching a few hours sleep in a comfortable cell between interminable interviews. I was there voluntarily so theoretically I could have left at any time but for me it was a huge relief to unburden myself of the truth at last. I didn't hold anything back. I hoped that Abbie would not be brought to trial but I knew that I wasn't clever enough to protect her by trying to fool my interrogators. They were the professionals and I was the bumbling amateur in this game. I knew that in other parts of the building the three Irishmen and Abbie were also being interviewed with, I suspected, less courtesy than was being shown to me. I learned from my interviewers that Angus was in a critical condition in intensive care. They wouldn't let me see Abbie. I phoned Gloria and explained roughly what had happened. She shrieked, and then sobbed, and then shrieked again. I asked to speak to Charlie but, predictably, he was out. I phoned Anne but when the call went through to her answer phone I was secretly relieved. I didn't leave a message. I didn't know what I would have said to her if she had answered.

Colonel Grange came in to see me. He was less openly friendly then he had been the previous evening in the immediate aftermath of battle. I got the impression from his questions that he was trying to see how willing I would be to testify against Abbie. Eventually I asked him if I could go home. He reluctantly agreed but requested that I remain contactable at all times. I asked whether he thought my house would be safe. His response was that as I was now equally despised by the BMI, the Karen resistance, and the London Irish mafia I would probably be safe from all three of them. It was not particularly reassuring. I got the impression that I was no longer the flavour of the month with MI5 either. Maybe the Colonel was having difficulty explaining why his golden boy had been colluding with wanted IRA gangsters for so long.

As both my bikes were still impounded at the Kilburn crime scene I walked out into late afternoon sunshine and took the tube to Brixton.

It seemed unnaturally quiet inside my house. There were a few junk letters and flyers on the mat inside the door. The bread in the bread-bin was showing the first signs of mould. I cut out the visibly green bits and put two slices in the toaster. As I waited for the kettle to boil I scanned through the mail. There was only one proper letter. The postmark showed that it had been posted in central London the day before. Inside there was a note in Abbie's handwriting:

Dear James,

I am not sure if we will ever see each other again after this evening so please accept the enclosed as a token of my thanks for all that you have done for me. I know that you didn't really expect me ever to pay you back so put this down as a deposit on your airfare. Hopefully a day will come when you will be able to visit me in Karen state. Then you can judge for yourself whether you were right to help me.

Love,
Abbie.

There was also a thin manila envelop inside. In my mind's eye I saw Abbie's sad eyes watching me as I counted out the 20 fifty pound notes inside it.

The phone rang.

'James?'

'Anne? Where are you? Can I see you?'

'I'm at the hospital. I can't believe this has happened.'

'How is Angus?' I asked.

'No change. Still unconscious.'

'I am so sorry,' I said.

'I don't blame you, James. I don't know quite what I do feel at the moment, but it's not blame.' Anne sighed heavily at the other end of the phone. 'I thought you should know that Abbie has asked to see me. I'm not sure if it will be appropriate for me to represent her professionally, but I'm going to see her anyway later this evening.'

'Abbie? How did she sound?' I asked

'I haven't spoken to her directly yet. They haven't charged her with anything and they will have to soon or let her go. I'll give you a ring when I've spoken to her.'

'Thank you. And Anne…'

'Yes?'

'Give Abbie my…' I struggled for the right word, testing several alternatives inside my head, '…love.'

I spent the next couple of hours either making or receiving calls. Jane, Julia, Charlie, Ben, my Mum and Dad. They all deserved to know the full story now that it was over. Then I walked next door to Jimmy's and gave him a version of the truth which preserved Abbie's sanctity. The chow mien was on the house. I took it back to my house and turned on the kitchen radio for some music to listen to while I ate. The news headlines came on as I was washing up; the presenter had moved on to the sports stories before I realised that I hadn't even been listening out for the word "Heathrow".

I suddenly felt overwhelmingly tired. My house was still a mess after it's turning over by Michael but it could wait until tomorrow. I was on the way upstairs to run a hot bath when the door bell rang. I opened the door cautiously. Anne did not say anything, she just came in and spread her arms wide for a big hug. I wrapped her in my arms and patted her shoulder gently as she rocked in my embrace. She pulled away from me and looked up into my face. There were tears in her eyes.

'James. I just can't believe it. I knew he was an arrogant man, but I didn't think he was a traitor.'

'Angus genuinely believed in what he was doing,' I said.

'Bollocks.' I was shaken by the violence in Anne's voice. She pushed herself out of my arms. I followed her into the kitchen. I was conscious that this was the first time that Anne had been inside my house. It was not a pretty sight, but then it would not have compared favourably with her docklands penthouse at the best of times. Anne only gave the room a cursory glance as she prowled distractedly around.

'Angus is a complete shit,' she said. 'That's the hardest bit about this. Half of me really hopes that he never comes round. The Firm are desperate to question him of course but I think that even they are secretly thinking that it would be better for everyone if someone just unplugged his life-support system.'

'Anne, we don't have to talk about him.' I said.

'He tried to murder you,' Anne said. 'He was always jealous of you but it never occurred to me that he would try to kill you. Do you remember William's reunion dinner?'

'Of course. That's when we met again.'

'Whose idea do you think that was?' Anne asked.

'William's I assume. He tracked me down at Pigeon Post and sent me an invite.'

'I think even William now believes it was his own idea. But it was Hanna who put him up to it. And it was me that suggested it to Hanna.'

'You engineered the reunion? To meet me again?' I asked.

'This is not quite the end game I had in mind,' Anne said slowly, 'although I do admit that I was interested to see if you had changed. The Friends Reunited thing may have been worming its way into my sub-conscious. But really I just wanted to see how Angus would react.'

Anne stopped pacing and slumped into a kitchen chair. 'Can we have a drink?' she asked.

'Still prefer Paddy's to Jameson?'

'You haven't got some in?' Anne asked, smiling for the first time.

'Of course. Old habits, and all that.'

I fetched the whiskey, poured us both a generous measure and sat down across the kitchen table from her. Anne took a large sip.

'Last summer I was presented with incontrovertible evidence of Angus's infidelities,' she said. 'I think I may have told you before.'

I nodded.

'It does odd things to you. It's not just the shattering of the dream. It's not even the thought of the physical act itself, although that is all that Angus claimed that it was. In fact somehow that made it even worse. If Angus had actually fallen in love with someone then maybe he really couldn't help himself. It might have all been for something. But he didn't. It was just sex. Which means that he was prepared to betray me for something which didn't even mean that much to him. After Cambridge he pursued me relentlessly; he can be incredibly charming and attentive as you know. The attention lasted for the first few years of our marriage. They were good years. Then I think that he just got bored. I was still his trophy wife but because I loved him unconditionally there was no longer any challenge left in it for him. He had won. The game was over. So he went chasing other game just to prove to himself that he could still win. I think in the end he actually despised me, as he despises all losers, because somewhere deep down I think he despises himself. He thought less and less of me the more I loved him, because he doesn't actually think that he is worthy of being loved. Sort of "I wouldn't want to be a member of any club that would stoop so low as to let me join it" kind of psychology.'

Anne was no longer looking at me. She was looking through me into the space which had once been her marriage. She shook her head as if to dispel the distant memory.

'Anyway,' she said 'the trust went. I went through all his emails and files at home. I told myself that I was trying to build the trust back up again, that I needed to confirm that he really had turned over a new leaf, that there were no more skeletons in his cupboard; at least none that were still alive. It wasn't easy to check up on him, given his line of work. Everything was very secure. They're not meant to bring sensitive material home but I found some stuff on his famous Emerald report and his subsequent deals with Michael. And then I found his file on you.'

'He had a file on me?' I asked surprised.

'He knows everything about you, from your grandmother's maiden name to the match report of your last rugby game. I know about your accident in Thailand,' Anne said gently. She reached across the table and squeezed my hands briefly. 'He'd became obsessed by you. I think it started as a sop to his deep insecurity. It made him feel superior to spy on you. He looked down on your dispatch riding as something with which to contrast his own high-flying career.'

'Did he know that you'd found his file on me?' I asked.

'I don't think so. My first instinct was to challenge him about it but, ludicrous as it may now seem, I still wanted to save my marriage. I hadn't seen you for years and you didn't seem to be a threat to our marriage. It was an obsession, but not of the kind that I had been frightened of finding. I let it drop, but it wouldn't go away. In the end I thought that rather than confront him directly with my knowledge I would see if I could get you back into our circle of friends and see what happened. Sort of "light the blue touch paper, and stand back". I couldn't just phone you up out of the blue and invite you to dinner, but I knew that if I gave enough information to Hanna she would feed it on to William and...'

'… The rest, as they say, is history,' I finished for her. I saw again the hatred in Angus's eyes as he levelled his gun at my chest. 'I think he really does love you, in his own way. It was his fear that you might leave him for me which finally pushed him over the edge.'

We looked at each other silently. It was the first overt allusion to what might be.

'I am not leaving him because of you,' Anne said very deliberately. 'I am leaving him because of him.' She took my hands in hers again across the table. 'However, having left him…' She stood up. I stood up. I pushed back my chair and it toppled noisily to the floor and suddenly Anne was in my arms and we kissed.

We kissed. And we hugged. And we kissed some more. Eventually I asked if she would like to stay and Anne looked around the kitchen as if seeing it for the first time and suggested that it would be better if I took up my convalescence where it had left off, back at her flat. Her car was parked outside. I asked if I could drive. She agreed as long as we could have the top down and she could do the gears.

★ ★ ★

'How is Abbie?' I asked when we were sitting in Anne's car putting on our safety belts.

'Remarkably phlegmatic. She says that she would welcome a trial as an opportunity to tell the world what is really happening in Burma but I'm almost certain that she'll be quietly deported to some neutral country. The shooting was clearly self-defence and she's a pretty small fish in the greater scheme of things. It's Angus and the IRA guys that they are really crowing about. Putting Abbie on trial would make the whole thing much too complicated. She gave me a message for you.'

I looked at Anne and braced myself for the vitriol.

'She said that she had sent you a ticket for a tour of the Karen state.'

I nodded.

'She says that the offer still stands,' Anne said.

'You're joking!'

'That's what she said. Will you go?'

'Will you come with me?' I asked. 'We can call it research for our campaign to save the Karen people'.

I remembered Jane's address from that morning: that life without a reason to live was not worth living. Maybe there is a God after all.

I pulled out from the curb without looking properly behind me and the car behind us had to break suddenly. I put my hand up into the air to apologise.

The car behind tooted its horn three times.

ND - #0083 - 290622 - C0 - 216/138/25 - PB - 9781844268511 - Gloss Lamination